Full of Clover

by

E. R. Millott

Full of Clover

E. R. Millott

Cover design and book layout: Book Cover Corner, www.bookcovercorner.com

Visit the author: www.fullofclover.com

Millott, E. R.

Full of Clover / E. R. Millott — 1st ed.

For: The Trinity who never gave up on me.

*Thank you, to so many friends who gave me the confidence
to tell my story and especially to my husband and children
for seeing me through this process.*

**All proceeds from this book will be sent to
John T. Massawe Tanzanian Mission Projects.**

1

Elaina leaned her bike against the towering gravestone that marked her childhood's magic place. The snow-dusted cemetery reminded her of an enchanted, frozen paradise.

Would they come? An involuntary quiver of doubt interrupted her shiver in the frigid, early-January wind.

If the Three did arrive, she would recognize their presence from the flame that would light deep within her, radiating warmth to her entire body. Their tenderness, like a bear hug, would feel more real than her hands in her pockets. They'd hold her while listening without comment or question, placing her heart's sensitivities foremost in their consideration.

If they came.

She swept off the snow collecting on the top of a grave marker as she searched for the memory of when she'd first met them. They'd made themselves tangible when she was a child, one at her right, another at her left, and the third inside her heart, as she'd skipped between the headstones. When she ran through the clover field beside the cemetery, they'd lift her on the wind. She learned to find them by lying peacefully in front of the tall grave marker that held a bluish marble statue of Mother Mary and three pink angels. After that, they had been part of every moment that mattered.

In the company of the Three, young Elaina had done most of the talking. They recognized that their ears were needed more than their words. They already knew her emotions and what she longed for: to matter and to be loved.

Their quiet presence neutralized the teasing and rejections of classmates and neighbors, calmed her ever-racing thoughts and negative assumptions, and lifted insomnia's hold on her nights. The Three crawled into bed with her each evening upon her ritual pat-of-the-pillow invitation, lending her the same comfort other children found in blankies or stuffed animals. Like magic, her narrow bed warmed and expanded.

The adults had reduced her Three to imaginary friends when she tried to explain, giving her good reason to stop speaking of them altogether. If only those grown-ups could feel what was as real as their own beating hearts, they wouldn't dismiss her or her friends. But then the hard lessons of second grade, with its truths about Santa Claus and the Easter bunny, had raised doubts in her mind about the Three too, until she'd found the courage to ask the new fine arts teacher.

Sister Immaculata, her delicate art instructor, had scooped Elaina onto her lap. *Your three friends who run with you through the clover field are the Trinity, belle fleur, beautiful flower. Think of your personal friendship with them like a secret club—your Clover Club, yes?*

It made sense to Elaina.

It was hard to understand Sister Immaculata because she'd just arrived at Saint Augustine School from Grasse, France. But because she was so nice and her red hair reminded Elaina of curling ribbon, she had pretended not to notice that Sister Immaculata didn't know how to pronounce *h*'s and made the *th-* sound like *z*'s.

"Blessed is your friendship with the Three, for you've reached beyond the confines of man-made religions. Most adults know only a small and demanding Trinity who they've limited by their definitions. They refuse to get to know the real Trinity, boxing them up with a 'Sunday morning' label and placing them on a shelf. There's a big difference between knowing *about* God and knowing God," Sister Immaculata had said.

Without the Clover Club, her childhood would have been unbearably lonely, but in their company, Elaina was oblivious to exclusion from other children. The Clover Club didn't care that her clothes were hand-me-downs and thrift-store finds, that she was the last of ten children from penny-pinching parents, or that she was never invited to the popular girls' parties. Rejection had no sting because they'd assured her that her fickle, impulsive, daydreaming self was wonderful just the way she'd been made.

But after she'd met Cole last year on her sixteenth birthday, the Three's love began to no longer seem like enough. An older man—who could have anyone he wanted—wanted her. It wasn't long before he'd told her she was the most beautiful woman in the world and that nothing else mattered.

The Three objected to the latitudes she'd begun allowing Cole. Through her guilt, she argued that they didn't understand the delicious longing enticed from as little as a brush of his hand. When touching turned to intercourse, she evicted the Three from her heart so Cole could live there at liberty.

The wind moaned through the bare trees, seeming to cry for her. She glanced down at her thickening abdomen, shivering harder. Denial was no longer an option. This secret refused to stay hidden with the rest, reminding her with morning sickness and exhaustion like she'd never felt before. Though the Three already knew, because they knew all, she would have to admit her foolishness before asking for their help.

Guilt seized every opportunity to remind her of the Three's faithfulness and her own selfishness, repeating the same thing her older brother, Eric, loved to jab: *It's all your fault.*

A guilty conscience needs no accuser, her dad prodded just as often.

Did giving guilt a dwelling place make her guiltier? What if she shoved it onto another person, as Eric did to her? What if she buried it?

There was no burying this baby, though. She dreaded giving Cole and her dad the news.

She'd give the Three a few more minutes before heading home. If only they would come to keep her company the way they used to. A firing squad seemed easier than bearing the weight of her parents' disappointment alone. Again.

2

She popped out frenetic enthusiasm for her dad's question about who'd gotten her in the family way.

"He's amazing, Dad. We love each other. One day, we'll be married, too. I met him at Tasty-Tote when I started working there—my sixteenth birthday."

They couldn't be too angry about that. All the Michaels were allowed to date at sixteen. In convincing her father of Cole's virtue, perhaps she'd find more assurance herself, ignoring the fact that Cole had only mentioned marriage a few times in the distant past.

"Does he go to Saint Augustine?"

"He's already graduated from Tarrock High and works night stock." She felt proud at being one of the few girls at Saint Augustine High whose boyfriend was an independent adult.

"So he's over eighteen and from the public school?" Her dad's tone implied the inferiority of a public school diploma. "Why have you kept him secret?"

"We weren't serious at first. Before that—"

"There've been others? I didn't know you were dating." He turned to Elaina's mother. "Paula, did you know?"

If he'd stop interrupting and jumping to conclusions, she could explain. Why did he care, anyway? Everything was about his damn nursery and landscape business. He never asked where she'd been or what she was doing. She couldn't remember the last time either of her parents had even asked to see her report card. Her cooking and other household chores "to earn her keep"—that's all they noticed.

Her father didn't wait for her mother's answer. "Does he know the predicament you're in? Do his parents know? Will he take responsibility?"

It'd be nice if he'd fire one question at a time.

"He has his own apartment, so his parents aren't an issue. And no, I haven't told him yet. I thought you'd appreciate being first."

"An apartment. That explains a lot. Get in the car. I want to meet him and learn his intentions."

Elaina's older sister, Kim, burst into the kitchen. "You didn't finish facing the HBA shelves before you clocked out. The non-foods manager complained to me like I'm your keeper. You were hired at Tasty on my reputation, but you can't keep riding on my shirttails."

She left the room just as quickly, oblivious to the tension as she focused on her more important life. For once, Kim had just helped her dodge a bullet, though. Cole deserved a warning before her dad's confrontation, and her distraction might help Elaina push her father off track.

She took up hesitantly where they'd left off. "He's at work. I told you he works nights. Please let me at least tell him first."

"What's his name?"

On any other day, she'd have sung his name. "Nicholas Charles Carter, but he goes by Cole. He's working crazy hours because—"

"How do you get to his apartment? Let me guess, he's in walking distance of Saint Augustine. How often are you at his apartment . . . fornicating?" He choked on the word. "Oh, Elaina, where have secrets gotten you? Have you learned nothing from ten years of Catholic education?"

Catholic education? Was he joking? Saint Augustine's sanctimonious nuns taught that God's purpose for man and woman was to keep the human race going through reproduction, yet a baby born out of wedlock wasn't a child of God but a bastard. A baby born to non-Catholics was a bastard, too, because their marriage wasn't valid. The world was filled with two kinds of people: Catholic children of God, and bastards. God-fearing Catholic women pumped out as many babies as possible.

Sex was wicked and naked bodies vulgar, according to Sister Ruth, but sinful sex and nakedness were what a good bride gave her husband on their wedding night out of duty, to honor God. People needed to fight sexual attraction because it led to damnation. Sexuality was a gift from God that could send you to hell, except within the confines of marriage and only for reproduction. Even then, women had better hate it or risk the eternal fire.

Elaina struggled to maintain a neutral expression. Her thoughts shouted what she'd never say aloud: *Your God is a hypocrite who gets a perverse pleasure out of messing with our hearts and heads. Your God sets people up for failure from the beginning.*

How could her gentle, compassionate, loving Three be the same God as the oppressor Saint Augustine's nuns spent so many classes preaching about? Her chest tightened, holding back a clutch of loosening sobs.

Where are you, my Three? Please come back. I've made such a mess.

* * *

Styx blared so loudly from inside the apartment she wasn't sure Cole would hear her banging. Why wasn't he sleeping? He'd have a bunch of excuses, lies just like the *I love yous* that dripped from his mouth when he wanted sex. He believed his own lies as long as he thought she was convinced too.

Come on, Cole, open up. Her dad was less than an hour away.

"Hey sweetheart, what a surprise!" He pulled her inside the smoky apartment and pecked at her forehead. Her aggravation vanished. His pecan-colored curls, pronounced square jaw, and strapping shoulders made everything unpleasant disappear.

Her momentary bliss extinguished itself in the overflowing ashtrays that littered the room. "Friends" had stopped by again for a game of pool before Tasty's nightly grind. Coats, beer cans, and wet shoe prints had left their mark in his pool hall as he called his front room. His top-of-the-line pool table, as pristine as the day he'd brought it here, mocked her efforts at yesterday's cleaning. Cigarette and pot smoke left a burning sensation in her throat—or was that her own irritation?

She'd have to get these pigs out, clean and fumigate this place again, and tell Cole the news, all before her dad arrived.

Deanne Jonis and Karmin Jacobs sauntered in, balancing trays like cocktail waitresses. "More shots."

What were they doing here? School was barely out, but it appeared they'd been playing barmaid all afternoon. She didn't know them well, but she knew enough. They were loose party girls from the public school who didn't pretend otherwise.

The harsh, metallic guitar solo aggravated her already festering worry. How long before Cole tired of her in his addiction for physical pleasure and women's adoration? Elaina certainly wasn't his first, nor his second. He'd admitted losing his virginity before his fifteenth birthday.

"I know that look," he said with a smirk. "You're jealous."

Would indignation hide her insecurity? "They skipped school."

"You sound like a prudish Catholic girl, but I know better." He teasingly pressed his body to hers. "Remember all the times you played hooky for our afternoon delights? How about a quick reminder?"

She kept her expression neutral. When had their magic faded and sex become their dates? Though Cole showed appreciation for her cooking and cleaning, homemaking took a back burner to his physical desires. She wanted their relationship to mimic marriage, not that of a client and call girl. The day she'd overheard him bragging about his name for the sweet talk she thought he'd reserved for her, suspicion began to sour her thoughts. *Honey butter*, as he called it, was merely bullshit on a sucker stick to get his way.

Her scowl at Deanne gave away her suspicion, prompting Cole to shepherd both barmaids out the door.

"We'll pick this up another time, girls," he called after them.

He pushed the door shut with his foot.

"Okay, sweetheart, what's up?" He intercepted the overflowing ashtray from her hands and put it back down. Then kissing her forehead, nose and quickly moving to her lips, his tongue pried her mouth open.

Would he take the news better if she let him have his way? There wasn't time. "My dad's coming at seven thirty to meet you—"

"You're kidding. In thirty-five minutes?" He stepped back. "Why now, after almost a year?"

She wanted to ask the same. Why had Cole shown no interest in meeting her parents after all this time? If they were to marry eventually, this day was inevitable. She groped through emotions, searching for excitement to cover her dread. The manifestation of her birthday gift to Cole was proof of their love.

She squeezed his hand. "We're pregnant!"

Silence crashed against her hope, sinking the little confidence she'd clung to.

His voice was barely a whisper. "How long have you known?"

"Just yesterday. I told Mom and Dad first because—"

"What happened to the rhythm method, or whatever you called it?"

"I don't know. Girls at school use it all the time. Nobody's pregnant there."

"How far along are you?"

Her enthusiasm squelched, she shrugged.

Before Cole, sex had been a strange activity in a shadowy, forbidden world. Lacey, her older neighbor and a self-proclaimed scholar on the subject, gave tutorials with Barbie and Ken dolls. They were Elaina's only reference for answers. Lacey had explained that every sexual encounter didn't necessarily result in pregnancy. She wondered if her God-fearing parents had partaken more than ten times in forty-one years of marriage, once for each Michael child. But Barbie and Ken had then demonstrated other things couples did instead of intercourse on the three days a woman could get pregnant.

A sick feeling churned in her stomach as she recalled Eric's slithering appearance that long-ago afternoon, his glassy, unblinking eyes watching Lacey's lecture. When she'd shared this disturbing story with Cole a while back, he'd busted out laughing and concluded that Eric had found watching Barbie and Ken sexually stimulating.

If God had invented intercourse only for procreation, then why did men want it all the time? Wouldn't it have been more practical for every sexual encounter to result in a baby? Then only two, three—or ten—encounters would then have been necessary for creating a family.

And men wouldn't be so obsessed.

"Are you sure it's mine?"

Like a firing squad, the first bullet pierced her heart.

"You expect me not to ask?"

Yes, actually. How could he forget her mortification at soiling his sheets and his assurance that the first time was always messy? After that, just as Lacey and all the sexually active girls she knew instructed, she'd kept track of the days between her periods, never refusing him except on days thirteen, fourteen, and fifteen. The irony: during all that counting, she had already been pregnant.

"Do you think I let this happen on purpose?" Tears burned her chapped cheeks and made dark dots on the toes of her suede shoes.

He lifted her chin and studied her sincerity. His beautiful smile emerged, instantly healing the injuries from his words. "We can get this little mishap taken care of for a couple hundred. No worries, sweetheart."

She squared her shoulders against his second round of fire. "No, Cole. There's nothing I wouldn't do for you—except that."

"If you're thinking marriage, forget it. We're too young. You said the rhythm method would work, but it didn't. There's a reason you don't see pregnant gals roaming the halls of Saint Augustine: it's called 'River Rock Clinic of Choice.' If you insist on having this baby, I'll stick around till it's born, but that's the only promise I'm making."

"You can tell my dad that in twenty minutes."

Rage and regret begged for a voice, but she and Cole had to appear united for her father's benefit. She grabbed the ashtray again and handed Cole several beer cans, sending a clear message that both their efforts would be necessary to make the place presentable.

Their efforts took every last second. The door hadn't fully closed behind her dad before he batted his first question. Several more were volleyed, and Cole leaped to spike his defense.

"She told me it was safe."

He cringed as her usually restrained father slammed his fists on the pool table.

"It's a sixteen-year old's fault because you decided to make birth control a minor's responsibility?" Her father planted himself inches from Cole, who stood a head taller. "You're equally to blame, if not more because you're a legal adult. How old are you, anyway?"

"I turned nineteen the last of October." Cole stepped back, reclaiming his defiance.

Her father lowered his voice. "It appears you have a good job. I expect you to be financially responsible, at the least."

"I offered to pay for the termination of the pregnancy, but Elaina refused." This had to be a stranger speaking. Where was the sweet, loving boyfriend she'd described to her father last night?

Her dad's voice held disbelief as he pulled her under his arm protectively. "Of course she's going to see this pregnancy through. We're Christians, Mr. Carter. Are you?"

The temperature seemed to drop as the two men's temperaments rose. Maybe Cole didn't want a home in her heart any more than she'd wanted the Three to continue living there once she'd met him. Now a baby nested there that nobody wanted but her.

Her father's question left a moment of silence that amplified the busy street noises just outside the window, the hiss of the furnace, the clicking of the jammed eight-track tape player.

"I'm a member of South Street Baptist Ministry," Cole said, "and I believe it's wrong to bring a baby into this world without happily married parents. My parents are divorced because my father cheated constantly, siring children with women half his age. I'm not ready for marriage nor to be a single father, and I can't afford child support."

"Then why did you have sex with my daughter?" her father thundered. "Elaina's not a toy for your pleasure. Have you learned nothing from your father's sloppy example? Unwanted pregnancies are only one byproduct of irresponsible sex and have led our country to legalize the murder of unborn humans for the sake of sexual satisfaction."

Oh no, not another moral tirade. She couldn't bear a lecture now.

Cole and her father fought with the same fury as her emotions had during intercourse. In the heat of Cole's initial desire, she'd felt beautiful and wanted—until his urge escaped the confines. Then worries about pregnancy and damnation kept pace with his thrusts. As he climaxed, she found herself transported to a place of deep shame formed long ago. This dark place had smoldered since childhood, slowly disintegrating her self-worth with its secrets. Sex with Cole had added fuel.

Another of her father's sayings splattered like a huge insect on her window of thoughts. *Just as darkness can't exist in light, secrets have no part in goodness.* Beneath her excuses, truth reminded her that she'd kept Cole a secret because her parents wouldn't have approved. A deeper truth confirmed their reasons.

"If you refuse financial responsibility, I'll pursue statutory rape charges," her father said. "An attorney can inform me of your legal obligations."

When her dad used white-collar verbiage, he meant business—but she'd had enough.

"That's all I'm hearing—money," she shouted over them. "I'll pay myself! I have eight hundred dollars, and I'll work more hours. I'll do anything. This is your baby, Cole, and your grandchild, Dad." She took her dad's hand in a plea. "With a little time, we'll figure this out. You won't have to pay a dime, Dad. I promise."

His shoulders dropped like a hundred-year-old's, and he left without asking when she'd be home. She'd show her dad and everyone that she *could* make this situation turn out properly. In believing herself the soon-to-be Mrs. Nicholas Charles Carter hard enough, she could disregard her father's negativities in ways Elaina Michael never could.

3

Pain shot through her abdomen so forcefully she twisted, but as quickly as it had arrived, it retreated. With her feet in the stirrups, she waited for another. The women in the waiting room had said something about Brandon's hex. Who was Brandon, and what was his hex?

So near her due date, full examinations were required. Elaina's face burned at the humiliation, increasing with every appointment like her girth.

Dr. Stoffer studied her chart. "Describe the pain."

It was hard to remember. She couldn't concentrate over the sour smell of medicine and the former patient's perfume. In the little room left beneath her ribs, her baby adjusted, lending her joy that surpassed her discomfort. This tiny one merited full credit for her smooth skin and silky, thick hair. Dr. Stoffer said pregnancy hormones were the reason, but Elaina knew better.

This baby, already her world, would think of her the same way. They'd be inseparable, extensions of each other, just as the Three had been to her before Cole. To experience love returned as passionately as given, to matter above all else, was all she wanted. She already knew the taste from her Three and Sister Immaculata, the five of them making up the Clover Club.

The doctor repeated his question.

"Oh, yeah. Just one quick stab. No big deal."

"That attitude may be the reason you're here, young lady. Your condition *is* a big deal, especially at your age."

Why was her pregnancy referred to as a *condition* by him, her parents, her older siblings, her coworkers . . . As if it were any of their business. She also hated *predicament, situation,* and *dilemma.* Pessimists like Dr. Stoffer were the problem. Yeah, yeah, she was still in school, only working part time, no health insurance and no financial help. But she loved this baby. *Love is a choice;* her dad repeated it so often it was tattooed on her brain. So she chose to believe that love would conquer all the little hurdles. She would prove every pessimist wrong.

With her pregnancy now old news, pursed-lipped adults turning their children's eyes away from her protruding belly as if she were contagious no longer stung. Dismissing Dr. Stoffer's disapproval became easier too, except for these examinations, naked save for a paper gown, her feet raised in surrender.

His hand pushed inside of her, bringing a storm of strange, troubling emotions that struck and then blew away so quickly she was left confused and shaken. Elaina wiped a tear before he could notice.

"I suspect Braxton-Hicks. Schedule an ultrasound for tomorrow," he instructed the nurse. "If there are no openings at Grace General, try River Rock Mercy. You remember the routine, Elaina?"

This would be her third ultrasound in two months. She remembered Sister Immaculata's encouragements from her early years: "Everyone worries at times, *ma chérie,* but worry sprouts from original sin—doubt in God's perfect love." She would tweak Elaina's nose and add in her song-like French accent, "Never doubt your Three's love for you, or mine, *ma jolie fleur,* my pretty flower."

This baby would never doubt Elaina's love either. The Three and Sister Immaculata—Imm, as Elaina had been calling her for years—had proven that the root of everything worth living for was love. Yet for all their love, here she was alone. She'd probably have to go to this ultrasound alone too, just like the others.

Would her little one's birth be a solo act as well? Had she traded Imm and the Three, her Clover Club, for Cole and a baby?

Dr. Stoffer extended his hand to help her up, and the stiff, paper gown slipped off. He looked away too quickly out of respect for her modesty. She likened herself to a sideshow monstrosity. Sometimes her swollen middle brought as much embarrassment as her emerging breasts had in fifth grade. Her assets, as her dad called them, had appeared about the same time as her sexual confusion and the denial of the uglies—or did it go back further, to the darker episode in the barn? Per her parents' unspoken guideline, she would let the sleeping dogs alone.

But her silence conflicted with the nuns' warnings. Failure to confess one's most serious sins was a sin of omission and mortal in premeditation. Sister Ruth said it was better not to make a confession than to withhold. The contradictory messages of her parents and the nuns tangled in her belly during every mandatory confession, but still, she wouldn't loosen the skeletons' ties.

As she pedaled home, concern, pollen, and exertion exacerbated her labored breathing, as if the twenty-nine extra pounds she carried wasn't enough. Allergies and this ancient bicycle made each turn of the wheels feel like her last. What if Grace General was too full for tomorrow's test? Who'd give her a ride to River Rock Mercy, forty-five miles north? Her parents would be working, and Cole would be sleeping or covering another stocker's vacation—or so he'd say. She'd rather walk than ask Kim for a ride; her sister's preaching was too righteous to stomach.

Commuting on this single-speed, balloon-tired rust bucket with a seat big enough for an elephant had been enough of an embarrassment back when the popular girls whizzed by in their convertibles yelling, *Don't get a speeding ticket, Elaina.* Now, she only conjured pity.

She hated how her parents settled for *it will do* and expected their children to do the same. Even now, with Walkmans, VCRs, answering machines, and those amazing home computers—apples or something— her dad insisted that "happiness comes not from having more but being content with little." Except, of course, for the money he hoarded.

Ceaseless productivity is the antidote for temptation.
—Edward Michael

An idle mind is the devil's workshop. —Edward Michael

Listing Edward Michael's endless quotes was a game all his children played, but she and Eric were the only Michaels who deviated from their father's mundane philosophy. Where Elaina dreamed of college, study abroad, and an apprenticeship under a great painter, though, Eric simply wanted life's pleasures as quickly and effortlessly as possible. He made cunning and conning a science.

South Street's steep hill loomed ahead, making an even taller shadow on the grassy slope beside her bike. She floundered off the bike, her feet hidden from sight beneath her mountainous belly. She needed to rest for just a minute, but would some Good Samaritan stop? She had a tendency to draw unwanted help lately.

The telephone booth beneath the huge, shady oak offered a breather. It felt like 100 degrees even this early in June, and her body felt fifty degrees higher. She cooled her forehead against the glass, beads of sweat cascading like gossamer ribbon. The first pay phone call she'd ever made had been from this very booth in the second grade, to Imm. How many times had she and Imm huddled in here after, pretending to dial heaven and request that the Three join them for a Clover Club meeting? How many times in the last six months had she wished for that time to come back?

The glass muffled outside sounds except those she focused on: children playing in the park, the squeaky wheel of a passing stroller. Dare she call Imm again? Other than hurried hellos between classes, she hadn't had a meaningful conversation with her beloved art teacher since Cole. Truth be told, she had avoided Imm, like the Three, for fear of disapproval. To ask for Imm's time now that no one else was around seemed selfish, yet never, ever had Imm refused her *précieuse* as she called Elaina. Elaina's confidence increased as she remembered how often Imm had scooped her onto her lap, swirling her magic paintbrush over Elaina's cheeks and sweeping sadness or exclusion away.

She dropped two dimes into the slot.

"I'm so happy you answered." Elaina cradled the phone as her nerves generated still more sweat. "It's last minute, but I was thinking of you . . . I miss you. It's so beautiful outside. I wondered if . . . if you'd want to meet at the cemetery, like old times. I'm—"

The hands of shame closed around her neck, causing her chest to heave. She caught the sob at the back of her mouth and pressed it down. Oh God, she was so thirsty for the smallest gesture of tenderness. Months and months of alienation inflated her lungs, yet her determination not to lay her troubles on Imm kept the tears from flowing. She wouldn't dump this on Imm. Not after she had ignored her so long. It wasn't right.

"I knew it was you, *ma chérie*, before the second ring," Imm said. "I've asked the Trinity for this call every day. You see, they do answer prayers, but in their time. I'll be under Mary and the angels in fifteen minutes."

* * *

Imm and Elaina stretched out in front of the towering grave marker, Imm's slender, freckle-covered arms wrapped around Elaina from behind. The blue marble mother of Jesus and three pink angels seemed content to watch.

"Close your eyes, my child. Just watch your thoughts come and go. We'll listen in on the birds' conversation until our minds have settled."

The past year and a half of negligence vanished as paint-stained fingers stroked Elaina's arms. Velvet grass and silky breeze, heavy with the perfume of so many flowering shrubs, lulled her senses. Her mind scolded that she'd forgotten her inhaler, and she realized she didn't need it anymore. Stirrings of her Three felt very near. Maybe because they were here, with Imm. Nothing more was needed.

"This is my favorite place in the world," she said with a sigh. "Less than a block from my house, I feel a million miles away." She pulled Imm's small hand atop her belly and whispered, "Give the wee one a minute, and you'll feel a kick."

"Your child will be *un œuvre d'art*, a work of art."

"You used to call me that. Remember when all five of us would lie here? You'd all surround me protectively while listening to me blubber about something stupid like not being invited to jump rope. Then you'd all climb inside my heart and bandage another ouchie. Sometimes we were so close it's as if we were one person."

"We are," Imm whispered. "It's Holy Communion. This is how we understand your wounded spirit that's not visible to others."

Elaina wiggled closer to Imm. "I've been so selfish . . ."

"I missed you terribly," Imm cut off Elaina's self-distaining, "but I knew you were only searching for what we all want, to love and be loved in an intimate way. Besides, patience defines true friendships—and with no expectations."

"The biggest mistake of my life started here." Elaina patted the grass beside her. "Last fall, I wanted to sketch Cole in front of Mary and the angels. He brought a bottle of wine, and I got light-headed. Every art lesson you'd taught me floated through my head like falling autumn leaves." Her voice grew pensive. "The human body, Cole's muscles and nerves wrapping around strong bones like ribbon . . . He's so beautiful, Imm, like the incarnation of Michelangelo's *David*. I asked him to take his shirt off. I just wanted to run my hands over his arms and chest. With my eyes closed, my fingers tried to memorize the rises and dips of his form like you taught me to do with objects before painting them—tactual replication, I think you called it."

She plucked a clover hidden beneath taller grass and handed it to Imm with a sidelong glance, checking for signs of disapproval. But just like old times, Imm tilted closer, encouraging every thought on Elaina's heart to pour forth. How much of her spirit had withered in the last year wishing for someone to listen like this?

"Remember when Sister Ruth found me with one of your nude art books? I still wonder if it was the pictures or my shame for being fascinated that brought her ruler over my hands. You were the only one who didn't throw naked paintings in the same pot of sin as porn. Sex and sacredness belong in the same sentence, you said."

"You remember your lessons well." Imm wound one of Elaina's black curls around her fingers. "Tell me more."

"Touching Cole felt sacred, so good that I should've figured it was sinful. Then when he said he loved me, wanted to marry me and that I was all he wanted for his birthday, I didn't want to stop him anymore. I swore that no one would come between us." She sighed and patted her middle. "So guess what came between us? Looks like the nuns were right about nudity leading to sin."

"A baby cannot be a sin, regardless of its beginning. And true sexual relations are merely a man and his wife's mimicry of God's love in a physical, human way. That's why Adam and Eve felt no shame in their nakedness and desire for each other. Have you told your Three what you've told me?" Imm asked gently.

Elaina floundered to sat up, putting space between them. "You mean confession?"

Hurt flashed across Imm's expression. Why did Elaina continually push the few who loved her away?

She sprinkled a peace offering of clover over Imm's head with an impish smile. "Remember when I asked you if my cemetery friends were related to the Trinity?"

Imm laughed, then carefully selected several longer stems of clover and tucked them into Elaina's hair. "I had only been in the US a few weeks. My heart heavily missed Grasse until the day I met you, *ma précieuse.* Then I knew God had sent me to Saint Augustine Elementary for a very special reason. I saw a halo around your little head when you asked me about your invisible friends."

Elaina raised a hand to touch the clovers in her hair. "I was so sad when you said they were everybody's friends, until you added that my personal relationship with them was like our secret club. And I loved your comparing them to clover that grows beneath the grass. People can't see it because they don't look."

"But the Trinity's love, like clover, is everywhere, deep-rooted and with the sweetest nectar. Once established, it spreads quickly and is difficult to contain. Clover remains green through heat and drought, long after the grass has turned brown." Imm's eyes turned up toward the sky.

"I felt so lucky the day I met you. You, with them, makes my four-leaf clover." Elaina buried her head in Imm's shoulder, fighting tears again. "Thank you for coming."

The Saint Augustine Church bells rang six times. Her parents would be home from the nursery, waiting for supper. She wiped her eyes, thoughts jumping to the day four years ago when her allergies would no longer tolerate working at the family landscape business. Her father had assigned her to take over the household and cooking tasks. Though she'd thought it a blessing at the time, it didn't feel like such now, now that it forced her to leave her beloved Imm after they'd finally gotten back together.

"I have to run. Will you meet me here next week, same time?" she asked hopefully.

Imm's tight hug was her answer, and the last stretch home seemed less breathless than before.

* * *

Elaina hurried into the kitchen to find her parents already seated at the table, looking completely lethargic. Pale pink liquid steamed in their bowls, a sure indication that her mother had added water to a can of condensed tomato soup even though she knew her husband liked it with heavy cream. Their grilled cheese sandwiches were black on the outside, the cheese within still cold—likely cooked on high for a few minutes saved.

They'd asked so little of her lately. Even her mom's rigid cleaning schedule had been relaxed due to Elaina's cumbersome size. Her dad pushed his sandwich away, increasing her guilt. Cooking was the one place she'd never let him down, butter-braised and sugar-glazed, deep-fried and king-sized.

How many hours of her parents' 126 combined years had been sucked up by Michael's Landscape and Nursery? They were too tired to even lift their spoons. In Elaina's opinion, their business had ruined the family, stolen her parents' every waking minute, every ounce of energy, and any desire to be a mom and dad. Their defeated manner reminded her of old dogs. Their only memories would be of working—to death.

Two sets of exhausted eyes followed Elaina across the kitchen, taking in her rumpled maternity top and thick, disheveled ponytail. Their quizzical expressions questioned if she'd been having sex with Cole again. The assumed answer disgraced her, all without a word.

"Your doctor called. He's scheduled another ultrasound for tomorrow at Grace." Concern broke through her mother's fatigue. "Is everything all right?"

"Yeah, it's just another way for them to extract money. I thought about not showing up, but they'd probably charge me anyway."

"Do you need me to go with you?"

In other words, could she ride her bike, right? Yeah, she'd get there by herself, just like the last two times. If they'd put their damn nursery aside for a moment, though, they could have come to see their grandchild.

Merciless reality diluted the joy of the last two hours worse than the water in her mother's tomato soup. She pushed back from the table and carried her bowl toward the sink. "I'll figure something out. Sorry about dinner. I met up with Sister Immaculata and lost track of time. Well, I'm going to—"

"Just a minute. Have you and Cole decided what you're going to do? Arrangements have to be made." Her dad kept his voice mild, and her mother got up and feigned busy with the dishes.

"I want to keep my baby. Cole's a little apprehensive, but once he holds his—"

"So he's helped you with the bills?" Suffused disdain said he already knew the answer. "That'd be a good reason to give him the benefit."

Would he ever stop interrupting? To be fair, she'd never asked Cole for anything, not after the initial confrontation between the three of them. She didn't care about the money. She wished her dad would shut up. It wasn't like he was picking up the bills.

Her father's no-nonsense voice took over. "How do you plan to finance baby care with a year of high school left? You couldn't earn enough for check-ups and vaccinations, much less all the other things a child needs."

She remained stonily silent.

"Your mother and I have already raised our children, and the nursery is more than full-time work for both of us. That doesn't mean we aren't willing to lend a hand, but we won't be parents to a baby again."

"I never asked you to." She harnessed her resentment and lowered her voice. "I'll do everything. I can apply for government assistance—just until I'm out of school. Child Services provides day care for unwed mothers, and I heard college tuition might be covered too. Eventually, Cole and I will be married, but—"

His fists hit the edge of the table, making ripples in the pink soup. "Government assistance? That's welfare! Welfare is a euphemism for the legal theft of one man's paychecks to support another who wants a free ride. I'm sick of hearing about Cole *eventually* coming around. Even if his intentions are good, the path to hell is paved with good intentions."

She looked away, rolling her eyes. He had a quote for everything.

"He's nothing but a politician who's handed you a pack of lies." Her dad's greatest insult: comparing someone to a politician. It felt like a slap to her face.

"Furthermore, the very mention of mothering and college in the same sentence is ludicrous. To keep this baby, you'd have to drop out of school, and dropouts can't go to college."

She examined the dusty toes of her shoes.

"Your mother will take you to River Rock Adoption Agency on Monday. A caseworker will guide you through the process." He left no room for argument.

Elaina's body would only allow for a waddle up the stairs, though she longed to run, longed to hide, longed to be back at the cemetery with Imm. No one but Imm understood her or even wanted to try. That exceeded any difficulty this pregnancy presented. If only she could sleep, the heavy, dreamless kind of sleep, perhaps she could also put to rest the heartache.

She could hear Kim come in the house and then a burst of her father's laughter. Why did her own presence seem to do the opposite?

Maybe she should call Jenny, Patty, or Sarah. Real friends accept all, Imm had said. They still sat with her at lunch, even though they'd had to learn about her pregnancy secondhand. Trusting Cassy, of all people, with the news before them had been a huge mistake. Still, they'd brought her crazy carry-ins for pregnancy cravings right up to the last day of school. If nothing else, Jenny had said, their concoctions would build up her baby's immunities. The world didn't seem so disparaging when remembering Jen's chocolate-covered beef jerky, Patty's peanut butter-mustard spread, and Sarah's soda crackers with vanilla icing.

* * *

Was there any place worse than a hospital? The odor of cleaning chemicals, normally one of Elaina's favorite smells, told of sickness, disease, and a host of other horrible possibilities.

The same ultrasound technician as before, kind and easygoing, squeezed jelly on her massive rise. His wide forehead, creased in concentration, reminded her of Cole. Had she been wrong in not telling him about this appointment? The probability of Cole flipping his standing excuse, *I'm too busy*, left her feelings more upset.

The technician twisted a knob on the monitor, and she could hear her heart's half notes make a natural duet with the racing sixteenth notes of her baby's. Individual fingers were easily identifiable when the miniature hands spread. Lips, always sucking, formed a tiny rosebud on the screen.

"Would you like to know if it's a Sally or Sam? Hold still in there, little one. They usually settle down by now. Not much room for him to play in there anymore."

"Him?"

"Oops, guess the cat's out of the bag now. He's a Sam, all right. Okay, I have what I need, and I'll bet you're desperate for the bathroom. That's a lot of water you're holding." He extended a hand to help her up.

Toddling down the hall, she wondered how much larger this baby could grow before she toppled over. Heartburn, swelling feet, and leaking breasts increased by the day, too—all worth it for her son. Before this moment, Elaina thought she'd reached her greatest capacity to love in what she felt for Cole, but this baby wriggled past all her limitations.

She tried assuming a voice of authority as she reentered the room. "Why did Dr. Stoffer order this ultrasound? The last two times, they just talked around me."

"Doctors do that, don't they? But I'm in charge here," the tech said with a grin. "First, here's your Sam."

As if pulling a rabbit from a hat, he handed her an ultrasound picture with a wave and a bow. Elaina blinked. He was perfect.

"Your baby's around seven pounds, and you still have eight weeks to go, we think. Usually, they don't get much bigger the last trimester, but we need to watch this bugger close. Your pelvis is small and shows no sign of spreading."

Panic or asthma constricted her chest. She wasn't sure which, because often the two collaborated to cause a third impairment when anxiety arose: hives. As if being allergic to pollen, ragweed, dust, and pet hair wasn't enough. She'd forgotten her inhaler. Now, combined with heartburn, the allergies and stress felt like suffocation.

Her pale color must have startled the technician. "Don't worry. C-sections are common, and you may not need one."

She pulled a reply from her dad's quotes. "Worry is a debt paid in advance for a bill that might never be owed."

He grinned. "Clever you, and very true. Now, if you can find your way out, I have another appointment." He stepped out the cold steel door.

With her son's first photo in her pocket and nothing else pressing, Elaina felt the morning begging for a celebration. Ice cream! The cafeteria awaited one floor down.

But oh gawd, Cassy's mom was heading her direction. She flushed at how fat and frumpy she must look.

"Good morning, young lady. How are you feeling? I haven't seen you in a while." Mrs. Adams's formality made the encounter worse.

Elaina ducked her head. *You haven't seen me because you forbid Cassy to associate with me. But Cassy still comes around, Mommy dearest, because I'm her ticket to Cole's parties.* If Mrs. Adams knew that both her daughters were having sex, Elaina would love to be the one to feed her crow. It just might happen, too, because both Cassy and her little sister bragged about using the rhythm method of birth control.

She tossed Mrs. Adams a crumb. "Fine."

"You look well. How much longer?"

"Two months." Brief replies build high walls, her dad liked to say, his superior guidance always one quote away.

"Well, it was nice seeing you. Take care." Mrs. Adams backed away, not sure what to do with so much silence.

Self-reproach stepped on Elaina's heels. She'd been so rude: no thank you or goodbye. Shame had generated nasty behavior, a weak excuse as a defense.

But both Cassy and her mother assumed they were better than the Michaels because of their bigger house in a better neighborhood, their higher standing at Saint Augustine—everything bigger and better, including a family of five rather than twelve.

Each step Elaina took kept time to self-berating words: geek, loser, trash. If a former friend's mother could make her feel this low, those words must be true. Why couldn't other people see her the way Imm did?

* * *

The ugly tangerine vinyl chair, an obvious relic from a decade past, forced Elaina to sit uncomfortably upright. She watched her mother's lips purse and relax, feeling like a beached whale trapped in this sweltering room.

The middle-aged caseworker, tightly buttoned in a long-sleeved polyester jacket, made the room seem hotter and the clock tick slower. The jacket's geometric pattern made Elaina feel nauseous. The caseworker's vein-puckered hand crept along a seemingly endless stack of papers as if she owned time.

"My name is Tannis Farrow," she finally stated, her face lacking expression. She reached across the desk to shake Elaina's hand, but the chair refused to release Elaina's disproportionate rear.

The woman turned to her mother, indicating no notice of Elaina's flailing.

"I'm the caseworker who'll help your daughter arrive at a decision for this child's future." She stared matter-of-factly at Elaina's belly. "Your parents have explained why they believe adoption is best, but it's your child and your choice. I'm here to answer your questions and witness your arrangement."

Had her mother actually taken off work to come here behind

her back?

"Do you know who the father is?"

Did she look like the kind of girl who didn't? Polyester Woman was starting on the wrong foot if she thought she was getting Elaina's baby.

"Of course I know who the father is."

"His name?"

Elaina sighed.

Numerous questions followed: the overall health of the baby's parents, the OB doctor's name, her due date, and so forth. This meeting seemed more like a business deal than a conference about the welfare of her child.

Polyester Woman pulled in air, her prelude to weighty words. "The headlines of late have shown heartbreaking legal battles between biological and adoptive parents over child custody. Women have relinquished their babies, then changed their minds and demanded the child's return."

Elaina watched a moth flutter against the window. It could see the sky, but no matter how hard it flapped its wings, the invisible barricade made it impossible to reach the place it longed to be. She was the same. She did the same stupid things over and over, hoping in vain for different results.

" . . . and these court cases have torn lives apart," Polyester Woman continued. "They're the reason we exercise every precaution. I'll explain the process. Stop me if you have questions."

Over the past year, Cole had left holes in her heart like the moths had in her mom's wool sweater. Warmth and love, the hallmarks of the Three, had seeped away. She shivered.

"If you relinquish your child to a more suitable home, it'll be a closed adoption." Polyester Woman made brief eye contact.

A more suitable home? Now she was insulting Elaina's mother, too.

"A closed adoption means no identifiable information can be exchanged between the adoptive and birth parents. Once you've signed the papers, you'll not see the baby again. This is best so everyone's lives can move forward."

Her mother leaned in, anxious after her own concerns. "The father has provided no financial assistance, and we have no health insurance. If the papers are signed before the birth, could the adoptive parents help with expenses, at least for the child?"

Elaina grabbed her mother's arm. She could speak for herself, for heaven's sake. What made Polyester Woman the authority on what made a suitable home? And why were her finances any of her mother's concern? It's not as if her parents had offered a dime.

Polyester Woman's nasal voice irritated like metal against a chalkboard. "That's a frequently asked question, Mrs. Michael. The law says that financial assistance from the adoptive parents, before or after the infant is born, is considered buying the baby. All medical bills from the infant and mother prior to the relinquishment signing are the responsibility of the biological parents or grandparents. Adoption papers can't be signed until seventy-two hours after the birth, ensuring the biological parents have ample time to reconsider."

Elaina jerked her chair back, scraping the floor with a chilling screech. "I don't want financial help. I'll pay for my baby's birth and care myself—and provide a suitable home. I'm sick of being talked about like I'm not here and my pregnancy reduced to dollars and cents."

She pounded her fists against her barely visible knees. Her breasts, achy and full, began to flow along with her emotions. Her top stuck to her belly. Months ago, she'd started expressing her milk into the sink to ease the pressure and avoid embarrassing leaks, but for some reason, the milk seemed to be getting more plentiful and the dreadful chore more frequently necessary.

Mascara stung her eyes; salty tears and mucus from her nose burned her cheeks. Absentmindedly, she lifted her maternity top to mop her face, exposing her swollen middle.

Her mom's hand reached briefly but was retracted as quickly.

Was it her mother's stiff German upbringing that wouldn't permit visible compassion? Imm would have known how to make this bearable. She would have rocked Elaina, urging her to let the pain flow until every drop had been released.

After what seemed an eternity, Polyester Woman began again. "I know this is difficult. You're upset because you understand the gravity of the situation. That's good, in spite of how much it hurts. It says you want what's best for this child." She patted the air above Elaina's head, avoiding contact.

"I'm going to tell you about three couples who want to give your child a home. Each has been waiting years for an answer to their prayers. All three couples are financially comfortable college graduates in established professions, yet each of these women would give up their careers to stay home with their new child." She paused to allow the words sink in.

Elaina tried to focus on the moth, the activity outside the window, anything but the description of these parents that her own were not.

"We've carefully screened each couple for happy, healthy marriages—the best environment for a child."

What *was* Polyester Woman's standard for a happy, healthy marriage? Did those couples' faces glow the way lovers' did? Did they laugh together? Elaina wanted her baby to be the addition and reflection of his parents' adoration for each other. She'd seen too many marriages that appeared more like business partnerships between reproduction workers designed to keep the human race going. That might have been a holy marriage, but it wasn't necessarily happy—or suitable for her son.

"I'll share a few details about each family to help you envision where the baby you're carrying would be happiest."

Vague but enticing bits of information tempted her to listen more closely. One family had a large, tree-filled yard. Her son could climb those trees just as she had loved to do as a little one. The same family had adopted a girl several years earlier, a playmate for her son to lean on if he ever wondered why his mother had given him away.

Tears collected.

"I'll need to speak with Cole soon," Polyester Woman said. "The biological father and paternal grandparents have equal say in a decision."

Elaina had never even met the paternal grandparents. How could strangers have this much authority over her child's future?

4

Elaina's head rested in Imm's lap as breeze carried away the heat creeping into the huge grave marker's shade. She could smell the clover field not a hundred yards away and see the wild raspberries beginning to swell at the fence row.

"Your parent's rose farm in Grasse grows flowers for perfume factories, right? So what do you think about a perfume that smells like clover? Oh, and lotions, and bath salts . . . I want Isaac Nicholas to identify his mom with the scent of clover." She patted her belly.

"Oh, *ma chérie*, it's a boy? And such a noble name."

"I've been dying to tell you, but I wanted it to be here. He's huge, Imm, and he's absolutely beautiful! The first two ultrasounds, he looked like an extraterrestrial, but this time I saw even his fingernails. I was so happy until—"

She swallowed the sour memory of the encounter with Mrs. Adams.

"Is everything all right?"

"Fine. I just—I ran into Cassy's mom afterwards. I was pretty rude. But she really hurt my mom and me when she demanded that Cassy stay away from me. Now that I look like a whale, though, she's all pity. Worse, she must've told Cassy she ran into me at Grace, because Cassy called faking concern so she'd have new dirt to spin."

"Those are strong accusations toward someone who's been a friend since first grade."

"Friends? Ha! Both of us would've pushed each other off a cliff if it meant an invitation from one of the popular girls. We're both wannabes.

Well, I was until Cole. Cole could have had anyone he wanted, but he wanted me."

Imm said nothing, but her uninterrupted stroking of Elaina's cheek said she wasn't judging.

"Cassy's MO is sniffing out slip-ups and blowing them into all-out sins. She sabotages others' reputations to eliminate her competition, all while gaining momentary attention. She does it to just about everyone, though, so I don't care."

"You sound angry for someone who's unperturbed," Imm said. "Harsh judgments, even when thrown in self-defense, are still stones."

"She played me for a sucker! I don't feel as much mad as I do stupid. Cassy found me in the restroom with morning sickness last December. I'd just found out. Her interrogation, a lot like confession with Monsignor Blaski or Father Krammer, caught me off guard, and I decided to trust her with the truth. You know, an olive branch. You've always said that trusting people makes them more trustworthy."

The pain of Cassy's betrayal still stung. "I asked her to keep her lips zipped until I could figure things out. But a few hours later, in the cafeteria, the frenzy of whispering may as well have been a loudspeaker announcement. I stomped over to Cassy's table, grabbed her, and called her a snake. That probably made it worse."

Imm massaged her shoulders as if to knead the pain away.

"My trust was less valuable to Cassy than the crumbs she gained dishing the dirt. Popularity is that important to her."

"If you tell yourself that enough times, it becomes your truth, *ma jolie fleur*."

Elaina rolled her shoulders impatiently. "I have too much time to think. Since Tasty put me on maternity leave, I constantly worry about how I'm going to pay for the tests the damn doctor keeps ordering, if Cole is going to change his mind about keeping Isaac, and even what people are thinking as they do a double-take at the prego freak on the hundred-year-old bike."

"You never used to fret when you talked to your Three," Imm said. "They've never betrayed your trust, either, have they? We all have demons that need expelling, some so ugly that our fear keeps them hidden. Through confession, you can unload—anonymously, if that's your comfort. But silence also shows your refusal to trust. You've closed yourself to the Trinity's peace and mercy."

Why wouldn't Imm let go of the whole confession thing? And how was Elaina supposed to make a full confession without rattling any old skeletons? The few times she'd tried to share the childhood uglies that tied her up inside, both Monsignor Blaski and Father Krammer used questions to twist her words. When she couldn't remember the details they demanded, they'd accused her of withholding. She'd left the confessional feeling more confused than before but sure that her buried childhood ordeals were somehow her own sins.

She hadn't taken Imm to the burial ground of the uglies, either, for fear that her beloved art teacher, friend, and fellow Clover Club member might find her at fault too. Expelling the uglies wasn't worth risking Imm's disapproval, nor would it stop the permeation of rot under every reminder.

As for the Three, they already knew it all, so she didn't need a priest. That they hadn't shown up at the cemetery last January after she'd begged told her they were fed up.

* * *

The only yellow Volkswagen Beetle in Tarrock sat parked next to Cole's Delta Eighty-Eight in his apartment lot, as it had for days. Everyone knew it belonged to Marsha, Tasty's deli manager.

Every day, Elaina pedaled by to see if it was still there, then home little faster than a crawl. She would never confront him, jeopardizing what little of him she had left. New space in the dark place inside her would have to be finagled to hold this hurt, too.

With every downstroke, she ticked off a what-if: what if he hadn't sown even one seed of love for her to nourish, what if he refused a change of heart about marriage and their baby, what if he left her for good?

Funny, they no longer seemed like what-ifs but whens and hows. When had Cole's face stopped lighting up when she came around? When had she stopped walking on air in his company? When had dreams of becoming a great painter and author begun to appear silly and worthless?

She pushed a stray lock of hair from her eyes and ignored the cars passing too close as she struggled along the shoulder. How would she plow through the days with no purpose beyond enduring time? How much longer would lonesomeness feel like her spouse? Life had no point without a loved one to share her pleasures with.

Every effort to pin Cole down had failed, probably due to Dr. Stoffer's warning that intimate relations could induce early labor.

> *The farmer will never buy the cow if he gets the milk for free.*
> —Edward Michael

Oh God, she'd been such a fool.

> *The only foolproof birth control is to place a quarter between your knees and not let it drop.* —Edward Michael

Before Barbie and Ken's demonstrations, Elaina had been sure that sex included cows and quarters. Her father had peppered his rendition of the birds and the bees with so many strange words—adultery, fornication, masturbation—that she'd decided sex was unachievable without a dictionary. Now, the cow and quarter quote said that the responsibility for sexual propriety and pregnancy belonged to women.

She coasted dangerously near Cole's car, and he materialized from nowhere, jumping between her bike and the passenger door and grabbing her handlebars. His face flushed, but whether from worry over his precious Delta Eighty-Eight or her, she wasn't sure. Or was he embarrassed to be seen with her?

She blurted the only thing on her mind. "Please can we keep the baby?"

He smoothed her wind-blown hair, and agony forced a burn to her throat, yet she didn't pull away. Even misery was sweet with him. How could she love someone so selfish? Did God ask himself the same question about humanity?

"Sweetheart, look at you." He shook his head, unable to hide his shock at how large she'd swollen. "You're too young to go through this. And why are you still on your bike?"

She hadn't been too young for anything on his nineteenth birthday. And she was still pedaling because he was never around to give her rides.

"We're both miserable when we're together anymore. Multiply that times ten with a screaming baby. That Farrow lady is right. Adoption is best so everyone can move on."

He'd all but said he planned to leave after the baby was born. The threadbare scrap of hope that he'd feel differently once Isaac was in his arms barely held together. Still, she refused to give in, except for the nagging fact that Polyester Woman had never said what would happen if Cole and Elaina couldn't agree.

"You can't go to college until you let go of this dream of playing house. I want to take some classes, too, and travel." Talking more to himself, Cole appeared to already have set the wheels of escape in motion. "Don't you want to get the hell out of Tarrock?"

"You mean us? Where?" Her heart jumped, but only one bounce before Cole shook his head.

"You have to finish high school, silly." He tousled her hair. "I promised to stay with you until the baby's born, but that's it."

He hadn't kept his promise, though. He'd been emotionally distant ever since he'd learned of her pregnancy. And cheating with Marsha and who else.

"We'll settle this at the next agency meeting."

Settle it? More like Cole getting out from under it.

Sure enough, at their next meeting at the adoption agency, Cole slopped honey butter over Polyester Woman before even being seated, reducing her to girlie gushing. Was it possible to hate the man she still loved most?

"Let me ask you a question, dear," Polyester Woman said. "Before this child's life began, what was your dream?"

Elaina blinked. "I thought about studying art. Or creative writing." It sounded foolish now.

"And how did you plan to make those endeavors happen?"

She waved her hand over her belly. "Well, this happened before I had a chance—"

"Will you attend college after this chapter of your life is over?"

She hadn't allowed herself to think beyond bike rides with Isaac in a baby seat behind her, and painting him in Cole's arms in front of Mary and the angels—or how to keep Cole in the picture. "Probably not for a while."

Polyester Woman and Cole were both staring at her.

"My dad says that until I've paid for this birth, nothing else can be considered."

"That's honorable. You have much to be proud of."

Nothing about this situation felt honorable, although it wasn't as if she had options. She had to give Isaac away because she had nothing to offer him and no one to help. But Polyester Woman's virtuous character crap was the last thing she wanted to hear.

Cole nodded in eager agreement with Ms. Farrow. "She's a sweetheart, for sure. They don't come any better."

Polyester Woman reached across the desk, taking Elaina's hands in hers. "Focus on the endless possibilities you'll be giving this child through giving him away. Don't second-guess yourself."

Why did the only hand extended in compassion have to be from Polyester Woman?

5

"Are you on your bicycle again?"

She shrugged, suspicious of why Dr. Stoffer was asking. Her answers always seemed to result in more tests.

"How far did you peddle?"

"I don't know."

"I'm not questioning but commending. Exercise will speed your recovery. I only asked because your pelvis needs measuring, and I don't want you peddling to Grace."

She'd give him the answer he wanted. "I'll call my mom, but I want to know why."

"Your baby's dropped and turned, but your pelvis isn't spreading in preparation for birth. A cesarean may be necessary. If your mother isn't available, I'll find you a ride."

"No, no, she's home. I'll wait outside for her."

Would he be disturbed to learn that his offer was more than she'd gotten from the father or grandparents of this child?

After a grueling test under a crushing machine, she was banished to a large, empty waiting room. Metal doors amplified emergency calls, ominous warnings of bad news, sickness, and death. And the smell. It must be the same as in a morgue: deadly clean.

Another nurse popped her head in to speak with her parents.

"I'll deliver your message," Elaina said, trying to seem confident on her own.

"How'd you get here, Miss Michael?" Suspicion frosted the nurse's words. "Your doctor was specific that you weren't to ride your bicycle. Now, where can I reach your parents?"

The alarm in her words said the game of pretending to be an adult was over.

Yet adults only pushed their noses in Elaina's business except where she needed their help. Memorized mumblings that the nuns called prayer distracted her from her worries momentarily, but eventually the pointless routine brought to mind the God she had no confidence in. She had traded her faith for a guy who barely gave her the time of day.

> *The gravest and most unforgivable sin is to turn your back on God.*
> —Sister Ruth

A dull inner voice reminded Elaina that she was no better than Cassy, who'd betrayed her for the popular girls' scraps.

Why wasn't she privy to her medical information, when she'd footed all the bills thus far? Ms. Farrow at the agency wasn't any better, giving Cole's decision for this baby equal weight as hers. How could Polyester Woman so easily dismiss what her mom had said that first meeting about Cole's lack of financial support?

She briefly considered how much easier Cole's proposal to end the pregnancy would've been, but just as quickly realized there would have been strings attached to that as well. The tight lips and acute sadness of two classmates just back from a "spa weekend" gave away their abortions. Both those girls' lives seemed a flawless, empty circus act for their parents' benefit. If either of them loved their boyfriends as much as Elaina loved Cole, then they must have felt some measure of joy in the difficult news of a forthcoming child. The guilt and emptiness after having their babies ripped from beneath their hearts was inconceivable. One of those girls had attempted suicide soon after.

Elaina's heart warmed remembering her dad's protective arm sliding around her when Cole had suggested an abortion. She could do far worse for parents. She wished she could loosen blame's grip, which had driven a wedge between her family and her future. Imm often reminded that bitterness builds the walls to one's own prison.

Forgiveness, like love, must be given and accepted freely for one to reach his soul's truest desire. —Sister Immaculata Lefevre

Elaina's mother rushed into the waiting room and hurried over. Questions deepened the lines on her face, but she tried to smile. Though she appreciated her mom's presence, Elaina knew better than to hope for a hug.

The nurse who'd gotten short with Elaina earlier escorted them to a cubicle. "Your daughter's pelvis is too small for a vaginal delivery. We've scheduled a cesarean for tomorrow morning."

It may as well have been a weather report. Her mom's mouth gaped, begging for answers, but the nurse had already left without leaving instructions or even a dismissal. Her mother jumped up and ran after her.

Relieved, Elaina sank deeper into the chair. Her visions of grueling labor vanished. When she woke up from surgery, she'd feel nothing but the sweetness of Isaac Nicholas in her arms.

Her mom reappeared several minutes later. "We need to pack a bag. Can you walk to the car, or shall I pick you up at the door?"

She'd been on her bike two hours ago. Why all the fuss now?

When they were finally settled in the car, her mom's foot barely touched the gas. She drove as if she were transporting fine china. Elaina found herself choking back pleas to speed up until there it was, a reason to stop altogether.

"Mom, pull over. It's Cole!"

Cole trotted across the street toward her shout, never looking for traffic. How like him to assume the world would wait when he needed to pass. He owned gracefulness.

Before he reached the passenger door, she'd already blurted everything out the window. "Can you meet me at Grace in an hour?"

"How 'bout a hi first, sweetheart?" He planted several pecks on Elaina's forehead, each sealed with an exaggerated smack and subtle challenge to her mother. "I'll come before my shift, if they'll let me in your room." His hard glance past her said he wasn't questioning permission from the hospital but from her parents. "I can't get there any sooner. This is awfully last minute."

Aversion curled her mom's thin lips, as irritating as Cole's breezy manner. Elaina tried to justify both their reactions, but in the tug-of-war between opposing sides, the father of her baby won. She beamed at Cole, who proclaimed his easy victory in the trophy smile he shot her mother.

By half past nine, Elaina lay in a strange bed, half the room dark where the hallway fluorescents couldn't reach. Like her life, her bed rested on the line between light and dark. She rolled from side to side, trying to get comfortable, but neither suited.

If the door had been closed, the darkness would have allowed her to sleep, but the staff told her it must stay open so they could check her vitals throughout the night. Sticky pads attached to thin wires tethered her belly and chest to a beeping machine. It flickered red dots on the wall like Sister Katherine had described in the Communist prisons that tortured priests. Her dad said if Ronald Reagan made president, he'd put an end to the Cold War and Christian persecution. How could her dad be so preoccupied with the oppression oceans away yet blind to the violations and perversions in his own domain?

The sounds and odors of misery, malady, and mourning filled her from every direction, telephones, pages to doctors, doors opening then quickly closing. A nurse clipped orders to her records, fueling her anxiety as the uglies packed around her already trembling body like ice. Her summer nightgown stretched to its limit under the thin white sheet, and she shivered under the air conditioner's blast.

The door swung wide to Cole's magic hand, and the dark half of the room disappeared. His gait, never hurried, was like a fashion model on the catwalk. His cologne, her favorite scent next to roses, chased away the other threatening smells, and his smile warmed the chill. Isaac stirred as Elaina's heart leaped.

"Hey, sweetheart! You're all tucked in. Scoot over." Cole wedged in beside her, then jumped back up. "It's freezing in here. I'll get you a blanket."

"No, stay." She patted the bed, knowing time with him was short. She craved his body heat like the sun in springtime, an intense warmth that soaked through her skin to the marrow in her bones. She wanted his arms to envelope her completely, as the Trinity had cradled her when she was small. Her eyes began to well.

"Oh, sweetheart," he murmured, stroking her hair. "I never meant for things to get so crazy. I love you, but it's not the kind a marriage could last on. You and I are like fireworks: dazzling, but we'd fizzle way too fast."

When she didn't respond, he continued. "I know I've been selfish in wanting you with no strings, but I've been honest."

Maybe it was her fault too. She'd taken his mentions of marriage and remolded them into promises. No, Cole hadn't been dishonest, but he had been calculating. She was easy, though not in the way the mean-mouths at school and her own family implied. "Her kind of easy" referred to her emotional shortcomings. She was apparently incapable of making a real love connection.

* * *

The room smelled vaguely different, and the ceiling pattern was off. Lights overhead made her squint, and mechanical noises bounced through the air. A plastic bag above dripped something into a thin, clear tube that stretched somewhere. Everything was fuzzy, including time.

Elaina squeezed her eyes tighter, then carefully reopened them, but nothing connected in her mind-fog until his beautiful face appeared grinning above.

"Hey, sweetheart, you're back." Cole's voice beckoned like a beacon.

Her enormous, salty-dry tongue blocked her request for water and raised a fit of coughing that flooded pain to her fingers and toes. Nausea overpowered in her body's effort to release lodged mucus. She felt a stabbing pain.

"Something's wrong!" Cole yelled.

A needle held by pink fingernails injected something into a plastic bag. "The anesthesia is wearing off, but this'll make it better." Sunburned cheeks that matched the nails pulled up in a smile. "You're gonna love this stuff, sweetie!" the pink voice cooed.

To Cole, the voice said, "When she relaxes, give her these ice chips."

Worry made wavy lines across his wide forehead, and his eyes reflected Elaina's fear. Was she dying? Numbness hung weights on her eyelids. Was she dead? It didn't matter, because the pain had passed away too.

"We had a boy! He's healthy and big as a beach ball. It's all over now." Cole's voice sounded far away.

People kept disappearing and reappearing. Had her parents just been here, or had she dreamed them? Where was here?

Sometime later, the pink voice hovered near again. "You're goin' for a ride to a more cheerful room with your chauffeurs, Freddy and Slim."

"On three—"

Freddy and Slim lifted. The movement thrust pain like a white-hot skewer. She writhed, her tongue blocking a scream.

"Hurts, huh, missy? We'll getcha there as easy as we can."

Freddy and Slim found encouraging words for every bump and groove they crossed in the hallway. Once she was settled into a stationary bed, she begged for whatever the pink fingernails had injected into the dripping bag earlier.

The pain could be contained if she remained still, small ripples dissolving before reaching her shoulders and thighs. Between vitals, visitors, and a vigilant watch on the bag's drip, the significance of this day unfolded. Today, July 18, 1980, Isaac Nicholas Michael-Carter had been born at 8:26 a.m., weighing seven pounds, eight ounces and measuring twenty inches long. He was somewhere in this hospital.

Her parents' small talk couldn't distract her. What color were her son's eyes and hair? Who was caring for him, and when would they bring him to her?

Giggles outside the room diverted her momentarily. Jenny, Patty, Sarah, and Cassy bounced through the doorway wearing huge foam hats shaped like fast food.

"May we take your order?" Cassy asked with a curtsy.

Wild laughter burst from their attempt to dance in the ridiculous hats that brushed the walls. She noticed her father smile as he pulled her mother from the room. Elaina's giggle loosened her phlegm-clogged lungs to coughing uproar; pain so sweet. The girls' shoulders shook and tears of merriment rolled. At any indication the laughter might subside, another hoot relaunched the hysteria.

"She's splitting a gut," Sarah yelled.

"She's in stitches," Patty said.

"She's doubled over in yuk-yuks," Jenny added.

"That one makes no sense." They laughed louder.

A tiny Grace nun erupted into the room like a hospital warden, so old she resembled a shriveled rag doll. "Ladies! This is a hospital. Miss Michael has been out of surgery less than nine hours. Control yourselves or you'll have to leave."

Before her footsteps reached the end of the hallway, more howling burst from their room.

These friends were like flashlights in the dark. They'd come when most needed and with no expectations.

When the silliness settled, Elaina watched Cassy fidget, clearing her throat and making false starts at conversation. After betraying Elaina's confidence about the pregnancy, she was a fifth wheel in their group, searching for a place to belong.

Demerol-induced repose or the Three seemed to fill Elaina, bringing the story of Christ's passion to mind, told in Sister Immaculata's fervent way. The connection had something to do with Cassy's unease.

"A rooster stretched himself, shook his feathers, and crowed," Imm had told her captivated students. "Jesus, surrounded by soldiers, looked full into the face of Peter, knowing this betrayal would be the beginning of great pain and anguish. Suddenly, the chief apostle broke into sobs, covered his face with his hands and ran.

"Exactly as Jesus had foretold, Peter betrayed him." Imm's eyes had pooled in sorrow. The students teared as well, both for Jesus and for their beloved teacher. "What Peter didn't know at that moment is that he'd been forgiven for this grave disloyalty before he was born.

"The next time Peter saw his teacher alive was after Jesus's death. As Jesus busied himself building a fire on the beach, Peter, from his boat, recognized his best friend and swam ashore. But face-to-face with the one he'd betrayed, Peter was speechless. Both Christ and this fisherman remembered the deception, but the reason Jesus came back was to forgive, extinguish shame, and encourage us to do the same. Jesus gives a million do-overs."

Elaina couldn't hold Cassy's betrayal against her, either. She and Cassy were so much alike: desperate nobodies who ached to be cherished but seemed to attract false friendships instead. Each would sell whatever they had—gossip, loyalty, even their dignity—for a taste. One day, Cassy would see it as clearly as Elaina did now.

If Elaina had a paintbrush, these four with her, so full of Clover, is how she would have painted the Trinity.

Relationship with people is Holy Communion too. Both in Eucharist and in friendships, we can take Jesus into our hearts physically.
—Sister Immaculata Lefevre

"We should get going." Jenny patted Elaina's hand. "But first, we brought you a gift."

On the corner of a tiny blue blanket, amateurish embroidery spelled out Isaac Nicholas Michael.

Elaina curled up, wishing to disappear. "You don't understand. I think I'm giving him up."

"We know," Jenny whispered. "Cole didn't think it was a secret. But we understand what Isaac means to you. The blanket is to help you remember him."

Four sets of helpless eyes watched her cry into the blanket as she struggled to face a future with empty arms.

* * *

"Did you see Isaac?" Elaina demanded before Cole had stepped fully into the room.

Carrying a stuffed lime-green elephant and cotton candy, he wore the expression of an excited child. He offered the fuzzy monstrosity and pink, sugary fluff with a bow. How many times had she told him she hated cotton candy, even the smell? The Demerol, almost worn off, made it worse.

"I won it at the fair. Isn't it—well, it's the thought that counts." He sighed and tossed the elephant on the chair.

"Did you see Isaac?" Elaina repeated.

"Yeah. He's perfect. Really fat. We sure made a beautiful boy together."

We? She waited for more, turning away from the cone he extended that was beginning to collapse into a gooey mess. "Did you hold him?"

"I didn't ask. It'd just make things harder. Remember what Ms. Farrow said? And with your mom and dad at the nursery window, I didn't hang around."

"Aren't I supposed to see him and feed him by now?" Her breasts were full, adding to her pain. "Ask who's feeding him and what they're feeding him. I'm still his mother until I sign." Her voice rose hysterically.

Cole scurried to the door.

He was back within minutes. "Apparently, you can't feed or hold Isaac as long as you're on pain meds. Something about the baby getting Demerol through your milk. Maybe I could take Isaac's place."

His attitude made her sick; worse was the flip way he spoke their baby's name. She had chosen his middle name, Nicholas, to honor Cole. Nicholas meant victory, and this baby was her victory alone. Cole played no part except—

"Did you bring your Instamatic camera?"

"I don't know about this, sweetheart. You need to let go."

"It's been easy for you, hasn't it, honey butter boy?" Her belly, empty of the baby she ached for, filled with hatred. "You're nothing but a reminder of how stupid I am. One day, you'll regret your selfishness." She tried to turn her back to him, but another stab immobilized her. Helplessness was worse than the pain.

"Get me up. I'm going to the nursery. Wheel the IV, and I'll carry the camera and this gross bag of pee."

"What is that?" Cole's nose wrinkled.

"I had to be catheterized. I can't get to the bathroom by myself." She lifted her gown to shock him—retribution for his insensitivity. "It's horrible, isn't it? And it hurts like hell. Now help me up."

"If they wanted you walking around, you wouldn't be connected to all this crap." He waved his hand at the bag.

"Please, Cole, I have to see Isaac."

Maternal need superseded the throbbing that threatened to bring her to her knees. With her jaws clamped, she focused on each step.

Cole supported most of her weight, but halfway there, she couldn't continue. What if Isaac was taken away before she saw him?

Cole scooped her up, instructing her to grab the IV pole. They moved awkwardly toward the nursery, tangled in tubes.

Karmin and Deanne ran toward them. "Are you all right?"

"I told you to wait downstairs." Cole cursed between clenched teeth.

"But we wanted to see your baby," Karmin protested.

Elaina watched in disbelief. She was like a tragic soap opera character, heavy in bad luck. Cole's one unselfish act, their only moment to witness the manifestation of his birthday gift together, was about to be stolen from them.

"Get out," she shouted. "Leave us alone."

Cole jerked his head toward the stairs. "Go."

The girls scurried away with a look of shock on their faces.

At the nursery window, Cole supported her from behind as she carefully positioned her feet on the floor. Isaac Nicholas lay bunted like a new baby doll waiting Christmas delivery. He had no hair, only downy fuzz the color of wheat. He was perfect.

"Take the pictures."

"How the hell are you going to stand up without me?"

"I'll hold the ledge. Go inside the nursery. Quick."

He accomplished his mission as she gritted her teeth by the nursery windows, and then carried her gracelessly back to her room. She winced at each jar in his arms.

A nurse entered just as she was getting settled again. "You look terrible. Let's get something to help you sleep."

"Are all the pain meds worn off? I haven't held my son yet, the Michael-Carter baby."

"If you think you can manage without pain meds, I'll bring him for a night feeding."

Elaina fought her tightening muscles and waited, silently calling to her Three. When was the last time they'd snuggled? This long day, so full of apprehensions, had filled her with a grogginess she couldn't fight. But if the nurse found her sleeping, they'd take Isaac away. She forced herself into a semi-reclined position she'd specifically been advised against, stabbing her back to full consciousness.

"Congratulations." The nurse helped her adjust her position upright and placed a sleeping Isaac into her arms.

Oh, dear God, she was holding heaven.

"Your baby's been bottle-fed, but I can help you get started if you want to give him a little more."

Elaina's breasts, so full and achy, begged for her baby. Milk flowed down her belly into the painful incision. Isaac's lips puckered in and out like a sleepy goldfish. He was beautiful beyond her imagination. Another spasm, either her abdomen or her heart, caused his tiny arms to jerk free of the bunting. His tiny face crinkled, and his fist latched to her index finger like a delicate vise.

A stern voice interrupted their bliss. "There's been a mistake. I'm sorry, but you're not supposed to hold the baby." A silver-haired nurse lifted Isaac from her arms before turning to the other nurse. "This infant is being placed for adoption. Didn't you read the chart?"

Could hell be this horrible? Sobs racked Elaina's body, shaking her into a coughing fit. Demerol was forced into the IV drip before she could protest, and the pain—and her baby—faded from view.

* * *

She had been dreaming about an auburn river, wild swirls cascading as a porcelain face dipped into and out of view. It reminded Elaina of the way Sister Immaculata's curls exploded when the rain was heavy or the humidity high, especially after Imm had given them freedom from the veil like so many other nuns after Vatican II.

Elaina cracked open her eyes. Tiny, paint-stained hands wrapped around hers. Imm *was* here, in the hospital! As if a motherly bond had called her to Elaina's side, Imm seemed to materialize whenever she was needed.

Elaina squinted at the sun streaming through the window, beams of yellow moving within Imm's riot of locks. Illuminated by her blazing halo, Imm reminded her of the picture in her First Communion book with the fire of the Holy Spirit descending onto the Apostles at Pentecost. She had always loved that picture because Imm said the apostles would never be frightened or alone again.

"Oh, *ma jolie fleur.*" Imm shook her head slowly, her tongue holding the last syllable, then lightly flicking it from her mouth. The chime of her accent made music for the sunlight still dancing atop the coiling cloud of red.

Elaina wanted to tell her she looked like an angel and that being here made her an angel, but the painkillers restrained her words.

"You look so forlorn," Imm said. "Have you found your Trinity?"

"They're gone, so long. I don't know where . . . how to find them." Despite the sunlight across her bed, Elaina felt pulled into gloom.

"Where did they used to meet you? In the sacred silence of your heart, yes? Is there quiet there anymore, or has doubt and self-criticism invaded their home?"

Elaina guiltily pulled her hands away from Imm's. "I kicked them out. I ditched everyone and everything for Cole. I'm a traitor."

"Maybe the problem is that you want their friendship but only when it suits you. Love can't be part time. It's a constant exchange in complete trust."

"I'm afraid to love or trust. Ever. The pain of this C-section is nothing compared to what I've been through with Cole."

"Did you evict your Trinity because you thought they wanted to spoil your relationship with Cole? Is your life better now without them?"

"Cole seemed like everything I needed and wanted, for a while . . ."

"Now you understand the abandonment your Clover Three must feel, yet they're still here, *ma chérie.*" Imm placed her hand over Elaina's heart. "Just as you don't love Cole any less despite his selfishness, and you can't love baby Isaac any less even though he'll call another woman Mama, so your Clover Club can't love you any less regardless of your disloyalty. It's impossible for the Trinity to desert you any more than they can desert themselves, because your heart, mind, and soul are also part of them."

"How'd you know I'm giving Isaac away?"

"Ah, *ma jolie fleur*, as I've told you many times, you and I are bound by similar heartstrings. I perceive much about you from my own experiences. Your ache to share a mother-child bond with your own flesh and blood is an ache I know, too."

Elaina frowned. Unless Imm had given birth and been forced to relinquish her child, how could she know this pain or guilt?

"Your heart's treasure is evident in what you feel most guilty about," Imm continued. "Guilt protects goodness and encourages growth, unless you twist it to shame. True love often comes at great cost and without reward, like the love you've given Isaac in choosing to give him life and a future. The Trinity gave you the same. The scars on their hands and feet are proof."

Imm gently placed her hands on the blanket above Elaina's middle. "The scar under your belly is your proof. Blessed are all women who bring God's reflection into the world by way of another human life. You're a holy woman."

But there was so much Imm didn't know. Elaina's state of mortal sin had begun long before she'd had sex with Cole. Eric had put her in mortal sin, yet the only way for her heart to be sparkly-clean again was to say it was her fault.

Elaina had tried to confess the uglies as a child, praying the priest would see how she'd been tricked. Taking blame would have made the confession go faster but it would have also been lying. So she'd simply omitted those horrors.

Yet every time she received Holy Communion in a state of mortal sin, the sin increased exponentially—years and years of mortal sins. Sister Ruth had said it would be better not to make a confession than to withhold, and better to refuse the Eucharist than to partake while in mortal sin, but Elaina had been forced. If she had refused, the nuns would have demanded a reason, compelling still more lies. Eleven years of forced daily Eucharist and monthly confessions equaled a mortal million.

At this point, hope for a priest's absolution was too great a stretch.

"You doubt your holiness? Then why did they choose you to bring Isaac into the world? Look at yourself with God's eyes. You're the mirror in which they admire their own reflection. When you finally accept how brilliant you are, you'll no longer feel unlovable and you'll find your heart's wishes. But first, you must rid yourself of that which blinds you."

"You mean confession, don't you? No, thanks. I'll go directly to God."

"But you haven't. You just told me you can't find them. Or is it that you don't trust them? Holding onto hurts allows the pain to abscess, but in releasing them through words, you purge their poison. Like radiation on cancer, casting light on dark things neutralizes them."

If Imm knew the extent of what Elaina had buried, she'd understand that even after exposing the contamination, the stench would remain. Sometimes she could actually smell it rising to the back of her nose.

Imm brought her shoulders up, pulling in air. "You fear. Fear extinguished the light in Lucifer. Now the dark one uses fear as his tool. If you trust light, it will bridle fear when you drop into the darkness. Confession is merely dropping into darkness and casting light on secrets."

Elaina's lips quivered. Yes, she was afraid to relive the horrors by retelling them, and she also feared judgment. Both her parents' and the two priest's reactions had been the opposite of what she'd needed and prayed for. She'd even tried talking to Imm once, but Imm's sharp response, using her formal name rather than the usual French endearments, had spooked her. *Elaina Michael, is there something you're trying to tell me?* It felt as if Imm were scolding her.

No doubt, this matter was too grave for anything but burial.

"Enough for now. Rest." Imm stroked her face as she used to do with her magic paintbrush.

For a second time since Isaac's birth, Elaina thought she felt her Trinity filling her. "Imm? This is Holy Communion, isn't it?"

"You're my smart one, *ma petite fleur*, my little flower."

She watched Imm's fingers go back and forth. Paint stained her neatly trimmed nails. What had she been painting in that shade of green, the shade of clover in springtime? Imm herself was green, the color of life and hope.

"*Tu billes comme un diamant,* you shine like a diamond, Elaina," Imm whispered, laying her head on the blanket above Elaina's belly. "Diamonds and gemstones grow like flowers in deep, dark places where it's frightening. Heat and pressure are necessary for them to form. Miners must venture into those dark recesses, find the treasure, and dig it out. Then the imperfections must be cut away with much force to bring out brilliance. Those stones that have withstood the harshest conditions reflect the Son's light the brightest."

Imm drew back with a smile. "Less than twenty-four hours ago, you produced a perfect gemstone through much pain, and now you're giving your treasure to another woman. Never forget who you reflect!"

"Sister Katherine and Ruth would call that lesson in pride." Elaina couldn't keep the heavy sarcasm from her voice. "Besides, I caused the conditions."

"The Trinity don't concern themselves with the origins of the conditions, only the results. Holiness—treasure—can be born from sin and darkness just as grace can. Grace is the call to cut away imperfections and the force that does the carving. Your Clover friends only ask you to trust them as you venture into dark places looking for treasure, and then to share it with others."

"Only ignorant and pious people define humility as covering one's brilliance," Imm added, "and it doesn't make other gemstones shinier. It takes many candles to light a room, the reason the Trinity are so recklessly extravagant with their gifts and grace."

Beeping monitors, humming lights, and the snoring woman in the other bed lulled like white noise. Elaina wrestled sleepiness.

"It feels like our Clover Club's together again, just like at the cemetery."

"Yes, *ma poupée*, my doll, they've been waiting patiently for you to invite them back. They've brought you the flowers just outside this window, and this morning's sky was painted in all your favorite pinks."

"They came with you, Imm. Remember when we started the club, how we'd eat wild raspberries we picked at the fence row while you told all of us your childhood stories? Tell me those stories again, especially the ones from your rose farm."

Another healing hour passed, giving Elaina strength to refuse more Demerol, not in hope of holding Isaac but because she wanted to heal with her friend's help alone.

"I talked myself into believing Cole would come around once Isaac was born. I wanted a family of my own more than anything. Now it's just shattered pieces of an illusion I created." Elaina sighed, speaking as much to herself as Imm.

"Wishes that come from your deepest feelings are your purpose," Imm said. "Your job is to find the seeds of your dreams and help them take root. In loving Isaac enough to give him life, you've brought a visible sign of God to the world. Now you understand why people are sacrament."

Imm squeezed her hand and peered at the clock anxiously. "There's another baby inside you, a spirit baby who's placed in each of us the day we're born. Her name is Need. As we grow older, we become more aware of her. Love is her nourishment. Our job is to feed Need, and she will guide each of us toward goodness."

"I don't understand." It seemed too theoretical, but she sensed Imm's urgency.

"Need is the swelling in your soul where God lives, making you aware of your hunger for perfect love. Need is demanding. She keeps you searching and dependent on the Trinity. The more you feed her, the more her appetite grows. She cries when she's hungry, and she's hungry all the time. There are days when she never stops crying, the days you feel swallowed by loneliness. It's tempting to feed Need substitutes for real love, but instant gratification only gives her an appetite for dark, ugly things. She'll become greedy and addicted to the poisons of this world. Don't ignore Need's appetite. Feed her pure love."

"Where do I find pure love? How do I know when to feed her? I still don't understand."

"You will, *ma poupée*. Just trust your Trinity."

Imm swallowed hard and pressed her hands to her face, as if try-ing to shield a loss of composure. "You're the daughter I've always dreamed of. Oh, *ma enfant*, my child, we're connected in a mysteri-ous way. The same colors swirl inside both of us. I knew you were the missing piece of my heart the moment I met you ten years ago. But I have something else to tell. I must say *adieu*. *Ma maman* is sick and there's no one to care for her. I'm leaving for France tomorrow, and I don't know when I'll be back."

Elaina gaped at her, stunned by this turn of events. Just as she was beginning to hope things would take a turn for the better . . .

Why did God keep taking everyone away?

6

Isaac was little more than seventy-two hours old when he legally lost his mother to her signature. How long before a stranger would rename him and call him her son?

"Wake up, sweetheart," said Cole. "We need to talk before I take you home."

Startled, Elaina lifted her head to see three pink angels around the bluish-gray Mother Mary looking down from their pedestal. Saint Augustine Cemetery was as beautiful as the day she'd started sketching the man beside her now, who'd brought her here to say goodbye.

Old habit compelled her to reach out, absentmindedly running her hand along Cole's jaw. How would she ever learn to stop loving him? She begged time to pause, soaking in the scenery as she remembered the beginning of the passion that had eventually created Isaac. How had they gotten from there to here?

"I gave notice at Tasty," he said.

"Do you remember when we—"

"Yeah, that's why I brought you here. El—"

"Please, Cole. Can we just sit quietly for a minute?"

The blue-gray marble woman seemed to know Elaina's heartache. She'd lost her firstborn to strangers, too. *Hail Mary, full of grace. The Lord is with you. Blessed are you among women . . .* The memorized words finally held meaning. *. . . and blessed is the fruit of your womb, Jesus, your firstborn.*

Oh, Mary. Elaina's throat tightened. *Please watch over Isaac. Imm told me to refer to him as my firstborn, because it holds hope for more children. Hope?*

Had the chiseled angels' wings just moved? She knew shadows could play tricks, but maybe they'd heard her.

Michelangelo's *Pietà* came to mind, and the replica at Saint Augustine. Imm had explained how the sorrow Michelangelo carved on Mary's face was not as evident as in the angle of her outstretched hand. If one gazed at the sculpture long enough, she'd said, Mary's heartbreak could be felt in her fingers' upward tilt. The gesture of her hand as she offered up her Son gave life to the entire masterpiece.

From this moment, the *Pietà* would always bring Isaac to mind. Could she ever release her son from her heart with the same generosity that the Mother of God had relinquished Jesus to the world?

"Sweetheart? Earth to Elaina . . ." Cole wiped her tears, bringing her back from escape. "I'm going to Texas. You can write me once I have an address, but this is goodbye. Remember what Ms. Farrow said. We have to go on living."

Yes, they did. Cole with his future full of exciting plans, and Elaina with . . . well, with Mary and the angels. Though their faces were stone, Elaina tried to believe that the Mother of God and her guardian angels wouldn't leave her, too.

* * *

"Yes, Dr. Stoffer, that's correct. Thirty-two pounds."

"In six weeks? What've you been doing, Elaina?" Dr. Stoffer sounded angry. "Diet pills?"

His skepticism reminded Elaina of Monsignor Blaski's interrogations. "The only thing I've taken is what you prescribed. I'm just not hungry. I've been exercising, too."

"You should have more padding. Your mother says you sleep all day in the sun—and it's obvious you're not using sunblock. Tanning can be as compulsive and dangerous as dieting." Then, more softly, he said, "Tell me how you're really feeling."

Elaina's lip quivered.

He reached out and clasped her hands in his. "This ordeal's been difficult. I know the father of your child has left and you're shouldering the financial burden. You don't have to pretend."

Her mom must have blabbed. Had she also told Dr. Stoffer that they hadn't given Elaina any help either, nor any choice but adoption?

"What you're feeling is postpartum depression, the baby blues—like you're falling into a black hole, huh?"

Tears collected, first in small drops, then flowing like the Niagara. Tomorrow was the black hole, and each day after a deeper abyss. Only one consolation lent Elaina any sense of control and determination: compliments on how great she looked. Her daily runs had started out as a way to turn off her brain for an hour, but the escape transformed into ego food. Turning heads and whistles propped up her beaten self-image. She wanted to admit how fragile this cover-up was, but how would Dr. Stoffer understand?

The dark one encourages us to appraise ourselves and each other on appearance and accomplishments. Fear laughs when a man sees a woman's value based only on her sexual allure. —Sister Immaculata Lefevre

And what did a nun understand about the real world, either?

"I'm giving you two prescriptions, one to level your hormones and one to brighten your spirits—and a release to return to work. Once school starts, life will feel normal again."

He hesitated. "One more thing—" He handed her another small white form. "Here's a prescription for birth control, with the assurance of my discretion. It's good for a year. Consider filling it *before* you become sexually active again, and insist on a condom to prevent STDs and AIDS. The fact is, once a girl's gone all the way, it's pretty hard to go back to holding hands." His eyes didn't meet hers. "Questions?"

What was AIDS, she wondered. She'd seen headlines but assumed it an acronym for some kind of disaster relief program. What did it have to do with sexually transmitted diseases? She certainly wasn't going to ask.

The silence begged for relief.

"And eat! You should be up at least ten pounds next checkup."

With no one left who really cared, why should she? She'd let Cole pound her ego into the ground, a natural follow-through after a dad who'd disregarded her for years. Her dad had said not to worry about what people thought but to concentrate on what she knew. Well, she knew that if she kept herself looking this good, she'd have more guys than there were hours in the day.

In the time it took to reach home, she'd boosted her own spirits.

"Elaina?" her dad called from the breezeway between the house and garage, the room he called his office. He handed her an opened envelope. "This belongs to you, but it's not pretty."

She took a long look at the bill and threw it to the floor. "How can Grace charge this? I was there less than thirty-six hours."

"Unexpected things happen, like your cesarean. Making a baby takes two, and raising one was intended to be a team effort."

This would take years to pay, unless—

"Dad, did you know I had enough credits to satisfy state graduation requirements last May? Saint Augustine's four-year religion stipulation is the hold-up." He'd know it was true if he'd taken the time to look at her report cards. "If you requested my diploma now, I could skip senior year and work full time—pay it off faster." She felt clever for having backed him into a corner. "You always say, 'The second sin is lying, and the first is carrying debt.'"

"You could also pick up more chores at home. I've always paid you well since you took over the house. Then you could graduate with your class."

She remained silent, hoping for a better offer.

"I suppose I could ask for your religion class to be scheduled the first period, leaving the rest of the day for work."

It was the most she could hope for. Still, there'd be no more recitations of the afternoon rosary, no more kneeling on the asphalt in a dress to say the Angelus, and no more forced confessions. Never again would she have to try guessing which priest was behind which sin-splattered screen, the one who instructed that she should only confess the top two sins or the one who wanted every detail.

Just days later, her idea panned out.

"Father Krammer simply needed a reminder of my annual alumni donation," her dad reported after his meeting on Elaina's behalf. "You'll be the first senior to attend for just forty-five minutes. I also stopped at Grace General. They'll freeze interest on your bill if the three-hundred-dollar monthly payments remain timely."

Did he expect gratitude for committing her to three hundred dollars a month? There'd be nothing left of her paycheck. It would be decades, the millennium, before she was off that ratty bike.

Maybe with feigned appreciation and agreement to the payments, he'd bend for her appeal. "May I buy a new bike first? Please, Dad?"

He sighed. "It's about the look, isn't it? This will be your downfall. 'Display is like shallow water. You can see the muddy bottom.'"

But the new ten-speed was sleek and light as a feather. Even the wind couldn't keep up when Elaina pushed her legs to their limits. Yes, it was about the look, something her parents had withheld by keeping her penniless in forced tuition fees for the private education she was given no choice in accepting. The only comfort to giving Isaac away was knowing that he'd always have the right look and be one of the privileged ones from the beginning.

Look the part, and the good life follows. —Cole Carter

* * *

Elaina strutted into the break room in her new, skin-tight Calvin Kleins. The crochet bodice of her midriff peasant top gave generous peeks of the lacey hot pink bra beneath, while doing little to cover her ribs. Every penny after the hospital payments, the prescriptions, and several choice over-the-counter pills was spent on wardrobe. The smell and crisp finish of new clothes pacified her umbrage at a lifetime of hand-me-downs, although they could never compete with the paint-stained T-shirts in the back of her closet. Those were the treasured reminders of time spent painting with Imm.

Kurt, Tasty's new meat cutter, jumped from the break table, dropping the book he'd been engrossed in for weeks. Eyes looked up momentarily from conversation, but seeing that he was simply holding the door for a senior employee, everyone went back to chatting.

Elaina watched from her corner, noticing how often this introvert had graciously taken last-in-line for the time clock and first-in-line to unload the meat trucks. He stood whenever there were limited chairs for employee meetings. His pleasant inconspicuousness brought to mind the happy but overlooked little girl whose invisible friends and French art teacher had been enough, as if he too were a charter Clover Club member. His kind usually wore a wedding band.

But being so nice often made one unappealing, she noted wryly. Nice also didn't spend time with girls like her—the reason the Three no longer came around.

"Hey, Elaina," Mark called with a whistle. "Lookin' hot. How 'bout you and me have dinner Saturday night?"

That presented possibilities. Deanne had had a crush on Mark forever, and it was Deanne and Karmin who'd ruined Elaina's last sweet moment with Cole at the hospital. Revenge jumped at the opportunity, and Elaina gave Mark an eager yes. She added a whisper to seal the deal that raised a grin on his face. Every eye in the break room was on her, every neck craned, wondering and wishing. They all wanted her.

This must've been how Cole felt when surrounded by women. No wonder he was so vain. Still, something deep festered—the spirit baby Imm had described? Were men's admirations enough to satisfy Need's hunger? Might any one of them give up everything for her and she for any of them? Was that kind of exclusive love a childish, Clover-shaped fantasy?

Mark would be another notch in her lipstick case. Men's attention simply postponed Need like the various pills she used to suppress her appetite, wake up, fall asleep, or feel more cheerful. Like all the others, Mark would resent paying for a dinner she would barely touch, but he would still want his arm candy looking magazine-thin. She wanted to slap him and every man who held onto this double standard. In the time it would take Mark to reach satisfaction, she'd go from gorgeous to garbage.

She knew all of this. But still, she'd follow through.

* * *

December 15, 1980

Dearest Imm,

Happy holidays, and thanks for your address. You sound happy to be back home and helping your mom. That doesn't make me miss you any less, though. From your description of the farm, it seems like little has changed while you were in the US.

I hope your mom feels better by Christmas. I laughed at your description of her temporary recovery to see who shot J.R. My mom and dad were glued to the TV too. My dad was so cocky when it turned out to be Kristin. "I knew it!" he shouted so loud I heard him upstairs.

Do you have plans for Christmas? I wish you were here. I keep hoping for something to make this season special, but without a boyfriend, I feel incomplete. I think 1981 might be a very lonely year.

I'm interested in Tasty's newest employee. He's quiet, unobtrusive, and considerate, so opposite Cole, which makes him very appealing, I'm afraid to show interest, though, for all the mistakes I've made with guys lately. (Let's not go there!) Any suggestions on how to get a nice guy to look my direction?

I try to remember everything you said at the hospital, especially about Need, but I think I suffer from selective memory. I miss you, the Three, and even Cole so much. Why do I still pine for a guy who brought me nothing but trouble? I want to love and trust again, but I wonder if a guy exists who's worth the gamble.

Happy Christmas season, to you, your mom, and your congregation of the Sister of Mary, Mother of God.

All my love,
Elaina

December 25, 1980

Ma chére enfant,

Happy Christmas to you, and happy birthday, Jesus.

Ma maman is better though still weak, but I have faith in our longtime family doctor. We'll pray for the best.

I suspect your difficulties of the past year are directly related to the "let's-not-go-theres", from recent disappointments to heartbreaks of much further back. Trust me enough to go there with me when you feel ready. The colors that swirl inside both of us, both the dark, muddy ones and the vibrant and spirited ones, allow me to under-stand you. The longing that burdens you cannot be lifted with the attentions of insincere men. (You see, ma jolie fleur, I do know!)

May I gently remind you that nice men want girls who honor themselves. Ask yourself why you don't feel worthy of respect, why you don't insist on it. The answer is what you need to purge from the dark place within yourself.

You never took the time to heal emotionally after Isaac's birth and Cole's abandonment. Give yourself the gift of your own com-pany, time to discover the young woman who doesn't need a man to prove her value. Do the things you used to love. Paint!

Find Elaina, and love will find you.

I've never left you in my prayers, and I love you,

Immaculata

* * *

The colors on her palette ran together like the shadowy images in her dark place. Without Imm to paint with, art had lost its power to restore. Weekends were hardest, when loneliness made Need inconsolable.

One morning in early January, Elaina asked her dad for a ride to a huge celebration for President-Elect Ronald Regan that was going on. Actually, she just wanted a lift the nearby ice skating rink.

"Are you meeting friends?" he asked as he pulled into Hurstland Ice Arena. "Or a guy? Isn't this place for hockey players? A girl alone with a bunch of—"

"It's open skating for anyone," she snapped, then quickly softened her tone. "It doesn't look like many people are here, but that means I'll have more of the ice to myself."

Was she imagining the strange looks as she checked in by herself? She pulled the laces of the rental skates tight. It seemed as if everyone was staring, asking each other why she was alone, and whispering pos-sible reasons.

But skating here was better than any memories could conjure. The ice had no protruding sticks or leaves, no bitter wind, and no worries about thin ice like the Tarrock quarry. A Zamboni-smooth film made her strokes as effortless as if her feet had never been out of skates. Ice shavings sprayed with each turn, cooling her sweat-soaked face and encouraging harder strokes.

She chased the swirling reflections from the rotating mirror ball on the ceiling, the dots apparently longing for someone to skate with as much as her. If only she could shut out the gaiety of other skaters, empty the rink of bodies tumbling on top each other in laughter, helping each other up and heading off to skate a double.

Doubles were for couples, though, and trios were for groups. She was alone. It weighed on her chest, made breathing harder. Oh gawd, was she going to cry again? What was the matter with her? She gave her last ounce of energy to a final lap, fighting her emotions, determined to win.

A power beyond her own began in her legs, rising like heat and lifting her solitude. Like a thousand balloons inflated solely for the purpose of release with every exhalation, joy and amazement joined in. It was her Three, one at her right, the other on her left, and the third inside her heart. She'd found them! They'd found her!

They raised her until she soared, and the ice became the clover field beside the cemetery when she was small. Exhilaration, euphoria, and unearthly happiness so overwhelmed that her trembling hands clamped over her mouth to suppress an explosion of emotion. The darkness looked so much blacker bathed in their light, her selfishness so much uglier in their great generosity, her life so profoundly desolate with them now accompanying her. She was so happy, so ashamed, so relieved. Wrapping her arms around her shoulders, she hugged them, gripping until her fingertips turned white. No questions intruded about why they'd waited so long, why they'd come, or if they'd have to leave again. She just wanted this moment to last forever.

I love you, my Three. I love you so much.

Her days were now counted to the next time she could snag a ride to the skating rink. Her long stretches on the ice so wore her out that she needed no more pills to fall asleep or suppress her appetite to maintain her shape. Neither the antidepressants nor the birth control prescriptions were refilled. By the end of January, she'd saved enough for a new pair of skates.

When Elaina was on the ice, nothing mattered but time with her Three. Skating transported her to a holy place, her heart bursting each time they lifted her closer to their world. When exhaustion required an easier glide, she'd collect her treasures of strength, self-confidence, and peace that lay like diamonds on the ice. Her Three were inside her and all around, reflecting each other like the lights that created a glittering holograph on the frozen surface of the ice.

7

The massive meat department window allowed customers to watch the butchers processing their meat, as Elaina did now. Kurt effortlessly hoisted sides of beef that were almost as long as he was tall. Strength rippled beneath his bloody T-shirt, reawakening her appreciation for the human form. Her inner artist pictured the muscles ribboning around bones under his skin's veil of protection. Imm had taught her well. Kurt was small and slender but sturdy. And unlike Cole, he was unaware of his impressive physique—probably the reason women didn't flock to him.

An eager, self-conscious grin broke from his deep concentration when he turned and saw her. "How long have you been standing there?"

"A couple of minutes. You're no slouch! How much do those slabs weigh?"

"I'm not sure . . ." He hunted for more words. "It gets pretty grungy in here . . . I heard it's your birthday. Happy birthday. The big eighteen, right? Bet you're going clubbing." He was nervous. It made him chatter just as she did.

"Actually, I have no plans. How about you? Maybe we could do something together?" She gave him an encouraging smile.

"What would you like to do?"

"Surprise me," she said. This guy was different—she could feel it— and she knew he would have something better in mind than another grappling session in the back of a dark car or dirty apartment. "Maybe someplace quiet?"

Two days later, she found herself frantically searching her closet for something demure. Disgust rose with each flip of the hangers. How much of this skin-tight faux leather and animal-print trash had been designed to attract the very thing she dreaded? How had filling the emptiness Cole and Isaac had left become so twisted? Or had this warped thinking begun in an earlier time?

Elaina's mother called with an excuse moments before they had promised to come home and meet her date. Why couldn't they make an effort when she was obviously trying so hard to do things right? She refused to sag under disappointment and commended herself for her effort toward making proper introductions.

When she invited Kurt in, the swish of his new slacks and jacket shouted his hope for something promising too.

"You look fantastic!" She ran her fingers down his ultra-skinny leather tie. "I barely recognized you without your bloody apron. So GQ!"

His eyebrows rose. "What do you mean?"

His cluelessness was utterly charming. "GQ is a men's fashion magazine, *Gentlemen's Quarterly*. When you look GQ, it means you're very stylish."

"Oh. Well, you look GQ too—I mean, you look beautiful. But I'm sure you already know that. I still can't believe that you'd actually—never mind."

Oh, this one was a gem, so different from the rest. And here she looked the same as always. She tugged at her embarrassingly tight mini and wished for lower heels in something subtler than neon pink.

They drove to River Rock the back way, passing snow-dusted fields. Drainage ditches edged in serrated ice looked like long black ribbons trimmed in silver. Elaina found the silence disconcerting. It usually signaled disapproval, but Kurt's chivalrous gestures told otherwise. He'd left the engine running to keep the car warm, fussed over adjusting her seat after he'd opened the door for her, and inquired after her favorite music before selecting a radio station.

So this was how it felt to be treated like a lady. Her dad had always done these things for her mom, but she'd never noticed until now.

Affection melted the frost that thoughts of her parents usually brought to mind.

Kurt had been born and raised in River Rock and started his meat cutter's apprenticeship right after high school, he told her. When Tarrock Tasty made him an offer, he jumped.

"The commute got tiresome, especially with gas at $1.19, so I moved. Tarrock's okay, but weekends are too quiet. Mark's invited me over several times, but the heavy drinking—been there, done that years ago. It's old. I suppose I sound old." He laughed nervously. "Anyway, it's great to have company for a change. Thanks for joining me." He reached over and squeezed her hand.

She sensed a loneliness beneath his cheerful manner and awkward attempts to fill the void with shallow socializing. He too seemed familiar with feelings of not belonging anywhere. If not for the formalities of first dates, she would have assured him she understood so well. What a waste of time proprieties were when the heart knew what was needed for healing. Why were unsuppressed emotions looked upon as pathetic or a failing?

They pulled into the long drive of Fête, an upscale French restaurant complete with a valet. Massive doors opened to a display of grandeur she'd never seen except on TV. Velvet drapes dressed massive windows and protected huge potted palms from wintry drafts. Gilded embellishments reflected candelabras on every table. It reminded Elaina of the light at the skating rink.

Immediately, anxiety over the prices pushed her astonishment aside.

While they waited for their server, Kurt reached across the table. "You have amazing eyes."

Her mom used to say her large, wide-set green eyes were her best feature, but so did Tasty's stockmen while staring at her chest. Imm had painted Elaina's eye more times than she could remember, and Cole had praised her eyes while peeling off her jeans. She wanted to believe Kurt, but experience said flattery plus an extravagant dinner was the price for sex later. Worse, she knew she would pay up—and then hate herself and Kurt, just as she had the others.

She was so tired of hating.

Dare she ask his intentions—or trust him? Would she ever find a man who understood that eyes were windows to the soul? In one of Imm's many art-religion lessons—always bound, as if two sides of the same instruction—she'd said that humans are God's only creation intended to make love face-to-face in order to see in each other's eyes while joined physically in reflection of heaven's love.

Her concerns vanished by the fifth course of creamy cheeses and raspberries. Raspberries—a sign? Kurt had hung on her every word like her Three, not just interested but fascinated. Need suckled peacefully, while Elaina desperately hoped.

"What about you? Where'd you graduate from?" She was eager to know more about him.

"Columbus High, east River Rock."

"Your class must have been huge!"

He chuckled. "Every place is big compared to Tarrock."

"Yeah, make one mistake in ol' Tarrock and it's never forgotten." Had she just steered the subject into dangerous territory? "Let's drive around River Rock before it gets too late."

Thousands of tiny lights illuminated the trees along a sidewalk that enclosed a skating pond. A few people glided around despite the cold.

"Let's walk on the ice. Pretend we have skates on," she said zapped with excitement.

A skating pond. Could it get any better? She linked her fingers with his and showed him how to twirl.

He looked deep into her eyes, and she knew her enthusiasm had charged him. His passion escaped in a deep, demanding kiss. The intimate contact tasted so delicious, but also so wrong. She wanted to be . . . desirable? Admired? A nice girl?

"I'm sorry. I got carried away." He looked away, red-faced at her reaction.

Disgust washed over her. Somehow, she'd conveyed a message of availability as she always did. Worse, he'd interpreted her startled reaction as dishonor. She couldn't get it right.

"It's okay," she said with a gentle smile. "You just caught me off guard."

Her attempts to convince him were futile. He remained stiff the entire drive home.

"May I see you again?" he asked formally after pulling into her driveway.

"Of course."

She moved closer and brushed his lips with hers. He relaxed into the kiss, so she pressed harder and deeper as Cole had taught her. Climbing onto his lap should come next, her hands cupping his cheeks. Experience told her he'd pull her into him just like—

But he pulled away with unexpected force, frustration written all over his scowl. "Not like this, Elaina. I won't take you like this, and I don't see any point in tempting what I don't intend to see through."

He hurried around to open her door. "I'll call you next week."

A quick hug was her dismissal before he backed out of the driveway far too fast.

He wouldn't call again. None of them did. She was damned if she did and damned if she didn't.

8

Kurt met her parents the following week. He arrived on time, dressed neatly in slacks and a collared shirt, and stood a courteous distance from Elaina. He accommodated her father's questions in a slightly submissive tone that gave every indication of his respect for elders. How different from Cole.

A long, speechless moment shadowed the conversation when Kurt mentioned he was eight years older than Elaina.

"I appreciate your truthfulness, and you seem like a gentleman," her dad replied slowly. "Elaina's a legal adult now so my concerns won't hold weight, but I expect you to mind my curfews."

"Rest assured, sir. And I appreciate your giving me a chance to prove myself."

Away from her parents' scrutiny, Elaina released a nervous giggle. "I'm glad that's over. Thank you for meeting them. I hate sneaking around."

"I agree. Secrets destroy everything."

Misunderstandings did, too. She kept her tone light. "Things got awkward on our last date."

"If I get tangled in you before learning who you are, I may never find out. You know, the cart before the horse."

She nodded. Was this coming from a man?

"Trust my reasons for wanting to go slow," he added. "The old-fashioned way prevents . . . Let's just say I have a war story there."

She'd heard Kurt was a recovered alcoholic and something about a friendship with another man. At first, the odd references made her wonder if he was gay. Discreet inquiries turned up that he was a member of AA, and "a friend of Bill W.'s" was a confidential way of identifying members, Bill Wilson being the founder. Was Kurt's war story related to alcohol?

If she was honest with herself, she'd have to count herself on the long list of people who'd fallen for alcohol's deceits, usually as a collaborator with sex. Together, alcohol and sex calculated the value of a relationship by its sexual intensity, after distorting emotions.

> *Sex, like fire, is good and productive until tampered with.*
> —Edward Michael

Still, it was difficult to slap a toxic label on any of it until it became clearly abused. She'd witnessed how insecure boys measured their manliness based on their sexual conquests, usually after plying their targets with drinks. Afterward, their loose tongues destroyed many a girl's reputation.

"I wish I could convince people that real maturity postpones the physical stuff in consideration of another person's value," Kurt said.

She was shocked at how closely his words echoed Imm's.

Over the next weeks, Kurt sacrificed his schedule to give Elaina rides everywhere she needed to be. As the Clover Club used to do, he waited patiently and cheerfully in the background while she skated, painted, or got together with friends, perfectly content in her happiness. She sensed his feelings for her increasing, and he filled her heart too in every way but passion. If only the chemistry she'd felt with Cole could be transplanted to Kurt. With her eyes closed, she'd try to imagine Kurt as the incarnation of Michelangelo's *David*, but even in her fantasies, the embers soon went cold.

Was the security of being loved worth settling for a simmer? With true love, giving seeped into receiving that soaked back into giving. This circular openness marked her early relationship with Kurt, but she craved fervor, urge, obsession. Cole.

Imm said the purpose of Need's craving for love was to bring her back to God. Before Kurt, the squalling infant felt more like an invading alien trying to pull her down, but since their first date, Need had been at peace. Should she take this to mean that Kurt's goodness could keep her united her with the Three? Maybe if she faked passion long enough, she could make it happen.

* * *

March 25, 1981

Dearest Imm,

I often think about your explanations of God during art class when I was young. They were so different from Sister Katherine's and Ruth's. They tied worship with guilt, as if a person's connection to God were directly correlated to the amount of shame felt, as if self-inflicted condemnation were the only way to bond with the Trinity.

Admit that it was your sins that drove the nails into his hands and feet.—Sister Katherine

You said that gratitude is the best way to worship and build on our friendship with the Trinity, because no matter how great our sacrifices and sufferings, they're but grains of sand on the ocean floor compared to Jesus's. The Three didn't endure the crucifixion to instill guilt. They tolerated all the uglies of this world for the love of us and with no need or expectation of return, yet they're always desirous of our love and appreciation.

If the Trinity don't need or wait for our love, then why is such a strong need to be loved placed within us? If it is meant to bring us back to them, then why is our craving for another human's love so overpowering?

The third week of Lent has passed, and I've yet to sacrifice anything. With the Clover Three silent again, I begin to wonder if Sister Katherine and Sister Ruth were right about suffering and shame. I can't feel the Three. Please help.

All my love,
Elaina

April 3, 1981

Ma chére enfant,

Feelings are not facts, nor is everything an ordained man or woman says. Great misinterpretations of God's word are part of the human condition that divided us from each other and the Trinity. They are the reason many choose to go their own direction.

Consider this: A child often attempts to run away from home when he doesn't get his way. The wise father won't stop the child but will follow closely behind to be sure of his child's safety. After venturing to strange neighborhoods and dark, frightening places, the child begins to feel very alone. Because he feels unaccompanied doesn't mean his father isn't but a few paces behind, though the father allows space so the child will recognize what his heart misses.

His father will remain just out of sight until the child calls, but Papa knows the difference between lip service and a heartfelt invitation, because grief and regret are always present in the latter. When Papa is appealed to in sincerity and true contrition, he comes running with open arms, just as Jesus told in his story of the prodigal son.

Our hearts were made for the Three. It is the reason our longing is so strong. Until we can be united with them again, though, we've been given each other for comfort. Each of us, as a reflection of the Trinity, can serve as a semblance of God's love for each other, but only through giving like God, with no need or expectation in return.

This is all God asks of us, to love as they do. Sometimes this requires sacrifice and suffering, but when performed in love, willingness and joy will accompany them. When you love others, you'll be confident of the presence of the Three, even when it's not felt.

I've never left you in my prayers, and I love you.

Immaculata

* * *

Kurt parked his tired Skylark in a narrow, abandoned farmer's lane.

"The Easter bunny left this for you." He handed Elaina a lacquered, Fabergé-style egg covered in tiny pearls.

"It's beautiful! So delicate. I'm almost afraid to open it."

She gently lifted the top. A small square of paper stuffed inside began to emerge before she could completely free it.

She read it twice, her face scrunching. "Hurstland Ice Arena? I don't understand."

"The entire rink is all yours tomorrow morning. After I make you breakfast, you're going to dazzle me on the ice."

"This is the best gift ever!" She threw her arms around his neck. "It says you understand how important skating is to me. Thank you, thank you, thank you." She planted a kiss with each thank you.

Sexual frustration revealed itself in his deep groan. She fumed at herself, her dark place hurling insulting names. Though there'd been times she'd tantalized him in an attempt to gain self-assurance, this wasn't one of them. But even genuine gratitude seemed to come out like a tease. She *was* a slut, and every other name the darkness called her.

"Don't pull away, Lanie. It's not your fault. Just looking at you drives me nutty, but I'd cut off every extension of myself before I'd take advantage of you. You're worth my discipline."

"I don't want your discipline. I want to give you something for a change. I don't have money—only this." She began to take her shirt off.

"No, Lanie. I'm not keeping score, nor should you. I love you, and refusing you—for now—is the best way I can show you."

She supposed she should feel honored, but concern and shame were all she could find as he buttoned her up.

Breakfast the next morning, complete with sausage and bacon, eggs and pancakes, and an arrangement of daisies, left her almost too full for skating. Her excitement burned through it quickly.

"The greatest part of having the rink to myself is going any direction," she shouted to Kurt, who watched from the bleachers.

She could pull reckless turns and sharp, spraying stops wherever she pleased. Alternating her pace between hard strokes and a leisurely glide, she cut swirls into the ice while imagining Imm's graceful, scrolling cursive. Optimism took her hands when her feet were in skates, bolstering her belief that decency was attainable.

The huge rink begged for a partner. She waved Kurt down and pulled him around the rink on his slippery loafers. They twirled as they had on their first date, laughing at the memory of their awkward first kiss.

Happiness came easily with Kurt. Surely chemistry would begin bubbling soon.

* * *

The assassination attempt on President Ronald Reagan seemed to stop everything but April showers. Elaina's parents, beside themselves with concern, attended weekday masses and prayer vigils. She couldn't believe it. Closing the nursery for a stranger—from Hollywood?

> *Without Hollywood, Satan wouldn't have a prayer.*
> —Edward Michael

So which was it, Dad?

Kurt frequently reminded Elaina that her school friends should take priority over Tasty overtime, especially with graduation so close. Though he meant well, she resented it. If he had an inkling of her debt—but her tight lips were the reason for his cluelessness. Still, she accepted his offer to invite her friends to his place for a night of cards.

The girls complained about calorie-padded hips as they stuffed themselves with desserts and sodas. Watching their sugar-induced sillies, Elaina wished to be as lighthearted, but carrying on felt phony in a mindset focused on pressing problems.

"Thanks, Kurt," Jenny said, popping the last bit of brownie in her mouth. "Your place is great. You and Elaina are perfect together—"

"—because you're both OCD!" her friends all yelled at once.

"Look at this place," Patty teased. "You could eat off the floor."

"You coming, Elaina?" Sarah jingled her car keys.

"I'm hangin' back. Kurt will give me a ride, but thanks for coming."

Confusion wrinkled Kurt's brow, but he'd never question her in front of friends.

"Lanie, we've discussed this," he sighed after they'd left. "I can't be alone with you here; I'm not disciplined enough. Your parents trust me. Down the road, when I ask your dad . . . I want to say I've respected you."

Elaina heard nothing past her waiting argument. "Can't we just talk? I've barely been alone with you in over two months. Is there something wrong with me?"

She knew better, but Need's squalls were beginning to make the nights unbearable. Though her feelings for Kurt hadn't increased beyond what she might feel for a brother, surely she could ignite passion with intimacy. She had passed too many nights remembering the sweet hours with Cole, before and after, the whispers of adoration and the kisses that said *I'll do anything for you.* In the face of that, intercourse was tolerable. In anticipation, she'd refilled her birth control prescription.

"Sit with me, Kurt. I just want to talk. You said secrets are lies. I want honesty for us."

She had no intention of disclosing last summer's events, nor any locked-away shame from further back, but she knew Kurt wanted to be trusted. Like the Three? She loved him for that, but trusting was risky. It gambled with rejection, leaving the loser with nothing but regret. When she'd tried to be truthful with her parents about Eric, she'd lost what little affection she'd managed to finagle from them. And though she'd never specifically confessed those secrets to the Trinity, they knew everything—and where were they now? If they were remaining just outside her awareness, as Imm's little story illustrated, she didn't appreciate their game of hide-and-seek.

Kurt reluctantly joined her on the couch. She scooted closer and began rubbing his neck and thigh simultaneously. She loathed being so forthcoming yet reveled in her power as the aggressor. How many times had Cole used this tactic to get his way? Except where he had wanted a moment's ecstasy, she wanted . . . reassurance? What did she want?

Kurt's muscles tensed, then relaxed, saying she'd learned well. Though Kurt was smaller boned, his neck and shoulder muscles wrapped in the same rises and dips as Cole's. His profile reminded her of the images on ancient coins. He was beautiful. Her hands begged him to steal her away from the memory of the man who'd broken her heart and still held it prisoner.

He gave her a small smile and moved to the other end of the couch. "You want honesty, so shoot. What's on your mind?"

"You never drink," she blurted. "Just coffee."

Surprise flashed across his face, but his manner remained mild. "I'm glad you asked, though I think you already know. I'm an alcoholic, but I haven't had a drink in four years. Before that . . . It was bad. I'll spare the details and simply say I can never drink again. If I do, I'll fall right back into that hellish place where my family found me."

"Is that your war story?"

"Yeah. I've never been to war, but the nightmares I've heard that come from being in combat remind me of coming off alcohol. You get delirium tremens, or the DTs, hallucinations of hideous catastrophes, devouring insects, and demons that seem more real than the air you gasp for as they're chasing you. Your body trembles until your teeth rattle, so violently you wish to die. I've been to hell, Lanie, and I'm not sure I'd make it back if I slipped there again."

"I'd never do anything to make you slip. I want to love you the way you deserve, as close as humanly possible, but you keep pushing me away."

Tears collected in his eyes. He didn't blink or brush them aside, as if he were distracted in searching for the truth in her words.

What kind of selfish game had she started?

"Sex isn't love, Lanie girl," he whispered. "You want me to take your body in hopes that I'll cherish your heart. But if I take you physically before I've committed my life to you, it could destroy the most important part of our relationship: trust. Self-indulgence dismisses the heart, one's own and another's, and always leads to abuse or addiction. Then it's not pleasure but a pain-inflicting vice."

His eyes begged her to understand. "I hate how fuddy-duddy I sound, but this is where my battle scars come from. I'm sure you have scars too; it's impossible to grow up without a few. But I won't damage you any further than the others' selfishnesses have, no matter how hard you try to convince me you're fine with a quick roll in the hay."

So there it was. It was her reputation after all. "What have you heard about me? Or is it that you don't trust me?"

"I don't trust myself." His agitation startled her. "Once"—his pause seemed to drag his heart over barbed wire—"I was indicted for aggravated assault for almost raping a girl."

She willed herself to remain expressionless. His need to unload outweighed her shock, validating Imm's conviction about casting light on the uglies.

"We'd been drinking; both of us were wasted. I assumed she was willing to, you know, because she didn't resist. Suddenly, she was fighting me like an animal. I was so frustrated, so angry, sure she'd played me. So I made no effort to control myself."

"I hired a slimeball attorney to portray me as the victim. He badgered her so mercilessly on the witness stand she couldn't look my direction when repeating the words I'd cursed at her while I beat her. I'll never forget how she cowered when she walked past me after her testimony."

Elaina could barely comprehend such ruthlessness from this gentle man.

"My attorney convinced the jury she was a tramp, but for a fast-talking attorney, when is truth more important than winning? Afterward, he showed me photos of her black-and-blue body, evidence he'd proudly gotten dismissed. He gloated over our victory, while I couldn't stop replaying the terror I'd seen in her eyes. I turned to the bottle for peace, but I went to hell instead."

She grieved for him as much as the other woman. His haunted conscience was proof of his goodness. A lesser man would have felt no remorse.

She leaned toward him across the couch. "It wasn't you; it was the alcohol. You've got to forgive yourself. Imm told me that if you lock up your heart to preserve it, it will disintegrate instead. Happiness and fulfillment are in direct proportion to the extent you're willing to make yourself vulnerable. She said those who've experienced the greatest heartache are best suited for joy. Let me bring you joy now."

The hypocrisy of her words weighed on her chest as she pressed into him. But really, was her pretense so wrong? If persuading him to give in released his demons while also bringing Need some peace, what was the harm?

She kissed him hard and when he didn't protest she tugged his shirt off. Her skin tingled under his soft but urgent stroking of her breasts.

She could feel his body's want for her as she slipped from her undergarments. Pulling him into her, aching to be filled, she beseeched him, "Please, Cole, don't leave me again."

Kurt shot up off the couch. Cold air rushed in to take the place of his warmth atop her naked body. His jaws were clenched so tight that the veins of his neck distended.

She clutched a cushion to her chest to cover her nakedness and shame. Blame tried to protect what she'd flagrantly devalued only moments earlier. "What's the matter? Why don't you want me?"

he said so ominously she shivered.

He picked up his clothes and left the room.

A cold prick of fear grew in her belly. Could she have said Cole's name out loud? Did he know about Cole?

The effort they'd made to adhere to her father's curfew had all been for nothing; the long walk home would take her past midnight. She gathered her things and headed to the door.

Kurt's hand shot past her and slammed the door shut. She shielded her face, an automatic reaction for a girl with nasty-tempered brothers. He pulled her hands away roughly and scooped her up with an unsettling strength.

The faceless monster in the pit of her stomach slithered.

"I'm not Nicholas, or Cole, or whatever his name is," he said. "If you want me, you'll have to give him up, even in your mind. He's your war story, isn't he? I know about him and the baby you relinquished, but I'd hoped you'd trust me enough to tell me yourself. I can't imagine what you've been through, but you'll have to make peace with your past if you want a future for us. I'm here, Lanie; they're not. I'll wait for you and try to help, but you have to try too."

They clung to each other, the monster no longer threatening. Safety and security enveloped her, yet it didn't come with the warmth she remembered from childhood nor the energy that made her soar over the ice. Tonight, it came in the reassurance she saw in Kurt's brown eyes.

Healing seeped through their entwined hands as Kurt whispered more comforts. "Isaac will always be part of your heart, your flesh, and your blood. The life you gave him will always connect you and Cole too. I only ask you to make Cole a memory instead of a futile hope. I want to marry a girl who only has eyes for me."

That word. Finally. "Marry?"

"Yes, Lanie, as soon as you can honestly say you love me the way I do you. I won't be a stand-in for Cole, though."

The possibilities opened by that word made her feel safe enough to expose the turmoil of her pregnancy. They moved back to the couch, and she poured out her story. Hearing her own voice giving words to the harsh conditions that had brought Isaac into the world, she finally saw through the paradox of Imm's words at the hospital. The difficulty in giving him life was directly proportionate to the difficulty of giving him away. Love born from giving didn't mean less pain but more.

Suffering and salvation go together. Our Savior illustrated this best on the cross. —Sister Immaculata Lefevre

The shames she'd partaken in after giving up Isaac were still too fresh for exposure, though. If Kurt didn't ask, she'd never tell.

She snuggled close enough to feel his body heat but left enough space to respect his resolve. His emotions seemed as spent as hers, evident in his sparse, drawn-out words and droopy eyes. Sleep tucked itself around her curled body, bringing dreams of possibility.

* * *

"Holy crap—wake up, Lanie! Call your parents and tell them you're with me and we have a good explanation, but it will have to wait."

They pounded out to the car, and he drove her straight to the school.

As he pulled up to the curb, she opened the door and leaned back to kiss him hard. "You're wonderful, and I *am* going to marry you!"

As good as engaged. She hadn't bothered calling her parents. If they asked, she'd explain—but when did they ever ask?

She skidded into religion class with a minute to spare.

"Sister Ruth is subbing," the obnoxious underclassman who sat in front of her snickered.

"Bet she's got more on the evils of pornography," his friend added. "Who'll be first to make Ruthie blush?"

Their crassness disgusted her, but last night's drama and the direction it had taken pushed ahead of other thoughts. As Sister Ruth bustled in and began her lecture, she settled back comfortably into her thoughts. Only one small knot spoiled her now neatly tied-up future in marrying Kurt: imagining a lifetime with him. As long as denial kept that knot tight, though, Need would never infringe on her sleep again.

" . . . and it's sinful to look at nakedness in the opposite sex unless you're married to each other," Sister Ruth droned. "After Adam and Eve ate the forbidden fruit, lust and shame were born. God saw man's lust and woman's shame, so they covered themselves in fig leaves."

"Which sin was greater, Eve sucking on forbidden fruit or Adam's fruit ripening?" asked Diff, the opening act of every trouble instigated by St Augustine's jocks.

"That's enough! You didn't raise your hand, and you're not listening."

Laughter quickly progressed to chaos. Wads of paper sailed over heads, and boys high-fived each other in appreciation for their foul comments. Diff grabbed a basket of wax fruit from the bookcase and began using them in lurid gestures then tossing them to the others.

A banana landed in Elaina's lap. She quickly shoved it under her desk as Father Krammer stomped in.

"Enough!" His fists pounded the desk. "This is religion class. Any further disrespect will result in immediate suspension."

Sister Ruth, satisfied with the silence, proceeded. "Now, I'll answer *dignified* questions."

With her thoughts so appallingly violated, Elaina's mouth took charge before her mind could hush it. "If looking at nakedness is a sin unless it's your spouse, then why did Pope Julius II ask Michelangelo to paint the Sistine Chapel with hundreds of nudes? Why does our Holy Father say Mass under those nudes every day? And when you say Adam and Eve covered their sin with fig leaves, are you referring to their genitals? Are body parts sinful?"

"You're being obstinate, Elaina Michael," Sister Ruth shouted over cheers.

"To quote Sister Immaculata, your personal condemnations and twisted version of God's intention for our bodies are completely opposite to the truth. She said only fools repress their cravings and impulses, and that we'll never be free of lust until we can look at temptation, rise above it, and see the beauty beneath peoples' warped perceptions of the human body. When we can look at nakedness without lust or shame, holiness is present."

The other students chanted. "Go, Elaina, go. Go, Elaina, go."

"Tell me, Miss Michael, do you believe the trouble you got yourself into last year was God's intention?"

The class went silent, waiting between shock and curiosity to hear her response.

Her painful disclosures from the previous night, lack of sleep, and hatred for this Catholic School ignited. "Your definition of purity has nothing to do with God. It's condemnations like yours that spoil God's song that our bodies are meant to play. I'm quoting Sister Immaculata again. Have you ever really looked at another person's nakedness? If you weren't so blind, the beauty of the human body would take your breath away. Imm said a woman's body is a tabernacle to bring God to our world in each new baby." Her voice rose hysterically. "Look at a woman's breasts—"

"Show us yours, Elaina," a boy hollered from the back of the room.

"Shut up," she shouted back. "A woman's breasts transform nutrients from her blood into food for her child. Blood given to sustain life. Who does that sound like? Mary, the Mother of God, brought our Savior into this world through her genitals. The prefix *gen–* in Greek means 'to give or produce.' Where do you think the word *generous* comes from?"

Sister Ruth smacked her ruler on the desk, demanding quiet, but Elaina wouldn't be silenced. "Mary fed her son, our infant Messiah, with her milk, transformed from her blood through her breasts. He in turn shed his blood thirty-three years later, naked on the cross for all mankind. Imm said this is what we should think of when looking upon nakedness." Tears collected, and she quickly brushed them aside. "Bones swathed in muscles with a network of veins lacing under the protection of skin . . . the velvet skin of a woman's breasts. It's God's own design to feed His beloved babies."

Her mind reeled backward. She'd never gotten to feed her own son.

"Stop, Miss Michael." Sister Ruth's hands covered her ears for emphasis. "I won't tolerate your pornographic talk."

"Go, Elaina, go," the students began again.

"Flash us your hooters!"

"Show us your milk titties."

The room began to spin as hatred stole the last of her control. She reached under her desk and hurled the wax banana at Sister Ruth. "This is what you know about sex and pornography."

* * *

" . . . and so we have no alternative but to expel your daughter, Mr. Michael."

"I can explain," Elaina interrupted. "I didn't mean what Sister Ruth told you the banana implied. I meant that she doesn't know bananas about sex or pornography—you know, like she doesn't know a thing. It was *her* interpretation that was vulgar."

"I fear how much you know, Miss Michael." Father Krammer's meaning was clear. "You can explain away, but my decision stands. We permitted you to continue school last year despite your . . . condition, risking our fine reputation, because charity is our motto. We allowed you to attend just one class this year—completely unprecedented—in order that you may receive a Saint Augustine diploma. We've bent the rules for you time and again, and this is how you thank us?"

Her father cut in. "I'll remind you that I never asked for a reduction in tuition even though Elaina's only taking one class. None was offered, either. I've faithfully pledged to this school for over twenty-five years. I'm asking you to let her graduate. There's less than a month left."

He donated to this school every year, but he couldn't help with any of her prenatal or hospital bills. Maybe she should remind him she was the one he'd forced to pay every penny of this school's damn tuition.

Father Krammer stood. "I'll reduce expulsion to three days' suspension, but only because of your generosity, Mr. Michael."

She followed her father meekly down the hall. Experience had taught her to wait and see what direction his anger would take.

"You've shamed me for the final time." He tossed the words over his shoulder like trash, never turning around as he exited the building.

Elaina trotted after him. "Dad, please, I swear, I—"

He stopped. "Where were you last night, for the entire night? Who are you sleeping with now? And what about your clothes? Half the time you look like"—disgust contorted his face—"like you work on a street corner. Now, this filth comes from your mouth—to a nun, no less."

His words pierced her to the core. How long had he been biting his tongue?

* * *

Guilt poked Elaina for wishing her gal pals weren't here. Kurt had been sweet to invite Jenny, Patty, Sarah, and Cassy to his apartment after commencement, and they'd been such good friends this final year at Saint Augustine. Who knew how the future would divide them? She shook off her selfishness and put gratitude for their loyalty ahead.

Kurt came out of the kitchen with five glasses of sparkling cider. "All right, ladies, we have something remarkable to celebrate. May this moment remain in our hearts as we journey ahead, and may success find each of us by our own definition."

Glasses clinked. "Cheers!"

"While we're together—because we're together," he continued, "I think Lanie would want you here now . . ."

He shifted his feet uncomfortably, the words obviously refusing to come. He pulled a small box from his pocket.

Goosebumps prickled Elaina's arms and neck. Could this be . . . ?

He reached for her hand and slid a large solitaire ruby onto her finger.

Five sets of hands flew to gaping mouths.

He stepped closer and took her by the shoulders. "Lanie told me about the blanket you gals gave her when Isaac was born and what it meant to her. I chose Isaac's birthstone for the same reason, because I want you to remember your firstborn always, Lanie. What you went through in carrying him has made you the woman I've fallen in love with. Will you spend your life with me?"

It was just as she'd always dreamed.

With Cole.

9

The hospital bill read Paid In Full. There must be a mistake, unless her dad had taken pity. Maybe he wanted to bridge their rift. They'd barely spoken since May. Even the news of her engagement had been accepted with flat congratulations. If her dad had paid off this bill, she'd have to meet him halfway in gratitude. But what if it was a mistake? Appreciation where it wasn't due might draw her father's attention to the error. Then he'd force her to do the honorable thing. Honesty was as overrated as hospital charges were inflated.

Before she entered Grace General, she checked the statement again: paid three weeks ago in cash. Cash was her dad's MO, but bailing Elaina out wasn't.

"Can someone tell me who processed this final payment?" she asked.

"According to this, it was Jason," said the clerk. "He'll be in shortly."

When the staff member who was apparently Jason arrived, he barely had his coat off before Elaina began firing her questions.

"Yeah, I remember because large balances are rarely paid in green-backs," he said. "And the person also requested anonymity."

"Just nod and you won't be breaking any confidences, okay?"

It took only three confirmations to give her the answer: Kurt. How had he known that she owed Grace? Even her mom probably wasn't aware; finances were strictly her dad's domain. Love was written all over this. In saying nothing about his gesture, he showed that he had no expectations in return—just like the gifts her Clover Club used to shower her with. Nevertheless, she wanted and needed to show her appreciation.

Kurt's tired Skylark rested on the side lot, reminding her of its owner's words: *It gets me around. That's all that matters.* It was rusty and had a dented bumper. Stepping up to a Vette or Camaro would carry far more significance, she thought, leaning her bike against the building.

The door opened slowly to her knock, creaking like the kneecaps of a 100-year-old. A stranger in faded, flannel pajamas answered. He looked vaguely like Kurt, red-nosed and with hair in every direction. His voice came out in a croak.

Her insides turned inside out, and all gratitude vanished. He looked like her dad after a twelve-hour work day—or her husband after twelve long years.

Could she spend a lifetime with someone this old? One day, this frumpy man would also sport a pot belly held up atop scrawny legs. Stray hairs would protrude from his nostrils, and nodules would sprout from his neck and back. His toenails would curl into crusty yellow claws. His bathrobe alone foretold her future, threadbare and dated. Once she had married him, her dreams of college, painting, and writing would wear out like that, too.

"I'm sorry to bother you," she stammered, drawing a blank as to why she'd come. "I'll come back . . . when you're feeling better."

Before he could protest, she dashed to her bike and pedaled away as if she'd seen a ghost.

Safely at the cemetery, she let out a scream. Weeks of accumulated misgivings tore from her throat. Hives began to rise on her arms; this time, her allergies were blameless.

She hurled herself to the grass in front of Mary and the angels, their stillness inviting her to unload. They seemed sympathetic to her thoughts. Maybe they were even offering prayers for her in this confusing state of second-guessing.

She regurgitated a glut of doubts onto the grass. Yes, tied-up tomorrows made the future worry-free, but in selling out for the promise of security, she'd forfeited the kind of anticipation that made her heart dance and the kind of euphoria that sizzled for days. Each life, the one of mundane security and the one of precarious passion, came with a price.

Could she close her eyes and make her apprehensions go away? Could she live on autopilot, pretending that ho-hum was enough? Would she ever find the peaceful satisfaction she'd known as a child with the Clover Club? Was compromise necessary to shut Need up, or could she abort baby Need from her soul?

She picked through the grass for clover, trying to guess what Imm would have asked to help her find the answers she craved. The fact that she hadn't told Imm of her engagement spoke volumes itself. Ambiguity was a plague—or was this merely cold feet?

If love was a choice, as her dad often said, she would choose Kurt. There. Settled.

She gave herself a day to solidify her decision and let Kurt recuperate before she biked back to his apartment. "I may as well tell you, my parents won't pay for our wedding. I can count on some money after the ceremony, but probably not much. The bright news is that somebody paid a huge bill of mine, so now everything I earn can go toward our wedding."

Kurt nodded but said nothing.

"I also want to apologize for acting weird the other day," she said shyly. "Your generosity overwhelmed me, reminding me again that I don't deserve you."

"But I deserve you." Kurt buried his face in her hair. "And you're everything I want."

Oh God, she'd heard those words before—the beginning of disaster.

"About our wedding," he began. "Don't give the expense a second thought. I live simply, so there's plenty in the bank collecting dust. That's the nice part about having money: spending it on those we love." He pulled her as close as possible without stepping inside of her, then pulled away and began to pace.

Elaina wished she could climb into him and never come out. He was safe. Predictable. If only they could make love now, her reluctance might disappear. But attempting to break Kurt's resolve had grown tiresome.

She changed the subject instead. "How'd you know I owed Grace money?"

"Your dad's a lot like mine with his lay-in-the-bed-you've-made attitude. I put two and two together. Grace was free with your information once they learned I wanted to square up." He frowned. "But it was supposed to be anonymous."

"Your help with a financial mess involving another man borders on sainthood." She tipped her face up to his.

When their kissing turned the corner, Kurt gently pushed her back. "Soon, babe—and it's going to be heaven." He held her at arm's length. "Do you believe what I say?"

"Especially that I'm beautiful," she said with a giggle.

"Then believe that your past is where it stays. I paid the bill for both of us, so we can start our future with a clean slate."

He was perfect. Unbelievably perfect. "You've done more than my parents."

"They did what they thought best. I'm sure it would've been easier to pay your bills, and I'm even more sure it hurt them to make you shoulder it. But they believed your character would grow. Honor develops in taking responsibility."

She looked away. She needed his unconditional support, not a defense of her stingy parents.

"Do you love them?" he continued. "Real love has no expectations. Too many kids know their parents can't say no out of guilt or because they want to relive their youths through their teenagers. It takes more love to say no than yes, just as your no did to keeping Isaac. When you accept this, you'll also believe how lovable you are to your parents, me, and the world. Then even if your parents' decisions were wrong, you'll thank them, because their nos and the hardships they required of you are the seeds of your character."

Imm had said something similar. *Real love puts feelings aside when making decisions because love is steadfast, where feelings come and go. Choices that cause the most pain are also the greatest acts of love: childbirth, defending one's country, willingly suffering on a cross to give eternal life. Would the Trinity wear those scars if it were just about feelings? What about the scar beneath your belly you earned in giving Isaac life?*

If you have no scars, there's much more digging to be done.
—Edward Michael

She couldn't look at Kurt for fear of losing her composure. "My baby's always one thought away. I must sound ungrateful, but the hospital bill was my last connection to him. And now it's gone too."

"You sound like the mother I want for my children. If I'd met you a year ago, Isaac could've been my son too. I would've asked you both into my life, but it didn't work that way. I don't want you to forget him but only to move forward, confident that your firstborn now has more than most." He tilted her face up and kissed her tenderly. "Let's have a baby as soon as we get your dream wedding out of the way."

Who was this amazing man who loved her *because* of her flaws? How could he resemble her Three in so many ways but say he knew nothing of a higher power?

Please God, help me love him the way he deserves.

The air felt holy, not so much for this moment between them but for a greater love's presence.

"Who is your God and where does he fit in your life, Kurt?"

"He's here, Elaina, the God you seem to breathe like air. I want to explore Him with you."

* * *

Mark relieved Elaina of her potluck salad and leaned against the front door, eyeing Jenny appreciatively. "No Kurt? What's the matter with that guy? You've gotta teach him how to party. Come on in. Make yourself at home in here or around back, where the keg is."

He ushered them into the raucous gathering. "I bought you and Kurt a congratulations bottle of bubbly, sure he'd be with you. Guess you and Jen will have to kill it instead."

"Lanie's on her own with that," Jenny said. "I'm strictly a beer drinker."

"As am I," Mark said with a leer. "Grab a place in line for grub, and I'll chase you down a cold one."

His eagerness grated on Elaina.

Based on the guests' staggering, this crowd must have been nursing the keg all afternoon. She should've figured, with Mark as host of this Fourth of July bash, that beer and booze would be the main course. No wonder Kurt wouldn't be persuaded to come, despite her persistence. His reluctant offer to consider a brief appearance later had left her sure he wouldn't come. Thank goodness. This was no place for a teetotaler.

She suspected the champagne might fizz over when she opened it, so she went around the back, where its spray could only water the grass. With Jenny being wooed by Mark—the last thing she wanted to watch—this gave her a reason to withdraw.

The tree pollen irritated her eyes and threatened to ruin her makeup, so she headed back into the house to find a quiet corner and nurse her bottle. The effervescence made her head feel bubbly, magnifying her consciousness of being alone again. Was there anyone single here? Here she sat, Elaina Michael, newly engaged, alone and watching others laugh and carry on. She felt sick, as if distress had been dropped into the sparkling wine, shaken up, and popped open inside her stomach.

Maybe she'd feel better if she found Jenny, but she felt so unstable in these heels. On second thought, she'd finish her bubbly and wait for Jen to find her. How was Kurt filling this evening? She wished—

There Cole stood, looking like a Grecian god. The sight of him slammed into her chest, stopping her heart, then restarting it with such force that the room spun. Everything went helter-skelter, crashing into disbelief.

"Sweetheart!" He lifted her chin and kissed both her cheeks. His eyes shined against a dark tan, his sun-bleached curls winding tightly the way she loved.

"Sweetheart," he whispered again. He brushed his chiseled jaw against hers, a gesture that never failed to weaken her. Absentmindedly and of old habit, she ran her hands over his shoulders, drinking him in. He still wore the same cologne. He still called her sweetheart. And he still made everything around him dissolve.

"Why are you here? When did you come back?"

"I found a bargain flight and wanted to be the big surprise. Mark's face looked as startled as yours, but yours is the best welcome home."

"Are you back for good?" The words felt wobbly.

"Just a week. The gods must be smiling—you and me, here."

Astonishment kept her speechless.

"Elaina Rose Michael, with nothing to say? Never thought I'd see the day. A drink'll bring back the chatterbox I know and love. Does the lady still prefer dry red?" He gave a deep bow like the first time she'd met him in Tasty's break room. "Let's find someplace quiet to talk. It's been so long."

He pulled her to a tucked-away room, snagging a bottle along the way. Every reason to avoid this temptation leaped to mind, trying to block his lead. He didn't want to talk, argument screamed. He didn't care about anything except what would benefit him, and that wine he was carrying was to *his* advantage.

She didn't need warnings, nor did she want them. She hushed the misgivings; a couple of minutes would be harmless, just enough to show off her engagement ring and describe the man who was everything Cole was not. A little wine, one glass, would strengthen her resolve.

The ruby on her finger flashed caution as she tilted her glass. Kurt's soft eyes bore into her conscience as if he watched from the shadows, but her guilt weakened under the sound of Cole's smooth voice.

"Not a day goes by that I don't think of you." He topped their glasses. "I pass an art gallery every day, and their displays remind me of you. I always loved watching you draw and paint. Do you still have the sketch of me at the cemetery?"

"No," she lied, "I never finished it, so why would I save it? You said we needed to move on."

"And you look like you're moving pretty well. All your baby fat is gone."

Baby fat? She knocked back the wine to wash away the burning, love-hate sensation. Yes, the extra padding on her belly and hips that had kept Isaac cozy and safe was gone. Everything was gone.

Strong hands covered hers, his silence saying he knew her thoughts. He refilled her glass, and they locked eyes. "I'm sorry, sweetheart. That was insensitive of me. Come here. Lordy, you'd think I had leprosy. I just want to hold you for old times' sake. Tell me everything that's happened since I left."

The ruby begged to be introduced, but each time she tried, her thoughts fluttered to the past. A shadow of something moved across her mind . . . or was it in the doorway? In the nook of Cole's arm, nothing mattered but the rise and fall of his voice, his chest, his scent—for old times' sake. One minute fluttered to the next so gracefully she wasn't sure when they'd started kissing. Maybe they'd never stopped since that long-ago autumn afternoon when desire had demanded the sketch be put aside so they could stretch out on the grass . . . the carpet?

A sharp cough from a silhouette in the doorway made them both jump. Her zipper refused to cooperate, nor would her balance as she tried to scramble to her feet, nor would her surroundings come to focus...

"A toast to happy reunions." Kurt raised a whiskey bottle sarcastically, then took a long gulp. He flipped the lights on and stumbled to the center of the room, forced shot glasses into their hands, and began to pour.

Cole stepped in front of Elaina, about to intervene, then hesitated. As the amber liquid spilled, Elaina grabbed for the bottle.

Kurt pushed her back into Cole's arms. Whiskey ran down his neck as he guzzled.

"That's where you belong, Lanie. Aren't you going to introduce me?" He extended a trembling hand. "I'm Kurt Trackwald, Elaina's fiancé. I take it she didn't mention me."

He turned and staggered out.

Elaina shook Cole off and ran before he could ask what had just happened. He didn't deserve another moment any more than she did a chance to explain to Kurt.

Darkness, the thief of sobriety, laughed at her clumsy attempt to chase after another victim. She had to find Kurt, but she wasn't sure where she was, or how to get . . . where? Home wasn't an option, drunk as she was, and she couldn't stay at the party after what had just happened. She had to explain to Kurt what she didn't understand herself.

She was hooked on Cole like Kurt was alcohol. Slick poison, Kurt called it, smooth and sweet at first—like honey butter, intoxicating—until the lies turned rancid. Promises that rotted to excuses. She'd guzzled Cole's lies, drunk on his appearance and charm, until his honey butter disgorged itself like bitter bile the moment he'd learned she was pregnant. But even after he'd shown his toxic nature, refusing to help her, sleeping with anyone who'd stroke his ego, she'd continued to make excuses for him and refused to give him up.

Imm had warned how evil lures with false promises, leaving just enough bait to entice and just enough string to give a false sense of freedom. The dark one's method of operation is euphoria, then despair, intoxication, and harsh reality, all while slowly reeling in the victim.

> *The surest sign of the dark one's presence is selfishness.*
> —Sister Immaculata Lefevre

Unable to balance in her heels—or was it the wine?—Elaina staggered under the compulsion to find Kurt. Need, always pressing. She lurched up the driveway toward the street.

Walking came easier once she removed her shoes, until a stab brought her down. In the wet grass, she wrestled her foot up to find blood oozing and glass lodged in her bare heel. She'd have to wait for help in this ditch with every creeping creature that made its home here: opossums, skunks, snakes.

The thought of snakes, camouflaged and appearing from nowhere when least expected, reminded her of Eric. Both were glassy-eyed and watched from hidden places. Both left her feeling trapped, like a nightmare when the mind screams to run but the legs are too heavy. Eric's presence had kept her in a state of dread in her very home. But only opening the dark door to the uglies would bring her face-to-face with the real reason he was such a snake.

Her skin puckered as she recalled her mother's standing excuse for every trouble Eric caused: *He has little man complex because of his small stature.* She shivered involuntarily like a knife scraping against china.

Young Elaina and the neighborhood had conceded to Eric's command of all their activities. His audacity and ability to persuade had earned him this position, and his skill at talking himself out of any corner—or at slithering into hiding—had helped him get away with the things he'd done to her.

Nausea forced up the sparkling wine and dry red, bitter with bile. She sprayed the street. The dry heaves followed. Her legs felt so weak she was sure she couldn't stand, but when blinding headlights brought hope for help, she hobbled into the street.

Deanne Jonis jumped from the car. "Holy crap, I almost hit you! What the hell are you doing? Wait, is that—Elaina? Oh God, are you alright? I'm takin' you to my place."

Everything looked hazy inside Deanne's apartment, but whether it was bad lighting or her blurred vision, Elaina wasn't sure. But even her inebriation couldn't have conceived the musty odor like old, dirty socks.

"Let's get your foot fixed."

She winced as Deanne yanked at the glass, ripping a larger hole in her foot. Deanne doused the wound in gin, and Elaina nearly passed out.

"Sorry, I don't have anything else. No first aid stuff, either. This orange T-shirt will do. Pretty sure it's clean." Deanne sniffed it to be sure before ripping it up to wrap Elaina's foot. "Which kind of tape do you want? I've got electrical, masking, and a little transparent. Or we could use 'em all."

Elaina shrugged weakly and remained collapsed against the back of the couch while Deanne completed her ministrations.

"You look like shit," Deanne announced after finishing the make-shift bandage. Elaina would've laughed at her nursing skills if she didn't feel so awful. "Let me spin one up."

Elaina hated pot—the smell, the buzz, how stupid people acted after they'd smoked it—but Cole had told her it was rude to refuse.

" . . . and I can't get over him even though I know he's not serious." Deanne's voice droned on like white noise. "He feeds me crap like how gorgeous I am to get me in the sack, and while he's getting off, my head's screamin' 'You liar!' You know how long I've been settling for his line of shit?"

"Probably as long as I did with Cole," Elaina mumbled. She could hear the bruises Mark had left on Deanne's heart. Deanne had been so helpful tonight, fermenting Elaina's guilt for all she'd thought and done in jealousy to a girl no different than herself.

Revenge will only boomerang bitterness back to your own heart.
—Sister Immaculata Lefevre

* * *

Sunshine seared through the grimy window, pressing heat and offensive glare through the thin skin of Elaina's eyelids. It forced them open to the pain of a new day. Measuring this hangover against previous whoppers, there was no comparison. Cole, the reason for every stupid thing she'd ever done, could take credit for this throbbing headache too. Even after moving a thousand miles away, he still managed to turn everything sour.

As she slowly raised her left hand to block the glare, the ruby on her ring finger reflected a red spot on the ceiling. The color of blood. She was the assassin of Kurt's sobriety. In her addiction to a man who left nothing but trouble in his wake, she'd sold out Kurt—and her own soul.

The magnitude of the destruction she'd caused reduced her to sobs. She dropped to her knees and begged God to have mercy on Kurt, excluding herself from her petitions. Asking anything for herself seemed like a mortal sin.

Never grab for love which isn't extended freely, she could hear Imm whisper. Cole had never loved her, yet she'd clutched at his imitations. Kurt had offered his entire life freely, but all she'd extended in return was a used and cast-aside body, rewrapped in flashy clothes as if she could pass herself off as untouched. So gracious in his love, Kurt was willing to accept trash as his wedding gift—to lift her dignity.

Something on the carpet stuck to her cheek. She'd awoken in grime and the smell of stale beer, sweat, and sex before, but this morning's foggy head wouldn't clear. Where was she? The drab walls of this room, free of any decor, were the color of unwashed skin. Oh, she needed to throw up.

She stumbled down the hall searching for a place to retch. Each room was filthier than the last, the bathroom foulest of all. Her body wouldn't wait, regurgitating sour wine and regret. A splash of cold water afterwards brought temporary relief as she searched for any remnants of last night that might give a clue as to where she was.

Snoring led her to the last room, where Deanne sprawled across the bed. If Elaina had been normal, she'd still be sleeping too, but an alarm clock in her head blared at 6 a.m. regardless of how late she'd stayed up or how much she'd had to drink. Her internal alarm clock had no snooze button, and it flashed thoughts, worries, and to-do lists until she got up. Her dad said it was a gift, but it felt like a cross.

The only place where stillness and contentment partnered was under the gaze of the blue marble Mother Mary and her pink angels. That was a lifetime ago. Childhood's simplicity, where right and wrong were obvious, was where freedom lived. No shadows blurred the lines between virtue and vice. There, she'd been sure of herself and her friends. It was probably the reason Imm used to say that innocence was bliss.

Pacing the apartment eventually gave way to cleaning, her cure-all for boredom, anxiety, and self-contempt. Her back-and-forth movements rocked her thoughts gently. She would need to return Kurt's ring and the money for the hospital bill. After that, she'd get a car . . . maybe move in here with Deanne . . . split the rent and keep the place clean. Deanne couldn't refuse that.

Life had promise when she held a sponge in her hand. She scrubbed harder.

10

Elaina's heart trembled as she weighed the wisdom of opening the box. Was she better off leaving these reminders alone? She pulled the blue blanket out slowly, aching for Isaac's sweet scent. Instead, she found that a year's storage had left only the smell of the Michaels' home. The dark, off-center photos of her firstborn were better than nothing, but time was shrinking Isaac to a stranger.

"Happy birthday, precious one," she whispered. "Are you walking yet? What kind of a party will your mother have?"

Every one-year-old she knew came to mind as a gauge for Isaac's size right now. What color were his eyes and hair? How many teeth did he have? What was his favorite toy? She hoped his parents weren't too old or too busy to play with him and hold him way more than necessary.

The truth, like oil, wouldn't sink or dissolve but made a thickness on top a year's worth of tears. Isaac was better off with them, whoever they were, because she had no ambition beyond finding any place to live but home.

Her parents' most recent announcement churned uncomfortably in her stomach: Eric had run into trouble again and would be moving back in. Even the thought of Eric lurking about the house sent a slithering sensation across her back. She refused to tolerate him anymore. So while her mother prepared for her son's arrival, Elaina plotted her own escape.

If she confessed the uglies to Kurt, would he take pity and let her move in with him, despite what she'd done with Cole? Desperation urged her to open the dark place to him, but even if she were brave enough to confess, she wouldn't know where to find him. He wasn't at work anymore. She'd heard that he'd requested a transfer as soon as he'd been released from detox.

Every Tasty employee knew why he'd lost his sobriety. She'd started taking her breaks and lunches outside, where the atmosphere wasn't so frosty. The distance from the store's rear to the time clock made for several late punch-ins, and management extended a final warning. The reason they'd lost their best meat cutter had become dispensable. It was only a matter of—

"You have a package," her mom called, "from Grasse, France."

Elaina quickly tucked the pictures back in the envelope and slid the box back under her bed. Could hidden heartbreak be hidden treasure, too?

She raced down the stairs, grabbed the box, and darted back to her room, taking the stairs two at a time. Her melancholy lay under the box springs, forgotten.

She traced Imm's swirling script with one finger, savoring every detail. She opened the box slowly to find two wooden boxes with wood-burned lettering in Imm's distinctive hand. Within were tubes of oils, brushes, inks, and calligraphy pens, all secured in leather loops. It must have cost a fortune.

She immediately recognized the Kolinsky sable label on the brushes. Running the thickest one over her cheeks as Imm used do to when holding Elaina on her lap, she imagined Imm's musical accent saying again as in childhood, "These are distinct because of the softness and strength of their bristles. If cared for, they'll last forever."

A crisp yellow envelope fell from the box.

> *To be read July 18, 1981*
> *Ma chére enfant,*
> *A year ago, you bore a masterpiece, the creation, manifestation, and reflection of your Clover Three's pure love. Happiness should fill you in being chosen the co-creator and tabernacle in which a piece of God was brought to our world.*

I know your pain, as I too have borne the sweetness and bit-terness of love and loss. Glorify your Clover Club's Great Three by painting your aches and joys, prayers and petitions, all while trust-ing that your pictures will come true. Praise them with the work of your hands, fueled by your imagination. Should you find yourself unable to paint at this time, write what the brush cannot express. Your words, like your paintings, will hang in their gallery, treasured like all your other objets d' art—works of art.

I've never left you in my prayers, and I love you.

Immaculata

In the days to follow, Elaina swirled the colors, remembering the comfort of Imm's magic paintbrush circling over her cheeks as a child, but the solace of painting couldn't be coaxed. The calligraphy box, with its firm, gray paper and blackest ink, enticed her instead. If she couldn't paint a thank you to Imm, it would have to be penned.

July 20, 1981

Dearest Imm,

Thank you for remembering Isaac's birthday with the most won-derful gift. I love it!

What did you mean that you too have borne the sweetness and bitterness of love and loss? You said something similar when I was in the hospital. How do you always know what I'm feeling?

I hope this letter will reach the rest of our club, too, because I love and miss you all. I remember the countless ways we used to commu-nicate with each other when I was little. As I got older, you reminded me that my personal relationship with the Three was beyond what could be formed from books, pious religion lessons, and man-made rules. Too often those things merely raise conflict, you said, and there's a big difference between knowing about God and knowing God.

Thank you, Imm and dear Three, for my imagination and cre-ativity. Even though you're all so far away, I think of you each time I listen to music and paint.

Are you still harvesting roses and making wine? How beautiful

Grasse must be! I dream of the day I'll visit and see for myself. Tell me where we'll go and what you'll show me.

Life here has been uneventful, but there's a bright note: most of Isaac's hospital bill is paid. I have much to look forward to now, including an apartment and a car. Independence, here I come!

All my love,
Elaina

The fib that life had remained ordinary sucked the joy from writing to Imm. Omitting unpleasant details seemed considerate, though. In sparing Imm the truth, Elaina wouldn't have to shoulder the guilt of having let her down again. She had enough on her back.

Honesty would also have required her to put doubt and vulnerability on the table. She'd tried that already with her parents, Cole, and Cassy. How much truth dared she risk before Imm gave up on her? Her parents had. *You've shamed me for the final time.*

As for the Three, they already knew everything. Their silence and continual hiding said they had given up on her, too.

* * *

July 27, 1981

Ma chére enfant,

I'm compelled to respond immediately, after reading between the lines of your letter. Though you think independence—control and having your own way—is what will bring happiness, self-sufficiency is just the opposite of what you need and what your soul (Need) craves.

As a child, your Clover Club took part in every aspect of your life by your invitation. You drained yourself of loneliness and rejection, and filled yourself with Clover love. They liberated your pleasures: painting, running through the clover field, and gorging on wild raspberries at the cemetery fence row. You never doubted their faithfulness, love, and support.

Three of the most frightening or freeing words are "I trust you." We're reminded of the broken trusts we've experienced, wondering

"Why will this time be different?" We know we'll be asked to rely on another to lead. There's powerful freedom in allowing our hearts to have a say. A true relationship depends on total giving, sharing, and receiving. Trust, too, must be circular. When you give your trust to another, that person usually becomes more trustworthy.

Your three friends, with one divine nature, are a community within themselves, yet so great is their love that it naturally expands to fill everything within their interlocking hands. Like clover, once love takes root, it soon fills fields and fields.

We are God's lambs who feed on Clover—love. When full of Clover, our greatest desire is to spread. When our bellies are full of Clover, there's no worry over tomorrow's supply. We share with no concern. Selfless giving frees us while also making us completely dependent on God, each other, our communities, and our nation. While on earth, loving one another is the closest we can get to perfect eternal communion with the Three, humanity's greatest longing.

Independence becomes our motive when we doubt God's desire for us to have those things that bring pleasure, things that are mistaken for happiness. Earthly pleasures and true happiness are vastly different, though. Would the Three who love you so much say no to anything (or anyone) just to flaunt their authority or withhold happiness? They say yes to everything except what will bring pain and confusion.

God the Three trust you so much that they allow you to choose brief pleasures or happiness. They're so confident in your ultimate potential that they continue hoping you'll make good decisions, while constantly forgiving your mistakes. Because of their faith in your ability to learn from your blunders, they also give you thousands of do-overs with each new sunrise.

Though your Trinity already know and have forgiven your self-indulgences, in admitting those wrongdoings, you pull sin from the recesses and make room for Clover to take root again.

Ma maman is struggling in her diminishing abilities. Like you, I'm a change-of-life baby now caring for the one who nurtured me, as you'll one day experience, too. Life is an unbroken circle, a halo, when we mimic the Three.

The harvest is almost over, yet the rose fields are still heavy with scent. Occasionally, while picking, I'll find a rare blushing rose with tinges of scarlet within the yellow petals, cross-pollinated with the crimson variety from down the road. They remind me of you, ma rose jaune avec un cœur rouge, my yellow rose with a red heart.

What will we do upon your visit? First, we'll paint together in my studio like old times. Every afternoon, we'll find a different place to picnic with local cheeses, honey, and wine, all containing floral hues from the cows and bees that feast on such a variety of wildflowers.

Until the day I wrap my arms around you again, trust your Three, especially in times of loneliness and temptation.

I've never left you in my prayers, and I love you.

Immaculata

P.S. Two more days until Prince Charles and Lady Diana's wedding. Write me your thoughts after you've watched.

* * *

Elaina continued stirring the roux, trying to ignore her dad's grumbling about the waste paying rent would be when Elaina could continue to live at home for the price of cooking and housekeeping. She wouldn't let the flour and butter lump and stick the way his negativity did.

He insisted that a loan for a new vehicle was frivolous too, when so many used cars were available. Her sister Kim, only three years older, owned her secondhand car *and* mobile home, he reminded Elaina. He never missed a chance to restamp "Perfect Daughter" across Saint Kim's forehead.

> *The need for the latest and greatest is a rabbit chase.*
> —Edward Michael

As if fate wanted to hold a salt shaker over the wound, Kim buzzed in and peered over Elaina's shoulder. "You're going to give Dad a heart attack with the crap you serve him."

She was just jealous. Dad loved Elaina's cooking.

Elaina wanted to scream that the reason for her prison break wasn't only her parents' dismissal of Eric's violations—leaving him free to resume them—but also their constantly placing Elaina in Kim's shadow.

Imm's persistence that Elaina should make a confession also brewed, but her inner turmoil came more from her excuses that didn't fully address why disclosing herself to a priest was out of the question. If she exposed the uglies, might her innocence be in fact not completely so? Or did it have more to do with the necessity to forgive if you wished to be forgiven? The fact that her parents had buried Eric's warped deeds said they were also liars, which only inflamed her distress.

A moment of pity for her parents flickered. They'd finally shaken their last child, only to have another move back in.

> *The only thing a parent owes a child is what he cannot do for himself.* —Edward Michael

She shook off the memory of her father's words. *So how's that working out for you, Dad?* Her pity quickly faded.

Imm portrayed self-sufficiency as darkness's lure yet Elaina couldn't remember a monologue of her father's that didn't uphold the honor of independence. So, which was it? Neither had said her new life couldn't include a little fun, though, so this is where she'd start.

Excitement rode the waves of the songs blasting from the radio of her new Ford Pinto. The car was just big enough for moving her things to Deanne's apartment, which was centered between three fraternity houses. Every corner of Tarrock's east side would be hosting parties to usher in the extended Labor Day weekend and a new college year, Deanne said.

A final pit stop on the way to her new life would close the door on last month's disaster. Once she'd paid Kurt back and returned his ring, she could concentrate on being a model self-sustaining, tax-paying contributor to society.

She pulled into the parking lot of Tasty and strode straight to the meat department.

"I don't have Kurt's new address. Can you get this to him?" She tossed the envelope on Tasty's meat counter, unsure how Kurt's former coworker would respond.

"When I see what's in the envelope," said Anne. Next to Kim, Anne was Elaina's greatest critic. "You're not going to play him a second time."

"Here, feel—it's a ring and a check with an apology. Not that it's any of your business."

"I'll deliver it if you take the apology out. You're not worthy of his forgiveness."

"Forget it, then." She grabbed the envelope. "But you can't say I didn't try to do the honorable thing."

"Honorable? If that isn't the biggest load of shit! Give me the envelope and get out."

Elaina tossed the envelope back on the counter and left, satisfied. Oh, the hypocrites, hiding behind their blameless black-and-white walls because reality's gray boundaries might force a face-to-face with their own flaws.

She couldn't think of anyone she resented more than the righteous, except maybe the privileged, wealthy enough to buy the ever-changing latest and greatest, all while purchasing beauty, influence, prestige, and the prerogative to thumb their noses at everyone; wealthy enough to own the reply, "whatever."

A bittersweet thought occurred: her firstborn would be rich, educated, and privileged. Polyester Woman had promised.

This was her new life, though. No negative thoughts allowed. The little Pinto's air conditioner was flipped to high and the windows cranked down because it was wasteful. For eighteen years Elaina had never before indulged extravegence.

She breezed into a parking spot, slammed the car door, and bounced up the steps to her new shared apartment.

The skin-color walls reminded her of her commitment to optimism. Maybe Deanne would go halves on paint. Other decorating ideas jumped around as she pulled the steam cleaner over the filthy, dated shag rugs. Deanne's cleaning standards, somewhere south of zero, were tucked under a loose corner of the carpet.

She wistfully remembered Kurt's habit of hanging up his coat, taking off his shoes, and placing his keys in a tray the minute he arrived home. His apartment, which had once appeared so simple and small, now struck her as a palace. But Kurt was another closed door, too.

Recalling the words of her apology that she'd included with the ring and check, she hoped it would heal them both a little.

> *Dear Kurt, You were right about my need to get over Cole, but I didn't try very hard. I'm infected with want for what I can't have; impatience and impulsiveness my downfalls, too. I lost you because of them, though all is not lost. In your love, the Trinity were also present. You gave me hope when I wanted to give up. I only wish I'd told you that sooner.*
>
> *I hope you'll explore the higher power we talked about on our all-nighter. You'll have no trouble finding the Trinity because you're patient, loyal, and trusting. Those things come hard for me, the reason I've ruined more relationships than just ours.*
>
> *I understand we're done, and it's with a heavy heart that I take the blame. Please accept the ring and money back for propriety's sake and for my dignity, which is currently in short supply.*
>
> *Thank you for giving me confidence in the male population and for your forgiveness, which I've no doubt is already mine. You're the mark of the goodness I want to reach someday.*
>
> Love, Elaina

The words she'd wanted to write were that she'd do anything to be given another chance. She was slick poison to nice guys. In her fear of rejection, she had managed to destroy even her oldest and dearest friendship. In being the one who sabotaged, there was no risk of being the victim. Crazy? Yes, because it hurt no less on either side.

Deanne burst in the door. Immediately, her nose crinkled. "Whoa, looks like my grandma's place, so clean."

Was that good or bad? Concern fed Elaina a gush of babble. "Your room's exactly the way you left it—except I did your laundry . . . because I couldn't tell what was dirty with everything on the floor."

Deanne wandered from room to room, shaking her head.

"The laundromat gave me hangers," Elaina continued, "so now your things are organized: jeans, shirts, dresses . . . See? Is it all right?"

Deanne's mouth opened as she weighed her words, but they wouldn't be denied. "Nothing's where I had it! How do I find my clothes hidden in the closet? Is there any place you didn't clean? And what's that horrible smell?"

"Ammonia. Oh, and bleach. Ammonia strips grease, and bleach is for the mold. I also put ammonia in the carpet steamer rental. Hospitals use ammonia and bleach because they're cheap and do the best job. I'm not saying this place was germy like a hospital, just dirt and . . . spirited living . . ."

She felt increasingly troubled by Deanne's scowl.

"Spirited living? What's that mean?"

"Living that . . . doesn't include cleaning. I had to do the carpets three times before the rinse water came out clean. The chemical smell will go away if we keep the windows open overnight."

Deanne sighed and took a serious tone. "First, I don't eat off the carpets, I walk on them—and so will everyone who's in and out with grungy shoes. Do you expect people to take their shoes off? If you want that kind of place, you don't belong here. I don't wanna hurt your feelings, but we better get this out now."

Elaina folded her arms in front of her. "Taking shoes off is practical, more comfortable, and eliminates ninety percent of the dirt that gets tracked in."

"Elaina, we live by three frats houses, not convalescent homes! You're setting yourself up for mega-frustration. I wash a dish when I need something to eat off of, and if I don't feel like washing a dish, I use a magazine as a plate. And about keeping the windows open all night, we're surrounded by frat houses—duh. Unlocked anythings invite hungry, horny men." She winked and pinched Elaina playfully. "They'll take you first, and then everything in your fridge! We have to button up tight at night."

Elaina scooped up a pile of wet rags. "Okay, I get it. I thought you'd like free housekeeping. I'll limit it to my room, the bathroom, and the kitchen."

"Excuse me, but your room is also the living room, and the bath and kitchen are *ours*. In other words, you just said you're gonna neurotically clean every inch of this place except my room."

"Well . . ."

Deanne kicked off her shoes and began walking away. "Okay, if you want to break your back for nothing, be my guest. But remember you're doing it for you. Don't get bent out of shape when things revert to a total pigsty overnight, because that's my comfort zone."

She nodded, confident that Deanne would learn to love a clean home.

But as soon as Deanne entered the kitchen, she burst into laughter. "Flowers? For real? Come here, wifey-poo."

She smother-hugged Elaina and stuck her tongue in her ear.

"Ew, a wet-willie. Back off." Elaina was more relieved than grossed out. This roommate situation had to work out; she couldn't go home. "Will you go halves on some paint? You can pick the color—anything except this shade of dirty skin."

Deanne shook with laughter and collapsed on the floor. "It's called peach, with a fifty-year overlay of cigarettes and weed. Any shade we pick will look like dirty skin in a couple of weeks unless we go with black. How about we leave the dirty skin and spend our bucks on spirited living?" With a wave, she dismissed the topic. "What we need to discuss is this holiday weekend. You up for clubbing, frat parties, or taking your sweet new green machine up to the lake—or all of the above?"

* * *

The clock read 6:02 a.m. as the bass music from the neighboring apartment continued to pound at her temples. She had to get some quiet. Where were her jeans? Where was the light switch? Three passed-out guys littered the living room floor. Had she slept in just her underwear with them in here all night? Had she done anything regrettable? Her throbbing head could only imagine.

Everywhere she stepped had become filthy overnight, just as Deanne had warned. The air smelled like a hangover yawn. Beer cans and cigarette butts littered the counters and floor. She picked up a jacket to find it covering a puddle of puke. Animals didn't live this way! And oh yuck, someone had puked in the sink, too.

Disgust stoked her charge next door to the neighbors. She pounded on the door to no avail and finally kicked the screen in. The frame fell off its hinges. She barged in, stepping over liquor bottles and a maze of passed-out bodies, and yanked out the stereo plug.

This was independence? She thought of the cup of coffee her dad used to hand her every morning, saying the same thing each time. *We need our caffeine like those in hell need ice water.* Hell must look like this.

Back outside, she sucked in the fresh air. Apparently, independence offered two choices: make coffee in the grimy kitchen, or cross the street and pay for a cup. The kitchen and her dad's saying won.

A penny saved is a penny earned. —Benjamin Franklin

Back at the apartment, caffeine and more scrubbing energized her. Thank goodness she'd raided her mom's stockpile of cleaning supplies. She had enough to disinfect this side of the planet. She cleaned right around the passed-out, puke-covered pretties who had seemed so pretentious last night. So this was how the educated entertained themselves. These future doctors, lawyers, bankers, and bigwigs, strung out on God knows what, looked no better than bums in the harsh light of morning. Their parents' money was the only thing that separated them from beggars. What a twisted world Saint Augustine's God had created! Her Trinity couldn't be the same as him.

Yet beneath her bitterness lay the wish to be one of them, well known, invited, significant. At least she could pretend. After all, they lived side by side in this ghetto. Except while these losers could call themselves Haisting College students, attending their $10,000-a-year classes, she was bagging groceries for minimum wage. And $3.35 an hour wouldn't cover even book fees for a single semester.

One-by-one, they woke and stumbled out the door mumblings complaints for the early hour and the noise from Elaina's cleaning frenzy. Just as they slammed her apartment door behind them, they would exit this hellhole side of town on their graduations into huge homes—and she could, too. She'd just have to find a different route.

"I smell coffee." Deanne hugged Elaina and yawned.

She pushed Deanne back with a gloved hand. "Your breath! Yuck!"

"Look at this place—you angel! Maybe I *could* get used to clean. How'd you get the frat brats out of here?

"Rags dipped in ammonia and placed by their head. The fumes will drive any size roach away." She grinned and waved her hand like a magician.

"You're weird," Deanne laughed and hugged her again. "No wonder every guy wants a wife eventually. I love my new one, and I'm takin' her out for breakfast. We'll recap last night's knee-slappers over something greasy and come up with a plan for this whole new day."

Deanne's optimism was astounding, even hungover. Nothing mattered but the next good time. No wonder everyone adored her. Elaina made a mental note.

> *Enthusiasm and determination will get you a lot farther than a sheepskin.* —Edward Michael

Something else Deanne always seemed to have enough of was money. Breakfast would cost at least eight dollars, because Deanne refused to do fast food. But Deanne hadn't just spent half of next month's rent on a carpet steamer and flowers, either.

They settled into a booth at the local pancake house, and Elaina squinted under the incandescent lights and even brighter sunlight pouring through the big windows. Before breakfast arrived, she had to cover all her bases from the previous night.

"So did I do anything, um, regrettable last night?" She pretended indifference.

"How would I know?" Deanne mumbled from behind her coffee cup. "Who cares? You're still breathing, and you're about to have hot waffles in front of you."

Elaina shifted, her thighs sticking to the bench. "There were three guys on the floor of my bedroom—I mean, the living room. I can't remember anything, and frankly, I don't trust myself after what happened at Mark's party."

"Oh," Deanne nodded knowingly. "You're wondering if you had one or maybe all three of them?"

Her loud, unabashed laughter forced Elaina's hands to her temples. It wasn't funny. Sweat ran down her back from the morning sun, yet she was shivering from the AC that blasted from a vent at her ankles.

The waitress dropped off their order. Deanne ate as if she hadn't had a drop of beer, wine, tequila, and who knew what else. Come to think of it, Deanne ate that way all the time and never gained an ounce.

Deanne reached across the table and patted her hand. "Lighten up, and I'll be more serious. Both Cole and Mark proved that you and I need a little lovin' sometimes, too. You'd better get that birth control scrip filled so you don't have a repeat mistake."

Elaina froze, a fork of waffles halfway to her mouth. "What mistake are you talking about? My firstborn? He wasn't a mistake. I hate when he's referred to that way. God doesn't make mistakes." She shoved her plate away.

"No offense intended. But spare me the God stuff."

"Religion lessons are the problem." She smacked the table with a fist. "Warped teachings, like unbaptized babies can't go to heaven. That makes God a monster!"

"Your hangover's gettin' noisy, not to mention that your day started in the middle of the night." Deanne's voice remained mellow. "You know I'm right about the birth control."

Once a girl's gone all the way, it's hard to go back to holding hands. Dr. Stoffer's words echoed Kurt's. *Sexual arousal, like the craving for alcohol, will master you if you don't muscle it first.*

Her hands dropped to her lap, sweaty in acknowledgment that every date with Cole had also been a rendezvous with alcohol. She'd been drinking twice as much since he left. Alcohol made the same ole, same ole of life without him tolerable. It quieted Need, shrank heartache, and lately it even washed recollections away. Except during her brief relationship with Kurt, she couldn't remember the last weekend that hadn't centered around drinking. Was this independence or a bad case of dependence?

"How can you eat?"

Deanne continued to fork Elaina's barely touched waffles.

"Feeling pretty rough? Try these." Deanne handed her two black capsules.

"I don't do drugs."

"Neither do I. They're prescription—for somebody. Just diet pills."

"Then why are you eating like a cow?"

"I spun one up before we left, and now I've got the munchies. These little wonders keep me svelte." Deanne gave a Zsa Zsa Gabor imitation. "Think of zem as a cure-all for hangovers, weight gain, and general blahs, dahling."

"Is that why you're always spastic?"

"Probably, but let's not analyze it to death. Do you want 'em or not?"

If they were prescription for someone, what could be the harm? That's what the FDA was for.

"I'll make a deal with you, wifey-poo." Apparently, the nickname was now cemented. "You keep our place clean—including fresh flowers—and I'll keep you in black beauties and anything else you want."

Elaina's stomach clenched. "You deal?"

"Of course not, but I have friends who do, so I know where to get what I want and what my friends want. Everyone needs an occasional perk, even the Haisting yuppies. Don't look so shocked."

Elaina wriggled on the bench and tried to look indifferent.

"Remember Steely, the guy with the long ponytail? There's a reason he lives right behind us: Haisting College. Steely heals the frats and sororities of their hangovers and hangnails, rushing disappointments and homesickness, not to mention exam overload and the freshman fifteen." Deanne's sarcasm couldn't be missed.

"The freshman fifteen?"

"Oh gawd, Elaina, you're so clueless. First-year college kids generally gain about fifteen pounds because their mommies aren't around to make sure they're eating their veggies. We'll never have that problem, because we can't afford seven-hundred-dollar-a-semester meal plans. When Junior and Blondie go home and step on the scale, Steely gains a whole new clientele for black beauties, coke, ludes, whatever cheers 'em up."

Deanne's dismissive attitude alarmed her, as did learning a drug dealer lived behind them. A feeble voice in her head reminded her of the reason she couldn't recall anyone named Steely: excessive drinking. She had no room to judge. She shrugged.

"Wow, you must've been really ripped," Deanne said. "You and Steely talked for quite a while. He couldn't peel his eyes off you until business called. Then he said, and I quote, 'She's the cutest thing that's hit our side of town in ages.'"

Elaina wrinkled her nose. "Which would mean he's either blind or high all the time. Let's face it, I can't hold a candle to the rich, bottle-blond sorority girls who swarmed the neighborhood last night."

"Are we really gonna argue about who's cutest?" Deanne rolled her eyes. "Let's talk about tonight. How 'bout givin' your new green machine some highway miles? There's a fab band at the lake. Ever been to The Lobster Trap, off I-26 past those new beachfront townhouses?"

"I've heard it's really expensive. With car payments, rent, utilities, groceries, I can't afford it." Oh gawd, she sounded like her dad.

Deanne leaned over the table, her face beaming. "I'll spring for gas and the rest—just follow my lead. When Karmin and I go, we never spend a dime. All you gotta do is strut your stuff, and you'll have more drinks than you can handle."

"Cassy wanted to get together. I've neglected my old friends." Her ears burned at the weakness of her excuse, but the last thing she needed was another night of drinking.

"Spare me, please. Cassy thinks she's all that." Deanne's voice dripped sarcasm. "I could gag when she whines about being hungry, then orders a teensy bag of popcorn." In an exaggeratedly high voice, she mimicked, "I'm so fat that I can't find any size 1 jeans."

"Wow, that was harsh." Elaina let her disappointment be heard, surprised at Deanne's nasty tone out of nowhere.

"Can we take your car or not?"

"Sure, but I'm asking Cassy to come along. Call Karmin, and we'll make it a foursome. And just a reminder, a year ago, you called me Cole's prissy, pain-in-the-ass girlfriend. Now I'm your wifey-poo. Never say never!"

They slid from the booth simultaneously, and she spontaneously hugged Deanne, happiness dissolving her hangover. She did have a friend after all.

11

The Lobster Trap, located at the north end of the casino strip, was packed. The smell of fish, motor oil, and money wafted through the rooms inside and out onto the deck. Men dressed in everything from satin parachute pants to peg-legged leathers lounged like colorful peacocks, a stark contrast to Tarrock's standard denim.

Elaina could barely hear over the band, but words weren't necessary when you wore the look. She felt invincible on a third black beauty, her stomach hollow but her body thrumming with a weightless, limitless energy. As long as the gals stuck together, she felt worry-free, too. Though the men's attentions, dance requests, and free drinks were wonderful, Elaina had made it clear on the way here that the girls would all be going home together.

After a third dance with the same stranger, the time to escape was a song ago. She pointed to the ladies room and slipped away. Deanne's hand reached through a thick pocket of people and pulled her to a table on the outer deck. Karmin and Cassy were already seated with three expensively dressed older men, the four-G logo shouting Givenchy on their puff-sleeved silk shirts.

Cole called this sort the beautiful people, with their deep tans from long afternoons on yachts decorated with barely dressed girls. Gold chains, chunky diamond rings, cuff links, and tie tacks set them above even the smartly dressed yuppies draped over the bar. Their confidence in word, gesture, and stride commanded the world to eat from their hands.

The girls squealed as the waitress presented a bottle of Dom Pérignon, all of them familiar with the legendary French winemaker's champagne from what they'd seen on the soap operas. To see a bottle up close and partake of the liquid gold was beyond anything Elaina had ever imagined. How could she get the label as proof they'd truly sampled it without looking small-town?

Ron, the kingpin, nodded to the staff and moments later, seven fluted glasses of the thinnest crystal arrived. The fizzy nectar with its fruity finish was emptied in one round, and a second bottle appeared immediately.

"What the hell, it must be obvious we're hicks, so I'll just say it: we need the label as proof we actually drank Dom Pérignon," Deanne blurted. She grabbed the bottle.

Ron laughed, seemingly enchanted by her candor. "Would you each like a label?"

The girls squealed again.

"It's going to cost you"—he winked at Deanne—"and you." He pointed to Elaina.

Elaina smiled back. Men near her father's age would never be interested in silly girls *that* way. Surely sex was a distant memory after fifty.

Two more bottles arrived on ice, missing their trademark. The waitress presented each girl with a label pressed to a Lobster Trap coaster.

"My gift so you'll never forget this evening," Ron said.

Something in his tone sounded off . . . as if he felt offended? Elaina wondered why men of these means would bother with red-neck girls unless some agenda awaited. Instinct raised goose-bump warnings on her arms. Meanwhile, the bubbles boosted her indifference.

"Tell us what all these bottles cost, big guy," Deanne slurred, draping her long, bare legs across his lap.

Elaina knew her friend would regret this audacious behavior tomorrow, but when Deanne threw back the last of the champagne directly from the bottle, she realized she was flying on more than just alcohol.

"These four bottles will cost you around seven hundred dollars," Ron purred into her face. "Are you good for it?"

What did he mean? Shivers rattled a premonition up Elaina's spine.

"Well, hell yes!" Deanne sloshed. "It'll take me ten years to pay you back, but I ain't goin' nowhere. You got some kinda yacht around here to take us sailin'?"

"This way, madam." Ron rose, sober as a lawman.

"Come on, you guys." Deanne stumbled as she motioned the girls to join.

"That won't be necessary." Ron snapped his fingers, pointing for the girls to remain seated. "Cassy and Karmin will stay and dance with the boys. And you, Elaina, will come with Deanne and me."

Elaina reached for Deanne's arm and tried to pull her back, but the tall, slender train wreck, giddy and blasé, trotted willingly alongside Ron. Her crazed laughter made it impossible to whisper a warning.

A sense of certainty shattered the last of her calm. Something gruesome would happen if they left the crowd. Ron's guiding hand grew rougher. If she ran, Deanne would never be able to keep up, and she'd never leave Deanne alone.

The brass and chrome on Ron's yacht reflected the lights across the harbor. To Elaina, they resembled demonic eyes. Ron's appearance also mutated in the darkness, from a debonair older man to a grotesque little troll.

The girls were pushed to a lower level of the boat. Elaina tripped and fell on top of Deanne, who continued her carryings-on as if possessed. Before she could regain her footing, Ron wrestled her against a support post, fastened her wrists behind her back, and shoved a rag in her mouth. The taste of motor oil gagged her at the same moment that terror coiled around her throat. Asthmatic panic threatened to asphyxiate her if she didn't gain control.

He grabbed Deanne by the hair. "Shut up." Two hard jabs of his fist brought her down, and her eye swelled like a ripening plum.

The gag and ropes secured Elaina. She was helpless but to watch as Ron tightened his grip on Deanne's jaw, forcing her head back so far Elaina was sure her neck would snap. The waves slapping against the exterior of the boat competed with Ron's goring as he raped Deanne, making the boat too shudder in his brutality. Except for his grunts of profanity, the viciousness continued in enduring silence, Deanne helpless under the power of his thick hands.

When Ron was through, he calmly zipped his pants and wiped the blood from his knuckles. Deanne's nose was streaming with blood.

"Clean up this trash." He spit on Deanne, yanked Elaina loose, and shoved her at Deanne. "Clean up this filthy whore mess and get off my boat."

He kicked Deanne for emphasis, his boot thrusting fresh fury into her friend's ribs.

From the darkest lessons of childhood, Elaina had learned how to appease the kind of demon that howled inside this man: submission and diversion. She slid in front of him and kneeled, then reached her hands up to receive his next kick. Ron halted. Slowly and purposefully, she removed her sweater and began buffing the embellished steel covering of his bloody boot tip.

Pacified, he nodded approval. "You have ten minutes. Once you've cleaned this garbage up, collect your friends and get out. I never want to see you baiting for drinks in my club again."

It took all her strength to drag a stumbling, beaten Deanne back to her Pinto, but Ron's order had shot enough adrenaline into her system that she didn't hesitate. Once she'd arranged Deanne in the reclined passenger's seat, she locked the doors and bolted back to the club.

Karmin and Cassy stood near the emergency exit, looking worried.

"Leave with me now, or find your own ride," Elaina shouted over the ruckus of the club. Without argument, they dashed behind her.

"Oh my gawd!" Cassy gasped at Deanne's barely recognizable face and oddly twisted body. Deanne lay frighteningly still but for the pulse on her long neck. She could've been mistaken for dead except for her bruises, reddening and swelling by the second.

"Hurry up!" Elaina already had the car started and in reverse. She weaved through the late-night traffic, trying to empty her head of everything but the quickest route to Tarrock.

"Slow down," Cassy yelled.

"We need a hospital. Stop this car now!" Karmin's fists pounded on Elaina's shoulders from behind.

Cassy grabbed the wheel, and the Pinto swerved past the berm and into the ditch. Elaina slammed on the brakes.

"What the hell happened?" Karmin demanded.

"Are we in trouble?" Cassy said.

Elaina gripped the locked steering wheel, resting her forehead between her hands. "It was so horrible—" She tried to block the image of Ron on top of Deanne. What could possibly be accomplished in telling Karmin and Cassy? Would it help Deanne? God only knew who Cassy would blab to or how she'd exaggerate the details. If word got out . . .

"What happened to your arms?"

Elaina lifted her head to find puffy scarlet skin circling her wrists. "Deanne and I tripped down some steps. They insisted we leave because we were drunk. We'll be home in half an hour and take care of Deanne ourselves."

"You're lying," Cassy said, her voice shrill. "Something happened on Ron's boat."

"We've all been drinking underage, and Deanne's had a lot more than champagne. You wanna get busted?" Elaina twisted around and gave Cassy a hard look. "If you tell a soul about this—"

"Fine. But Deanne's your problem. Just get Karmin and me home. My mom was right—you *are* trouble."

12

Deanne's head rested on Elaina's lap as it had for days, eyes closed—one from the swelling, the other to shut out the horrible images that continued to haunt her. Elaina swept her fattest paintbrush over the gray-green bruises, a motion that comforted both of them. Neither had spoken of the defilement. The pain was still too fresh for words. Nighttime was worse, as both their unconsciousness minds replayed the rape in slow, distorted motion. Daydreams too inflicted torment—a 24/7 ordeal. The girls slept together now, comforting each other when visions led to choking sobs.

The outside world hovered over them. Unless Elaina could produce a doctor's excuse for calling in sick, she'd be fired, but telling the truth held far worse possibilities: a police investigation and Ron's retribution. The gravity of her poor choices pulled in a downward spiral, just as Kurt said it would, a painful descent into a self-made hell. *Between binges, sobriety brings mindfulness. It's terrifying to watch your own wreckage unfold. It drove me to drink more, giving the pull greater force.*

Elaina watched Deanne's restless sleep and willed her heart to the cemetery beneath Mary and the angels. If she could find the Three, they could tell her how to bring her friend peace.

Imm's story of Christ's passion wafted through her mind in a voice like wind chimes. *Mary couldn't be persuaded away, so they brought Jesus, newly taken from the cross, to his mother's arms. The floodgates opened for tears she'd held back while her son hung dying. Gently wiping the blood from his face, she couldn't ask why any more in her utter defeat.*

How had Mary forgiven the unspeakable horrors she'd witnessed? Elaina continued to softly sweep her friend's bruised face with the brush. Maybe, with enough strokes of the paintbrush, she could restore Deanne's self-image the way Imm's magic brushes had healed her childhood hurts.

"Imm used to say that letting the pain flow can allow it to wash away," she whispered, cradling Deanne's head. "Let's just cry again until you're ready for me to listen."

If only confession could be like her conversations with Imm and the Three when she was small. They had listened, just listened, without questions, comments, or solutions. Sharing her problems with them had always given her a sense of healing and forgiveness, unlike the worry the nuns had instilled in her over messing up proper confessional procedures and prayers or being unsure of whether her heart was in a true place to be forgiven. Before confession, the nuns would give warm-ups, grilling the children for details under the pretext of helping with an examination of their consciences. Once they'd finished assigning blame, Elaina found her list of sins was always twice as long.

Deanne's silence added weight to her almost unmanageable guilt. What had motivated Ron to rape Deanne rather than her?

Imm said Need could mutate, growing multiple, ugly heads in its hunger for significance. Ron fed his soul-monster money, possessions, and the control he gained from inflicting fear.

That which seems satisfying can never replace the meal we crave: love. We consume garbage, refusing to acknowledge why we're still starving. Find love, and nothing else will be necessary.
—Sister Immaculata Lefevre

Every man needs the self-worth, which is acquired through the respect and esteem he's earned. When honor is deficient, he'll steal it through dominance and control, but true dignity can never be gained this way. Unscrupulous imitations soothe momentarily, but the God-given hunger for worthiness can only be satisfied with what's gained through merit.
—Edward Michael

* * *

September 11, 1981
Dearest Imm,

Here's my new address. The apartment is small but okay. Anything is better than home, now that Eric's back. His presence simply isn't tolerable.

I've been thinking about the things you've said, and I believe love and happiness are synonymous, like Imm and Elaina. It's simple: the Trinity is love, and in reflecting them, I will be happy. I want to give of myself the way they do, completely. But what if a person only wants a part of me? Do I give only what they want? Something slithers through my gut each time I struggle with this. Knowing that my complete self isn't wanted makes me feel worthless.

This morning, I noticed reds and oranges on the edges of some leaves. Do your trees change color? Remember when we used to press leaves in waxed paper for collections? I miss those days as much as I miss you!

All my love,
Elaina

* * *

Weeks passed before any semblance of normalcy returned. Deanne's bruises turned muddy yellow and then faded along with the nightmares.

"Another day off?" Deanne asked. "Spend it with me, wifey-poo!"

But being given so many days off in a row had Elaina worried. By cutting her hours close to nothing, was management hoping she'd quit?

"I have a surprise. Come with me." Deanne tugged Elaina's arm, and then a shadow darkened her expression. "You know, you saved my life. I couldn't have gotten through the last weeks without you. I'd marry you if you came in a guy package."

"Imm said dark places can produce treasure. The night I trashed Kurt was also the start of our friendship. We survived The Lobster Trap together. And you're the first person in a long time who accepts me the way I am: a flaky, compulsive clean freak."

Deanne took Elaina's hand. "Let's skip like you and that nun used to. I loved the stories you told me about her rose farm, especially the one when she got a contract with Chanel. So cool!"

Elaina's heart smiled. She'd had no idea Deanne had really listened. She allowed Deanne to lead her down the alley to whatever the surprise was.

They stopped at a dilapidated apartment, and Deanne knocked softly. Wasn't this the drug pusher's place? What the hell was Deanne's surprise?

His long ponytail looked ridiculous on the man who answered, but his warm greeting reminded her not to judge. Minus the beer belly and plus a bath, a shave, and better clothes, he could have possibilities. This place on the otherhand, needed to be condemned. Crumbing drywall and peeling wall-paper gave the same haunted appearance she remembered from the abandoned house at the end of her street in her childhood. Once, Eric had threatened. . . Oh God, she didn't want to think about that any more than she wanted to be here.

"Hey, stranger! You brought your roomie—Elaina, right? I can't remember what we was talkin' about our last meet-up but I sure enjoyed the company," he winked at Elaina.

"We've been a bit out of commission lately," Deanne said.

"If you're talkin' 'bout a bender, I can relate," Steely nodded .

"Speaking of, can I have the weed you offered? It's my surprise for my bestie here."

"If you stay for a minute. I only got beer but you can pretend its coffee."

It wasn't even mid-morning. Alcohol's black line was noon, but Elaina supposed she could make an exception. Deanne's infectious smile was finally back, and she'd do anything to keep it around.

She'd also excuse this Steely guy's poor grammar and disaster of a front room to make room for his more flattering qualities: eyes that bored into hers, unsettling and soothing, and a subtle yet seductive flirtatiousness, curiously out of place with his childlike enthusiasm.

Need suckled the same potion she'd sworn off after Cole.

"I smell fireworks," Deanne teased. "Is my girlie-girl is blushing?"

Baby Need bounced around Elaina's empty heart, thrilled at Steely's attention. The painter within her woke up, too. Steely must have once been a faithful weightlifter. Though beer, junk food, and lack of exercise blanketed his powerful muscles, it reminded her more of a Santa suit that disguised his darker allure. The longer she scrutinized him, the more attractive he became, and under his gaze, she felt beautiful too.

"Excuse me." Deanne cleared her throat. "I'm gonna cool you guys' sparks 'cause I wanna get going. We have a busy day ahead of partying, getting silly, and doing nothing."

Steely's affirming gaze left a tingle through Elaina's entire body, and this was the first time in weeks that Deanne seemed her old self, excited and full of mischievous anticipation. Elaina gave Steely a goodbye that made her reluctance obvious. Though she would never put a guy over a friendship again, maybe this cake could be tasted at a later date.

Deanne crinkled the baggie of pot inside her pocket as they walked back home. "You're to do nothing today. Let's just be lazy together, okay?"

The late September breeze blew peeling paint off the back gate as the girls reached their apartment. Elaina itched for a broom.

Deanne laughed. "No sweeping. Sit here." She pointed to the postage-stamp plot of grass inside their fenced back yard. "I'll get your sketchbook, and you'll draw me every picture in your crazy head. I want more stories about your nun friend's farm, too. That's why you love yellow roses so much, huh?"

Deanne returned a few minutes later with a curtsy and a bottle of Beaujolais. "Look, I got you boo juice, or whatever you call it."

"My favorite! You remembered. I love you, Deanne."

"I love you, too." Deanne's voice quivered. "How do I thank you for—"

Elaina hugged her and stepped back to look squarely into Deanne's eyes. "You already have. If you need to talk, I'll listen, but if it's too horrible, we'll just . . . Will we ever forget?"

Deanne held up the marijuana and giggled. "That's what this is for. It's laced with angel dust—'for the two angels next door,' Steely said. I don't know what angel dust is, but what the hell, it was free."

Elaina crinkled her nose. "I'm passing. Pot makes me nervous and tired all at once. Besides, angel dust sounds like a fancy name for chemicals."

"Fine," Deanne said, looking hurt, "but I got it for you. You had no problem smokin' the first time you stayed with me."

"Cole used to tell me I looked like a Saint Augustine snob when I refused. That's the only reason—"

Deanne plopped down and pulled Elaina onto the grass beside her. She brushed Elaina's hair from her eyes. "Cole's an idiot. I'm not offended, but I'm gonna be just as honest. I hate the crap you drink, so you're on your own with the boo juice."

Elaina was relieved that the dry air and breeze neutralized the smell of Deanne's joint. Even with a fence to hide their activity, she worried that a pedestrian might detect the odor. She began sketching Deanne, who stretched out on the blanket-sized patch of grass, and thought back to a time Cole had reclined the same way at the cemetery.

"Tell me about the Cole you knew, Deanne. Did he ever talk about me?"

"He was like a big brother; nothing romantic. Karmin and I used to clean his apartment for weed and liquor until you came around. We hated you, Lanie, 'cause Cole didn't tire of the prissy party pooper who just wanted to play house—like you still do." She laughed. "I know you're still hung up on him; it's why that I can't understand. He thought himself God's gift to women, all of 'em. One day, he's gonna regret his Don Juaning, though."

"Did he ever mention Isaac?" She longed to hear that Cole had shown some measure of love for their baby.

"He cried so hard when the three of us left the hospital, saying something about how badly he wanted to help you, even marry you, but if he did, he might never get out of Tarrock. The choice came down to saving himself, or you and the baby. Not really a choice, he said, because if he stuck around, your relationship would probably end miserably anyway. I'll never forget his last words: 'Elaina has a heart of gold that seems to buy disaster, and selfishness keeps me rolling in luck. She and I are dynamite and matches—useless apart and even worse together.'"

Elaina's sigh closed the subject. The wine scattered her thoughts like the breeze sprinkling paint chips across the walkway.

"You're so . . . Does anything worry you, like not finding a husband or never finding a place to belong?" she asked. "When I was little, I had this club—make-believe, but not. When my art teacher, Imm, became a member too, that's when I knew my invisible friends and club were real. They were always happy when good things happened to me and supportive when I was sad. They convinced me I was special and talented, so fitting in at school and the neighborhood didn't matter. Strange, when it didn't matter, loneliness didn't exist. When the club was around, right and wrong weren't an issue, either. I wanted to be good and wanted to please them—and everything was good. They intensified happiness and dulled pain, the way you described that angel dust."

Deanne gazed at the overhanging tree branches, deep in thought, then suddenly jumped up and scampered away. Before Elaina could rise, she was back with a bouquet of jewel-edged leaves. "Fresh fall leaves— for you. Not roses, but it's the thought. Oh, Lanie, some guy is gonna be so lucky to get you. But until he snatches you up, you belong to me."

Tears gathered, and she quickly brushed them aside. Though Jenny, Patty, Sarah, and sometimes even Cassy had been good friends, she'd never had a bestie. Deanne was beginning to fill the hole her Clover Club had once overflowed from.

"Why'd you say I saved you?" Elaina detoured, before her emotion got away from her. "I stood there doing nothing while Ron—"

"You were as helpless as me until he untied you. You were going to take his boot for me, the very thing that calmed him. Then you had the good sense to skip the hospital, get me home, and stay with me. I wanted to die. I thought about . . . If you hadn't been there I would've—"

How long they'd stayed outside, what liquor she'd consumed after the Beaujolais, and what time they'd finally climbed into bed were a blur. The only sure things were her raging headache and belly cramps.

Hungry but unable to eat, exhausted but incapable of sleep, she'd finally woke her snoring roommate in the middle of the night for the reds Deanne had offered earlier. They'd lent her some shut-eye but no real sleep, apparent in her anxiety and rubber legs as she now stumbled to answer the door. Deanne had warned her that jitters were an aftereffect of reds—after she had swallowed them. Steely leaned in the doorway blocking the sun that announced the morning was half gone. The struggle to appear composed under his piercing gaze only aggravated her already pounding heart.

The screen door refused to open, as if urging her to reconsider welcoming a drug pusher into the house. Then again, she was a drug user herself now. The world of black-and-white had bled to gray. Separating the good guys from bad wasn't as clear on this side of town.

"You okay?" Steely guided Elaina's chin up to meet his gaze, a gesture so gentle yet dominant that it instantly calmed her. She felt small and safe. Still, the dots didn't quite connect. She couldn't remember what day it was.

"Did you like the angel dust?"

"It was nice, except for this hangover and jitters. I took a couple of reds last night to sleep. I normally would never—"

Would he get the idea she was a possible client? Her voice sounded strange to her own ears. "It's stupid to use one drug to remedy the effects of another, and a waste of money. I should just stay away from everything." Including this drug dealer.

"Waste of money? Did Deanne charge you? The dust was my gift."

"I didn't smoke it. You misunderstand. I don't need drugs to have a good time."

"You wanna stay clean. That's cool. I expected that, comin' from a Saint Augustine graduate. I could tell where you were schooled just by the way you talk. Classy."

What was it with men's Catholic girl fixation? As if she were a princess or prize. She supposed by these eastsiders' standards, she did seem privileged, yet on the south side of Tarrock, her home was the smallest and oldest. Her family was the biggest and likely the poorest—no, the most frugal. On the south side of Tarrock, you were either rich or not, Catholic or not, college educated or not. Anywhere in between couldn't survive the black-and-white attitudes and judgments.

Here on the east side, dilapidated apartments housing welfare recipients cuddled next to frat houses accommodating college students with more money than morals. Each street to the east demonstrated greater poverty, yet deprivation partied with wealth, turning everything to shades of gray. Relaxed expectations and exceptions to rules prevailed not only because of hardship but because parents encouraged their students' sowing of wild oats before it was time to take over Daddy's corporation.

Could privilege be in the eyes of the beholder? Steely thought Elaina was somebody, but she felt like nobody. She found the east side's relativity far more appealing than the south side's absolutes.

"Elaina? Lanie? You with me?" Steely was looking purposely into her eyes. The smell of beer, cigarettes, and cheap cologne made her stomach curdle.

"Come here. You're tremblin'."

He picked her up like an infant and carried her to the sofa.

"You need a cold rag."

Relief seeped through the nap of the washcloth, alleviating her thumping temples and washing away her hot-cold nausea. With her eyes closed, she could feel numbness begin to relax her tight muscles. Her thoughts went blank.

When she opened her eyes again, the sun's place in the window said she'd slept for hours. Steely was in the same spot, still gazing down at her as if time inside of her apartment had frozen. The coffee-colored hair falling over his copper skin reminded her of the Native American Indians in history books. With braids and a couple of feathers, he'd look like a warrior.

Need arched in Elaina's belly, begging for Steely to enter her fantasy. A smoldering image burst into flames before she could stop Need from fanning the inferno.

Play with fire and you'll get burned.—Edward Michael

A good Catholic girl never feels sexual cravings.—Sister Katherine

Sex is a committed wife's duty, no more, no less.—Father Krammer

Elaina had met this Steely less than twenty-four hours ago. She didn't know his last name—his real name—only that he sold drugs and had been so compassionate during the last hours that she'd finally gotten some sleep. She reached up and stroked his hair, shutting out all thought except how silky it felt.

"Let me braid it," she murmured, twisting the strands together.

Steely leaned down and kissed her, cautiously and then ferociously.

She curved to meet his body and mumbled a protest. "I shouldn't be doing this."

His skin, warm and soft above a deeper strength, overtook her anxiety, beckoning and blanketing. Physical hedonism silenced decency. She welcomed his hands inside her shirt. Before she could stop their deep kisses long enough for a breath, her shirt and bra lay on the floor.

A flash and a finish, like the destructive zap of lightning, left her feeling only shame, as exposed as her body. She'd use this man solely for physical pleasure. Her dad said a woman gave sex for love and security, but she didn't love this man, nor did she even know him enough to form a like or dislike. She was trash, sticky and sex-covered like thick, black oil that left stains on everything it touched.

Worse, his eyes told of the hope for a relationship that she'd carelessly planted, no different than the barren seeds she'd scattered over Kurt's heart and Cole had sown on hers.

Oh God, untwist this perversion that people called lovemaking.

She turned her face to one side, but Steely wouldn't be looked away from. Angrily—or urgently, she wasn't sure—he jerked her face back. "Look at me like you did before."

His strange, overpowering demand felt almost reverent, as if she were an exotic flower. Her apprehension electrified her as it had in Cole's arms on the Fourth of July, and Elaina pressed herself hungrily against him again.

* * *

September 26, 1981

Ma chére enfant,

Mon pére used to tell me that it's easy for a child to obey because he trusts his daddy. It's the reason the Bible says to believe like a child. He keeps a safe distance from the cozy hearth because his father has warned of popping embers. But as a child grows, independence draws him nearer to the flames. When he is burned, his father can and will help, but healing requires time and space from the fire. The father cannot be faulted for injury. The child's disobedience is the error.

Menacing feelings are God-given grace that protect us when we're walking in darkness. Pain too is a gift, alerting us of the need for healing but healing cannot happen if the injuries are hidden under bandages, void of light. The inclination to cover what's painful is the most troublesome part of dark secrets. In our concealment, we lose sight of boundaries. Darkness begins to feel safer, all part of evil's plan, because when in light, he can't keep us isolated and continue his lurking. Light takes his freedom and power away.

I've sensed your buried childhood hurts for many years. Do you remember coming to me with troubling questions when you were eleven or twelve? I still feel distress over my reaction, sure it frightened the beautiful little girl who wanted so badly to unburden herself. Is your unwillingness to reveal your secrets because the child within you fears being blamed for something for which she is innocent? I'm with you always, ma fleur. Like the rest of your Clover Club, I'll wait as long as you need, and I'll be here when you're ready to step into the light. Feed your Need what grows in the Son.

Yes, our leaves change too. In just a few weeks, I'll gather all my favorites, press them, and send them to you.

I've never left you in my prayers, and I love you.

Immaculata

* * *

Life had become a command performance except in Deanne's company. Promptness, productivity, and detachment made work tolerable, but she would arrive home to find Steely visiting with Deanne. He'd become the mistake that wouldn't go away. She worried over how much he may have told Deanne about their fling.

"He's not comin' around for me," Deanne teased.

"I know, he wants a date and interprets my excuses as encouragement." Elaina rolled her eyes. "What's his real name, anyway? What do you know about him?"

"Phew, he's either admired or detested, considered a legend or a bottom feeder." Deanne's tone sounded like a groupie. "His real name is Steve Johnson. He earned his nickname for steel-knuckling a kid almost to death. After doin' a year in juvie, Tarrock High wouldn't take him back, and he's been dealing ever since, like almost a decade."

Deanne seemed amused by her shock.

"The cops hate him because of his connections, especially up at the lake, the reason he's been busted more than anyone I know but hasn't done any long jail time. Occasionally, he'll pick up a job till the heat wears off, but then he's back to witch-doctoring the Haisting yups."

"Whoa, sorry I asked. There's no way I'd go out with him."

Deanne's expression darkened. "You're too sainted for eastside trash? Well, Catholic girl, if you're so holy, why'd you seduce him? And why are you living with eastside trash? Steely's had a hard life. You haven't seen poor till you've spent a day in his old neighborhood. He's had to fight for everything, even food, yet he'd give anyone the shirt off his back and the sandwich in his hand. He's loyal to the people he calls friends. That's how we get by around here."

"So it's wrong to steer clear of drugs and dealers?"

"If so, you'd better stop doin' black beauties and reds—and drinking. Alcohol's a drug, too, remember? And while you're at it, stop toying with the most vulnerable guy I know."

"What the hell did he say?"

"Nothing, 'cause he'd never discredit you. But I'm not stupid. Your dirty deed is obvious by the way he looks at you. You're not gonna shrug him off that easily, either. He's very protective of those he loves. You slept with the wrong guy if you're not serious, 'cause he thinks he's in love."

Elaina shuddered. "You're kidding. He sounds like that John Hinckley dude, trying to off the president to impress Jodie Foster."

"You know why he took steel knuckles to that kid? 'Cause the idiot was messin' with his sister. Look on the bright side. Nobody's gonna bother with you, ever, 'cause you're his lover now."

Elaina shook her head slowly, like an addled bull. "Stop it. This

isn't funny. If he had a legal job, I might consider a date. But a drug
dealer? No, thanks."

"Then why did you have sex with him?" Deanne yelled.

Goose bumps mushroomed along Elaina's arms.

"He's fixated on you for the same reason you can't get over Cole. You
make him feel better about the cruddy life he's been dealt. He thinks
you're a step up in the world. So use his high regard to clean him up,
Saint Elaina. You know what they say: behind every good man, there's
a better woman."

Deanne's words, though sarcastic, dangled truth. Imm too had said
Elaina would never fill the black hole until she started giving without
thought of return. Was Steely her opportunity, her penance? Or was
he a leap into the fire?

* * *

October 11, 1981
Dearest Imm,

*Is the pure love you said Need craves God's love? Is God's purpose
for us to absorb pure love and pass it on? I can only soak up their
love in loving others selflessly—the paradox you explained to me. In
giving we receive, right? I've met a person who needs to be cared for
as much as I want to care. I want to get it right this time.*

Please write soon.

All my love,
Elaina

October 18, 1981
Ma chéri enfant,

*You've got it! "Unless a grain of wheat falls to the earth and
dies, it remains a grain of wheat. But if it dies, it bears much fruit."
(John 12:24)*

*You are full of Clover when you desire to serve. Be patient and
remember the example Jesus gave us in his total sacrifice (to death!)
on a cross. After dying to your own wants for others' sake, you'll feel
the Three tangibly again—but make no mistake, they've never left*

you. Without them, life is just a series of hit-and-miss pleasures. To find pure love, everything that's treasured more must be surrendered. They are simple words but difficult to practice because we are so marvelously complex.

Saying yes to Three also means giving them your trust and dependence.

Enclosed are the leaves I promised. Do you remember your science lessons on photosynthesis? These leaves have transformed themselves to jewel shades by turning sunlight to sugar, then reserving that sweetness for a darker, colder season. In this way, life cannot be taken. We can do the same by storing the Son's light for strength when times turn bleak.

I've never left you in my prayers, and I love you.

Immaculata

* * *

Dating Steely would bring Elaina so much criticism, but it's not like she had a shining reputation. She'd have to replace her judgments of him with affirmation while also accepting what others would think and say about her.

Patience, service, and surrender, Imm said—and choosing to trust. Did service and surrender mean sex, too? Because she knew Steely would never accept no. Father Krammer said sex was a wife's duty. Oh Lord, did service and surrender mean she'd have to marry Steely, too?

Kurt's words echoed in her head. *Love and sex are not the same thing.*

Maybe she was getting ahead of herself. Steely just needed someone to believe in him. He could be her reparation, helping her pass over the whole confession thing.

Imm's voice came to mind. *People who continue their efforts despite mistakes are God's race horses, even when the world calls them losers. We're always winners until we give up.*

Elaina would make the entire Clover Club proud.

* * *

Dear Lanie,

Thank you for the kind and uplifting words. I'm in short supply. We both have much work ahead in pulling ourselves up to a place of self-respect. One day at a time, as AA says.

Your need to return the cash and ring is because, under lots of hurt and confusion, you're a decent person. I never doubted that, only your ability to see beyond the moment. By the way, your dignity can't be lost, but you can give it away or throw it away. Take it from an expert!

I'm exploring a higher power as you suggested and am drawn to Christianity because of your stories of Imm and your Clover Club. Unfortunately, I've tried several churches only to find congregations so bent on their concepts of who God is that real spiritual growth seems impossible. The leaders demand that their perceptions be accepted blindly, reminding me of the twisted teachings of those misguided nuns from your school days. Like your Imm said, no question is a bad one; thus, any faith group that frowns on my questions is not for me. I'm sure of one thing about the Highest: he has no expectations of perfection and asks only for my honesty regarding my past and present.

With that, may I return a suggestion? Don't give up on your Three, and release your harsh judgments on your Catholic faith because of a few arrogant and erroneous leaders.

Last week, I read something that made me think of you: "In allowing the darkness of past mistakes to cast a shadow on the possibilities of today, you suffocate all potential for tomorrow. The seeds of yesterday (especially those from personal blunders) can sprout wisdom."

I guess this is it. We both know it's over. I got your new address from Tasty management, wanting to let you know your package arrived safely.

I hope the future brings you what you're looking for.

Affection and memories,

Kurt

P.S. Don't stop skating, painting, trying and caring. It's what makes Elaina Lanie! Congratulations on acquiring your own place and a car.

13

"Anyone home?"

Elaina tapped on the door again, wondering what she'd say if Steely actually answered. Hesitation argued with impulsiveness, reminding her there'd be drugs and dirty money inside. Her reckless generosity had left a trail of setbacks that defined her past. Was making Steely her mission and redemption a pact with the devil in hopes of salvation?

The door hinge creaked a final warning as she pushed inside. Steely lay on the beat-up sofa, as still as dead. She scanned the place in disbelief. Deanne's apartment at its worst was relatively clean compared to this. As she groped for reasons to excuse the filth, another of Imm's sayings came to mind. *Free the fault-finder locked in your head. When you assume the best of people, it often becomes prophecy.*

Steely would give the shirt off his back, the sandwich in his hand, the roof over his head, and even his stash if someone were in desperate need, Deanne had told her. When she'd argued that giving away drugs helped no one, Deanne had snapped back: "When you have no job, no money, and no place to lay your head, tomorrow may as well be next year. It's about getting through the next hour. Poverty's the reason we're overrun with drugs. How can you judge his generosity so narrowly?"

Was Steely's charity worthless simply because it wasn't conventional? Elaina begged the Three for an answer. This place and his life seemed useless, but were they really? Maybe this place was trashed because of the homeless people Steely had welcomed. Wasn't every heart's generosity the same from heaven's perspective?

No one can be faulted for poverty, but there's no excuse
for being lazy. Only that which is paid for by the sweat
of one's own brow is treasured. —Edward Michael

Oh, how she hated her dad's sayings, popping up in her head for every situation. They'd reignited the anger at the servitude he'd kept her in, forcing her to make tuition payments to the school she hated, claiming that the privilege of superior education would only be appreciated if it had been purchased by her own labors. She had never been offered any alternatives, just as with Isaac, yet he grumbled about the fruits of a man's labor being stolen as taxes. What was so different about compulsory tuition?

She headed for the kitchen. Warm, soapy water calmed her nerves. Washing dishes led to scrubbing the counters and the floor; that led to cleaning the bedroom, which reeked of dirty laundry. Only the chilly late October air, rushing through the window she opened, could neutralize the stench as the furnace banged to keep up.

Hours later, Steely's apartment was spotless except for the area around his lifeless body. Perfectionism, always discrediting her every attempt, nagged her to wash the blanket that covered him too. If she had really indulged her obsessions, she'd have removed his clothes and washed them as well.

This was madness, cleaning the apartment of a man she barely knew but had already slept with. Then again, reason had nothing to do with these compulsive frenzies she worked herself into. Making small spaces spotless in a big, ugly world worked like an analgesic.

Satisfied, she closed the door behind her and headed to work.

At half past midnight, exhausted after eight hours of stocking shelves, Elaina fumbled for the entry light at her apartment. The quivering fluorescent bulb gave pulsating peeks at a riot of color inside the door, and an odd smell, like her dad's greenhouse, greeted her nose.

She took a hesitant step inside.

"Like 'em?"

She leaped back and crashed into the entry table. Steely caught the pot she had sent flying a mere inches from the ground.

Mums in every color imaginable filled the apartment.

"You did this for me?"

Steely whisked her up, pressed his lips to hers, and pried her mouth open with his tongue.

Flowers or none, this would *not* be a repeat of last time. To spare his ego, she pulled away gently. "What's this is about? How'd you get in?"

"Deanne. And this is about the woman who's been more caring than anyone before. Thank you for cleanin' my place. Deanne's right, you're a strange one, in the best way. I might frighten you, Elaina"— he pulled her close and locked his arms around her—"but I knew the first time I laid eyes on you that I *am* going to marry you."

He was a strange one, too, in a most frightening way. His childlike eagerness conflicted with his dominance, leaving her both intrigued and apprehensive. His quiet surety was far more appealing than Cole's obvious grabs for the stage, but it was ominous as well. Where Cole persuaded with honey butter, Steely motivated by force.

"Well, I hate to disappoint," she replied as brightly as she could, "but I've no intention of settling down anytime soon."

"I've got all the time in the world to wait."

Her growing anxiety prompted her to squirm until he released her at arm's length. "I don't know why you clean my dump, but—"

She couldn't remember either and was already regretting it. "No biggie. Just some thanks, for the dust . . . Even though I didn't partake, I wanted to reciprocate . . ."

Damn it all. He looked hurt. She wanted him, and she didn't.

"I don't know what 'reciprocate' means. Keep the words simple, and we'll do fine."

Her foreboding melted.

"May I kiss you?" Assuming her answer, he brought his mouth to hers quickly.

Need returned his every move. Ravenous for affection, she found herself the aggressor, tugging off his clothes and pulling him in as if he could plug the holes in her heart.

Afterwards, they lay naked, sweaty, and short of breath, like two animals that had just copulated. She couldn't look at him, appalled at her lack of control. Lower forms of life behaved this way, with no dignity or discipline and no thought beyond the moment. This was the root of all her problems. What was it Kurt had said? *Under a lot of confusion, you are a decent person. I never doubted that, only your ability to see beyond the moment.*

Steely stood up, lust still evident in his hard male dominance, victoriously pointing at her weak will and vulnerability. She could hear darkness laughing, and her stomach tightened in memory of every other time she'd been pointed and laughed at. Images seeped beneath the dark door: the flashlight and stick Eric had used to humiliate her, his tormenting hands.

Oh God, please make it stop.

"Phew, that wasn't supposed to happen till after I'd set the mood." Steely laughed and lit the candles.

Was it his nakedness or hers that she found more disturbing? The fact that they'd . . . fornicated before he'd even set the mood proved she *was* easy, loose, and all those other things people had called her.

He uncorked a bottle of sparkling wine, and a geyser of poison memories sprayed forth, from the bottle Mark had given her the Fourth of July and its troublesome results to the hellish night of Dom Pérignon. She quickly dressed while he was distracted in pouring.

"What the hell are you doing? No clothes. Take 'em off. Now!"

Why was nakedness such cause for anxiety now, after they'd been intimate twice?

She looked away. "I don't want to."

"Don't play games." He grabbed her and worked her blouse buttons open. "I'm not goin' to hurt you. Just finish undressing."

His order, like Ron's on the boat, left no room for negotiating. She couldn't shake the image of Ron zipping his pants: *Clean up this filthy whore mess and get off my boat.* And another figure stood just outside identity's reach.

Trembling, she stumbled backward.

"Holy crap, you're afraid of me. I never meant to—"

She fled to Deanne's bedroom, slammed the door, and wedged a chair beneath the knob. She'd stay here safe until he gave up and left.

Recollections of sexual shame filled the silence. Each new hour urged her to wait for another. At the first peek of the sun, she opened the door and stumbled into Steely's arms.

"I told you, I have as long as it takes." His protective hold left no room to escape. "I'm sorry." He pressed several blue mums into her hands. "I don't know what's got you so spooked, but I'd never do anything to hurt you, and I'd kill anyone who did."

He pulled her to the couch and into his lap, drawing forth two of her fondest memories: being in Imm's arms as a child and in Cole's arms on the way back to her room from the nursery window. She could almost believe she was precious and treasured.

In this place of warmth, she found herself telling him about that night at The Lobster Trap.

"What did you say his name was?"

"Ron."

His face went white.

Had he really meant he'd kill anyone who hurt her? He was no match for Ron and those thugs. Regretting the disclosure, she pressed her lips to his neck to divert him.

"What's your nationality?" she asked. "I love your skin, the color of chocolate raspberries."

"Cherokee on my dad's side, Polynesian on my mom's."

"What's your real name?" She wanted him to believe it was his own disclosure.

"Steve. Stephen Joseph Johnson. Why?"

"I like Stephen," she whispered, twisting his hair into a braid. "Did you know there's a Saint Stephen? You have such great hair, Steve. May I call you Steve? It suits the guy I want to start seeing."

"Call me anything you want."

Every thought, craving, and desire, when simplified, is about love or worry about its loss. Hatred is not the opposite of love; fear is, and the evil one is fear. If he can make you doubt love, he can destroy you.
—Sister Immaculata Lefevre

"Tell me about Saint Stephen," he urged. "Just talk to me, Lanie. Don't stop talkin' to me, ever."

His plea echoed the pain of his dark place. It took one to know one. This awareness seemed a grace that implored her mercy. Aching to comfort him, she painted a narrative just as Imm had for her.

"Saint Stephen lived in the thirteenth century. He had beautiful, long black hair almost to his waist that looked best in braids—"

"Really?"

She giggled.

"You're a liar, you witch. Do you know what saints do to witches?" He tickled her until they fell on the floor laughing.

Then like lightning in a rainstorm, he bolted upright, his eyes moist and voice hoarse. "You're like a porcelain doll. I'm afraid of breakin' you, yet I can't let you go. I break everything I love."

She pulled him close and took off her clothes. Isn't this what Imm had said to do, to give and love, especially when it felt like a sacrifice?

"I want to hear about Saint Stephen, Dolly." He stroked her hair, which lay spread across his chest.

"He was a prince," she began, airbrushing the story. "His dad, the king, decided to pass the throne to Stephen and join his other son at a monastery. Stephen ruled the kingdom with love, protecting the oppressed, feeding the poor, and helping the needy, just like you. He treated his servants like brothers. Everyone was happy because Stephen made all the kingdom one in faith. There were no arguments over whose beliefs were right or wrong and who was or wasn't following the rules. Their only guideline was pure love and their goal to imitate it. With pure love, rules weren't necessary, leaving no fear of punishment and damnation. Stephen's kingdom didn't need police, either, because everyone shared everything. He had churches built so people could love God together . . ."

She paused, remembering a fragment from childhood. "When I was in first grade, this church in California got two relics of Saint Stephen. It was a huge deal and made all the newspapers. Just think, his remains were over eight hundred years old!"

"A relic?"

"It's like, if I died, wouldn't you want something to remember me with? A picture or something I wore? If you died, I'd braid your hair, cut it off, and save it to remember your generosity. A relic is the same. Saints are so compassionate and faith-filled that we like to keep their things as a reminder of their goodness."

His eyes had misted. "You're somethin', Dolly."

"So are you, Saint Stephen. Deanne told me how dearly you paid for protecting your sister's honor. I don't condone beating the crap out of anyone, but doing the wrong thing for the right reason is better than doing nothing. That's why your apartment is always trashed, isn't it? Because you don't turn anyone away. But Steely—Steve—why sell drugs?"

"I can't make a go of it otherwise. I'm a felon; saw more jail time before eighteen than most ever will. Who's gonna hire a dropout with a record? So I sell to rich kids who dabble recreationally. It's no worse than alcohol, which the government says is legal so they can tax it. If anyone starts getting hooked, I cut 'em off."

"Isn't it too late by then?"

"I watch pretty close. They're just poor rich kids who want some fun before they hafta fill Daddy's shoes. I like to get high, too, for the same reason you probably drink more than this hot little body of yours should."

"But alcohol is legal, and the stuff you sell isn't. And I drink because I enjoy the taste of wine." She decided to add a drop more honesty. "Yeah, I like how I feel after a couple, but I don't need drugs for that."

He shook his head. "Remember your school lessons. Alcohol's a drug, too. Besides, you have a job and a private education and grew up on the south end of Tarrock. That makes it easy to judge. Stick around here and you'll understand why people want to forget, even for a couple hours."

She snorted. "Deanne said the same thing, as if private education and living on the south end makes everything easy. Well, guess what? I was trash at Saint Augustine, the last of ten Michaels whose parents squeezed every penny till it bled. Speaking of which, how'd you like to meet my parents? Thanksgiving?"

"Whoa!" He threw his hands up in the air. "No girl's ever asked me to meet her parents. I'm a lot older than you. And where do I tell 'em I work?"

"I'm an adult, so age doesn't matter."

"You're not old enough to be drinkin' this!" Steely teased pouring her more wine.

She ignored his contradiction. "Who knows, maybe by then you'll find a job—if you look. If we're going to be a couple, I'd like my boyfriend to be legally employed." She hoped her tone sounded compromising.

"My future wife's wish is my command," he whispered.

After just one night getting to know him, her confidence cheered her for steering him in a better direction. This was going to work out after all. With a little more TLC, Steely would come to see that he could make a better life all by himself.

14

Elaina raced to the door, annoyed at the dogged rapping.

"Cassy! Hurry, get out of the rain. You're soaked." Elaina pulled her inside. "What's the matter?" She grabbed a blanket and wrapped it around the slightly taller girl.

Cassy's garbled blubbering made it impossible to decipher what she said.

"Sit for a minute. I've got hot cocoa and tea. Which one? Or both?"

Elaina dried Cassy's bottle-blond locks and smeared mascara as her trembling subsided.

"I'm pregnant," Cassy blurted. "What am I going to do? You're the first person I thought to come to. This is old hat for you."

Knowing the insulting words weren't meant as such, Elaina stomped down the temptation to gloat. "I'm glad you're here, Cass. First, it's not the end of the world, though I know it feels that way right now. Once you get used to the idea, it's the most amazing experience. I suggest you be sure before you tell anyone, though. I can make an appointment for you with my OB, if you want. Whatever the outcome, I can help. Like you sad, I'm old hat at this."

She laughed and tried hugging the devastation out of her friend.

"Oh, Elaina." Cassy's little-girl whine found its way out. "You should be mad at me. I pretty much stuck you with Deanne after The Lobster Trap."

Pretty much? She wanted to tell Cassy that best friends don't consider themselves stuck at helping when the other was in need. Poor

Cassy wouldn't know anything about that, though.

At that moment, Elaina realized how exceedingly more difficult service and surrender would be with Cassy than with Steely. Why should a poorly educated eastside drug dealer have a greater tug at her sympathy? The answer, she knew, was in opportunity and need. Cassy had every advantage, yet in her bitterness, jealousy, and need for ever better, she made everyone around her pay.

The question that came stepping on the heels of the last asked why she didn't send Cassy packing. The answer, she knew, was her hope that mercy shown might lead to greater mercy for herself.

* * *

Over the next weeks, Steely insisted that Elaina accompany him everywhere. He exploded in curses every time Cassy called or stopped by. Though she wished for more time with Cassy, which gave her a chance to relive Isaac's first days vicariously, Imm's words echoed. *The greater the sacrifice, the more it reflects the Three.*

Time with Steely was certainly that, wearing scanty outfits he'd purchased to display her like a trophy. Surely this wasn't the selflessness Imm had spoken of. His friend's leering eyes confirmed the message she'd been telling herself for years: that beyond the desire she could rouse, she was worthless.

Steely pestered her to quit Tasty. He found her coworkers threatening and resented everyone who set foot in her apartment. His possessiveness made him redouble his efforts at convincing her to move in with him, but she held tight to the small piece of righteousness she had left, that she would never shack up with someone before marriage.

Spending several nights a week down the alley at his place pacified him until, inevitably, alcohol stirred up rants about her "Catholic hypocrisies." His hands grew rougher, resulting in bloody lips and bruises, which he followed with excuses and pleas for forgiveness. His abuse left her helpless, for she understood the fear that enslaved them both: being alone and feeling unlovable.

The very reason forgiving Cassy was more difficult than forgiving Steely left her guilty, too. Elaina's life had been blessed with greater advantages. How could she hold his insecurity against him?

In having more, more is required. —Sister Immaculata Lefevre

* * *

Tiny Tarrock, population 19,000, had an eastside subculture that took no heed to race. Steely's apartment brimmed with people of many skin pigments, labeled not by ethnicity but only for their poverty. Their muddy shade was a blend of the dropouts, unemployed, welfare recipients, and homeless people who lacked dignity and hope, forming a color even a rainbow didn't include. Like crayons missing their wrapper, they had no compelling name or label from a job title, degree, or career success to group themselves with the energetic reds, creative yellows or intelligent blues. Steely's friends were like broken crayons, tossed in an old box, only to leave a stain of resentment on the taxpayers who supported them. No wonder the eastsiders wanted to forget, even if briefly.

Just a block away, in the manicured courtyards of Haisting College, the same multicultural skin tones enjoyed a key advantage: the green of money. That green, when mixed with any color skin, created a shade called privilege.

How could one street, a pile of green paper, and buildings called Haisting College make that much difference? How many eastsiders owned brilliant minds, too, but had no means or reason to apply themselves. The way Elaina saw it, wealth and education (or the lack thereof) created the dark casts of prejudice. The strays and strung-out who gathered at Steely's brought to mind Matthew 9:36: "For they were like lost sheep without a shepherd."

Perfect love in color is white—not the lack of color, but the inclusion of all colors. If we looked at others the way God does, all humanity would be without pigment. Prejudice, oppression, acts of terrorism, and genocide all began with one person turning on another because of our contrasts, which is God's gift to humanity. Love is the only force that can disarm these evils. Love everyone: those who think, look, speak, and pray

differently. See people as God does, a brilliant inclusion of all colors.
                                          —Sister Immaculata Lefevre

The people who hung out at Steely's tolerated Elaina, but she knew they were bitter. He wasn't generous with handouts anymore because he spent all his money on her. Extravagant flower arrangements, expensive jewelry, and clothing absolved his temper and lack of trust. They also made her feel beholden.

His obsession with her was affecting his sales, as well. There were plenty of drugs to be found elsewhere.

"What's the hurry to leave? You and Deanne got somethin' goin' on?"

Elaina pulled her coat on, wondering how much more she could take. His constant pressure for sex, insisting she disrobe like the strippers he described after drinking—this couldn't be how she was supposed to reflect the Three's love. She'd allowed it to go too far, and now she didn't know how to turn back without taking a beating.

She hadn't held a paintbrush in months. Ideas for Christmas gifts couldn't dance if she had no time to give them. Steely's whims were no different than those of a spoiled, bored child who demanded his nanny's entertainment.

"You a switcher?" He pushed her against the door and yanked her coat back off. "I watched you and Deanne on the sofa together, her head on your lap while you rubbed her face with a paintbrush. A real turn-on, especially when you two started sleepin' together. But you belong to me now, and I ain't sharin'."

"You make me sick. I told you what I was doing with Deanne. I trusted you! Now I get your truth, that you were peeping in our window and imagining sicko stuff. You've been in the whiskey again. I can smell it. First thing in the morning, you're chugging beer to get over the shakes so you can open the hard stuff without spilling. You're nasty when you're sober and worse when you're drunk. I have bruises everywhere from your constant grabbing."

"You're a mouthy bitch." He slapped her, and his ring sliced her brow. The sight of blood startled him, as if another guy had just manhandled his girl.

She pushed down her fear and calmly picked up the buttons that had popped off her coat. "I'm done. Thanksgiving's off, too."

He blocked her path. "You don't understand."

His song and dance after every beating had grown old.

"I'm so afraid of losin' you that it makes me crazy. Girls like you never stick around, at least not with guys like me. If you'd just move in, I wouldn't be so jealous. I drink 'cause you're gone so much, and when you're here, all you do is neurotically clean. My friends don't come around anymore 'cause they think you're a snob. I don't care, though, 'cause I'm ready to make you a promise. If you'll move in, I'll stop dealin'. It's as good a time as any, bein's that half my business is across town."

He pulled her stiff body to his, burying his face in her hair. "I think I found a job hangin' iron in River Rock."

She melted as the words sunk in. She'd done it. He was going clean.

She hugged him back. "You've made me so happy. Yes, I'll move in, but it's only fair to give Deanne some time to find another roomie so she's not stuck with all the rent. Do you really think we were lesb—"

"Heavens no, you were just comforting Deanne. Sometimes you piss me off so bad I want to do the same back. I feel like Dr. Jekyll and Mr. Hyde."

Then why had his implication that she and Deanne were homosexual been so troubling? Imm said that all hearts crave the same thing: pure love. Sometimes, she added, desires go awry due to unique proportions of hormones, the use of pornography, or sexual abuse.

Sexual abuse. Elaina's gut churned at blurry recollections of gender boundaries crossing.

"Come here, little doll. Let's make up."

Steely thought sex was the remedy for every argument and spurt of blood. Each time she complied, he assumed he'd received absolution. And now she was moving in.

This was a downward spiral.

"You look so sad. Let's do some happy dust."

If sex wasn't the elixir, drugs and alcohol were. Considering he was going legit, though, she could look the other way one last time.

The razor's reflection bounced on the wall as he chopped the white clumps. Like her mother mincing nuts, he pushed the powder into rows and began again. The fuss made her anxious; she wanted to get it over with before she changed her mind.

"Hold your other nostril closed and sniff hard."

Her eyes watered and her nose dripped from the burn. She flapped a hand in front of her face and grimaced.

"I told you to keep your nose pinched. You're wastin' the goodie. Sniff it up."

The bitter liquid dripping down her throat made her gag.

"Now the other side."

Would the numbing in her throat cut off her breath?

As if someone had adjusted the tint on reality, every color went brighter. The grapes Steely offered to cover the chemical tasted were sweeter than ever remembered. Energy flooded her, with no jitters or stomach grinding. Her legs begged to skate, run, or peddle her bike at the speed of the wind. There was nothing she couldn't do.

"Ah, the girl loves it, don't she?" Steely inhaled the second line and came to her. "You want to move now, don't you, Dolly?"

He turned the stereo up high until the vibrations became visible on both speakers. The walls shook to all Elaina's favorite eight-tracks: Styx, Queen, Boston. She danced until she was soaked with sweat, then bounced outside to cool off. Her cheeks, red both from the chemical's fire and cold outside, gave away her body's confusion.

"Let's practice the hustle," she said. "I know you hate disco, but you're the best dancer at Sixes."

"My dance card is full," he said with a wink, "but you're the exception. How 'bout some Starship and then a slow one before you pass out?"

The crowd at Sixes dance club said they moved perfectly together, and at this moment, Elaina couldn't tell where her body left off and Steely's began.

"You want me, don't you?" she murmured as he twirled her again.

"I can't wait anymore."

The cocaine dulled the impact of his strength, but hours later, when she was coming down, pain reverberated with each move. Elaina stood naked before the mirror, barely able to straighten for an inspection of the damage. Like a beaten dog, her neck, arms, and breasts were covered in bruises.

"I can't be seen like this," she said with a moan. "I'll lose my job if I miss again."

A slow smile raised on Steely's face. "Tell 'em you fell off a ladder or somethin'. Deanne will back you up. Just don't let 'em look too close."

As it turned out, he was right. Management bought the alibi, leaving Elaina, Steely, and Deanne to snort coke and dance for the next two days. But afterwards, coming down, spasms, dry heaves, and hellish images trapped her between reality and a twilight zone, leaving her feeling far worse than merely bruised.

She had to get away from this world before it got the better of her.

* * *

By Thanksgiving, makeup and a turtleneck were able to cover the marks cocaine and lust had left. The iron-hanging job in River Rock had come through, as good a reason as any to introduce Steely to her parents. In directing him toward family, maybe she could continue influencing more wholesomeness.

She popped through the side door of her parents' home shortly before noon, Steely timidly lagging behind. As she took his coat, she could see dark circles under the arms of his shirt and smell heavy perspiration overtaking his deodorant. She agonized, more worried for his anxiety than her family's reaction to a stranger who would be lucky to sell a blue-collar status.

"What's with the hair?" Eric asked Steely, his condescension unmistakable.

"He looks like a girl," Elaina's nephew shouted.

Ever the notorious windbag and killjoy, Eric pitted question after question designed to expose Steely's lack of education. His bullying was a simple pretense to flaunt his own greater knowledge. As the youngest Michael, she'd been a pawn to her older brother's game too many times, seeing them for the put-down they were. Yet her mother remained silent, seemingly taking pleasure from Steely's struggle at small talk.

When she couldn't bear Steely's discomfort any longer, Elaina made their excuses and they escaped. Her heart felt as bare as the trees and gloomy as the early winter sky. She hated her family's boorish behavior. They were the trash for refusing to give him a chance.

"I'm sorry, Steve. If I'd known—"

"I told you, I'm not the kind of guy you take home." Defeat was clear in the slump of his shoulders. "Your family wants better for you. I've always known you were too good for me."

She forced a cheery tone. "People who think they're better are the problem. With what you'll soon be earning, you can thumb your nose at everyone. And if it makes you feel better, my family has a pretty low opinion of me, too."

On the drive home, old insults oozed beneath the dark door and leeched through her head. *You've brought disgrace to the most precious thing Dad gave you: the family name. Loser. Tease. Slut.* But the harshest resounded in her father's voice. *You dress like someone who works on a street corner. You have shamed me for the final time.*

Imm was the only person she'd ever confided those last devastating remarks to. Holding Elaina's disclosures like treasure to be polished, Imm had found the perfect words to cut away her pain. *When we hold on to demeaning words, our actions often validate what we have been told about ourselves. Self-sabotage happens over time, ma poupée. Malicious words have caused you to doubt your holiness and that you are a reflection of the Trinity. Forgive their unkindnesses, because they don't know how their words have damaged you. Forgive yourself, too, for giving credence to their words. And remember, self-reclamation also takes time.*

"I don't want to thumb my nose at anyone or prove anything."

Steely's remark brought Elaina back to the present unpleasantness. As cars passed, probably on their way to their own loving family celebrations, she couldn't shake a sense of overwhelming isolation. Only the Three could administer the antidote she needed.

"I don't give a crap about money, fancy houses, cars, all the stuff people slave for," he continued. "Yeah, I want some dough to buy the things that make you happy, but for me, it's just crap that takes up space."

She loved him for that. Kurt had said almost the same thing, too. Maybe one day she'd get to a place where money didn't matter, but right now it did. She wanted a family, and she wanted to give her children every advantage. Her kids would have the best educations so they'd never have to climb forty-foot beams in subfreezing temperatures, risking their lives to hang iron. They'd never have to live like eastsiders. They'd be able to invite friends to a home they were proud of, and their dad wouldn't need alcohol and drugs to get through the day. He'd love his life and his job, not need to escape from it.

But Steely couldn't give her any of that because it wasn't important to him. Worse, she couldn't tell him that for fear of his backlash. No, she'd never marry Steely, but she'd stick around until things got better for him.

"A famous guy said the same thing about money." She kissed him in genuine affection. "He was a classic rebel who didn't give a hoot what people thought. He had long hair, too."

Steely looked intrigued. "Who?"

"Swear you won't laugh?" She grinned. "Jesus."

His expression and tone flattened. "I'm not laughin', Dolly, but the whole Jesus thing ain't for me. You don't go to church anymore, so why you bringin' religion into this?"

Sister Katherine and Sister Ruth's years of guidance on guilt-grabbing grated her conscience. "I used to go to church every week. I loved Mass, being in church, and—a few other places where I'd meet up with church friends, but they don't come around anymore."

She was so tired of remorse for not going to Mass, for not tithing, for not confessing—and for driving another nail into Jesus with her sins. Had any Catholic found a way to raise themselves from the pit of loathing? No wonder so many abandoned Mother Church; self-condemnation remained her most zealous demand.

* * *

"Elaina, I want to come over and talk. When's a good time?"

She knew exactly where her mother must be standing: in the

Michaels' dated kitchen, pacing, then winding the long cord of the wall phone around its hook before resuming her pacing and pulling the cord loose again. If only she could hang up on the woman who'd been so rude to Steely, who was no more flawed than alcoholic Eric, high-horsed Kim—or herself.

"Whenever."

"Your friend worries me. He's trouble and from the other side of town." Elaina's mother said before she'd completely entered Elaina's apartment.

"You're standing on the other side of town, Mom. I live on the other side of town. Who cares? Let me guess—it's his hair. You know what Dad says: don't judge a book by its cover."

"You forgot to mention his age."

"So? I'm an adult now, and self-supporting."

"Elaina, please listen. He's into drugs, possibly trafficking. He grew up on the most undesirable street, quit school—correction, was expelled because he almost killed a boy. Did you know his nickname is Steely because of the weapon he used? If you don't break things off, the consequences could be devastating."

As if drugs made him the devil. How conveniently her mother dismissed Eric's problems with alcohol.

"Where'd you get your information about Steve, Mom?"

"Your brothers."

"Really? Which one? Your son with the anger management problem, or the one you've bailed out of more alcohol-related troubles than I can count?"

Her mother sucked in air as if she'd been slapped.

How many times had her parents paid Eric's fines, lawyers, and bails yet wouldn't give Elaina a penny's help for their own grandson? They'd forbidden her to soil the family name by accepting government assistance, leaving her no choice but to give her son away. How could they love Eric so much but not understand her same love for Isaac?

The door to the dark place expelled foul air into Elaina's chest. Her brain recoiled, warning her away.

"This is futile. I insist you stop seeing this Steve character, and I don't want him at our home again, either." Her mom delivered the demand in a manner cribbed straight from her dad.

"You know nothing about him. You haven't given him a chance."

Silence.

Her mother turned sharply and walked out.

"Are you listening to me?" Elaina shouted after her. "I love him, and I'm going to marry—"

The sanctimonious bitch. She would marry Steely if for no other reason than to get back at her parents. Her mother refused to release her grudge against Mrs. Adams for forbidding Cassy to pal around with Elaina after Elaina's pregnancy became public, yet she was doing the same thing in turning her nose up at Steely. She may as well reject Elaina too, because both Steely and Elaina wore the same muddy shade of indignity and lack of hope.

15

"I can't feel my feet," Steely muttered as he hurled a steel-toed boot at the wall. "This job stinks."

Elaina rubbed his blue-gray toes while praying. *Please, God, not frostbite. He's trying so hard.*

But conversations like she used to have with the Three were lost on the God the nuns had drilled into her as a child. That God only heard an occasional plea on someone else's behalf, buried under double standards, endless rules, and devotional requirements.

For Steely's sake, however, she'd give it her best.

She hadn't been to Mass or even inside a church in a year. She didn't miss it, even the glorious stained glass windows, paintings, and altar carvings. Religious art that once represented an artist's love and devotion to the Trinitarian God now appeared in her eyes like sacrifice and surrender to a dictator.

The pictures and descriptions Imm had given of the Renaissance artists' work in the grand cathedrals of Europe had once so beautifully illustrated multiple generations who'd sacrificed their entire lives to declaring their love for God. They worshiped under and on top of scaffoldings and were baptized, married, and buried in their unfinished churches, none more glorious than Saint Peter's Cathedral in Rome. As they ambled up the aisle of Saint Augustine, sometimes even venturing into the sanctuary, Imm's art and religion lessons had seemed one and the same.

The dedication of those men and even the unfinished churches teach a most valuable lesson that becoming a work of art for God, a true Christian, is a long and often painful process. The masterpieces we are meant to make of our lives won't be completed until we die.
—Sister Immaculata Lefevre

Without the Clover Club, the church had become a hollow reminder of faraway friends she missed as much as she missed her firstborn.

"Wiggle your toes," she said. "You've got to get the blood flowing."

Steely threw back a flask of whiskey. "Don't give me that look. I'm tryin' to warm up."

"I don't care what you drink here. But you take that crap to work too, don't you? If, God forbid, you fell off a beam and they found that you'd been drinking, you wouldn't get a nickel."

"But you'd be here, wouldn't you, Dolly? We'd have all day and night to—"

"Not if you're paralyzed."

His visible annoyance reminded her how much she sounded like her mother.

"Let me get you a glass," she offered in self-reproach. "How's it going otherwise?"

"Not good. I get up there and freeze, not from the cold but fear of heights. I can't pass beams or rivet. It's gettin' old."

"Didn't you say the newer guys will have to hang iron up top in a couple months? You only need to hang in there just—"

"I'm sick of it."

Sick of it? He'd been employed less than three weeks. His defeatist attitude was getting old, too. She was sick of making excuses for him, sick of keeping his and Deanne's places clean, sick of working full time. She'd never get their Christmas gifts finished. At least Steely had backed off about when she would move in, but she was spending most nights at his place anyway to pacify him. She went back and forth between her apartment and his like an itinerant.

Deanne's boyfriend, Raphe, had practically moved in, too, making another person to clean up after. Elaina didn't mind because he

passed his pricey Haisting art lessons to her in exchange for her cooking. But if Steely learned that Elaina was doing domestic labor for
another man, she'd have added problems. Lately, however, he'd been
too tired to notice.

Raphe had helped her with an abstract painting for Steely: blue
mums woven into rope-like braids. Once she'd grasped how highlights
could create depth, Elaina had used the technique on Deanne's painting,
too. Curtains, bedspreads, and pillows for both Steely's and Deanne's
apartments still waited for their final stitching.

The dark pink color returning to Steely's toes told her blood was
flowing. She gave his feet a final brisk rub and stood up. "Please,
please, will you sleep at Deanne's a couple of nights so I can finish your
Christmas surprise? She said it's no problem."

"Only if you keep me company."

"I'll try, but I can't promise. It'll be quick if I stick with it." Before
he could change his mind, she changed the subject. "Have I told you
how great you look? You must've dropped ten pounds. Umm, another
favor? Get yourself some warmer work gear. It would make the job
more tolerable."

"Yeah, yeah. You remind me of a crabby old hag who sits on her
rocker, constantly bitching. Now you're decorating my place like an
old battle-ax, too. I want my hottie girl back, the one who couldn't
get enough sex."

Who was that? Certainly not her. Sex with him had always been a
sacrifice. She smiled and turned to go clean the kitchen. Again.

* * *

Elaina's early Christmas gift for Steely hung on the freshly painted
wall, spotlighted by the sun streaming in. The blue mums with silvery-
white highlights popped against the otherwise muted tones of the apartment and seemed to sway in the shadows of the tree branches outside.

Deanne's painting, autumn leaves on overhanging branches,
included every fun, splashy color that her friend radiated: oranges,
reds, purples, and gold. Elaina hoped it would bring to mind their lazy,
shared afternoon a few months back. Confidence had inspired her to

spray-paint huge tropical flowers, graphic patterns, and lively words exploding in turquoise, fuchsia, and lime green on Deanne's bedroom walls. She wanted them to scream her joy for their friendship.

She wished Deanne could wake up to her surprise Christmas morning, but practicality wouldn't allow that. Elaina would have to show her early. How lovely it would have been to put her friend up in a five-star hotel until Christmas morning. But then again, Tarrock didn't have any five-star hotels.

Deanne shook her head. "Oh Lanie, why are you at Tasty when you could be a famous decorator? You're that good." She grabbed one of the pillows Elaina had sewn and rubbed her cheek against it, laughing and crying simultaneously. "My old T-shirt, the one I cut up to bandage your foot!"

Elaina hugged her. "A reminder of the night we became friends."

"I love it. I love you, too."

Raphe looked up from studying Elaina's work and high-fived her. "The graphics in the bedroom, wow! You do have talent. Mind if I bring some classmates over for a look-see?"

"I'd be honored. In fact, I'd like to hear their comments."

"You fixed up Steely's place too, right? Can I see it?"

Apprehension jumped along her shoulders. Steely would interpret Raphe's interest as a come-on, as if she were useless except for sex. "Don't bother. I rushed it."

"Describe it."

His eagerness got the better of her, and her enthusiasm found its way out again.

Deanne hugged her again. "It's obvious you love doing this. You should go with it."

"Doesn't sound like you rushed his place to me," Raphe said. "You sure I can't see it?"

"Maybe while he's at work. When he gets home, he's pretty tired."

"What was his reaction to your painting? Abstracts bring all sorts of stuff to mind, even to an untrained eye."

Deanne was so lucky. Raphe's thought-provoking questions perfectly illustrated his higher education.

"Well, he thought it held a sexual message, but that was the furthest thing from my mind."

"Don't blame the man." Raphe winked and pulled Deanne close. "Us guys see sex in everything."

She shrugged, wondering how a painting she'd intended to bring the story of Saint Stephen to mind could make Steely think of sex. Another example of how mismatched they were.

Men use affection to get sex, and women use sex to get affection. The problem is using sex for self-serving gain. Sex is for procreation. If you don't want a child, you don't have sex. —Edward Michael

Sex is God's most beautiful gift, but without unconditional love, it can't be three-dimensionally fulfilling to the body, mind, and heart, as God intended. Sex for physical gratification only or to buy devotion will always leave one hungry. —Sister Immaculata Lefevre

So why did sexual hunger feel so physical? Imm suggested it was because so many people assumed that since humans were created with the urge, it couldn't be wrong. Casual sex, she said, steals love and emotion from the act.

When marriage is no longer criteria for the privilege, sex also is robbed of its special, exclusive, and sacred characteristics.
—Sister Immaculata Lefevre

Steely wanted sex on command with quick climaxes, but Elaina's hunger sprouted slowly from a place much deeper. Maybe this is why so many marriages failed, because the couple's hopes were actually about satisfying their individual cravings. Could two individuals really spend a lifetime focusing first and foremost on what was best for the other? Her parents' relationship more closely resembled business partners or coworkers in a baby factory. She wanted the kind of sex and marriage that connected souls. Did that even exist?

Once, she'd walked in on Steely watching porn flicks. Finding her shock amusing, he'd forced her in front of the projector. A protest would've only enraged him, so she sat quietly and looked at the floor until his angry hands forced her head up. The graphic display of dominance and subservience brought back Deanne's rape. In her disgust, she threw up on Steely's projector. His rage exploded in an unprecedented string of curse words and ranting about her crazed mental state caused by Catholic brainwashing.

Was she psycho? Why did porn knot her gut, but nude art made her heart soar?

Whenever a human body is merely an object for pleasure and selfish gain, that body is raped of its spiritual value. Pornography shows only the physical, but human beings are also spiritual and emotional—trinary. Darkness blinds mankind of a full view because darkness fears how true awareness would light the world. Evil uses pornography to show a twisted and limited version of God's creation while also blinding us to the harm of our limited vision. —Sister Immaculata Lefevre

* * *

"You ready to bake cookies, wifey-poo?"

Elaina came in to find Deanne pulling ingredients from the cupboards.

"According to Raphe, you're wasting your talent," she announced as she plunked the bag of flour on the counter with a poof.

Though she knew Deanne meant it as a compliment, Elaina felt annoyed. Without a degree, her chances of success were about as great as winning the lottery with no ticket. Was the wager worth a mountain of student loans? Asking her dad for help would be a one-in-million gamble, too.

And where had taking chances gotten her thus far, anyway? *Pessimism* seemed a far more practical way of staying safe from futile hopes, like her silly dreams of keeping Isaac or finding a friendship like the one she'd once had with the Three.

"Steely doesn't give a crap about your Christmas gift, does he?" Deanne began cracking eggs into the bowl.

"He's just exhausted. The job isn't what he expected." Why was she making excuses for him again?

As if Deanne read her mind, she asked, "Do you love him?"

"He's a good person, like you said, generous, loy—"

"But do you love him enough to marry him?"

She squirmed, remembering Deanne's accusation about her thinking herself above eastsiders. "Mmm, I think we need more cinnamon in this batch. Cinnamon, ginger, evergreens—what's your favorite Christmas smell?"

"You're not going to get off that easy, Lanie. You need to break up with Steely. Now. He won't give up without a fight, literally, but it's not like he hasn't bruised and bloodied you before."

"Geez, don't sugarcoat it."

"I never do, which is why I also need to confess my part in this. I pushed Steely at you to see if you could prove that you didn't think yourself better. The day you moved in, all that cleaning—I felt like the trash you couldn't wait to clean up. But you've succeeded in doing exactly what you said you would. Everyone who comes around here has learned that, with a little effort, nobody has to live in filth, and that fresh flowers aren't prissy, they're mind-altering and motivating. So are you."

Elaina had no reply.

But Deanne, who rarely cried, was fighting with deep emotion. "I hate myself each time you come home with another mark on your face from that lunatic. He's not worthy of you, the reason he's threatened by everyone. That's why you won't show Raphe the art in his apartment, right?"

"Well, yeah. I'm not going to risk Raphe's free art lessons. An artist's hands don't stand a chance against steel knuckles." Her attempt at humor fell flat.

"No worries. Raphe's a gentle soul but not stupid. And as long as I'm around, he will be, too, because we're crazy about each other. But Steely is just plain crazy—scary crazy. Each sweet-talkin' he pulls off after another one of his wallopings is a preview for the next. One day, you're not going to come out of his place alive."

* * *

December 13, 1981
Ma chére enfant,

Maman is sleeping, so my thoughts can be put to paper. I'm always aware when your musings and mine are in sync. Across an ocean, I feel your joyous anticipation of this holy season and the creativity it's roused in your imagination. Tell me what you've painted.

Grasse is quiet, everyone having settled in for the cooler months ahead. The landscape is beautiful in a solemn, lonely way. Grays, iron blues, and dull greens make stripes against the horizon, sleeping in layers while waiting for spring. Painting winter scenes requires few colors and less blending, lazy work until new life leaps over the mountains next March.

Whatever the season, we must drench ourselves in every kind of art. In allowing other's visions to motivate ours, every artistic impulse becomes a spiritual movement. Don't shy away from that which you find unappealing; fertile soil nurtures both crops and weeds. But in God's eyes, which are which?

Allow yourself to become intoxicated by music, drama, dance, anything that helps you connect with the inner child whose imagination is the Three's grandest creation. Don't lose sight of little Elaina, whose insight was able to capture the incomprehensible: the Trinity. The painting you gave me your second-grade year can never be topped. It's also one of your finest prayers and acts of worship. Your creativity is the window for their light to penetrate, making your soul a house of mirrors to reflect them. Imagination is the greatest fuel and the fastest transport back to your Three.

Tell me you've found the Trinity, chérie. Write me soon.

I've never left you in my prayers, and I love you.

Immaculata

December 22, 1981
Dearest Imm,
Merry Christmas!
I'm happy your mom is doing well and you've found peace in

all the changes of the last year. I'm at peace, too, when a paintbrush is in my hand.

My new friend, Raphe, who's an art major at Haisting College, passes lessons to me. With his instructions, I've complete two of my best paintings yet, both abstracts. I'm most proud of the first because of its depth, texture, and movement; the flowers seem to sway.

My Three are not here. I stretch my hand to meet theirs, but it feels like groping in a black hole. I've even tried sacrifice and service in an effort to find them, but now I question if my intention wasn't really for hope of finding the kind of love I've begun to doubt even exists. I go through the motions of each day, losing sight of something better, but I will continue to be patient and remember what you said: God isn't bound by our understanding of time.

On a brighter note, I've included your Christmas gift: memories of you represented in paint chips I mixed and named.

Puff, the Magic Dragon: The color of Lake Erie when the sunshine dives into the water (third-grade field trip). It's the color of Imm's eyes and gentle, magic dragons. Remember singing that song as we polished the brass instruments?

Full of Clover: The color of the field next to Saint Augustine Cemetery in late summer. Full of Clover is a soft, creamy pink with a hint of lavender, reminding me of all the times our Clover Club ran through that field together and suckled the sweetness from the clover blossoms beneath Mary and the angels.

Forever in Blue Jeans: Da-da-dah, singing Neil Diamond with you in the art room while watching the breeze tickle your paintbrushes. This color reminds me of the first time I saw you in blue jeans. Forever in Blue Jeans is my name for classic indigo with a faded gray undertone. It makes me feel as cozy as when I sat on your lap.

Chilled Beaujolais: Imm's wine of choice, pink with a hint of purple. It's the color of my first pomegranate, with you at Christmas of seventh grade. The juice never came off my sweater, the reason it's still my favorite. This pink brings visions of crisp French wine, soft cheeses, and crusty bread on the pique-niques you promised when I visit Grasse.

Imm's Heart: Deepest red with just enough purple to give it oomph. In this color, I taste raspberries and hear your heart in my ears as my childhood head rests on your chest. This color is elegant, bold, and the tiniest bit goes a long way, the reason I'd love to paint an entire room this shade.

Walking Down the Aisle: Trust in your promise that one day I'll have a husband and family. Some would call this color cream, beige, or ivory because it looks like the other neutrals until you look closer. It is purity, trustworthiness, and dependability, a color that wears forever.

May 1982 be the year that brings me to you.

All my love,
Elaina

* * *

A thin slice of moon allowed a million stars to shine as she walked to the mailbox. The east side of Tarrock resembled the rest of the world under a blanket of powdery snow, a giant greeting card.

"Just a few days until your birthday, Trinity," she whispered. "Thank you for Imm. If you can hear me, please let me know."

Christmas morning arrived in silence but for Steely's gifts shouting reminders that he expected her gratitude and company today. Four porcelain dolls, a fur coat, and a car stereo, the gifts he'd insisted she open last night, still lay like overdue bills. The money he'd spent could've purchased warmer work wear, a better apartment, even time in detox—all the things she really wanted for Christmas.

Because she'd been forbidden to bring him to her family's home, how was she to make an expected appearance while also accommodating his wishes? A case of the flu might excuse a visit home, but then she'd have to spend Christmas having sex and watching him drink.

She cradled the receiver with her eyes closed, waiting for her mom to pick up. The smell of fresh paint from Deanne's bedroom lingered, but even that spot of brightness couldn't lift the dread she felt about making this call. Her ears filled with all the previous lies and excuses she'd invented since hooking up with Steely, drowning out her voice as she fabricated another to her mother now.

She sagged against the wall as the call ended.

"You're not sick. You just don't want to take me to your family dinner, right?"

She dropped the phone, spooked by Steely's sudden appearance. "Let's not do this again, Steve."

"Either I embarrass you, or you were told not to bring me around. Which?"

"The truth?" This truth was dangerous territory. "My brothers know how you got your nickname, and about your selling. Mom suggested that I—that we—slow down."

"I'm working my ass off for you, the obedient blue-collar worker who does exactly what his bitch demands, and I still ain't good enough? I didn't take this hellhole job for my health."

His frustration was understandable. One's past could never out-distance peoples' memory. Maybe, at least for today, they could just agree to say whatever. She reached to hug him, but he slammed her against the wall first. His fist flew by, missing her face by inches and crumbling the drywall instead.

The door banged shut, confirming his exit.

Now that she'd already lied, she supposed she was free to go home. It would be awkward, but anything was better than spending Christmas alone.

But loneliness wanted company, tugging at her heart as she sat in her mother's kitchen struggling toward an exchange, even small talk. Her mom feigned busy to justify her lack of response, although she didn't miss an opportunity to fire some nasty comments about Steely.

After an hour of this game, Elaina cracked. "Can't you find a drop of kindness, even on Christmas? He's not a dealer; he hangs iron in sub-zero temperatures. Let's see Eric work that hard instead of you and Dad bailing him out."

The snow looked flat and dull as she stormed outside again. Apparently, she would be spending Christmas alone after all.

16

The time clock stamped completion of the first shift of 1982, and her Pinto's speedometer betrayed her excitement for the painting taking form in her imagination. Steely wouldn't be home for hours, giving her time to slip into his apartment and study the technique she'd used in his abstract.

She pulled up to the curb near his door and hesitated. This didn't look good. Two zoned-out bodies without coats propped each other up on Steely's steps. It couldn't be more than thirty degrees. His door hung open, and music poured from the front room. Had the place been broken into? She backed up a safe distance and watched.

Steely stumbled into the doorway, yelling something. Instinct urged her to stay away, but her desire to review the painting won.

Beer cans and booze bottles lay between a half-dozen or more bodies strung out on the floor. The unshaven man at the table looked vaguely familiar, but why she couldn't grasp. As if she were watching a horror movie, her eyes would not avert from his teeth pulling a rubber hose tight around his upper arm, leaving his hands free for a spoon and hypodermic needle. He pushed a spurt of liquid into the air, the tiny droplets shooting out like glitter into a ray of sun. He jammed it into his arm, leaned back, and moaned. The needle and hose fell to the floor, and saliva ran from his gaping mouth. Slowly, he slid off the chair as if melting into a surreal, gruesome puddle.

Another familiar figure snatched the needle and began mixing white powder and water in the spoon. Hasty hands held a lighter beneath it, and the solution began to bubble. The liquid was drawn through cotton. He followed the process as the one before, who was now twitching on the floor.

Elaina bolted, her stomach lurching with sour fear.

"Let it up, Dolly. Your belly's gotta be empty to get the full effect." Steely held her hips from behind as she continued to vomit. "Who fired you?"

"I don't understand." She turned and flinched, terrified at the sight of Steely's satanic smile. She tried to back away and stumbled over another body.

"Who gave you the bang? You used a new needle, right?"

She knew better than to correct him. "That guy on the floor."

"No worries, then. He's the best. So how do you feel? Radical, huh? Man, I was wrong about you. You're a rock-and-roller."

"The party's great, but what about work?" She took another step back.

"I never planned on goin' back after Christmas, but I didn't want to disappoint my Dolly, so I got myself fired this morning." He pushed her against the wall and pressed himself into her. "You bein' here says I don't need to bullshit my babe, though. It'll be just us from now on, 'cause you're gonna quit Tasty and move to the lake with me."

"You're on my foot, Steve." She pushed him back, grateful for the excuse.

"Oh, sorry. Hey. Wait, you seem pretty straight. Let me smell your breath. I can tell if he gave you enough fire. Maybe you need a little more."

She backed toward the kitchen. "I need a beer."

"Oh yeah, that's my Dolly. Jammy did you good if you're thirsty."

"Jammy? I've seen him and that other guy before." A shiver tripped across her back as the answer began to loosen.

"Jammy brought the stash for my welcome back party." Spit frothed at the corners of Steely's mouth like a rabid animal. "Ron took me back, baby doll, 'cept now I'm head of transportation."

Her head spun. Transporting drugs? The lake? Ron! The two on the floor were the thugs from The Lobster Trap. Steely had known exactly whom she was talking about when she'd told him about Deanne's rape.

No wonder he'd looked as if he'd seen a ghost. How long had he worked for Ron? What had she gotten herself into?

Hallucinating bodies sagged around her, supported haphazardly by the walls. Their hands waved through the godforsaken nothingness in front of them; mumbled gibberish slipped down strings of drool. The apartment was freezing, yet it reeked of an outhouse in the heat of summer. The dry winter air couldn't support such a stench except in a room filled with sweat, vomit, urine—and a clingy, slithering kind of evil.

Steely's painting sat atop a bar stool, serving as a makeshift table to hold paraphernalia, begging for rescue. A cigarette smoldered through the canvas. She watched a black hole grow like the deprivation consuming the room. How to escape? If she knocked the painting over, the bottles would crash to the floor, causing enough distraction for her to run.

Steely pulled her into the kitchen. "I want to fire you myself. Nobody's gonna give my Dolly treats but me. Sit while I find a clean needle."

As he turned away, Elaina bolted. He wheeled and blocked her. "You didn't shoot, did you, you lyin' whore? You think you're better than this? It's time you get an education, bitch."

One day, you're not going to come out of his place alive.
—Deanne Jonis

Sirens blared nearby.

"I hear cops." Elaina prayed for deliverance.

"Cops!" Steely yelled.

Bodies jolted as if his warning were a defibrillator. The junkies scattered like rats, running to the door, climbing out windows, and hiding in closets. Others, too far gone, continued staring through hollow eyes.

Three uniformed men stormed through the door, knocking Steely down. His hands were swiftly shackled, his Miranda rights bellowed over his shouts. More police swarmed in, restraining lifeless bodies in handcuffs and beating them to consciousness.

Elaina remained frozen among all the commotion. A nightstick came down on Steely's back over and over as he tried to writhe away. Blood splattered the walls, blotching the officers' clubs like scarlet paint.

Elaina pulled at an officer's sleeve. "Please stop. He's helpless in cuffs." She fell to her knees in the same submissive posture that had earned her past successes.

Another officer grabbed her collar. "He's resisting arrest, and you're obstructing justice."

They tossed her in the back of a squad car as the brutality continued. Every window provided a front-stage view of cruelty beyond comprehension. Elaina whispered the prayers of the Rosary she'd not spoken with sincerity since elementary school. The repetitive words still held no meaning but came as automatically as the breaths she gasped for between sobs.

Time held no mercy for the victims of these lawmen's ruthlessness. Tirelessly, they flogged the anger monster within themselves, projecting its face on the drug-addled desolates.

Every man craves the kind of respect acquired through self-esteem and the high opinion he's earned from others. When a man's honor is deficient, he'll steal it through dominance and control and by instilling terror. However, honor can only be gained by merit. —Edward Michael

* * *

Tarrock's finest wanted information about Steely that Elaina simply didn't have. Hours of interrogation brought nothing. When toxicology found her clean, they had nothing to hold her on, but she refused to leave until she could see Steely.

Steely had been provided with a thin cotton gown for visitation purposes but was naked beneath it, trembling from the draft in the visitation booth. "Some bullshit about clothing being a threat to my safety. They're liars. It's about humiliation," he shouted.

He made great effort to form his distorted words, his muddled voice climbing to a fury. He raised both middle fingers, waving them like a madman. Perspiration dripped from his goose-pimpled arms. The cuts and bruises on his swollen face rendered him barely recognizable.

"I'm so cold, Dolly." He reached out a quivering hand, seemingly unaware of the glass between them. Withdrawal was setting in.

Was this God's answer to her plea for deliverance, animals brutalizing Steely after he'd already been cuffed? He was still a human being.

A crushing revelation struck Elaina from nowhere. God had witnessed this before, at the hands of the law on his innocent, only begotten Son.

An involuntary wail escaped her throat, and she sagged in her chair. She cried out for Steely and the others who had been apprehended. She cried out for herself and for all for whom right and wrong had turned murky in the sludge of sin. She cried for the entire east side, who owned no color, no dignity, and no place to belong. In this washed-out place, the good guys and the bad weren't identifiable by the silver stars, white hats, and dark masks.

The ache for her Three swelled until it seemed to crush her lungs. Despair filled her airway, inflating reminders of more innocent years when nothing could interfere with the happiness her Clover Club lavished upon her.

Her father's sharp, judgmental voice, always a thought away, admonished her that consequences were necessary for people who sold drugs.

"That savagery was inexcusable," she screamed over her dad's sanctimonious words in her head. "They beat those men *after* they were cuffed. I saw everything."

Dumbstruck, Steely stared at Elaina through the glass, making her conscious of her tirade at the empty space around her.

Two guards pulled her from the visitation booth.

"Your sympathy is restin' on the wrong side, lady." The taller officer squeezed her upper arm roughly and guided her into another small room. He turned to the other cop and smirked. "A strip search will remind her to keep her piehole shut."

* * *

The second half of January was slow, cold, and empty. Elaina missed having Deanne's company to herself. With Raphe, three made a crowd.

Her feeling of isolation increased each time she passed Steely's apartment. His friends who kept an eye on the place had trashed all

her decorating efforts. Tattered curtains and upturned furniture bar-
ricaded the windows; the Harleys parked outside revved their engines
at all hours. The police were nowhere to be found, having put who
they wanted behind bars.

In addition to possession and trafficking, Steely was charged with
assaulting a police officer and resisting arrest. His defense attorney,
compliments of Deanne's rapist, Ron, insisted that Elaina testify on
Steely's behalf. His near-threats fell on deaf ears. Elaina sure the back-
alley lawyer would do anything or use anyone to get his client off. She'd
be insane to trust any of Ron's employees, including Steely, who'd tried
to force a needle into her arm.

Yet she also refused to be a witness for the prosecution. How could
she trust the lawmen who'd beat people already so high they were harmless? How could she trust those who'd strip-searched her after toxicology had found her clean?

By now, all of Tarrock knew Elaina Michael was Stephen Johnson's
girlfriend. Elaina's mother, beside herself with worry and shame, lec-
tured endlessly, while Edward's silence shouted his disdain. Elaina
wished to explain her irrational heart in a way they could understand,
but she didn't understand it herself. Besides, how could she trust the
two who'd done nothing to stop Eric?

Even her hope for the Three's compassion was close to extinguished.
They'd come out of hiding long enough to answer her prayer for rescue,
or perhaps their plan had actually been to burden her with more guilt.
If so, it had worked. Her fear of supporting either side left her stained
with dishonor perhaps as great as the shames Eric had laid upon her,
perhaps as deep as the shame of failing to mother her firstborn.

She trusted no one. She was entirely alone.

With nothing else to fall back on, Steely's attorney used the lack
of a proper search warrant to win a plea bargain for Steely of one year
at River Rock Reformatory.

Replays of the police interrogation invaded Elaina's thoughts
constantly. In her nightmares, she fled from policemen masked with
Monsignor Blaski and Father Krammer's faces. Both the police and the
priests' incessant attempts to extract the things she'd so carefully shut

away only strengthened her determination to remain silent. Whether on the cold, metal chair at the station or on her knees in the confessional, Elaina's secrets would remain buried. The truth was far worse.

Why did she pity those who broke the law and abused their bodies? Eastside education had taught her that moral absolutes don't exist under dire circumstances. Did God judge by definitive rules or from the perspective of each man's heart? How could one make the proper choices necessary to survive in such an ambiguous world?

We can't see white without the contrast of black or know love without experiencing heartache. Success cannot be achieved without failures along the way.—Sister Immaculata Lefevre

God, grant me the serenity to accept the things I cannot change, courage to change the things I can, and wisdom to know the difference.—Reinhold Niebuhr

By the end of the month, vines of gossip reached Elaina with tangled stories of Cassy's forthcoming wedding to the father of her unborn baby. Why hadn't Elaina received the news firsthand? Why hadn't she received even an invitation? Stupid questions, she chided herself; she was Steely's girlfriend, the drug dealer who'd made every newspaper for counties. Mrs. Adams couldn't have a drug dealer's girlfriend soiling her daughter's ceremony.

How had Cassy managed to finagle a white wedding—at Saint Augustine, no less—already four months pregnant? The answer to another stupid question rang equally clear. Cassy was the daughter of a church pillar. She had clout. Privilege. Jealousy and more hatred masked the deep hurt Elaina felt from being rejected yet again.

With nowhere else to turn, Elaina climbed into her car. New Year's resolutions for fence-mending, a bit overdue, drove her to her parents' house.

Hope puffed a breath of warmth into her chest as she stepped inside, but her parents' loose, brief hugs said her presence here was pro-bationary. She knew what to expect next: threadbare comments about the weather filling the spaces between long pauses.

"We were just about to watch our Wednesday night shows," her mom said when the last dish was washed, dried, and put away.

Any conversation was drowned out by her mother's stupid sit-coms: *Archie Bunker's Place*, *The Jeffersons*, and *Alice*. If she turned the volume high enough, she might forget Elaina was there altogether.

Her dad finally excused himself, she suspected to escape the super-ficial chitchat during the commercials.

Her mother didn't last another five minutes. "What's taking your dad? I'll see if he needs help while you make popcorn."

Her excuses were as old and tired as her boots and plaid coat. So was their relationship. Elaina wandered into the kitchen. Hot, buttered popcorn wasn't exactly the balm she'd been thinking of.

A scream broke through the tightly caulked window. Elaina yanked the pan off the burner and ran through the snow to the barn. Her mother knelt over the man she'd spent the last forty-five years in loving partnership with, rocking his head and murmuring, "No, please, no."

Elaina tore back to the house to call 911 and then back to the side of the two who, before this moment, defined unbearable. Her dad lay lifeless, waiting for an ambulance that would carry him to his dead on arrival pronouncement at Grace General Hospital at 8:28 p.m., January 20, 1982. The cause of death: a massive heart attack from arterial plaque. Was butter-braised and sugar-glazed, deep-fried and king-sized the reason?

* * *

After the funeral, there weren't enough hours in a day for sleep, even though Elaina slept most of the day. Sleep gave sadness a rest and nudged the hands of sluggish time. Sleep shortened mile-long minutes and made mechanical days tolerable.

The morning of her third day back at work, she woke up still feel-ing listless. As she rolled into the sun's reach, her body begged her to pull the covers back over her head. Maybe she would. She'd just give the clock a peek first.

"Oh, no!" She dropped the clock on the floor, leaped out of bed, and scrambled to find a clean, white shirt. Being late again meant probable termination, and deviation from Tasty's required dress would seal it. She had already leaned on the grocery union to save her job before. There was only so much they could do.

She slipped into Tasty's back door and retrieved her time card inconspicuously. She'd have to sign herself in again and fudge the time a bit, but if management saw her timecard punched late, she'd be fired. There was nothing to lose in trying.

She hung back by the soda bottle return area, busying herself separating Coke from Pepsi bottles. It was the worst of all jobs, touching the glass necks covered in sticky old soda. God only knew whose germy lips and hands had been there before. Why couldn't people take an extra minute to rinse them?

"Elaina Michael to the office, please," the intercom called.

This was it. She took the long way through produce and passed Kim, who was refilling the apple display. Eye contact with her sister brought a hostile shake of Kim's head. Bad blood needed no words.

The grocery manager and two assistants waited in the room she'd only seen once before, the day she was hired over three years ago.

Mr. Tizer, small and overly confident and reminding her of Eric, jumped for the first word. "We have three witnesses to validate that you didn't arrive until 6:38 a.m., yet your time card is signed at 6:00. We're letting you go."

"But if you quit, we'll give you a reference for future employers," added the head manager in a gentler voice. "You're a hard worker when you choose to come in."

"I'll quit." She could barely hear her own voice. Unexpected calm and acceptance slowed the thudding of her heart. Sorrow, worry, shame? She felt nothing. Her luck had flatlined for a smooth slide to ruination.

17

How much longer could Elaina remain at Deanne's without a paycheck? The reality of the recession hit hard now. Still, somewhere amidst the endless unemployment lines, she'd found a tiny bright spot. Each morning, the newspaper's skimpy help wanted section, hot coffee, and her mom waited for her visit.

"Sometimes I still consider college, but I've been reading about these two guys, Steve Jobs and Bill Gates," she said, as much to herself as her mom. "They've both started big companies, yet they're both college dropouts. It makes me wonder—"

"I know someone who needs a housekeeper," her mother said. "It'd be cash. You need something right here, right now. All that technological stuff is just another short-lived flavor of the month."

She sighed. Her mom was probably right. She had no alternative if she wanted to remain independent.

"That'd be great, until something more substantial turns up."

Once she'd taken a position as domestic help for a wealthy family, word traveled, and soon she had enough clients to remain independent. Housekeeping revealed the double standards of many pillars of the Saint Augustine community: pornography and birth control between sheets that needed changing, overheard conversations about tax hedging and extramarital affairs, and even several propositions from one husband. These hypocrisies only amplified her indifference for the church's definition of right and wrong. Why were these people, who dropped pennies of their millions into the collection baskets, exempt from the rules? How many church rules had no biblical backing, anyway? If you had enough wealth, man-made laws in the name of God were negotiable with no risk.

Jesus was crucified for exposing hypocrisy. He said rules are only necessary where there's risk of wrongdoing. With genuine faith, rules are pointless. Many have tunnel vision where right and wrong are concerned, using their hard line for personal gain or for judgment. Tunnel vision blinds us to God's perspective of our hearts and makes us spiritually lazy. —Sister Immaculata Lefevre

Elaina hid her despondency with bitterness and rebellion, but they couldn't bring her solace for her string of ruined relationships. Obedience and the love-filled no's that she'd never questioned as a child had all become open for debate since she'd ousted the Three from her heart. Fear moved in, making Need cry nonstop.

When we lose faith in the Trinity's eagerness for our happiness, we begin to grab for our own satisfactions and solutions.
–Sister Immaculata Lefevre

Elaina kept her head down and concentrated on pleasing her employers. Winter passed into spring. The temperature rose to the 70s, and homes unbuttoned to let six months of stale air out. Shorts and tank tops were pulled from bottom drawers so pale skin could gorge on sunshine, and squishy tires on bicycles were hastily filled for afternoon rides.

It was one of those weekends that the walls shrunk, leaving Elaina to pace the tiny apartment for something to do. The Harleys a block over antagonized her, continually revving their throttles. She loathed those man-boys who based their masculinity on the size of their engines. They lived like animals in Steely's apartment full time now, refusing to bathe or cover their beer-swollen stomachs. In their world, females existed only to appease their physical urges and fetch more beer.

Elaina decided to stretch her legs along her new running route. After her last run past Steely's, the filthy suggestions from the bikers who'd called themselves Chuck and Butch left her shivering. When she'd tried to get around them, they'd blocked the sidewalk, their comments bordering on threats.

A run around the campus lowered her agitation, but back at the apartment, she had to face the task she'd postponed for weeks.

"I can't freeload off you and Raphe anymore, Deanne. You've let me slide on rent, groceries . . . I have to move back home."

"No, Lanie. Don't leave me. This place will revert back to a pig-sty overnight. I don't have your wifey-poo knack, and I can't live the way I used to."

"I'll visit so much you'll never know I left. We'll talk while I clean, just like always."

Elaina's mom, short on words and oriented toward solutions, sent her daughter to bed as soon as she arrived, insisting they'd unpack her things in the morning. Just like in childhood.

Thoughts rained on her pillow, making sleep impossible. She wanted to pay Deanne and Raphe back, at least a gift certificate and flowers. They'd been so good to her. She'd not been in touch with school friends since shortly after graduation, soon to be a year. Her track record with men was disastrous, starting with Cole and stretching to the moments before her father died when he'd gone to the barn to escape her company.

Like the shadows of the past, worry for the future dulled her sense of possibility. She clutched at Imm's words. *It's a waste to spend even a moment in a time that doesn't exist. Now is free of everything but goodness, unless you fill it with past mistakes or worry about what's ahead. Now is where the Three shower their blessings, but your hands must be empty of the rest.*

As the weather warmed, Elaina took full advantage, riding her bike to save on gas. The days passed on autopilot. Her housecleaning work grew to almost full time. When she got home, she spent her time stomping down the loneliness that filled the hours between work. Only five miles separated her and Deanne—plus her mom's single demand: *Have nothing to do with that eastside trash.*

As much as Elaina missed Deanne, she also longed to see Raphe. He was the brother she'd always wished for, fun, protective, and eager to share another art lesson. She'd phoned several times, but there'd been no answer.

One long afternoon, she pedaled slowly down the sidewalk of the shopping strip, balancing a bag of cleaning supplies on the handlebars of her bike. She could barely see over the bag, but at this pace, pedestrians would have time to get out of her way.

"Hey, Lanie! How goes it?"

She fumbled to a stop to find Raphe peeking over the top of the bag. He relieved her of its weight and helped her with the kickstand, and they embraced like old war buddies.

"You've got a handful here. I just saw your sister at Tasty. Why aren't you hitching a ride with her?"

"Oh, Raphe, it's so good to see you." She squeezed him again, pretending she hadn't heard his last question. "It's going, you know, day by day—same ole, same ole. How are you and Deanne?"

"Actually, I'm glad I ran into you. Come to the jewelers with me. I could use your take on an engagement ring."

She halted, stunned for his news. She'd be the only single gal left on earth.

"This is where you're supposed to say 'congratulations.' Geez, Lanie, say something."

"I'm—surprised and happy. I haven't heard from either of you—"

"It's not like Deanne hasn't tried. The last time, your mom basically told her to drop dead. Deanne swore she'd never call again."

"I had no idea! If it weren't for Deanne, I might be locked up beside Steely."

"You gals better get you versions straight, because Deanne blames herself for hooking you up with Steely in the first place. Your mom's tirade didn't help, either."

She felt her eyes tear up, and he pulled her into a bear hug. "Deanne's going to be so happy to hear this. She misses you terribly. But let's not spoil this occasion with bygones. Karma crossed our paths for another reason, too. I have a job to offer, if you're still looking."

Elaina pulled back. "I'm all ears. And desperate."

"Deal. First, I'll show you the ring. Then we'll get a burger and talk shop."

The large princess-cut diamond he chose was magnificent. Deanne would love its simplicity and show-stopping size, beautifully contradictory, just like her friend. Jealousy threw flames at her joy, mocking Elaina's feeble attempts to put out the fire. It wasn't fair. Deanne had done more drugs, slept with more guys, and stirred up more trouble than anyone, yet talented, responsible, sweet Raphe, who had everything including a wealthy family and a future, wanted her for keeps.

Demeaning her friend's character comforted her momentarily, but it offered no justification for why yet another person had obtained what Elaina wanted most: unconditional love and commitment. She could hear Kurt's voice. *Judging others will only result in feelings of superiority or inferiority, and both will lead to resentments. Enjoy others' successes but remain confident in your uniqueness. Thank creation we're all different; repetition kills magic.*

"She's going to love it! You two are perfect together." Elaina found sincerity in the embers of her envy. "And I'll take you up on that burger to celebrate."

Once they'd eaten all the fries they could hold and Raphe had tossed the last bite of his burger aside, he pushed back, fidgeting.

"About the job." He scratched at the explanation as if it made him squirm. "I'll just come out with it, but let me finish before you say anything. My art instructor needs models for semester finals. He's not crazy about advertising, which can attract desperate people who are too . . . large. The class was asked to watch for someone who could do this kind of work, who appreciates . . . nude art."

Ah, the reason for his hesitation.

"Professional nude models with decent figures are expensive. The art department could afford large-size models if we have no other options, but a smaller frame gives a better perspective of the bone and muscular system. Models are required to stand in dignified positions for two-hour sessions. Of course, there'll be breaks, but it still takes stamina. Professor Nevous wants each model for three classes."

She blinked, keeping her expression carefully neutral.

"It's totally legit. In fact, you'd have to sign contracts. And it pays one hundred dollars an hour. Okay, I'm done."

A hundred dollars an hour! Every mistake she'd ever made had been through impulsiveness. Raphe would never mislead her, but she had to think beyond the money here. But this was almost a week's earnings.

"How many students are in the class? Correction: how many guys?"

"It's advanced art, so there's just eighteen: eleven gals, seven guys, and Professor Nev—"

"And who'll see the finished drawings? Will they be displayed for the whole stinkin' campus to gawk at?"

"We keep our work after it's graded. I can't promise an exceptional one won't be exhibited, but generally, facial features aren't the focus. I doubt you'll recognize yourself in most finished sketches."

She didn't know who was looking back at her in the mirror most days, anyways, thanks to the poor choices she continued making. Maybe this would turn out to be one of her better ones.

* * *

The room was bright behind the pulled shades, but the soft, yellowish illumination eased her nerves. Elaina stood on a platform in the center of the room, naked except for a sheet, easels surrounding her on three sides. Professor Nevous, a formal older man, didn't waste time. His instruction, gentle and efficient, said he'd done this many times, which helped loosen Elaina's knotting stomach.

"Please remove the sheet, and I'll arrange you." He adjusted her as if she were fragile glass, slightly protracting her hands, wrists arched upward and fingers spread. He placed one foot in front of the other, toes extended.

Her misgivings heated her face as she realized she was completely exposed to eighteen strangers. What had she gotten herself into? And just for money? A vague memory of another time she'd exposed herself for money left her hands trembling.

"Elaina," Professor Nevous said, "you must be very still."

"He wants you to stop breathing." Raphe's humor drifted out from behind an easel. Several students chuckled. Their mild manner stated that the human female they saw was good and without shame.

Quiet serenaded the clock's ticking and pencils' scratchings. Elaina's thoughts played hide-and-seek with lovely memories of Imm's art room, the cemetery and picking wild raspberries at its fence row, and runs through the clover field with the club. As she looked around the room, she caught students looking at her as if they were medical scholars studying a cadaver. To them, she was a subject to be duplicated on paper.

Under their earnest gaze, she felt free to analyze her own uncharted emotions. Childhood returned, the days when her exposed body was of no more concern than finances or fashion, when being unconfined by clothing was liberating, and when worry over sexual sin was non-existent. She could hear Imm humming as they flipped through nude art books openly. The naked figures, painted in photographic likeness to the human form, left Elaina in awe of the great wizard of all creation. In that time, nudity meant anatomy, anatomy meant beauty, and beauty was God.

> One's appearance is a reflection of her heart's purity.
> —Sister Immaculata Lefevre

Sex meant only the difference between male and female. Sex was good, by the Master's design. Elaina felt beautiful now as a reflection of the Three's model.

She could hear Imm's voice in her heart. *You are part of the Three, ma precieuse. Your friendship with them is also your friendship with yourself; thus, when you're critical and unkind to yourself, you inflict the same hurts on them.*

The students' furrowed brows gave no indication of artistic arousal, so she feasted her eyes on tubes of paint, jars of brushes, and boxes of oil pastels—a slice of heaven.

Imm had described heaven as complete vulnerability while also the total certainty of one's sacredness and grace. Heaven was free of all binds and coverings, she'd said, where God and man, man and woman, family and community saw each other as different pieces of a puzzle that were all made to fit together. A long time ago, that place had felt real to Elaina, when she was at the grave marker with Mary and the angels. Standing here, the possibility of getting back there seemed obtainable.

Still stiff from posing, Elaina bumped into Professor Nevous as she exited the dressing room.

"I'm pleased with your ability to hold a pose, Miss Michael. Raphe tells me you're a budding artist. Perhaps you'd like to audit our class with the next model. You can watch or try your hand, whichever you please." Not waiting for an answer, the professor walked on.

College art classes! Could it get any better?

She arrived early for the next session. The students milled around with coffee and small talk, in complete disregard of Elaina's nakedness under her sheet. Not one male art student had commented or hit on her after the first class; in fact, they were friendly and seemingly appreciative. Was this for real?

She climbed onto the pedestal and Professor Nevous lifted her arms high, reminding her to grasp the beam when she tired. He twisted her at the waist with her chin resting on her shoulder, assuring her she would receive several breaks from this challenging pose.

Daydreaming helped. Her sister, Kim, and Elaina had had no concern for nakedness as little ones, playing together in the tub for hours. Their bodies were merely tools for experiencing and expressing the joys of living. When had Elaina started worrying that Kim was thinner, her legs longer, and her chest flatter? Why were Elaina's swelling breasts so troubling, and when had shame taken residence in her budding body?

An invisible presence slithered around her tiptoeing thoughts. She tried to shake the troubling flashbacks from her head.

Professor Nevous's tongue clicked. "Be still, please."

Her parents had never prioritized appearances or outstanding accomplishments beyond respectable middle ground. Her dad often said it took boldness to be a nonconformist and find success by your own definition. One day, if she had a daughter, she'd repeat that message, adding that beauty and self-confidence begin in the heart and in doing the things you love.

Like skating. Why had she stopped skating?

Her third modeling session was much easier, lying on her side with her head propped on her palm. She watched the hands of the clock move slowly around the face twice, tethering her impatience. Professor Nevous had invited her to view the student's finished works when they were done.

"Fifteen minutes left. When you leave, your sketches will remain for grading. Before we wrap it up, though, I want to point out Elaina's muscles here." Nevous used a dowel rod to direct the students' focus to her upper thighs. "You'll find how distinctly the sartorius muscles wrap from the center of the upper thigh at an angle rather than . . ."

His mouth continued to move, but Elaina heard nothing over the mental alarms triggered by his pointing stick. Perspiration ran down her back, and the room swirled in a gush of internal sewage. Nausea threatened to bring up the reason.

She repeated Raphe's words in her head. *You're a natural, Elaina. Art is in your blood.* Imm would be so proud upon learning of Elaina's courage in the face of this modeling experience.

The students filed out promptly at the end of the period, with Professor Nevous on their heels. Before closing the door, he called over his shoulder, "Take your time. It's been a pleasure working with you. You're very professional for a first-timer."

Feel the pencil depressions, smell the charcoal, and look beneath the sketches. Immerse all your senses into the energy of their perception. Imagining Imm's words, Elaina's anxiety dissolved in the face of the beautiful being that each drawing depicted. She saw herself from the students' eyes, and the figures that gazed back came alive with the characteristics of her inner child, before a time of self-consciousness and shame. Each nude wore a fluid grace, each the matriarch of her mystique.

There wasn't accuracy in many, but likeness wasn't the point. Each student gave Elaina expression through their personal interpretation. One figure appeared moody, the muscles drawn taut and the jaw clamped. Another looked earthy, as if her nudity was her essence. But the figure Elaina loved most, though more rounded than herself, obviously loved her own shape.

What astounded Elaina most was that she was exquisite in every student's eyes.

Imm had once told her a story about a female model of Picasso's. After inspecting his finished work, she complained that the painting didn't look like her. He replied, "Don't worry, it will with time."

These sketches seemed a promise and prophecy that someday Elaina would love who she was, inside and out. She'd appreciate her short, muscular legs that said more about strength than grace and her small hips that could have belonged to a boy. One day, she'd wear her soft, flabby tummy, with its scar from her firstborn, with pride.

The last sketch on a corner easel had a note attached: "*To Elaina.*" She unfolded it eagerly.

> *My depictions are biased because Deanne told me about your former struggles. You're an incredibly beautiful woman because your heart radiates sensitivity. What courage you have. You're an artist at living. These sketches are for you to keep once they're graded. They come with gratitude from Deanne and from me for your friendship, which has exceeded any before.*
>
> —Raphe

Tears ran as she gazed at Raphe's work. Her palm rested on the scar that ran from her belly downward, and her outstretched fingers tilted upward in the same heartbreaking gesture as Michelangelo's *Pietà.* Only an artist would know the meaning of Mary's outstretched hand in that masterpiece: resigned acceptance at losing her son.

Divine presence, wonder, and peace enveloped Elaina. The Three filled the air with the scent of clover.

Renewing a friendship with the Trinity no longer seemed contingent on her efforts alone. Perhaps this experience was their message that she was dearly loved, wanted, and missed and that her potential for goodness was limitless, as long as she trusted their hopes for her.

* * *

April 15, 1982
Spring has arrived, Imm.
I found them! They were waiting in the strangest place: an art room at Haisting College, where I modeled nude. The fact that I can tell you this with pride says what a wonderful art teacher you are.
At first, I was overwhelmed by self-consciousness, but by the third session, the Three overtook me in their vast, loving embrace. I saw

the Trinity's reflection in every sketch of myself.

The art professor invited me to audit the next class with Haisting's prize freshman runner as the model. Lumumba is on scholarship from Tanzania. Oh, Imm, he's a wonder, with ebony skin stretching so tightly over the most defined muscular system. I tried to replicate his Olympian body, but my sketches weren't doing him justice.

Then, from nowhere, the urge to write overpowered me, yet the words I scribbled were ridiculously limited for the beauty that filled my head. Eventually, I gave up and just listened to the professor lecture. Need fell asleep for the first time in weeks, nursing on grace. I wanted to stay in that moment forever.

Professor Nevous had a weird look when he asked about the random swirls covering my paper. After a moment, he smiled and whispered, "Awe has overshadowed you. Every masterpiece begins with wonder. Without it, attempts to replicate creation are futile. You've been graced with the ability to gaze on nakedness the way the Creator sees our bodies."

Normally a rather dry man, he began passionately addressing the entire class. "A true artist will remain forever a student. Just before dying, Michelangelo wrote in his journal, 'I'm still learning.' Art isn't what we produce but how we live and what we feed our bodies, minds, and souls. What we focus our attention on will flourish."

Here's the strangest part: he'd spoken the word that had filled my head just before. I heard your singsong voice like background music quoting Matthew 6:21: "For where your treasure is, there also will be your heart."

I feel the Three within and all around me now, but it's been so long that conversations with them seem awkward. I want our old friendship back but keep remembering my disloyalty and all the stupid things I've done.

Thank you, Imm, for your faithful and frequent letters. Tell me what you're doing now that the weather is warmer.

All my love,
Elaina

April 26, 1982

Happy spring, ma enfant,

My prayers for your family continue in the loss of your father. Mon père died when I was just a few years older than you. I bore resentments similar to yours because, like you, I was the youngest in our large family, a place where the parent/child relationship often suffers. Appreciation for his wisdom will come with time.

How wonderful to experience being the subject of art as well as the artist. It's good to be the passenger as well as the driver, the audience as well as the speaker, the student as well as the teacher. We must open ourselves to every side of life to learn acceptance and broad-mindedness. You're growing wise, ma poupée. I love watching your soul bloom, even from this distance.

Many years ago, I too had the privilege of being a nude model. It helped me put to rest confusions about my sexuality. Like you, I felt a sacred, beautiful reflection of divinity. Now you understand why pornography is so insulting to human dignity, dismissing one's mind and soul for only that which inspires lust.

No details of your life could cause me to think less of you. As a young woman, I experienced the gift and cross of being young and physically attractive, too. Need's cravings were insatiable and caused me to also make mistakes. I love you just the way you are: passionate, impulsive, and full of Clover.

Remember, Jesus is most compassionate with sinners of the flesh because he knows condemnation is the surest way to turn his beloved ones from truth. "It is not the healthy who need a doctor, but the sick. I have not come for the righteous, but the sinners." (Mark 2:17) Human desires bring the greatest awareness of divine need. Jesus doesn't need to convince the starving of their hunger; it is through our sinfulness that we're most suitable to receive salvation. The Father doesn't tell us to clean up first before coming to him but loves us despite our messes and begs us to come so he can cleanse us.

Now that you feel your Trinity's presence, simply open yourself and receive. "Gifts will be given to you, a good measure, packed together, shaken down, and overflowing, spilling over into your lap." *(Luke 6:38) You cannot rebuild your relationship with them by what you do; give them the hammer and let them carve new facets in your life.*

Maman sits on the sun porch every afternoon sipping wine and watching butterflies as I prune the roses. We must trim away what winter has hardened, if we are to have more numerous and fragrant blossoms. The grapevines' new growth is promising this year, too.

I've never left you in my prayers, and I love you.

Immaculata

* * *

"Oh, excuse me, I habitually hog the middle of the track but—Lumumba?"

The slender runner was already twenty yards ahead, a blur but for the music blaring from his Walkman.

Halfway through Elaina's first lap, he came around again. "Hello to you. Yes, I'm Lumumba."

"Holy cow, you shot past me like the wind. I could still hear your music, though. It's beautiful. What is it?"

"Just a classical arrangement, but I find the harmony intoxicating. It actually makes me feel a little drunk. Run with me, and I'll play you some more."

He slowed to her pace, indulging her questions about the themes and variations of the music. She felt smart in her questions, thanks to Imm. The conversation about classical composers led to their shared experience in modeling, filling the spaces between stretches of heavy breathing. Before her legs tired, they'd already done five laps, one discussion bleeding to another, unusual for strangers.

"Shall we run together Thursday?" he asked.

And so they met every other day at Haisting's track, Lumumba teasing that their leisurely trots between serious training days recharged his legs. Whether by his culture or his education, he gave small talk no place and fired personal questions with such sincerity that it felt like an honor for Elaina to answer. As with Raphe, the intellectual discussions stimulated her old dream of going to college.

"What's holding you back?" he asked.

He shot down each reason she gave. "The quickest route to real-ized dreams is trusting Papa to drive. Too many people grab the wheel, then get lost or wreck and *then* want Papa to steer."

"Papa?"

"God, Yahweh, Abba, Jehovah, Allah—he's everyone's papa," Lumumba said. The Father's only requirement for being part of his family is to love him who is also them completely. Jesus said arguments about whose path to his father is best only distract us. It's more about the effort we make trying to find a direction and our patience and trust while waiting for Jesus to show us the route he wants us to take."

"Once you've been burned, trusting becomes a tall order, though." Elaina slowed to wipe her brow.

"Another excuse. Trust is a choice without guarantees, but real faith can do nothing else. When faith, like love and gratitude, are heartfelt, they can't be silenced. Jesus thanked his father out loud before per-forming miracles because he had complete faith in Papa's generosity. Gratitude before the gift shows the greatest faith, just as trust is better than wishing or hoping. Both wishes and hopes leave room for doubt and make us settle for less."

Easy for him to say, with his athletic skills, a full scholarship—

He must have been reading her thoughts. "Who doesn't think their burden is heaviest? I have the whopper of all excuses, the color of my skin. Poverty is strike two. When people see a poor black man, their suspicion becomes their truth. The only thing they want from me is to prove them accurate. I have to dig myself out of the hole they put me in. Does that exempt me from trusting Papa or justify behaving like a hooligan? I'd only feed their truth, that I'm worthless because of that over which I have no control, my race. If I wait for someone else to pick up my cross, I'll get nowhere because nobody cares about my excuses. But if I try, eventually when people see black skin, they won't assume that person is lazy or morally lacking."

Elaina stopped, reached for Lumumba, and pulled him into a hug. "You're amazing. I love how you see people's equal value while also rec-ognizing their differences. I love your God, too."

Lumumba smiled and turned his music up. "People are the strings, woodwinds, brass, and percussion of God's orchestra. The great maestro gets frustrated when the strings claim they're the most important or the brass insists that everyone play like them. He asks us to concentrate less on our individual parts and work harder to play in harmony."

Lumumba waved goodbye, explaining that he still had several miles to go to complete the day's training.

Lighter steps carried Elaina home in spite of her burning muscles. Surely Lumumba was a gift from the Three, allowing their voice to be heard through his words.

* * *

Mother's Day 1982

Dearest Imm,

You're like a mother to me, so happy Mother's Day. Have a wonderful day with your maman. (Does France celebrate Mother's Day?)

Lumumba had to leave for summer, but on our final run, I found the courage to tell him about Isaac. I was worried what he'd think. It was proof, he said, that the psychological harm of casual sex tops unwanted pregnancies, STDs, and so on.

"Our bodies were designed to play the notes of love, but sex without love is only a screech," he said.

He began a story about a lanky adolescent boy who was constantly taunted for his virginity. When that kid gave his frustrations to God while running, God not only showed him that real men prove their masculinity by exercising virtue—Lumumba said the Latin "vir" means man—but that God also gave that kid a track scholarship in the United States, at Haisting College.

Lumumba thinks that the celebratory attitude toward uncommitted sex is the largely to blame for the AIDS crisis. "My job is to protect every woman's holiness as if she were my intended bride. And you deserved a real man too, Elaina, not a sex-starved weakling."

Cassy Adams asked me to babysit her newborn. At first, it angered me. I wasn't good enough for a wedding invitation, but now I was suitable when she needed a favor. Then it occurred to me this might be Cassy's olive branch.

I thought I'd arrived at peace over giving Isaac away. Having made such a mess of the last two years, I know he's better off with another mother. When I held Cassy's baby, though, the old ache tore open. Days later, my sister Kim had a boy. He's so beautiful, but I still can't hold him. I'd lose my sanity.

It's so hard, Imm, especially today when another woman is celebrating being Isaac's mom. Everywhere I go, I study each little boy for something to identify him as my firstborn, until I see his contentment in his mother's arms. It reminds me that Isaac isn't mine. If I could see him happy, just once, maybe I could let go.

One day I'll get to Grasse, and the Clover Club can hang out in your rose fields and eat chocolate-covered raspberries. Meanwhile, I'll continue to look for work and sock away my housecleaning money toward college. I will get there.

All my love,
Elaina

18

Tarrock's unemployment had reached eighteen percent, but Elaina managed to parlay her housekeeping experience into a position with the state Family Services as a nanny. It broke her heart to watch financially struggling moms have to leave their children in the care of a stranger deemed suitable by another stranger. Most were single women with children from different fathers, beautiful babies resulting from attempts to feed Need feigned love.

Lust will lie to gain sexual fulfillment, and Need will believe the lies to feed the heart. —Sister Immaculata Lefevre

At the hospital the day after Isaac's birth, Imm had mentioned the day Elaina's puzzle would be complete. Elaina realized that a picture was beginning to emerge from those who'd influenced her life thus far: her parents, the Clover Club, Cole, Isaac, Kurt, Lumumba, Raphe, Deanne, and so many more. Whether each was a rose or a thorn, they all wore the face of the Trinity as she whispered gratitude for their friendships and life lessons.

Need's hunger was pacified by the satisfaction of her new job. Her heart warmed in the pleasure of mothers who arrived home exhausted to find the kids fed and bathed and the house spotless.

All things are fulfilling when done out of love because love removes all burdens. –Sister Immaculata Lefevre

Elaina had been working for Penny, a single mother of three, for over a month now. Unlike some, Penny didn't take Elaina for granted.

"I'm home," Penny called, closing the door. Her kids scampered to the kitchen and wrapped themselves around her.

How must it feel to own a child's pure love? Joy and misery tangled each time Penny arrived home to little arms so eager for their mother's embrace. Elaina retreated quietly, hoping to leave without interrupting the holiest moment any woman could wish for.

"Wait a minute," Penny called. "I've been rehearsin' this speech for the last two hours and need to get it out. I know Family Services doesn't pay squat, and the kids told me you've brought groceries in several times after I've left."

Penny took Elaina's hand and pulled her down on the chair beside her. "I've been lookin' for a way to thank you, and I think I finally found it: a big-ass payin' job this weekend. You interested?"

"Could you tell me more? If the pay's so huge, there has to be a reason."

"It's pourin' beer at a swap meet."

Alarms went off in Elaina's head at the mention of beer. "What's a swap meet?"

"Like a festival or a flea market, lots of bikers selling biker stuff. Wild but harmless. All you gotta do is pour and mind your business."

In her experience, bikers spelled worse news than beer. Putting the two together meant sure trouble. Her mind flashed with highlights of the drug bust and the bikers still squatting at Steely's apartment.

"We'd start at nine for eight to ten hours, but time'll fly 'cause it'll be crazy busy," Penny continued. "Nine dollars an hour plus tips. And tips are where the real money is. Once those bikers get loosened up, gratuities rain. Wouldn't surprise me if we clear three hundred each."

Three hundred dollars would go a long way toward college, but not if she got herself into a bind in some sketchy situation. What to do?

She prayed she wouldn't regret this. "Okay, I'm in."

Penny gave her a long, evaluating look. "What you wear makes a difference in tips. If you dress too skimpy, you'll look like a biker chick and be treated the same. But if you dress too frumpy, well, that's no good either." She pointed to Elaina's baggy sweats.

Elaina frowned. No way was she going to dress like a tramp again. "Suggestions?"

"I'm not sure. I've never done this before, either. Maybe jeans and a snug tee, but it's gonna be so hot. Something comfortable, cool, and girly. Maybe a sundress?"

Elaina's struggle to find the right outfit continued the rest of the week, right up until the moment Penny arrived to pick her up. Should she preserve her commitment to decency, or dig through the sleazy clothes she had packed away? Her right brain said college would bring dignity and respectability, while the left side reminded her which out-fit would earn tuition fees the quickest.

The doorbell decided for her. She threw on the sundress already in her hand.

The huge swap meet at the old raceway held more Harley Davidsons than she'd ever seen in one place. An old Honda Scrambler leaned against an outbuilding with a sign above: A Dollar a Pop. Several sledgehammers lay beside it, and fifty or more unshaven men stood in line for a chance to put a dent in the already dilapidated, foreign-made motorcycle. How many of these idiots didn't have jobs yet were flushing money on this?

Stands selling T-shirts, motorcycle parts, riding accessories, and greasy carnie food circled a flatbed semitrailer that served as a stage for the emcee and bands. Beer trucks dotted every space in between.

Penny and Elaina were quickly instructed on how to pour and where to collect their pay at the end of the day. "You can stagger a half-hour lunch if help shows up. If not, you'll have to manage, 'cause there's no way one of you can handle this crowd alone," the beer truck owner shouted over the noise. "Be careful. It *will* get rowdier."

Elaina grinned confidently. *Nothing to worry about, boss man.* She wouldn't be caught dead leaving this spot. Her thin denim wrap dress now seemed ridiculously flimsy for this environment, which more appropriately called for armor and a chastity belt. She gasped the first time a topless woman strolled past on the arm of her owner, drawing raunchy remarks from gawkers. Though drawing attention seemed to

be the purpose in leading their bare-chested pets around, the domina-
tors shook angry fists at those who commented.

Their displays of sexism sickened Elaina.

"Their masculinity is defined by how thoroughly they can repress
their women," she whispered to Penny.

"That's nothing. Some rent their girlfriends out for an hour or two
in exchange for bike parts and leathers. Just concentrate on the money."

How, after everything she'd witnessed at Steely's, was she still so
easily shocked? The depths these women had allowed themselves to
sink gave new definition to self-sabotage. They mud-wrestled in the
skimpiest of swimsuits, ripping them off each other on their masters'
orders. The men placed bets on the winner while standing far enough
away to prevent flying mud from soiling their new riding leathers. The
women were held in no higher regard than roosters or bulldogs. The
urge to rip their chokers off almost overwhelmed Elaina. They were
like dog collars, with the boyfriend's name engraved on a dangling tag.

Queasiness churned and premonitions of evil loomed every time
her glance met the edge of the woods, where couples copulated like
animals. Other bikers watched in groups, laughing and salivating, grabbing at each others' binoculars.

*The dark one laughs when humanity looks upon each other only for
the sexual benefit.* —Sister Immaculata Lefevre

Stiff taps made it difficult to control the flow of the beer, and the
tall plastic cups left too much room for foam. As much beer spilled
onto Elaina and the ground as into the cups. The smell of warm beer,
perspiration, and depravity hung on a smog of cigarettes and pot. As
the morning wore on, complaints about too large a beer head settled
into impatience for a quick refill.

Close to noon, Penny handed Elaina a sandwich. "Find some shade
and eat this PB and J. It's not the greatest, but it's the only thing I could
make that won't spoil in the heat."

Exhausted, Elaina didn't argue. She looked about for someplace
close but discreet enough where she could count the tips that bulged

in the lining of her dress.

"Take your tips to the ticket booth," Penny said, reading her thoughts. "They'll trade your small bills for twenties so you don't have such a wad. I'm already up over a hundred."

The beer she'd seen consumed before lunchtime was mind-boggling, like the heinous dark ages when orgies, drink, and overindulgence were the order of the day. Was she an accomplice to this barbarism, making money from their gluttony? Apprehension rumbled as Elaina perceived the mark of the beast in every direction. She felt slimy. Her mind begged forgiveness, trying to explain to her Three the reason she was here: college, a career, a decent life—

Imm's most recent letter sounded in her heart. *Be still and know that they are with you. It's your trust that comes and goes.*

Elaina squinted at the sky behind for some indication of their presence until a familiar face blocked the view.

"Steely? Steely!"

Her heart leaped from the wicked place the throngs of bikers and the blinding sun held her captive in. As long as he was here, she was safe. Despite the tribulations of last January, she knew he'd protect her with his last breath should anyone even look at her sideways.

Thirty pounds thinner and with skin just a shade lighter than Lumumba's, Steely's hair was braided the way she'd once done it, in two tails hanging almost to his waist. His physique, so powerful beneath the once soft exterior, reminded her of a warrior returning from victorious battle.

He picked her up high and swung her around. Need lunged for his inviting eyes. Though she knew a yes could hurl her back to the place she'd barely escaped, her heart loved Steely's arms more.

"Oh, Elaina, Dolly, look at you! Beautiful girl!" His words swept her beyond reason, as did the deep kiss he took as his due. "I've been watchin' you all morning. You look so hot, both ways if ya get my drift." He winked and tugged at the tie on her dress. "I oughta unwrap you right now."

"I double-knotted it for a reason," she shot a wink back, Need gobbling his garbage. "Seriously, Steve, I'm not who you remember. When did you get out? Why haven't I seen you around?"

"Shh, Elaina, too many questions." He kissed her again. "Waiting for this moment was the only thing that got me through lockup. I was released early for good behavior. The prison is so full, they'd shorten anyone's stay for a pretty smile. Oh, if those swines knew—"

His eyes flashed hatred, and just as quickly, his boyish grin returned.

"Do a line with me." He guided her toward the parking lot. "We can't talk over this noise."

Misgivings stirred in Need as much as Elaina. That he'd been watching over her all morning was reassuring, but drugs? Never again. She recalled the bruises so severe she had to lie for time off work, only to stay home and abuse the drug more—and then coming down: chills, shakes, hallucinations . . .

"I don't know what's been harder on you, babe, slingin' beers or watchin' the bikers socialize," he chuckled dryly. "Your pinched face has 'Saint Augustine princess' written all over it. Just do a little snort to soften those ugly wrinkles."

Wow, had his sense of humor always been so viciously sarcastic? "Coming down was horrible last time. I don't want—"

"That's what this is for." Steely slipped a tiny square of paper between her lips. "It's like a lick-and-stick tattoo from the gumball machines. Fixes everything. Now, what were you askin'?"

She couldn't remember. Her head emptied of everything as buildings and landscapes turned upside down, then flipped back up. She could see the trees breathing, exhaling colors that blended into indescribable shades. Joy was a flock with tiny, jeweled wings that went fluttering everywhere, even landing on Elaina's arms. Steely cursed, swatting them away until Elaina begged, "Let them go. They're beautiful."

"You're so easy, Elaina."

Why wasn't he calling her Dolly?

"Damn it, you're wasting my stash. Put your head back till your nose stops dripping."

She inhaled through her numb throat. It felt as if frozen rain was surging through her veins. "It's like the temperature dropped thirty degrees. I can touch my happiness."

She turned around slowly, her heart glittering in his company and pumping shiny feelings through her body. "Can we leave? I want you to myself. These bikers make me feel icky. I'll take you out to eat anywhere you want."

"You too good for bikers, Saint Elaina?" There it was again, that nasty tone. She wanted to be called Dolly.

He pulled her closer, but it felt more of a yank. "We're stayin', but you're done pourin' beers."

"Okay, but just a little while. I should help Penny eventually." Worry, gritty and uncomfortable, blew away with the dust sparkling in the breeze. "You look wonderful, like you've been working out in the sun."

"Like a slave. They made us carry . . ."

Steely's tirade about River Rock Reformatory saddened her, not the words but his facial expressions. The creases around his eyes looked jagged and dripped muddy sweat. Spit from his loud, indiscernible curses exploded against her, cutting through her happiness like shards of glass.

Colors flashed and sounds intensified as he led her back into the crowd. The urge to laugh brought another lopsided recollection: Deanne's shrill laughter on the way to Ron's boat. Had Deanne used a tongue tattoo that night? Paranoia and elation brawled like the women in the mud, splattering her lovely, clean mood. Thundering drums pulsated in the sky, and the clouds mimicked her emotions, dark and then bright, in strange, twisting forms.

Steely yanked harder, impatient for her rubbery legs to keep up while steering her through throngs of people. His face registered recognition of so many they passed, a nod to one and a scowl to another. His grin seemed to lead the crowd's happiness, and when hostility filled his eyes, the mob wore an angry frown, as if he conducted everyone's mood.

The sun left a chilly blast on her sweat-soaked shoulders. She gratefully drew from Steely's flask of honey-color liquid. Whiskey? Ginger ale? It was wet, so whatever.

A dozen or more girls onstage laughed and screamed as a man sprayed them with . . . glass? Liquid diamonds burst from a hose, glistening in the air before soaking their filmy T-shirts and making their breasts translucent like the angels on the ceiling of the Sistine Chapel.

Elaina was in heaven. That's why everyone was dancing. Dancing would make Steely happy, too, like when they'd danced at Sixes.

The emcee's voice sounded like an old 45 vinyl record set on low, then rapid and high as if he'd inhaled helium. He continued to call something Elaina couldn't understand, making her laugh harder. Why wasn't Steely laughing?

He pulled her up the stage steps impatiently, and the angels flew away. Applause exploded—for her! Though she wasn't sure why they loved her, it made her ecstatic. As he raised her arm to the crowd's praise, she squinched her eyes, unable to make anything out but a sea of heads below intense sunlight.

"Showgirl, showgirl!" The emcee led the mob's chant to the rhythm of the drums. Their clapping caused the air to tremble. "Dance, showgirl, dance."

Swoosh. Silver cut through the sunlight like a shooting star and sliced down her side.

Her sundress lay on the stage floor. Steely tossed the tie into the crowd. Trees, clouds and the crowd's shrill call spun in a cyclone that rose from the bowels of hell: "Dance, showgirl, dance!"

Delusion smashed into reality as awareness waterboarded her. The knife moved to her hips as the mob's beastly howl grew hysterical.

The world went black.

Steely's face, inches away. Angry. Something slapped her in the face. Men in white coats, floating above.

"Elaina, you've gotta get up!" The fog wouldn't clear for an explanation of what her eyes took in. "Stand up and refuse treatment. Once you're in the ambulance, I can't help. They'll find drugs in you, and we'll both get busted."

Steely's words gurgled beneath the dull thud of her heart as if from underwater. If she was alive, then who were these people in white?

"*Elaina.*" Steely pinched her arm so hard she winced. "Get up. If they take you to Grace, you'll be slapped with another hospital bill. Is that what you want?"

Those magic words brought her to shaky feet, each step a

concentrated effort. This place certainly wasn't a hospital and the loosely hanging thing that barely covered her looked more like a dress than a hospital gown. All she knew was that she had to get to Isaac before they took him away.

Steely's support was rough and hurried. People jumped out of the way as he cursed and threatened. Everyone was staring at the commotion she'd created.

"Slow down," she begged, struggling to maintain her balance, hold her dress closed, and arrange the piecemeal events not yet connected.

They stumbled into the parking lot, and Steely shoved her to the ground. "You stupid whore, fakin' that blackout could have landed me back in jail."

His foot rammed into her back, and the pieces snapped together. She'd chosen this hell. She'd willingly followed the monster here.

"Why, Steve?" she asked, not really wanting the answer. "Why'd you give me—whatever it was that made me feel like this? Why would you cut off my dress in front of . . . of . . . What've I done to deserve this?"

Where was the vulnerable, hurting little boy who'd stirred her sympathy before? Who owned this face, twisted in malice, as ugly and hateful as the troll who'd raped Deanne? His breath came in short snorts, and his curses rolled from a forked tongue.

"Your innocent act doesn't cut crap with me. You're a whore, and you know it. While I marked time in that stinkin' jail, forgivin' your refusal to defend me, countin' the hours until I'd hold you again, you were posin' nude for a buncha rich Haisting boys. You'll do anything for money, won't you? After I heard, the only thing that kept me from goin' crazy was plannin' how I'd teach you a lesson."

The demon inside him grabbed her hair. "Posin' for rich art students ain't no different than gettin' naked for this crowd. I fixed it so you'll never be able to sell yourself to those fat cats again. Now nobody's gonna want you."

He let go, and she reeled back.

His depraved smile turned menacingly sweet. "Believe it or not, I still want you, though, Dolly. Move to the lake with me, and we'll make Tarrock and today ancient history. I'll keep you in style—but this time, I'm callin' the shots."

She lunged at him, no longer caring what he did in return. The worst had already happened. There was nothing ahead to lose.

She went for his face, scratching like a cornered cat. "I'll never go with you. You'll have to kill me first."

A massive, tattoo-covered man trotted in their direction. "Hey, everything all right?"

Steely backed away, his face striped with blood and apprehension. He held both hands up, and his tone took on deference. "No worries, man, no worries. You know how they are when they got too much party. I'll think this bitch needs to chill. How 'bout you give me a lift and let me buy you a beer?"

Steely never looked back as the truck pulled away.

Her hands shook, and her thoughts flashed in and out of focus, making it impossible to figure out what to do next. Only one fact stood clear: word of this afternoon would reach Tarrock before she could hitch a ride home.

Faltering steps took her to the raceway exit. She continued down the first byway she saw. How far she walked or even if headed in the direction of Tarrock didn't matter. Where would she go once she got there, anyway?

Dust blowing off the fields made her eyes feel grainy and tongue taste like sandpaper. Heartache throbbed, keeping rhythm with her despair.

"Hey, Elaina," someone called from the passenger window of a beat-up Chevy. "Need a lift?"

She ignored the offer until a faltering clutch lurched the car back and then forward again in step with her. Names floated at the edge of her memory. Chuck? Butch? The two who'd used Steely's newly sewn pillows to rest their oily boots on? Hairy images scampered: their vulgar tattoos, their obscene comments as they blocked her running path, the motorcycle throttles that violated the neighborhood peace.

"You look like crap, girl. You know how hot it is? Climb in before you drop dead."

Surviving or dropping made little difference, but her exhaustion couldn't turn down the offer.

Chuck handed her a beer, seemingly concerned. "Wanna smoke one? Might help."

She shook her head, careful not to make eye contact. She clutched her dress tighter. Had they seen her on the swap meet stage? They couldn't have, or they'd have already said something.

Brain freeze pierced her temples, but thirst accepted a second and third icy beer. Chuck handed them back as fast as she finished them, yet their conversation continued as if she weren't there. Grateful to be ignored, she considered where to ask to be dropped off. Should she say something now and risk drawing unwanted attention?

Chuck laughed as they pulled into Saint Augustine Cemetery. "The magic of a couple beers. You look much better. Maybe you can dance for us now, showgirl."

Goosebumps chilled her hot skin.

"A couple beers? I think she's downed five," Butch said with a sneer.

She tried to open the car door as they pulled deeper into the grave-yard. It wouldn't budge.

"You'll have to use a front door if you want out," Chuck said ominously.

The other door was locked or jammed as well. She'd gotten in the back passenger's door? Random pieces of information wedged between any semblance of a solid plan.

Four hands grabbed her, and panic made the effort to break free cumbrous, as if she were trying to run in deep water. They pinned her quickly. Her dress fell open, and a jackknife sliced off her panties, as Steely had attempted to do onstage.

Butch yanked her ankles up, his moves so efficient she didn't think to scream or fight until the hot spear of Chuck entered her. Shuddering and begging him to stop provoked his thrusts to a frenzy. Surely the next ram would puncture her lungs.

Her screams came in a coughing wheeze as terror squeezed her chest. She gasped for the foul air he expelled above. The intense pain and degradation of this moment frightened her less than the invisible snake constricting around her airway.

Butch yanked her ankles higher and farther apart, as if he were splitting a wishbone.

The world went black again.

Choking attempts to extract air from the putrid confines of the car brought her back to consciousness. She was facedown in the back seat, the sticky paws of a beast pulling at her hips. Fresh air caressed her behind and made its way up to her gasping mouth.

Butch's monstrous form blocked her escape. He crammed her head into the seat, the filthy upholstery hindering the release of vomit. Frantic for breath, she jerked, provoking more curses from behind her. Butch shoved her face deeper into the stench of cigarettes, beer, and mold. A protruding spring jabbed into her forehead.

Her mother was just a block away, waiting for her arrival, but Elaina had gone to hell.

Another joust from behind shot fire through Elaina's racked body. She couldn't separate revulsion for what he was doing from the pain. This wasn't intercourse. Did humans really indulge in such an act? Animals didn't. Horror took full possession of her senses.

He gored her with fury, releasing a vile creature who tore her with his enormity.

"You gotta stop, man. Her ass is bleedin' like a French whore."

"Not until I've gotten off, God damn it," Butch swore. "You got her first. Now it's my turn."

"I'm serious. Stop. I'll pick up the tab for a visit to ole Sally. You need the real thing. Let's dump this bitch and get the hell out of here."

The engine started and the car lurched forward, leaving Butch no choice.

They threw her limp body not a hundred feet from her father's grave.

19

The battle to restore her breathing was almost more than Elaina could manage. Oh God, she needed her inhaler. Willing her mind to go blank, she concentrated on drawing deep breaths. When she'd released the last drop of bile and the coughing subsided, so did her detachment. Manic sobs constricted her lungs, and the choking returned.

She had to be silent, or someone might find her. Her shoes and underwear were gone, her dress bloody and hopelessly torn. This had to be a nightmare, yet the blood oozing from her forehead and down her inner thighs proved her wrong, as did the purple handprints beginning to swell on her legs and arms. Everything throbbed, but nowhere more than her backside, making it excruciating to sit up. The deep ache where her legs joined her hips caused her to wonder if they were broken.

Early evening, marked by long shadows, cooled the grass and a breeze turned her shivers to spasms. She crawled behind a large headstone so Mary and the angels, just to the east, couldn't see her.

She begged the dead to pull her under.

Eerie silence and the setting sun swallowed daylight, dragging with it her will to live. The world was too hideous a place. But death would mean sure damnation.

Voices from childhood called out insults, but *Let's dump the bitch and get the hell out of here* repeated the loudest.

Another voice stole her back to the summer after first grade.

* * *

As if she were watching a movie, she gazed at her child-self smoothing mud pies in her mother's garden. She could hear the little girl's thoughts. *Why had Kim and Lacey shooed her away again?* The same voice as before called again, and little Elaina followed its direction. It was Eric in the barn. He wanted to play with her! There wasn't a kid on the street who wouldn't jump through fire to be sought out by Eric.

"Wanna make some money and buy tons of candy? We'll split what we earn."

The only thing better than penny candy was Eric to share it with. A master of money-making schemes, he constantly found new ways to get ahead. Thanks to his cunning, the plots generally involved minimal effort, too.

"What are we going to do?" She clapped her hands in excitement.

He pulled her deeper into the barn and closed the sliding door, making the windowless outbuilding a murky haze. Sunlight penetrated slats of siding like grabbing golden fingers.

"All you gotta do is stand here and wait quietly. We don't want Kim and Lacey in on this, do we?"

No Lacey? But Eric had a crush on her. As the oldest neighborhood girl, Lacey was Eric's only competition for know-hows and know-alls. Kim and Lacey were inseparable from the first day of summer until autumn's first day back to school. This made Kim Eric's second favorite. Her older brother and sister's bond was solidified in their father's special affection, making it a distinct honor to be chosen as Eric's partner in crime.

"I'll round up the guys and have them stand here." Eric drew a line on the dusty floor just beyond sunlight's creepy fingers. "Do exactly what I say."

The thrill of it made the little girl squeak, this mysterious scheme balanced between mischief and daring.

The boys filed in front of the slivers of sunlight, rendering their faces unrecognizable. She knew David and Mickey by height, the three of them having walked to school together since kindergarten. Sometimes Elaina even played with them at recess. Maybe they would include her more now that she was Eric's collaborator.

The last boy in closed the door, leaving a crack. Eric pulled Mickey over. "You watch. If anyone comes, whisper 'run' and we'll get out the back door—except you, Elaina. Pretend like you're playing or something."

Disappointment weighed on the seven-year-old's shoulders. Why couldn't she run with them? Sometimes Eric played tricks on her. Was this another?

He shined a flashlight at her. "Take your shorts and underwear off. Hurry."

She must have heard wrong. Good girls never let boys see *that* body part. She didn't know why, but some nevers should never be questioned. Her uncertainty, a sure sin in itself, couldn't surpass her worry over angering Eric.

"Do it now or we'll make you go inside the Brommel house alone. You want that?"

The abandoned house at the end of their street was haunted by tormented ghosts. Every story of the murders that stained its walls filled her head. Tears blurred the barn's haze further, but she dared not cry. She was already labeled as the neighborhood bawl-baby. Refusing Eric's demand would bring lifelong exclusion because he was the leader of all neighborhood activities, and summer was a long time to spend alone.

Slowly, she pulled her shorts and panties down.

As Eric focused the flashlight between her legs, eight boys' breaths sucked in as one.

"I told you that's what it looks like."

"Like a knife gash," the oldest Hoffbrow boy whispered.

"And it bleeds every full moon," Eric proclaimed, proud of the shock he'd conjured.

Elaina panicked. She would bleed? When? To death?

"Sit down and spread your legs," Eric ordered. He shined the light directly on her privates and used a stick to point, the same way Sister Katherine and Ruth directed their rulers at maps. "That's where babies come out. You can touch it for another quarter."

"Kim and Lacey are coming," one of the boys whispered. Run!"

Before the girls reached the barn, the boys had vanished, leaving

Elaina as wide-eyed as a deer caught in headlights.

"It's just Elaina," Kim said dismissively.

The girls moved on to find the neighbors.

Elaina sat as still as a mouse in the gloom. When was she allowed to come out? How would she ever face the neighbor boys? It was going to be a long summer.

Eric leaned in the barn what seemed like hours later. "You still in there? Here's a quarter." The tossed coin missed her by several feet and rolled into a dark corner. "If you tell anyone, we'll all swear we had no idea you were going to pull your pants down. Then you'll be the one in trouble."

She didn't want the quarter any more than a child with flu wants chocolate. It would be a sin of omission to pretend she was still a good girl.

Maybe if she cleaned the barn, God would let her keep this a secret.

* * *

Though she didn't know it, the slithering sensation inside her stomach whenever Eric came near had a name: shame. Elaina found countless ways to avoid him to make being at home tolerable. Dinner time was the exception. His leering eyes refused to leave her newly budding chest. The only accepted excuse for skipping meals was cleaning, which helped her find dirt in places even her mother wouldn't have thought to look.

She lay in bed sweating, not a sigh of a breeze to thin the humidity in her tiny room. Upon her mother's insistence, the bedroom windows and door were open in hopes of circulating the evening's cooler breeze.

Tomorrow was the last gym class of fifth grade. She mentally reviewed the excuses she'd already used to get out of the dreaded class; repeats might be questioned. Disappointing Jesus with her weekly fabrications was far less bothersome than scrunching in the corner while changing to hide her swelling breasts from the other girls' curious eyes. She hated the lumps, which seemed to grow like Pinocchio's nose. If only she could bind her chest like Chinese women did their feet.

Then there was her shabby, rib-hugging underwear, gray from wear,

to amplify her embarrassment. Why wasn't she allowed to wear flow-
ered satin bikinis like everyone else? "Granny panties, granny panties,"
the other girls chanted.

The worst of gym class, though, was running laps. Since her chest
had begun flopping, the boys snickered and mimicked the sway of her
breasts.

A pattern of soft footsteps announced Eric before he snaked into
her room. Her breath instinctively quickened.

"Shh," he whispered. "Boy, do I have a story for you. Dad's so mad."

He nudged the door closed and knelt beside her narrow bed. Elaina
pulled the sheet up.

"It's so hot in here," Eric pulled it back down. "My room's cooler.
Take my bed, and I'll sleep on the floor."

"I'm not hot, and I was almost asleep." She turned her back to him,
tugging at her short nightshirt.

"Kim's so in the doghouse." He rested his hands on her stomach
and described how Kim had dragged the hose over her father's new,
costly seedlings, sparing no detail of their dad's tirade. Somewhere during his account, his hand crept to her breasts. Distress warned her to
protest, but curiosity begged to hear the rest of the story.

"Perfect Kim wasn't Dad's golden girl today." Eric's hand moved
downward.

Recollections of her shame in the barn loosened from their deep
hiding place as his fingers entered the place where babies came out.
Lacey said sometimes boys put something else in there too. Was Eric
going to do that?

"I'll scream if you don't stop." She wondered if she had the nerve.

"And then how will you explain what you started? I'm in *your*
bedroom."

He had a point. Who'd believe her over Eric?

He came to her room almost every night after that, pretense no
longer necessary now that he'd backed her into a corner. Even so, he
continued with his phony flattery and lies, partnered with the abuse
of his hands. Each night, his sweet talk grew more saccharine as the
roughness of his hand intensified.

Counting the nails along the ceiling trim or picturing herself in Imm's art room, Elaina attempted to make a mental escape from his entrapment, but after months of his abuses, even pretending to be at the cemetery with her club friends no longer helped.

Maybe his violations were punishment for the satisfaction she'd felt in hearing about Kim's trouble that first night. And now, in trespassing at the borders of the sixth commandment, dirty deeds with boys, she'd collaborated in a much greater sin than the silence and denial of the barn humiliation. Her Three, who knew all, must be so angry and ashamed of her. That must be the reason they remained absent, even from her mind.

She had to be firmer with him.

"If you touch me again, I'll tell," she insisted.

Eric smirked. "Even if you had the guts, Dad will know it's your fault 'cause you've got boobs now. That's when girls start doing dirty stuff."

Was that why Kim never did wrong, because she was flat-chested? Her mother was, too, and she knew her mom never sinned. Maybe it really was her assets, as her dad and brothers called breasts, that made Eric do those bad things. Maybe they were the reason she liked to imagine being kissed by Joey in science class. Sister Ruth said kissing is the start of wickedness.

When Eric dared another visit, she told her parents, braced for their questions, anger, or blame. Instead, they dismissed her from the room without a word. She'd anticipated everything but this, leaving her feeling even more forsaken.

That evening at the dinner table, her dad asked his last four children if they understood the sixth commandment. Without waiting for an answer, he passed them a grim dialogue of strange words: licentiousness, fornication, incest, lechery, and masturbation. Elaina felt more confused than before.

Only the last of his lecture stuck: "A girl will never have to worry for her purity if she places a quarter between her knees and doesn't let it drop." He looked hard at Elaina and added something about cows who give their milk for free.

What did cows and quarters have to do with her brother's vile infringements? Eric was right; her dad did blame her.

"We'll not speak of this again."

By the sharpness of his tone this must include confession, too. The fourth commandment: honor thy father and mother, demanded her lips remain sealed.

* * *

By eighth grade, changing for gym had finally lost its humiliation. She could buy her own underclothing now that her dad was paying her for taking over her mom's household tasks. With laundry a part of her chores and her mother at the nursery all day, her satin-and-lace barely-theres could go unnoticed. At school, the other girls' figures had finally caught up, and they flaunted them with frilly trim peeking out from the lowest necklines the nuns would tolerate. At slumber parties, pretty, colorful lingerie were the uniforms of acceptance.

Elaina's confidence grew along with her pricey collection of personals until the day she found her pink satin bra and panty set buried in the laundry. She hadn't worn them, and Saint Kim would never wear such things, nor would they have fit her slender frame.

Her gut twisted as she approached Eric's room to put the clean laundry away. She nudged the door open with the basket. The air reeked of beer and marijuana, and she could hear a soft, rhythmic beat. She flicked on the light switch.

There was Eric, wearing another of her bra and panty sets, masturbating on his bed. Her heart stopped as Eric eyes locked with hers. He laughed, then climaxed, and Elaina screamed and ran.

Later, when she was sure he was gone, she snuck back into his room dreading what she'd find. Several sets of her personals and a bathing suit were wadded in his bottom drawer, their use obvious. So now her space and belongings were Eric's prey, too, which left her in greater distress than his previous violations.

Her threats only enticed more perversions. They both knew she wouldn't tell. If her parents learned she wore anything but modest cotton tighty-whities, she'd receive the blame.

One evening, she found him on her bed naked but for her bra, waiting for her stunned devastation to stimulate his excitement. But Elaina refused to be his victim anymore and stammered the details to her parents, praying they wouldn't ask for proof. They'd never understand the mortification in granny panties.

Her mother excused herself, an unreadable expression on her face, leaving the matter to her husband.

"I'll take care of it," her father said simply, his expression as stony as his voice.

It wasn't an overdue library book or clogged drain. Eric's actions were deviant. Wasn't *it* worthy of her parents' rage and disgust? Wasn't she worthy of their protection, even if it meant punishing Eric?

The next day, her dad mounted a lock on her door and gave her clipped instructions to use it whenever she left her room. And that was that.

With no recourse, the dark place inside her would have to store this affront, too. She mopped up the ugly details, including her painful emotions, and dumped them into the pit within herself. She bolted the door on uglies, hoping never to have to deal with them again.

* * *

But here in the cemetery, bloodied and defiled beyond anything memory or comprehension could summon, the uglies flooded out once more. Mary and the angels' shadows, faint but morbidly tall, loomed like gruesome giants.

Elaina shivered in fascinated horror at the visions that had escaped her mind. So Eric was the faceless demon that slithered whenever anything of sexual nature arose. It was his violations that marked the infancy of her shame.

She hated her body, the tool she'd used to gain the devotion she longed for but that brought abuse instead. Had Eric's violations paved the road to the godforsaken hell of today? Any hope for a fresh start would be gone once Tarrock learned what had happened today. And she'd never get her Three back, much less find a husband and have a family.

Sex was the filthiest, most animal act God ever put upon humanity. How could he be so depraved as to make it necessary for the creation of a baby? He was the twisted one. No wonder her mom always
looked unhappy, spending a lifetime in "duty"—sexual servitude—to
produce the Michael family.

Her Three couldn't be the same wacko God that members of Saint
Augustine worshiped. They couldn't be capable of such hideous con-
tradictions. She didn't want to be Catholic nor spend her life in holy
wedded obligation.

The sun was almost down. If only she could shower and boil her
putrid body in bleach and ammonia, a suicidal cleansing. Her obsession for cleanliness appeared transparent now as a way to control her
immediate surroundings, the only thing she could manage to keep pure.

A hundred feet away rested her father's body. His soul had witnessed
her rape from heaven's view. He'd been wrong two years ago; today was
his final shame. She would promise him now, on this sacred ground
she'd desecrated, that she would never be intimate with another man.

She gave him only one thanks, and that was for forcing her to relinquish Isaac. She wasn't fit to be a mother, although that was actually
his fault for having given her such limited affection. He wasn't worthy
of being called a father any more than the one who insisted the world
call him Heavenly Father. She hated them both for doing nothing to
stop those animals.

Why hadn't they intervened?

20

July 18, 1982
Ma chére enfant,

On your firstborn's second birthday, I pray time has brought you peace regarding his future. I'll always to be with you in prayer on this day. Enclosed is a memento: preserved roses. Look at the bases; they blush the same shade as little Elaina's cheeks when she used to play in the snow. You're *ma rose jaune avec un cœur rouge*, my yellow rose with a red heart.

Utter dread came over me last weekend, somehow connected to you. I feared to call your mother and cause alarm in case my imagination had taken flight. After beseeching the Trinity's intervention, calmness washed over me. I believe our grace-filled bond allows me to sense both goodness and malevolent that enter your life, and I know when you're in need of intercession. Tell me you're safe.

Maman is in assisted care and eager to join the Lord. My sisters from Sisters of Mary, Mother of God, will take possession of the farm when Maman is safe in heaven. I'll continue to reside here, overseeing chores. My childhood home will serve as my sister's getaway, which brings me great joy.

I've never left you in my prayers, and I love you.

Immaculata

Elaina unfolded a carefully prepared packet of porous paper to find a dozen dried yellow roses with scarlet bases.

Her heart swelled. The day Imm wrote of feeling such dread was the same day Elaina had been raped. Was it Imm's intercession that guided her resolution not to end her life? Had the Three been with her the entire time, the very reason she was here this moment to still wonder?

The Trinity aren't bound by our understanding of time. Prayer supersedes the clock .—Sister Immaculata Lefevre

* * *

July 19, 1982
Dearest Imm,

Your love delivered the roses on the very day of Isaac's birth, and I think it was your prayers that escorted the Three to my side when I was most desperate. I too believe we're connected in the same unfathomable way that I am with the Trinity. I ache to be sure they are the residents of my heart again.

I've decided to withdraw from the nanny service so I can pursue massage therapy classes at Tarrock Technical Institute. The two-year course begins this fall and will leave little time for anything else. A second blessing: I already know most of the muscles in the human body, thanks to my art teacher.

Deanne asked me to be her maid of honor. She says her wedding will be a prom for those of us who never went to prom back in high school. Her colors, and I quote, are "every fun, splashy color my best friend painted on my bedroom walls." She insists everything be secondhand, too, challenging the thrifter in all of us. How can I not love the girl who's able to squeeze joy out of penny-pinching?

Your mom inspires faith and moves me to pray with confidence that goodness can be mine, in this life and the next. I choose to trust the Three again.

I'll pray for her quick and peaceful trip home.

All my love,
Elaina

* * *

Long, dark weeks pulled at Elaina's tenuous grip on optimism. Trapped in the black hole of time, she hung a smile over her despair, faking composure and contentedness. Even her letter to Imm had been filled with half-truths about her emotional state. Pretending served as an anchor, pulling her down to a deeper place that felt void of oxygen. How much longer could she hold her breath against pent-up misery?

Her one small light, Imm's confidence in her, illuminated her days through blurry, distant words that spelled loved, worthiness, and promise. Imm's faith in her was the tiny matchstick flame that would help her find the switch to activate greater light.

"I want to call Imm, Mom, please. I'll keep it short and pay the charges."

"International long distance is very expensive. What's so important it can't be said in a letter?"

She wanted to scream at her mother, spilling every detail of Eric's torments that had come to light after her rape. Elaina longed for compassion, someone to listen and encourage her. But her mother had lived in denial for so long, she'd probably dismiss Elaina's words now just as she'd chosen to before. Or she'd trivialize Eric's abuses as the exaggerations of Elaina's memory. Why would now be any different than before?

"Person-to-person, three dollars and sixty-five cents for the first three minutes and ninety-five cents for each additional." The operator's voice sounded robotic.

"Thank you," Elaina whispered and hung up.

The first three minutes was an hour's wages, worth three gallons of gas. But it was also three minutes with Imm. Imm's wind-chime voice sounded in Elaina's head, lending comfort simply in the imagining of it.

She waited until her mom left before she dialed the strange, eleven-digit code. Each thud of her heart felt like fists on bruises. How would she manage to unload twelve years' worth of uglies in three minutes? But if she couldn't speak to her heart-mom, getting through another hour of living seemed impossible.

Each French endearment that flowed through the telephone washed over another ugly detail of the drug bust, the swap meet, and the rape. Elaina exhaled every trapped toxin and spent her final sobs on Eric.

With no tears left and no secrets to divide, she looked at the clock: an hour and twenty-three minutes had passed.

The fragile peace she'd found hung by the finest thread, but the forthcoming phone bill was an unavoidable knife. "I have to go, Imm. Mom's going to kill me when this bill arrives. I love you so much. You're the only person—"

"I love you too, *ma poupée*, more than you'll ever know."

As she hung up, the Son reached through the darkness in her head for the first time in what felt like forever, making the imminent phone bill weigh far less than the uglies Imm had lifted off her heart. Only two weeks left until classes began.

* * *

August 21, 1982
Ma chére enfant,
You're the lost lamb who's been found again. "What man among you having a hundred sheep and losing one would not leave the ninety-nine to go after the lost one? And when he finds it, he sets it upon his shoulders with great joy. I tell you just the same way, there will be more joy in heaven over one sinner who repents than over ninety-nine who have no need of repentance." (Luke 15: 4–5, 7) Your club friends never left you; it's you who wandered. They're rejoicing, for it's your suffering that's brought you back. Trust the part of yourself that's also a part of them.

The morning after Isaac's birth, I told you that real trust is a leap of faith, making me a hypocrite for not confiding to you the reason you're so precious to me. I hope my (late) disclosure will assure you that no one is perfect.

I too was once young, physically beautiful, and unsuppressed. Baby Need confused me with her cries for the taste of God. I too discovered that she could be temporarily pacified with men's attentions. The sexual revolution of the 1960s had exploded here, as in the USA. Morality was flipped on its head. Society said sex and love were synonymous and that momentary gratification was enough a reason for intercourse to be commitment-free and unrestrained.

Once, at a party, I drank too much. Hours later and semi-sober, I realized my clothes were torn and bloodstained. My head knew I'd been raped, but the sexual revolution's lies said I'd simply lost my virginity unconventionally. Fear persuaded me to continue my denial until I learned I was pregnant.

The scandal traveled quickly in my village, no different from Tarrock or any other provincial town. Mon père searched for the man who'd impregnated me but found that three men had violated me while I was unconscious. Mon père sent me away to The Sisters of Mary, Mother of God. He rebuked my value to my face. I wanted to end my life, but the Great Three had another plan. My sisters of the cloth washed me of shame, convincing me how innocent and beloved I am.

Like myself, you're an extraordinary jewel, chérie. Our facets sparkle all the same for the pressures and dark conditions we've endured. You lost your first child through relinquishment, and I lost my twin baby girls in childbirth just hours before you were born.

How marvelous are His works, that when I'd finally handed bitterness and heartache over in exchange for a relationship with the Three, they knew I was ready for the child of my dreams. They asked me to travel over an ocean, because their gift waited in Tarrock: a beautiful little girl who needed une mére spirituelle, a spiritual mother, much as I needed a daughter. Imagine my joy when I learned your birthdate.

Because the Trinity aren't bound by our time, my offerings of pain and shame so many decades ago may be the catalyst for your comfort and strength now. My prayers for you, from the day we met and when I sensed your desperate need a few weeks ago, were your lifeline. Prayer is simply love, bringing help and absolution, regardless of time.

It's unthinkable for me not to trust the Three, because of their gift of you. You filled the hole left in my heart when my girls went to heaven. Our mysterious Holy Communion is also how I know that one day you'll have the most wonderful husband and children, by His design and beyond your farthest-reaching dreams.

Never doubt that you'll meet your firstborn again, too. On that day, you'll find evidence of your unselfishness in relinquishing Isaac. You'll praise God as I did on January 31, 1971, when you tilted your cherubic face up and said, "Today's my birthday."

Indulge me in one last thought, ma belle fleur, my beautiful flower. For years, I nurtured bitterness toward mon père for sending me away. I blamed my parents for my crushing loneliness and my baby girls' deaths, and I made the Three scapegoats to salve my grief. My wounds only festered, though, because resentment feeds heartache and destroys the bridge of forgiveness that is essential for crossing over to peace of mind. I lost precious time, not only with mon père but also with tranquility.

Maman was called home last night. I rejoice in her fortune but am left with an ache for what could have been. Regrets can't survive if now is lived to the fullest. I'm still learning.

I've never left you in my prayers, and I love you
Immaculata

P.S. I reversed the international long distance charges, an inadequate but genuine token of my gratitude for your trust in me.

August 30, 1982
Dearest Imm,

I'm so sad for your loss, knowing there'll be a void in your days without your mom. I'll pin your regrets to my heart as a reminder not to waste time on blame. Thank you for sharing your most personal experiences so I can learn. Your faith, friendship, and trust in me exceeds any gift I've ever received.

Your mother must have been a remarkable woman to have produced such a wonderful daughter who became my spiritual mother. In that way, I have lost a grandma. I look forward to the day I'll meet her and your twins because of the Three, who I know by your introduction. Thank you for filling me with Clover.

All my love,
Elaina

July 18, 1985

Dearest Imm,

Thank you for your mom's prayer book and for remembering Isaac's birthday. One day, I hope to pass it to a child of my own. Isaac is five today and has probably registered for kindergarten. I imagine him as small but sturdy, and I'm happy when I remember the few details Ms. Farrow told of his family.

Thank you too for your steady correspondence over the last five years. All your letters fill two shoeboxes so far, my favorite collection.

I love picturing your fields of roses unfurling in the morning sun as you paint on the shady side of your studio. Through your descriptions, it's easy to imagine, but I want to see it for myself.

I've had my massage therapy license for almost a year now but can only find work doing factory labor. With the recession still clawing its way up, this third-shift position is better than no job at all, but sometimes I wish I could go back to nannying for Family Services. I can't afford to work for minimum wage with my tuition debt, though. The time and money I spent earning my massage license feels like a waste when every massage therapy interviewer says they need experienced masseuses. How do I become experienced if no employer will give me a chance?

Three years of reclusion has eliminated the wild Michael girl from Tarrock's memory. I disappear behind a book at breaks, guarding my hard-earned dignity while praying for the newest victim of coworkers' tongues. Like a rabbit that hears danger in the wind, I feel menaced by overheard gossip. I only feel safe when I remain unnoticed. I wonder if having fake friends or staying invisible feels lonelier. Though both are awful, solitude, especially on the weekends, is unbearable. Kurt once told me how he'd watch the clock, willing the hands to bring Monday around.

My peace has become the six-day work weeks and twelve-hour shifts. Exhaustion keeps me deaf to Need's cries and worries over my dead-end direction, and self-imposed isolation is also where my self-respect grows. I water the seeds of character my parents planted, but there's no one to share the fruit with. I hold to your words: "Feeling lonely doesn't mean you're alone, because feelings aren't facts. If Need could be satisfied by one's own efforts, no one would need God. It's baby Need's hunger that drives us back to them."

I wonder why the Three don't tell me what they want so I can get on with it. Waiting seems pointless while everyone else my age is married and starting families. Being the only single bridesmaid at a wedding is the loneliest place of all.

You've lifted me up a thousand times, but I need you again. Please write!

All my love,
Elaina

August 3, 1985
Ma chère enfant,
Your gift is your pen, allowing me to hear the rise and fall of your voice as I read. I feel your every joy and ache as I watch your life unfold like a rose transforming from tight bud to full flower. You're too close to see that your relationship with the Trinity is growing by leaps. How uniquely and wonderfully you are made, ma belle fleur!

Our answers aren't given to us upon request but are found in the search itself. The answer you long for is not inside yourself, either, but outside your walls, outside the city on a hill. Your answer is in the crucified Christ. Keep your eyes on him. Christ in the storm gives us grace and trust that we'll be given what we need when the time is right. Grace is accepting what is, while the Trinity fills you to their measure.

You can't grab at them, or they will remain just beyond your reach. Love is patient, as Jesus demonstrated through entering Earth's time and putting on skin. For thirty-three years, he struggled with heartaches, temptations, and Need. Though he ached to be with his other two, he persevered to fulfill his Father's request so we could recognize the Trinity and the way back to them.

The hours Jesus waited on the cross must have seemed a lifetime. In his worst pain, he called for his Father just as you have, but his *human side, like yours, heard no reply. This doesn't mean the Father and Spirit weren't present and listening. They hear you, Elaina. With patience, you'll hear them too, and all your waiting will make sense.*

Place your loneliness, uncertainty, and dark memories in their light, for your peace and for the redemption of those who've desecrated you with their darkness. Remember, God the Three's time holds no boundaries for the forgiveness of perpetrators' wickednesses, but when you bury the atrocities, light can't disintegrate them.

Give the Three your limitations; they'll give you limitless strength and possibility. Giving them control will either be your greatest comfort or deepest fear, depending on your level of trust. Control is an earthly illusion. Darkness laughs while watching humans struggle to steer their sinking boats in their self-made storms. Even the dark one knows that only God can decide our first and last breaths.

Though we flip-flop between wanting God's way and our own, the Trinity are unchanging in their love and desire to be loved. But don't assume reciprocal love is a requirement. They love us regardless of who or what we put first. This is the reason perfection isn't a stipulation for a relationship with them. If you hold their hands, they'll hold your heart. Through your physical, mental, and spiritual self, be their reflection. Show the world who they are.

I've never left you in my prayers, and I love you.

Immaculata

21

Only two hours into Elaina's shift at the factory, time lagged, yet scraping flash from molded auto parts was still preferable to pretending to be engrossed in a book at break time. One minute of required breaks felt like an hour of menial labor.

She wrapped her hands around the steaming cup of coffee, its aroma stirring fond memories of that first cup her dad used to hand her every morning. If only the other memories of him were as warm.

A man several tables away was studying her. Was he sizing her up as a good prospect? He'd better think again.

"Hey showgirl, give us a dance," he called.

The others at his table erupted into laughter.

It took a moment for the boiling tar of his words to fully adhere, singeing through her skin to her core. As instinct dictates when hit with such excruciating pain, she jumped and ran like a person on fire.

She couldn't find her car. *Oh God, please.* His black burning words clung to her, refusing to loosen.

She squealed from the parking lot. She had to escape the shame that was raping her again. She pressed harder on the accelerator.

* * *

"Deanne? What's wrong? Why are you crying?"

Elaina reached up to wipe her friend's smeared mascara, but an unfamiliar numbness prevented her from lifting her hand. Deanne slipped out of focus. She turned her head to the left, and Deanne's face reappeared.

"She's awake!" Deanne turned quickly. "Raphe, get a nurse."

Why was everything to her left black?

Her nose identified an oddly familiar, unpleasant smell. She heard a flurry of sounds: doors opening and closing, brisk footsteps, telephones ringing, something beeping, a continual cough, background voices all talking at once . . .

Oh God, she was in the hospital.

A nurse hurried in and slipped a blood pressure cuff onto Elaina's arm. As it squeezed tighter, she squirmed for answers.

"Shh, be still," the nurse ordered. Satisfied with the results, the nurse asked Elaina if she knew the date.

"January . . . 1986 . . ." Elaina faltered. What day was it?

The nurse disappeared, and Deanne stepped back into view and began gently rubbing her arm. "You drove underneath a semitrailer three days ago," she explained. "You've been unresponsive since Tuesday."

Elaina shook her head as if to settle floating pieces. The only detail that fell into place was the word *showgirl*.

"It was crazy foggy, and there was a white semi with no backup lights blocking both lanes of Route 99. You must not have seen it. The detectives think it happened around one in the morning, but they're not sure because the trucker left the scene on foot. You were trapped in your car for hours. When they finally located the trucker, he was plastered."

Why couldn't she remember? Why didn't she feel any pain? She reached for her head to be sure it was attached, but Deanne pulled her hand back. "Let your face alone for now; you're pretty banged up."

"How did I get here?"

"Somebody called 911 from the pay phone near that closed-down gas station. The dispatcher never got his name, though. Whoever it was must have lit the flares and stayed with you, too, but when the EMTs finally cut you out with the jaws, there wasn't a soul around. They said you were talking to yourself. Man, Lanie, you know how lucky you are?" Deanne hugged her.

"Maybe an angel?" Elaina whispered.

Deanne laughed. "You told the cops the angel was middle-aged, smelled like tobacco, and asked you a bunch of questions about skating."

Her confusion was bad enough without Deanne's sarcasm.

"He saved you from goin' into a coma, though."

"Once you're standing, I hope you sue that trucker bastard," Raphe said.

During her next days in the hospital, the newspaper headlines brought in well-wishers Elaina hadn't seen in years. How often in self-pity had she imagined attending her funeral to see if anyone cared? This accident seemed a gift in learning how truly loved she was, all as life was spared.

The blindness and deafness on her left side were permanent, as was her left side's nerve damage leaving a numb sensation to the touch. This explained the strange lack of pain she'd had after such major trauma. With therapy, she was assured that her body would compensate, though she would carry scars and an oddly cocked left eye for life.

She woke one afternoon to a sound different from the usual collection of hospital noises that had grown familiar over the weeks. Swelling still obstructed the vision in her good eye, but eventually she brought Cassy into focus.

"You look horrible," Cassy cried, dabbing her eyes to salvage her makeup.

"Thanks." How like Cassy, diplomacy and subtlety lost in the moment.

"What if you'd died? I would've never had the chance to apologize . . . for the things I've said about you . . . for breaking your trust . . . for not inviting you to my wedding." Tears ran down Cassy's face, and her sincerity tugged at Elaina's heart.

"Come here." She pulled Cassy into a hug, just as Imm and the Three had to her after a hundred of her own betrayals and refusals to trust.

***

February 14, 1986
Dearest Imm,
Happy Valentine's Day.
Thank you for calling. I couldn't believe when the nurse said it was from France. I kept pinching myself to be sure it was really you.

Mom told me about your frantic call in the wee hours after the accident, before the police notification. I'll never doubt our mysterious connection again.

The coincidences within this accident are like strange magic, too. If I'd been one inch taller, I'd have been decapitated, but that morning was one of the few times I didn't use my booster pillow. The fog cleared just as Life Flight arrived and thickened again as soon as we lifted. And they still haven't found the man who called 911 and stayed with me. I'm left both humbled and affirmed in love.

To be given more do-over-days, as you call them, puts my disabilities in perspective.

The neurologist insisted on a six-month leave from the factory for healing and therapy. As soon as therapy is over, I'm on the next flight to Grasse. No more put-offs.

May I never spend another day without gratitude.

Thank you for your prayers.

All my love,
Elaina

April 1, 1986

Ma chéri enfant,

This day was one of my childhood favorites. Every April Fool's morning when the family was gathered for breakfast, mon père would say it's Atheist's Day. Then he'd hand us his Bible, and within the pages we'd find new, gold-edged prayer cards with our names. Enclosed are all of mine. One day, please pass them to your children.

Our steady correspondence in thoughts, prayers, and letters has been my greatest joy. Helping you separate guilt and shame has been my privilege. I'm confident you understand the difference now. Still, fear will continue to use your shame as a tool, twisting the lessons you've learned from God-given guilt, which helps us recognize wrongdoings and oversights. Shame will continue trying to bind you in inadequacy and doubt of forgiveness and attempt to divide you from your Three. Let go of the things you can't undo and shame will lose its hold, as well.

I'm overjoyed that you have your driver's license back and assume that sight from one eye is adequate. Does favoring your right side help with hearing?

I pray you will be awarded an out of court settlement that will cover the medical bills and leave you with enough to compensate for your limitations, but don't forget: in the true picture, it all belongs to the Three.

Though your mother may use pride as her safeguard, we know it's really a prison. Try to look through her walls into her heart. Some people hide behind arrogance and independence because they think loneliness is a weakness. Actions often attract what is most dreaded— in her case, maybe alienation. Perhaps her devotion to Eric is rooted in her need to be needed. Yes, she's turned a blind eye to his viola-tions of you, but whether that's sinful or saint-like, I can't judge. God is merciful in even the most horrific crimes. Let go of your feelings of betrayal, and remember how faithful the Three are despite how often we've deserted them.

I've never left you in my prayers, and I love you.

Immaculata

* * *

She bent to shake hands with the frail, silver-haired woman in the wheelchair. "Hi, I'm Cassy's friend, Elaina. She invited me to tag along to your family reunion and help with her little ones."

She needed to stop chattering. The old woman's gentle smile soothed her nerves.

"Cass and I were classmates at Saint Augustine starting in first grade," she continued, seeing that the woman enjoyed her company. They began talking more about Saint Augustine, and before she knew it, a half hour had passed.

Elaina navigated to the corner of the room where the children played and welcomed her with laughter and eager acceptance. Watching the kids was why she'd come, anyway, so that newly divorced Cassy could enjoy some adult time.

Cassy's baby nursed the bottle slowly, content in Elaina's arms with kiddie chaos all around. Elaina melted into the bliss of cradling a baby in her arms and watching Cassy happily hover between cousins.

She couldn't have gotten through the past months without Cassy. Cassy had hauled her to and from physical therapy before Elaina could drive again, helped her with exercises, and broke up the long days of recovery with her companionship. Not a day had passed that they didn't shake their heads in laughter and disbelief at their former on-off relationship. Tough life lessons had finally brought them together with maturity and sensibility.

A tall man entered the room, stopping conversation among young and old. He wasn't handsome, although he was pleasant enough to look at, but his smile overtook his entire body. Even with his back turned, she could tell when he laughed by watching his hands, open and extended as if offering humor for everyone to share.

"Vince!" the kids yelled. They clung to his arms and legs.

"Did you make chocolate chip cookies?"

"Did you bring your magic tricks?"

"Can we piggyback?"

The adults, too, surrounded him like moths to light. Though Elaina couldn't hear through so many voices talking at once, when Vince spoke, everyone hushed. Bursts of laughter followed. The energy of this man emitted fascinated her.

Cassy's little one emptied the bottle and began gumming happily on the nipple as Elaina watched Vince work the room. With the aunt in the wheelchair, he knelt and placed his hands on her fragile knees, conversing at her level. With the thick, acne-peppered teen who sat alone, he plopped down and ten minutes later, the young man's hands were still flapping excitedly to his passionate dialog. Vince engaged with each person as if they were the only one in the world. The children continued to swarm him, begging to be tossed in the air. Screams of delight tugged at her Need, who ached to be played with too.

Cassy finally pulled him her way for an introduction. "Elaina, this is my cousin Vince."

He took Elaina's hand between his and beamed. The cliché "twinkling eyes" no longer seemed trite. Heat rose to her face, leaving her speechless. She felt ridiculous. She wasn't sixteen anymore. She tried to reason with a rising sense of alarm, knowing her ruinous past with men was the cause.

Moments later, he was pulled away again. Elaina was left with a peculiar longing different from anything she'd experienced before.

"You never mentioned him." She hoped she sounded casual as she scooped up Cassy's daughter from the sofa. "Based on his long sleeves and corduroys despite this heat, I'm guessing there's no significant other to help him choose appropriate attire."

"He's been divorced a couple years. And yeah, he definitely needs some fashion sense, but don't you think his ineptness is endearing?"

Irresistible is the word she'd have chosen. "Tell me about him."

"Hmm, I only see him at our annual reunions. He's in his mid-thirties, has a house in east Cleveland. The sweetest guy on earth. Besides childhood stories, I can't tell you much, though. He's usually the listener in conversations and rarely talks about himself unless he's cutting up. And he's the funniest guy I know."

Divorced, at least eleven years older, and lived two and a half hours away. She should keep her net far from this fish.

"Let's get the kids down for a nap and then go outside for a glass of wine," Cassy said.

Once the little ones were tucked in, they headed for the deck adjoining the pond. Elaina had just settled into her chair when an icy splash drenched her, prompting a shriek.

Four heads popped out of the water.

"Sorry, but we couldn't resist." Vince pulled himself onto the dock, grinning and shaking like a wet dog. Behind him, three teen boys copied his every move in obvious adoration.

Though she'd spilled her wine and her shirt was soaked, she felt no more annoyance than if it had been a puppy. Time stopped as her eyes took in Vince's body, free of everything but denim cut-offs and dripping water. The artist in her remembered just one other man so muscularly defined, Lumumba.

She looked down, wondering how long she'd been staring. Oh God, she didn't want to reduce him to the merely physical, but he was a masterpiece. On second thought, she'd found him stunning in his winter clothes—the moment the kids had raced into his arms, and when he'd charmed the acne-covered teen out of his shell. So far, he bore the wrapper of the kind of man Imm described as *wears forever*.

These were crazy thoughts. She'd not shared more than four sentences with the man.

Vince appeared over one shoulder with a bottle of wine. "A peace offering." He filled her glass, his smile warming her deep inside.

She wrapped her hands around the bowl of the glass to stop the quivering of her fingers and scolded herself for the silly, adolescent fluttering in her belly.

But then he covered her hands with his, casually yet intimately, and her heart began pounding so hard she wondered if he would hear. Was it visible on her shirt? Surely her every thought was evident on her burning cheeks. Men had often said she was easy to read. Did his attention arise out of pity, flattery, or patronization?

She fumbled for conversation. "So, um, what line of work are you in?"

"I'm a mold maker. Ever heard of one?"

"Yes!" Excited and relieved that she was familiar with this, she rushed in with an explanation. "I work in a compression molding factory that makes car parts. Well, I'm not working presently—long story."

"What do you do to pass the time?" he asked.

His eyes explored hers. Was her left eye doing that weird floating thing? She stooped and fiddled with her sandal in case it was.

"I love to ice skate, but I haven't done that in a while, either."

"You're kidding."

"I'm not sure how well I'd do now, but I used to be pretty good."

"Let's find out. If you're up for the drive, there's a double hockey rink near me, one of the biggest in the country. I skate every Thursday on adult night. The organ player's incredible; worth a trip just to hear him. We could meet there."

A squeal almost escaped her before she could remind herself to look calm. Oh, dear Three, he skates! Her skin tingled as she wondered if this was really happening.

A surge of hope filled her from her core.

* * *

December 14, 1986

Dearest Imm,

Merry Christmas, and happy birthday, Jesus.

Most of the prayer journal you sent last July for Isaac's sixth is filled. Looking back on the pages, though, I see more questions than thoughts and events—about Vince, of course.

For the last five months, I've tried to be patient, but he's like this big, warm ocean that begs me to come for a swim. My toes are wrinkled from wading and I ache to dive in, but with each step deeper, I feel my feet lifting from the safety of the sandy floor. Should I throw caution to the surf? I know how to swim, but I fear unexpected breakers and undertow. I have no life preserver for my heart. I try to float above the worry waves, knowing I must trust again or spend my life alone on the beach.

Dancing on the ice with Vince is like skating with the Three at Hurstland. We move as one. I pray our shared love for skating is more than coincidence and that Vince is the one they've been saving for me.

I drive 120 miles to meet him at the rink each week. The drive home is brutal, especially when I've skated only a few songs with him. But in his kindness, he won't turn down any dance request, no matter how slow, heavy, or old the woman is. It's the very things I love about him most that drive me crazy.

Why is anxiety my bed partner when I've found the perfect man? Long-distance dating is hard enough, but my track record with men brings real apprehension.

I found some pictures of you and me from elementary school. Enclosed are copies. May they leave you feeling the same warm fuzzies they do me. Thank you for the pictures of your farm. Sister Thérèse is amazing with a camera! I love looking at them and imagine the day I'll visit.

All my love,
Elaina

P.S. Have you heard Madonna's "Papa Don't Preach"? I think it was released this summer. Does it tug at your heart like it does mine?

* * *

"I'm sorry, love, but we've got to leave. My allergies are getting bad." Vince rubbed his swelling eyes and hive-covered neck.

She felt bad knowing how long he'd looked forward to this football game at his best friend's house. Goodness knew she could sympathize; allergies were her cross, too.

Elaina took the wheel. Vince's face and arms were completely inflamed. "What do you suppose triggered it?"

It took several minutes for him to frame a reply after being possessed by an itching frenzy. "Well, I'm allergic to everything, so it could've been anything. It's why I suck on an inhaler constantly and my skin's always torn up. You must've noticed."

She had wondered, it was true, but she never would have embarrassed him by mentioning the blood that sometimes marked his collar and matted his hair. His poor skin was the driest she'd ever seen. Maybe that was why he always wore long pants and sleeves. Divinity had to have been the mastermind of this relationship. Only someone with asthma and allergies could understand, sympathize, and support another with this painful and socially debilitating curse.

Vince needed someone who knew the necessity of clean—deep clean—and who was willing to forgo pets, who would vigilantly read labels for taboo ingredients, and who understood the importance of keeping medicine, tissues, and a ready exit always on hand.

Vince needed her.

"When I was twelve, I had such a bad asthma attack from tree pollen that I couldn't work at my dad's nursery anymore," she said. "I thanked God on that day, because my dad let me take over the household chores instead. It was the first time I remember breathing normally for more than twenty-four straight hours."

"Wow, you do understand! That's the reason I'm a bit of a health nut: clean eating, exercise, and moderation. Sort of a gift to self. Is that why you run?"

Only Vince would counter allergies with *a gift to self.* His optimism made everything seem possible. If only this drive were cross-country, because then he'd never be more than a hand's reach away. Every time he shared another story of his work and personal life, she felt privileged. No detail was too small, yet Vince eliminated the kind of specifics that others would have bragged about.

"I just learned at the party tonight that you're the foreman of your company tool room," she said. She hoped the change of subject would distract him from the itching. "You never mentioned that."

"I sweep floors, too," he said with a laugh. Then more seriously, he added, "A good leader only asks of his help what he too is willing to do. I don't like titles. They elevate one while lowering another."

She glanced over at him and smiled. "I've never met anyone like you. Is there anyone you can't make laugh? And you listen as if it's your only purpose, yet you're slow to give advice."

When he did speak, he magically tinted himself to the speaker's shade though empathy while never losing his true color by compromising his principles. In this way, he softened opinions and criticisms and brought consideration to different perspectives. She suspected a difficult childhood and failed marriage had fed his compassion for minorities, the financially struggling, and those burdened with addictions.

They pulled up in front of his house, and she sighed. Each time they parted, the drive home seemed to increase, as did her desire for him. But real love fed her passion for this man, pure, blessed, and patient. Vince had weaned Need from shallow affirmations and feigned affections, and her inner baby now hungered only to be the person Vince thought she already was, honorable and pure. She prayed that his faith in her was a prophecy.

* * *

February 14, 1987

Ma chére enfant,

My valentine to you, the most precious person in my life, is assurance that your heart does have a life preserver: your Clover Club. No matter what happens, we're here for you always and beyond this world.

Cynicism isn't a mark of wisdom but rather a tool fear uses to nail us to doubt (fearful = full of darkness). The uglies, as you call them, make life feel threatening and help suspicion try to shift blame and refuse to trust again. Believing in others even after you've been lied to, cheated on, or sexually violated isn't a failure, but a leap of faith. Trusting yourself and others again would be heroic.

Please look at and accept the worst of your past. When you can put them to words, you'll dissolve their ability to bring pain and suspicion. It's frightening to make yourself vulnerable again, but this is also the place where your Three work their miracles. The risks and rewards are always high for that of great value. Risk is the gap that begs the leap and the very reason we feel so gloriously weightless after landing safely on the other side.

Your letters are heart gifts that paint pictures in my mind. You must love the pen as much as a paintbrush to write as you do, leaving no doubt it is of God. You are an artist at living, ma precieuse. It takes one to know one, just as the faithful recognize the faith-filled.

Allow yourself happiness. Watching your joy is the Three's greatest delight.

I've never left you in my prayers, and I love you.

Immaculata

* * *

Vince handed her a glass of wine and an envelope.

"Sit here"—he fluffed the sofa pillows—"and put your feet up here"—he pulled the ottoman over—"and read my valentine." He squeezed in beside her and pulled her into the crook of his arm.

Oh, his scent: sandalwood and cedar, like the scent of blankets newly pulled from the wooden storage chest in her bedroom.

She could feel tears collecting as she scanned his words. "The things you notice that I give no thought to . . ." she said. "I didn't realize my doodles are always the same three things or that I sigh whenever I see roses. And that you took the time to write them down . . ."

Vince dabbed her eye with his sleeve. "You'd think I just gave you a Tiffany's trinket. You're a cheap date."

If he only knew. But the time when those words would've scalded no longer existed. Vince's Elaina wore, moved, and breathed like a lady.

She loved who she was under his gaze when they were alone.

She knew his married friends objected to her age. She'd overheard their warnings about her lack of life experience. They whispered of her insecurity when they thought she was out of earshot. But they assumed that she and Vince had already been intimate. She found their cautions not to let the physical get in the way of good sense doubly irritating when they offered only a single bedroom for overnight invitations. She and Vince were forced to curl up fully clothed and keep their kisses light to protect their commitment to postponing what they craved more than food or water.

Vince smiled indulgently. "What's a little more time before eating the oranges when I get to sleep beside the tree? I get to watch us transform from a tight bud to full fruit. It's senseless to eat the blossoms or green oranges. When the time is ripe, I'll have my heart's content. Hunger pains are manageable when I think of what's to come."

He didn't speak seriously very often, but when he did, his profound and sometimes poetic words left her breathless. How could such a deep thinker also be such a funny man? Oh God, she so wanted this to be real.

* * *

Elaina cradled the phone as she paced, excitement tingling at the thought of her news.

"Hi, Vince. Guess what?" She heard her voice squeak.

"You tell me." His response sounded . . . withdrawn?

"The lawsuit is settled out of court. All my worries over what I can't remember were for nothing."

"Wow. Must have been an open-and-shut case. I suppose the trucker's career is over?"

"Well, yeah, but it was his third DUI. My attorney said we did right by getting him off the road for good. The settlement is enough to cover my medical bills and car and still leave plenty for my limitations."

"I'm happy for you, really, but I still feel sorry for the trucker. His job was probably the only thing that gave him dignity. He has no reason to sober up now."

God is all-forgiving, but he's also all-just. We must lie on t
he bed we make. —Edward Michael

Where did the Almighty draw the line between pardon and a just penalty? God had certainly spared the rod with her, but her medical bills and disabilities had destroyed another's livelihood. Kurt, so gentle and good, had also been an alcoholic. Had she taken away the trucker's reason to get clean?

"Elaina? You there? This is good news, love. You can start over with the means to do just about anything. So I guess now's as good a time as any to tell you . . . Elaina, I want you to start dating others."

Her breathing stopped. Had she heard him right? Panic crashed down. "Because of the settlement? The distance? Somebody else?"

"Shh, I care for you so much. That's the reason. I'm buried in bills from my previous marriage that'll take years to pay off, and I can't strap you with that. I won't steal your best years while you wait for a commitment I may never be able to make. Frankly, I'm afraid of marriage."

She'd wound the phone cord so tightly around her fingers that they were turning purple. "But if money's the problem, I've got plenty now. Everything I have is yours, with or without marriage. I love you that much."

"But you'd always question if I had stayed with you for love or financial gain. Find someone who can give you what I can't. It's goodbye, Elaina, for your sake."

The dial tone hummed in her ear.

Had he somehow learned of her past? It couldn't have been Cassy; she'd proven her friendship and devotion over and over during Elaina's months of recuperation. Maybe Mrs. Adams? No way.

Then who? What?

Why?

She'd just lost a man with more integrity than she'd ever hope to have. He'd refused her money, her body, and her heart—all that she'd offered unconditionally—not because he didn't want them, but because he believed it was wrong to take them. She loved him for the very things that were tearing her apart.

Only one certainty remained, and she'd swear it to the devil himself: Need would never be fed filth again. She'd starve her inner baby and watch her die before she'd ever be naked with any man again.

* * *

June 28, 1987
Ma chéri enfant,

May this letter and my prayers arrive on angel's wings. Just breathe, and let your club friends do the rest. Crying is the soul's exhalation, so let us shed tears together. Answers will come, though not as swiftly as you may wish. Trust, especially when it's most difficult, is powerful worship.

Instinct tells you to cling to what you have because so much has been taken. The Three urge you to give it all away, though. Sometimes they'll even pry it from your hands so there'll be room for what you truly desire. You'll never find what your soul aches for until you give your needs to them and give up what's keeping you from them. Nothing can come before God or nothing of real happiness can follow. As some wise person once said about God, "Until you're satisfied exclusively in him, you won't be able to experience the love that exemplifies your relationship with him." Give boldly of all you have. That's heroism.

I am with you in prayer and love you so much.

Immaculata

November 18, 1987
Dearest Imm,

Lumumba received my Moneygram and said it's enough to dig several wells for the people in Mwanza there in Tanzania. The settlement money feels less tainted when I give it boldly. Enclosed is his letter, which I wanted to share because, besides you, he's my greatest hero for devoting his life to such vulnerable people.

I was dismissed from my factory position with a generous severance package. Management felt I could no longer do the work required with my limited vision.

Cole made a surprise visit to Tarrock. It's been seven years. His startling good looks haven't faded, but my heart felt nothing more than an acknowledgment of Isaac's father. He asked me to join him for dinner as friends. I'll let you know what happens.

My every thought centers on Vince. Breathing hurts, and my heart feels black and blue. When will it get easier?

I'm sure you're busy planning Christmas projects. Tell me everything that fills your days and especially about your pageant with Grasse's children. Your letters are my only joy these days.

All my love,
Elaina

* * *

The Chinese restaurant was almost empty as Cole steered her to the far end and into a booth with poor lighting and no windows. Her nose wrinkled at the odd smell, ripped vinyl upholstery, and stained tablecloth. She'd stick to a drink—something with alcohol to neutralize the germs.

After their drinks arrived, Cole shooed the waitress away, asking for more time. He continued his monologue about unfulfilled dreams, people he'd hurt, and things he regretted, then began musing in wistful tones for the life he and Elaina could've shared.

Pretty odd ponderings for a guy who'd never given a thought beyond himself. She didn't remember Cole ever talking this much. Or was it simply that she had nothing now to say?

When he finally asked about her life, only Vince came to mind. Her enthusiasm rose as she described the man who listened more than he spoke, whose schedule was never more important than an old lady struggling with groceries or a child who'd misplaced his parents. Her eyes began to pool. Vince was no longer hers.

"Oh, sweetheart, I'm sorry," Cole said. "But if my advice is worth anything, don't give up. I flushed my future flitting from one relationship to another. Keep trying and praying."

Cole talking about prayer? Where had I-own-the-world Cole gone?

Reading her expression, he looked down. "Elaina, I'm HIV positive. Guess I loved one too many. I wanted to see you again before it gets . . ."

Allowing her to swallow her shock first, he reached across the table. "Please hold my hand, for old time's sake. I ache for our youth back and for the son I'll never hold or even gave much thought to until now. Do you know anything about him?"

Rage forced its way up from a deep place she didn't recognize. She stormed from the restaurant, Cole on her heels. He grabbed her shoulders just before she reached her car and spun her around into a tight embrace.

She pulled back and pounded his chest with her fists. Fury shouted things she knew she'd regret.

"You cheated constantly. You had money for everything but to help me. You never asked to feel him kick. He might be the only child I ever have, but because of you, I couldn't keep him."

She crumpled under the weight of grief. Her life was one heartbreak after another. Would it ever end? She just wanted it to end.

He was breathing heavily. "I know, I know, and now retribution has caught up. Your forgiveness is all I ask."

Her chest fell, exhaling hatred and blame and refilling with something beautifully peaceful. Cole's eyes revealed true remorse and showed her a person she could still love, not because of who he was but because of the Trinity who were in her. Love urged her to hold dear the part of Cole who'd made her stronger, wiser, more compassionate, and forgiving. Her Three gently nudged her to the starting gate, a place of pardon where nothing was expected in return.

"Eight years ago, a beautiful boy was created from our selfish choices, Cole," she said gently. "Isaac *is* grace, the manifestation of God's forgiveness."

Liberation like the light November snow swirled around them.

Back in her car, she knew the Three were near. She sat very still, trying to hear them.

Had she put Vince before the Three, or was he their gift? Had that been the Three telling her not to give up through Cole's words, or was that her wishful thinking? It was time to either call Vince again or move on.

"I can't, I can't." Her forehead dropped to the steering wheel, "I can't live without him."

22

Cole's words echoed the song her spirit played: *Trust yourself without wavering. Time is precious. The symphony that fills your heart is exceptional.*

Another rejection couldn't be as bad as never knowing for sure.

Elaina reached for the phone, curling her fingers tightly around the receiver. No more deliberations, rehearsals, or summations could replace this leap she had to chance. The plunge and potential result, solitude, wasn't unfamiliar. Yet this time, it seemed an all-or-nothing gamble. She could never love another the way she did Vince.

"Please Vince, give me a minute. I know it's only been five months—but I miss you." She sucked in a sob.

His voice held anguish. "Oh God, I miss you, too. Can you meet me Thursday night to skate?"

As when she ran through the clover field with the Three as a child, she and Vince's bladed feet seemed to lift them to holiness.

"We could star in the new movie, *Dirty Dancing*, except on the ice," she said with a giggle as their feet cut to a stop in perfect sync.

Vince was her Johnny Castle, Patrick Swayze's character, the talented but financially struggling man who refused to compromise honor in spite of life's hard knocks. Vince was the treasure she'd been looking for all these years.

* * *

The day Imm prophesied had finally arrived. Today, April 1, 1989, Elaina Michael of Tarrock would become Mrs. Vincent McCroy of

Cleveland. She sealed the envelope to River Rock Adoption Agency containing her name and address change. It would simplify the search if Isaac wanted or needed to find her once he turned eighteen.

If only Imm could see her dress, the color of Walking Down the Aisle—Imm's promise and Elaina's trust that the Three would bring her a soulmate who'd wear forever.

Vince had enthusiastically agreed with Elaina's wish to keep the ceremony and reception simple. "Today should be about you, me, and the Three who led us here."

As Deanne adjusted her halo of baby's breath, Elaina implored the Trinity, "May I one day feel my own baby's breath on my neck, and may I meet Isaac again."

"Oh, I almost forgot." Deanne handed Elaina a note.

The block letters of an engineer gave Vince away: "TONIGHT, I'M SHAKING THE ORANGE TREE."

"What's so funny? Stop laughing, Lanie, your makeup is smudging. What, what?"

But Elaina tucked Vince's note deep inside her cascade of yellow roses, refusing to share this precious intimacy.

She handed Deanne one of the prayer cards Imm had sent her three years ago on this day. "I need someplace to carry this."

Deanne looked it over and shrugged. "Tuck it up your sleeve."

The tattered corners had lost their gold edging, but Mother Mary, in aquamarine, was clearly visible with her angels above. It was old, borrowed, and blue. Elaina slid it up the sleeve of her dress.

Now she was ready.

* * *

"I love you, Mrs. McCroy," Vince padded to the bed where Elaina waited and handed her a large, heavy box wrapped in foil.

She lifted the lid carefully and burst out laughing. "Oranges!" Her laughter came so hard that several rolled from the container.

"Not just any, though. These are blood oranges imported from Sicily, thanks to Imm. She said they're legendary for increasing fertility."

A tremble behind her grin warned her of pending joyful tears.

"How did we wait?"

Vince was so close that their thighs pressed together. "In high school, the priests used to repeat, 'master your body, or it will master you.' Don't you think it got easier because we didn't tempt temptation?

"No," she shot back, pulling him down, "but I always felt honored. Imm warned me that fear of losing you would try to make me lure you to bed before our wedding. The devil in my heart didn't help, screaming how prudish postponing intimacy was, all while stirring up my fantasies. But it was our conversations that brought me to a frenzy. It was as if you'd injected yourself into my every thought."

She paused for his kiss: long, slow, and savored.

"Yet it's how you listen that gave me patience," she continued afterwards. "I've experienced greater intimacy talking with you than—well, you understand. Even when we're apart, a piece of you stays with me. But let's not talk when we can finally—"

He rolled aside and pulled her on top of him, her curtain of hair shutting out all distractions. They locked eyes as his fingers trailed down her neck and over her breasts. Blood rushed to her womanhood, which was aching to hold his masculinity and swelling a dewy welcome for her new husband. This was the purpose of her body's design, to receive her bride groom's gift of self so their fulfillment could be total, fruitful, faithful, and forever.

* * *

July 20, 1990

Dearest Imm,

I love the yellow rose grafts from your farm, a piece of you in my back yard. Thank you for remembering Isaac's tenth.

You've always referred to your home as "the farm," but does it have a name? If not, I've thought of one: La Terre de Mon Coeur—The Land of My Heart. In my imagination, it's paradise. If only I'd taken the opportunity to visit last year after the wedding. Travel to Grasse will have to be postponed again, though, because we're going to have a baby! I'm absolutely bursting with joy.

Will you be his or her godmother? Say dis oui.

Guilt reminds me how undeserving I am of the Three's generosity, but as you said, it only interferes with gratitude. It took a lot of tangles to convince me that temporary abstinence and waiting with them might work better. They really do want the best for me.

Each time Vince and I are intimate, it's not only physical glory but an indescribable euphoria in my head and heart too. Vince makes coffee tastes richer and voices sound sweeter. Long ago, you told me that sexual intercourse is meant to be three-dimensional, allowing a husband and wife to experience a part of how perfect communion will be with the Trinity in heaven. And now, Vince and I have partnered with the Three in creating another reflection of them. I wouldn't have believed it can get any better, but once my baby is in my arms—oh, Imm, I'm so excited!

I'm so thankful for you too, my spiritual mére, fellow Clover Club member, and friend for teaching me true sex education.

All my love,
Elaina

March 21, 1991
Ma chére enfant,
Thank Vince for calling me. My heart is full of Clover knowing you and your baby girl are healthy and happy. That she was born on the vernal equinox, the sign of spring, says much about her future. My godchild and namesake, Immaculata Rose McCroy, will be blessed with infinite potential. My mind can picture her pink perfection and foresee a woman of distinction. Have my prophecies been wrong yet, ma belle fleur?

Vince said you were up and walking several hours after the cesarean, wanting to know when you could go home. That's ma precieuse. Once you're settled and your precious one has found her routine, tell me everything.

I have never left you in my prayers, and I love you.
Immaculata

P.S. I'm glad that you and Vince will call her Max. No little girl should have to wear the name Immaculata, except on very formal occasions.

July 19, 1991
Dearest Imm,

I love the potpourri from La Terre de Mon Coeur. As every year on Isaac's birthday, thank you for remembering. Your gifts assure me it's okay to hope that one day I'll hold him again.

With the Gulf War seemingly over, I think about the mothers left to grieve their lost sons. I know Isaac is safe from war for seven more years, but should there be another, how will I know he's safe?

When I told Vince how I count on your thoughts, prayers, and little gifts, he said the surest sign of good parenting is a child who takes his or her parents for granted. How many children wonder when their parents will come home, who'll be sleeping in Mommy's bed or which bottle of booze Daddy will have for breakfast? They're the ones who take nothing for granted, he said. With that in mind, I pray Isaac can take his parents for granted, at least for the next seven years.

Max is finally sleeping through the night. In other words, Vince and I are rested.

I think you're right about Max's potential. In her impatience to get on with life, she kicked so hard she broke my water. My cesarean wasn't scheduled for another week. Now, as she burrows in my arms with her eyes squeezed tight to shut out distractions, I'm sure she's formulating a strategy for the next twenty years. When her forehead smooths and her rosebud lips stop puckering, I know her plan is all worked out. She's brilliant, Imm. I can already tell. She's the visible sign of our love. How miraculous!

Yet in this awesome responsibility to protect our helpless bundle of beauty, the world has become a scary place. Thank goodness for all your letters, eleven years' worth and growing. Every bundle will be passed to Max when she's old enough; your wisdom and prayers are our best insurance plan.

All my love,
Elaina

* * *

Vince rolled to his other side after a reassuring pat on her hip. "I'm tired, too. There's always the weekend."

He was so patient. How many more times could she expect him to accept lame excuses or play along with her feigned interest in intimacy? He wasn't fooled. He knew her better than anyone.

When had his affectionate touch begun to bring back snippets of the past she'd tried so hard to put behind? When had her dark place begun to spew out spores from the uglies? The thought that Vince might blame himself was bad enough, but what if he grew tired of her games?

Each evening as she watched Vince dance with Max, now close to four years old, gratitude for him overwhelmed her. She loved him more than she'd ever thought possible simply from watching him hold his daughter. The Three had gifted her beyond her wildest imagination, yet random occurrences could plunge her so deep in self-reproach it took days to find her way back.

Still, living with her secrets seemed safer than letting Vince learn who she was. Though her past had become a chasm between them, unloading her uglies on him for peace of mind might only bring more pain.

She forced her thoughts back to the present. Tomorrow was Halloween. Max's costume still needed hemming—but before all else, the pregnancy test.

Fifteen minutes later, she draped herself over the back of his big chair. "Say you're happy, Vince." She thrust the little white stick in front of his eyes.

He scooped her up, assuring her with his kisses, his merry blue eyes, and a grin that rose high on his cheeks. "Guess I'll have to put off early retirement." He paused, counting. "I'll be sixty-six before we get this one out of college. But what a reason to keep on truckin'. Happy? I'm ecstatic."

"I calculated years too, only backward. Fifteen years ago today, Isaac's life began, and four years ago, on Isaac's birthday, I learned that Max was on her way. It's about as coincidental as my birthday being just hours after Imm's twins danced their way to heaven. This is the reason I don't believe in coincidence. It's God's timing."

"I can't imagine being able to love another baby like I do Max, but I've no doubts." Vince pulled her close.

Elaina kissed his cheek softly. "It's as if the events of our lives intertwine for a purpose we can't see while it's happening, like the crocheting of a doily. The perimeter expands as new blessings loop themselves into the lacings of old, except that we already have a tablecloth."

He kissed her again. "You better write Imm and tell her there's another godchild on the way."

"And that we'll have to postpone that trip to Grasse again."

* * *

July 8, 1995

Dearest Imm,

Liam Galway was born this morning at four pounds, ten ounces and seventeen inches long. They took him early, the reason he's so tiny, but the doctor isn't worried about his underdeveloped digestive system. Still, neither Liam nor I can leave the hospital until he's gained a half a pound. I pray it's soon. Hospitals make hell seem like a resort. In fact, if I had to choose hell or a hospital, I'd choose hell and send the sinners to the hospital.

We fell in love with our beautiful boy at first sight. All my misgivings about guiding him to manhood seem silly now when I hold this baby, who's smaller than a bag of sugar. With Vince as Liam's role model, I'm sure he'll grow to a gentleman of dignity and distinction.

My friends who have sons insist that boys love their mothers like no other. That's a bittersweet thought knowing that Isaac will never love me like the woman who adopted him.

Vince paces while I feed Liam, wanting to hold him and cement a father-son bond, but he also seems terrified of breaking him. It's sweetness too holy for words.

Life at La Terre de Mon Coeur sounds anything but dull with the addition of the baby animals. How fun! Your last letter might be the most hilarious yet. I can't wait to meet your three-legged goat.

I'm thrilled that you've finally gotten a home computer, though

I hope we'll continue using snail mail unless there's a pressing issue. There's such satisfaction in pretty stationary, a nice pen, and a bit of a wait. Have you read about the new floppy disks? They can support 100MB of memory. What's next?

All my love,
Elaina

* * *

The challenge of keeping Liam's tiny stomach full made for hourly feedings. He cried as much as Need. Apparently, Elaina's soul baby hadn't grown up after all, as if maturity weren't nearly as stimulating as watching her jump between distrust and despair.

Sometimes paranoia overwhelmed her so completely that she was sure Liam would be snatched away if she put him down. Other times, she resentfully questioned why having Liam hadn't alleviated her ache for Isaac. Liam and Isaac often became the same baby in her mind, and when reality exposed her confusion, her crying jags left Vince and Max helpless but to watch.

"I'd be a wacko without Max." Elaina dug deep for cheerfulness on her monthly catch-up phone call with Deanne. "She does half of Liam's daytime feedings. We recently nicknamed him Fat Man for the little folds beginning to jiggle on his arms and legs."

"Looks like Max is headed in the wifey-poo direction. How could she be anything but a girlie-girl with you as her mom, though?" Deanne said with a laugh.

But a dark cloud above conversation rained misgivings on Elaina. Max's preschool teacher had recently commented how unusually serious a child Max was. There hadn't been much opportunity for her to be a little girl, between Elaina's exhaustion and mood swings.

Elaina sighed. That wasn't anything Deanne needed to hear now. "Give Raphe a hug for me. My turn to call you next month. Watch your mailbox for pictures. I love you, Deanne."

* * *

Vince and Max were patient as Elaina worked through her dark days, but she wondered if her outlook had been murky for so long that she couldn't spot goodness even when it shined directly on her. Prayer helped until something prompted a memory of her reckless years. Then all she could see was a world suffocating in instant gratification.

Her kneecaps, red from scrubbing the hard, cold ceramic tile on the kitchen floor, couldn't distract her from frenzied progress.

Vince shook his head. "Why aren't you using that newfangled mop I bought?"

"Because newfangled is the problem." She stood up and staggered slightly from the stiffness of her knees. "No time, effort, or commitment is required anymore to have everything we think we can't live without. Don't dismiss this as simply the age that blames the younger generation for a world gone to hell, either. It's about political correctness. Tolerance claims that if it's legal or everyone's doing it, it can't be wrong." Her tirade caught fire. "We confuse compromise as compassion, numbing people's conscious when we cross ethical lines and—"

"Well, I can't cast stones," Vince argued mildly. "I've shrugged, yawned, and looked the other way too. Sometimes we're just too tired to muster up any more than indifference."

"Or has selfishness erased the lines?" She bent back down, wincing at her aching knees. "It scares me. My dad's sermons, once such a thorn, turned out to be truth. He said that money and our materialistic, success-driven lives were the evils that blind us to other's needs. When evil can slither around unrecognized, using apathy as a tool, our indifference affirms the dark one's power. Our present-day deceiver counsels us to live and let live."

Vince sobered. "Where's all this coming from?"

"I'm scared for our kids. Our national debt is in the hundreds of billions! What will it be when they're our age? Even these high-tech computers, I doubt, will be able to—"

"There's that word."

"What word?"

"Doubt."

She glared at everything and nothing. "Yeah, I know. Doubt's the apple, and I think I've eaten a bushel."

Vince pulled her close. "Remember that slump you went through after Isaac was born? Postpartum depression or something? Maybe that's the reason for the funk you've been in."

Oh God, how much longer could she, should she, remain silent? The problem was her need to control, her secrets and deceptions . . . her disregard for—

"My thoughts are constantly—oh, Vince, what have I done?"

His soothing stroke on her back altered to a grip of apprehension on her shoulders. Doubt cut between them, replacing the woodsy scent of her husband with the tang of fear.

"When I told you I was pregnant with Liam, you joked about being sixty-six before he was through college. What if something happens to you? I can't earn enough to put the kids through college without you. I want them to have everything we didn't . . ."

Vince's fingers raked through his hair and ended with a tug at his crown, a sure indication that his patience was thinning. He saw her excuses as a buy for time.

"What if I got pregnant again? I think I'm fertile ninety percent of my cycle. My mom had ten kids, and they had probably abstained ninety percent of the time, too. Please try to understand."

Vince's clamped lips insisted she stop stalling. She had to tell him the truth. He had to understand.

"I . . . I had a tubal ligation."

He stepped back, disbelief turning his face white. "You made our family planning your sole decision because of money?" His head shook as repeated no's fell from his mouth onto the wet tile, shattering his hopes.

"It's not that simple." She reached for his arm, but he twisted away.

"Who are you? Some days I don't know who I married." One hand covered his mouth as if to cut off the words his mind wished to hurl.

"It's not as if I cheated."

"No, Elaina, it's worse. Though I'm sure it didn't occur to you, by sterilizing yourself you've said that you want me but not all of me, because you don't want any more of my children."

She was crying now, no hiding it. "I just wanted everything to stay perfect."

"You call this perfect, your mood swings and lack of confidence in me, your vague answers about your past? Try honesty for a change, so we can both be free of your damn secrets."

As hard as she tried, the words came out garbled. Her sobs increased to hysteria. "You married a whore who's been pretending at wholesomeness. I'm trash, Vince. You married trash."

He took her face in his hands and kissed her quiet. "I don't care what you did or who you were. I know who you are: my crazy, beautiful, imperfect wife who tries harder than anyone. Your past has made you wise and compassionate. And you didn't come to my bed as trash or whatever you think. You were pure when I first made love to you. Your passion and energy drive me wild, but you'll never believe me until you forgive yourself."

To forgive herself and the people she believed put her in this desperate place was too much.

"Oh, love." He stepped back for emphasis. "Do you think I'm clueless every time you go to that place, to your hell? Have you considered that your family are victims, too? When you arrive at your prison, you slam the door, leaving the kids and me to wait and wonder when you'll come home. I don't demand a confession, but I'm tired of being shut out. Your inability to be vulnerable and flawed is your biggest mistake. You're no different than your mother, and it's killing our marriage."

She gaped at him, speechless.

"Self-imposed persecution is still narcissism. You build a moat around your damaged ego as if it's sacred, leaving us to tiptoe around the perimeter like it's holy ground. Heaven forbid we try to break down your walls, much less scale them. Are your sins so grave that they're unforgivable? Wow, impressive."

His sarcasm slashed her heart. "You don't understand."

"No, *you* don't understand! You've already been forgiven—for everything, even having your tubes tied. There's nothing I wouldn't forgive you for. There's nothing God doesn't forgive you for. Do you believe that? Be careful how you answer, though. If you say yes but refuse to forgive yourself, you're putting your transgressions above God. If you answer no, then you're saying Christ's crucifixion for the forgiveness of all sins is a lie. You have to forgive yourself and then your prison walls will crumble. It's not a one-time act, though, but a choice you'll have to remake each time a hurtful memory invades."

She wrung her hands. "I thought they'd go away once I had a husband and a family and lived a decent life. I've tried to look beyond—"

"No, you haven't. You didn't consider anything beyond yourself when you decided on sterilization without including me in the decision. It's all about your need for perfection and what *you* want for our kids. What if I wanted more children? Stop lying to yourself and me."

He sucked in air and collected himself. "I've given you everything I am, but I'm still waiting for all of you. It seems you'd rather sit alone in the dark than turn on the lights. You can't see the truth of who you are—how I see you, and how the world is meant to see you—until you flip the switch. But only you know where the light switch is in your prison. In your determination to be anyone but who you really are, you've become what you loathe. If you'd just give your lopsided vision to your Three, as you call them, they'd beam back a reflection of brilliance. Their truth is that Elaina McCroy is incredibly attractive inside and out, talented and priceless in her devotion."

She wiped her eyes, seeing her husband for the hundredth time as if for the first. His strong, small hands, extended to her freely—those hands were also the Three's. Vince was their grace, dressed in wavy salt-and-pepper hair, eyes the color of denim, and ruddy skin that told of tormenting allergies for which he never complained. No matter what she did, he still called her his love and waited patiently for her to get it right, while giving himself to her as spontaneously as he drew air. With him, her hope for the uncomplicated, unconditional, and lasting love she once knew in childhood had again come to pass.

She sagged into him like a limp rag.

He wiped away her tears tenderly. "God's favorite tools are mistakes. The Master Mold Maker reworks every banged-up cast to fulfill its potential and promise. Look at his Son, who was considered a bum, an outlaw, and a friend of hookers. When Jesus finally committed the crime that society said justified capital punishment, God remolded his heinous death to glory. If God can do that, think how simple a project you must be."

Vince was right. Before the old reminders and recollections had come back, she'd already felt like the person they echoed. Until she changed her self-image, she couldn't expect others to see any different. Why were other peoples' opinions the measure of her worth, anyway? She rubbed her burning kneecaps, feeling contrite for having refused to ask this critical question and relieved to finally look truth in the eye.

There'd always be criticisms related to the past, but chaining herself to them was her choice. She could take them as truth or use them to find her own truth.

She pulled the new mop from the pantry, examined it, and handed it to Vince. "So how's this thing work? I'm going to give it a try."

He picked her up and swung her around. "Hallelujah! Now promise you'll make an appointment with your OB and take what he prescribes so I can have my love back. There's no crime in using what's available to get to a better place—or maybe a new starting place."

23

January 7, 1997

Dearest Imm,

I've read your letter twice, but it doesn't make sense. You're only fifty-one. Why so sudden and progressed? What about a second opinion? Cancer has symptoms, and you've had none. If we're extensions of each other, shouldn't I have felt something wrong, too? I refuse to console you because that says acceptance, and I don't. You can't give in to a diagnosis that could be beaten. Please fight.

I've put off visiting you for seventeen years. As soon as I mail this, I'm booking a flight.

Meanwhile, as you requested, I'll fill this letter with news of your godchildren.

Immaculata Rose is your child as much as Vince's and mine. You helped in her design by way of prophecy and prayer long before I'd met Vince. She shares our artistic flair and appreciation for beautiful things, making her an extension of yours and my love as much as of Vince's and mine. The day she was conceived, stars from Grasse's sky dropped into her eyes, and rose petals from La Terre de Mon Coeur became her skin. At seven, she has more poise and grace than most adults. One day, just as you foretold of my future, the Three will surprise Max with a man who'll exceed her dreams. We'll know he's the one because he'll see her exquisite soul and never be able to settle for another.

Liam, like Vince, is a natural funny man who loves making

people laugh. *Because of his genial way, he can only go up. One day, I've no doubt, he'll be as wonderful a father as his dad.*

These are the children you foretold. Your vigilant prayers were God's inspiration for Max and Liam. They're such happy children. And largely due to your correspondence with them, they're so confident in the Three's adoration and devotion to them that their requests of the Trinity are bold and broad. When we pray together and they extend their appeals, I think of how a toddler stands on tiptoes at his father's feet, reaching high to be picked up, with no doubt it will happen. Max and Liam honor God in their lengthy and large petitions because of their certainty in his extravagance. Thank you for teaching them to pray that way.

I'll be at your bedside soon, as you were at mine on that day of such need.

All my love,
Elaina

January 18, 1997
Dearest Imm,

When your mother superior called on your behalf to ask me not to come, I was forced to accept your diagnosis. I'm sick with regret at my selfishness in my previous letter, but I know you forgave me before you finished the first paragraph.

It took some time and tears, but I understand your wish to spare me the toll cancer has taken on your body. As you've asked, my mind will hold tight to the image of the delicate young woman with porcelain skin, copper curls, green eyes, and paint-stained hands who smelled like roses, sounded like wind chimes, and touched me with pure love. Your words have etched a million treasures of wisdom on my heart.

I read this in a magazine and wanted to share it with you in the hope that it will lend the comfort I so selfishly withheld in my last letter: "Cancer is so limited. It can't cripple love or shatter hope. It can't corrode faith or destroy peace. Cancer can't kill friendships. It can't suppress memories, silence courage, or invade the soul. It can't conquer the spirit or steal eternal life."

Your mother superior said the doctor is keeping you comfortable while you wait to be with your twins. I love you so much and can't imagine life without you, but there's such comfort in knowing we've communicated so beautifully across five thousand miles all these years that I can say with trust, "What's a few more?" I'll write you every day until you've gone home.

You've waited so long to be with your girls that I promise not to cry when the most wonderful mother in the world is taken from me. You are ma mère spirituelle as much as Paula is my biological mother.

Sister Lillian described the joyous anticipation on your face each time you speak of your welcome home party. Your faith and fearlessness in coming face-to-face with God encourages me to keep battling doubt. I postponed visiting you for too long and now it's too late, but this will serve as my reminder not to delay living in a way that will transport me back to the Clover Club. Then we'll suck on clover, eat raspberries, and be lazy in the grass together every day.

Be at peace, knowing I'll never leave you in my prayers.

You own so much of my heart.

Elaina

* * *

Typewriter ink replaced Imm's beautifully penned scroll on the next letter that arrived from Grasse. Elaina's chest collapsed. She lifted the flap with trembling hands, releasing yellow rose petals and the scent of Imm. The wording was unmistakably Imm's; the writing was not.

Ma chére enfant,

Because you and I are connected spiritually and because heaven knows not time or distance, soon you may talk to me night or day, and I will be no further than your heart.

I ask you one last time, if for no other reason than your love for me, to eject the demons from your dark place. Yes, ma poupée, go to confession. You've shackled yourself to the desecrations of your youth for so long that they're cutting off the breath of God.

Just as our bodies must eliminate toxins and waste, so too our souls must disgorge spiritual and emotional poisons. Jesus lowers himself to receive it all, regardless of how putrid, through the service of his disciples. Find a clergyman you're confident in, and put your secrets to words. In allowing your voice to regurgitate the darkness into the willing ears of another, you'll find yourself weightless enough to leap into light. That's all confession is. Then you'll know peace and reconnection with your blessed inner child.

When you've joined with little Elaina again, her imagination will soar, inspired by Holy Communion with her Three. She will be free again to depict the impossible—the Trinity—through pen or paint. I know this gift lives inside you, because as I dictate this letter to Sister Lillian, I look upon the painting you gave me your second-grade year. It is my greatest earthly treasure. Those five stick figures feasting on a basket of raspberries by a towering grave marker wear purple smiles that are larger than life. Though the genius of an eight-year-old, I clearly see the promise of all to come.

When your heart can forgive, you'll live in the present again, just as little Elaina did each day when she lay in the grass with her Three at the cemetery and allowed them to fill her with Clover.

You've been my greatest joy in this world, and soon I'll be closer to you than ever before.

Ta mére sprituelle,

Imm

Another note nested within.

Dear Mrs. McCroy,

Sister Immaculata Lefevre arrived home February 14, 1997, at 8:57 p.m.

I penned her final words before she closed her eyes peacefully with her entire congregation praying over her. She is loved beyond verses, and though our grief is heavy, it's with greater joy that The Sisters of Mary, Mother of God celebrate Immaculata's welcome into heaven.

Please look forward to a package containing the contents of

Immaculata's studio walls. Upon entering her room to clear her things, we were dumbstruck by the vast collection of paintings and notes from you and your children, covering almost every centimeter. This was her greatest testimony of love.

In addition, please accept our open invitation when a visit suits you. To meet you would be our honor and privilege.

Sincerely,
Sister Lillian Volez, Mother Superior

Elaina fought the tears she'd promised not to shed. Imm was finally holding her beloved twins. This alone should be cause for elation, but it also meant Elaina's mailbox would be forevermore empty of Imm's letters.

The ring of the phone sounded distant for the buzz in her ears and inconsequential for the weight on her chest.

Composure gave way to anguish and regret. Again and again over eighteen years, Elaina had procrastinated away the chance to paint with Imm. Time had raced until now: a slow, dull throb.

Strong hands cupped her shoulders from behind, and Vince brought his arms around her.

"Oh, Vince, thank God you're here. How did you know?"

"When you didn't answer the phone, I had a feeling . . ."

She turned around in his arms and looked up at him. The man with the smiling hands couldn't fix or heal her, but he'd come home to share her grief.

Her chest tightened with opposing force to Vince's embrace as he pressed his mouth to hers. Her trembling lips begged him to kiss her harder, trusting in his ability to dance the step she needed.

He'd bring her ecstasy as only he could, because the security he'd worked so hard to give her had removed her obstacles in reaching fulfillment. Each time Elaina risked exposing her emotions and found safety, rapture was free to lift her to holy bliss. Over eight years of marriage, Vince had carved spiritual and emotional facets on their physical intimacy to gift her with an image of the Three, just as Imm had when Elaina was a child. Their dance, sacred and supernatural, was enough for Elaina to hang onto even when life's cruelest courses were served.

Vince lay beside her, grayer for the toll of long hours and thicker for accumulating years. Beads of sweat on his forehead glistened like pear-cut diamonds. Elaina wiped his brow, watching the fluid gems dissolve on her fingers and remembering Imm's words. *Dew on the morning grass is how we know the Trinity has been watching over us all night. Dew is the condensation of their breath. Did you ever notice how their breath condenses on your forehead in times of stress or exertion? We call it perspiration, but sweat is proof of their life-giving water that flows from inside each of us.*

"I see their breath, Vince; you're covered in their breath. They're here, inside of you," Elaina whispered. "The first time I skated with you, our feet moving as one, the icy water spraying up like liquid diamonds, I knew they were skating with us. I imagined making love with you would be like ice dancing, and waiting made me sure."

He could ease her pain even when he didn't fully understand it—nor did he need to. Until she was ready to share, he'd told her, it only lent her greater mystery. Her pain was also her gift, he'd said, making her strong yet fragile and always his love. Vince made her feel as vast and deep as the Grand Canyon and beautiful beyond.

Familiarity with her womanly cycles told her that had she trusted her Three, this union would've resulted in a baby—maybe the child saved for this moment, the thumbprint of Imm, a great artist, naturalist, and lover of life. Maybe this child that fear had prevented had been intended to replace the great life called home.

Elaina nursed a new ache for this baby she would never know because of her doubt. Still, the Three had lifted her in euphoria with the man of her dreams, her lover, husband, and treasured friend. Through Vince's body, the Trinity brought assurance of forgiveness and pure love. Through their intimacy, she had learned that erotic and holy were intended to mean the same. Their dance would never grow old, because time taught new steps and brought new music.

"Thank you," she whispered to the Lord of the Dance, whose presence she could feel in her husband's body.

She snuggled into Vince's arms and lay her head on his shoulder.

His warmth invited her to bring him inside her thoughts.

"I want to write a story about Imm," she said. "The world deserves to be told what she convinced me of, that sexual wrongdoings can be the route to redemption as much as the reason for it. Sin doesn't create the need for forgiveness as much as it's the tool God uses to open our hands to his mercy. That's the message I want to pass on."

His fingers winding her curls signified his agreement.

Maybe her story could reflect light, hope, and truth, a radiation to cure hurting hearts and emotional cancer. But to give justice to truth and the honor to Imm that she deserved, Elaina would have to reveal her deepest humiliations—things even her husband still didn't know. Was there any doubt about Vince's unconditional love, though? He often said her heart read like a book; maybe that was his foretelling.

When Imm had told of her rape with such joyful appreciation for the twins it had produced, she'd demonstrated that true gratitude is surviving the worse and finding blessing in it. She'd then proven that in expecting only the best, attitude became the creator.

Imm's final request must be honored, too. For the umpteenth time, Elaina questioned why she so dreaded confession. Could she really blame her parents' unspoken instruction to leave skeletons in the closet? *We will not speak of this again.* Was her reluctance really fear that she'd be blamed for Eric's violations?

Wind chimes sounded the answer. Twenty-five year of alleged reasons were merely excuses to refuse forgiveness. The only requirement for the pardon of one's own sins was to forgive offenders too. Blame had supported her for so long that she didn't know how to stand without those crutches.

* * *

Nicholas Charles Carter, 37, passed away Sunday, March 23, 1997, at 3:36 p.m. at Central Hospice Care Center, surrounded by family members. He was born October 31, 1960, to Carl Thomas Carter and Marcia Kay (Diller) Carter. He was a 1977 graduate of Tarrock High and worked for Tasty-Tote grocery before moving to Austin, Texas. Survivors include his father, Carl, of Tarrock, two half-brothers, Thomas and Mark of Austin, Texas, and three half-sisters, Jill Mercer of Tarrock and Dianna Logan and Katlin Phillips of Grand Rapids, Michigan.

A celebration of life will be held on Friday, March 7, at 4:00 p.m. at the home of his father, Carl Carter. Donations may be made to the AIDS Crisis Center of River Rock or to the charity of the donor's choice.

Elaina received several obituaries mailed from old friends as they conveyed their condolences for the death of her firstborn's father. To be thought of at this bittersweet time touched her deeply. Worse than the horrific pain Cole must have suffered toward the end was people's stupidity, insensitivity, and fear where AIDS was concerned.

Elaina cradled the letters in her lap. *Thank you, dear Three, for welcoming Cole home. And Cole, I love you for being one of the intense conditions that formed two gemstones, Isaac and me. God made a beautiful boy from our puppy love for the woman Isaac now calls mom.*

Cole was probably sitting with Imm and the twins at this moment, all watching over Isaac.

Heaven knows neither time nor distance.
—Sister Immaculata Lefevre

But here, a calendar still marked the days to remind her that over a month had passed since Imm's final request. Procrastination had taken enough away from her.

She looked up from writing her reply to Deanne's sympathy note. Vince was leaning back in the living room, one arm thrown up to block the glare of the early morning sun.

"Vince." She blew him a kiss. "I'm going to do what Imm asked today, but I'm going to Saint Augustine. I might not be home in time for supper."

"Really? That's a long drive for—"

"Imm and I spent endless afternoons at that church together when it was empty, talking about artists, religion, everything. That's why it seems appropriate."

"I remember when she told me how Saint Augustine, as a young man, craved the peace that comes in surrendering one's own way, but every day he would procrastinate."

Complacency thrives like mold when we remain standing in sewage because we see others swimming in it. —Sister Immaculata Lefevre

She moved to where he was reclining. "Oh, Vince, I hurt all over."

"I'd offer to come along, but we both know you need to do this alone. Take back roads, love, and let your mind wander, even where it's painful. When you can look at the past without aversion or self-reproach, you'll take its power away."

"Imm said our search for peace, for God, is like a game of hide-and-seek. As soon as we think we've found them, the challenge begins again. I think it's me who's been hiding though—behind excuses. As the excuses became lies, I needed bigger places to hide from the truth and deny the damage I was causing myself, you, and the kids. The crazy part is that God knew all my hiding places, which was my greatest comfort while I hid."

He stood and wrapped one arm around her shoulders. "My dad used to tell me that God doesn't count the times we wander but the times we come back. Once you've worked through this, my love, you're going to find something amazing—maybe even the book you want to write. And there's a big difference between confessing and unburdening. Let go of your misdirected guilt, and this won't be so hard."

He walked her to the car and opened the door for her to climb in. Pressing his lips to her forehead, he held them there while cupping her cheeks. "I'm proud of you, Elaina."

* * *

The late March sky reminded Elaina of Vince and Max's eyes, flecked in powder blue and periwinkle. Pillow clouds made the sky seem bluer. As Vince had suggested, she allowed thoughts to drift, suspending the dreaded task ahead.

As she entered Tarrock city limits, sweat began to collect on her upper back and under her arms. Her mind was a complete blank of the proper steps and prayers necessary for confession. If forgiveness depended on the proper recitation of penitential prayers, then this trip was wasted. She tried to laugh. Had Sister Katherine and Ruth really believed that blind obedience for fear of punishment or in anticipation of reward had any part in God's plan? It completely contradicted free will and unconditional love.

Holiness, according to Imm, wasn't about memorized religious facts and rules but about finding and thriving in a place where temptation didn't exist. Yet if temptation led to sincere prayer, it could be the path for sacred living. Love was the destination and the constant companion, helping all seekers to untwist Need's hunger so that all decisions would be in accordance with love.

Prayer is lip service to an idol unless we act on those words. Actions are a thousand songs of validation, where speaking his name is but a single note. —Sister Immaculata Lefevre

Imm had accompanied her in the search for that place of peace. Her prayers and letters had been Elaina's guide. She'd allowed Elaina's stubborn sidetracks and shortcuts, sympathetic over the messy results, all while helping Elaina extract a lesson.

Imm had never forced Catholicism on Elaina but respected her enough to merely demonstrate the blessing that faith could be. Her quiet yet vibrant reflection of the Clover Three had enticed and enchanted young Elaina like a song. Only when Elaina had asked had Imm shared her music and its Great Composer. And now it was time for Elaina to sing the song she'd been waiting decades to sing.

24

Saint Augustine Church, though still astonishing with its stained glass, creamy marble, and gold, wasn't the overwhelming size of Elaina's memory. She tiptoed up the aisle while gazing at the magnificent sanctuary. Like old times, her eyes shifted to the east transept where the replica *Pietà* rested; this corner of the church had been young Elaina's favorite.

She could feel Imm urging her over, and Elaina's chest tightened at she gazed at Mary and her son. An art lesson of almost three decades prior came to mind like yesterday. *Why did Michelangelo, depicting Jesus as dead, carve his veins distended as if blood still flowed? Why did he make Jesus's body relax fluidly in Mary's arms, when Christ's body should've appeared stiff with rigor mortis after hours of hanging? Why did Mary wear the face of a young woman, yet her son's face was that of a middle-aged man? No other Renaissance masterpiece can compare in such thought-provoking paradoxes. When Pope Alexander VI complained about the age discrepancy, Michelangelo replied, "A pure woman never ages."*

Mary's face, so innocent and sad, held resigned acceptance that she'd fulfilled God's will in giving her only son for the world. Her head, bowed at such a heart-wrenching angle, like her upturned hand, offered all her pain to the Father.

Had giving Isaac up fulfilled God's will, too? Elaina had certainly loved him in the reflection of the Three, with no expectation of return. In his helplessness and need had come her strength to give him away. That God had trusted a seventeen-year-old to transport Isaac to this world was a validation of how worthy she was. No wonder Isaac still owned a piece of her heart; he was her first true love.

Seeing your own glory as a reflection of them is a beautiful form of worship. —Sister Immaculata Lefevre

Like a colorful welcome mat at the confessional door, jewel-toned fragments of light streamed down from a stained glass window. Still, panic unnerved Elaina, reminding her that a stranger sat inside the dark closet behind the sin-splattered screen.

The burden of her guilt for decades of negligence in confessing eased as she heard Imm's voice in her heart. *You can only understand God's freedom and forgiveness when you untie guilt, stop focusing on your flaws, and love yourself.*

Sunlight hit the polished screen and illuminated a silver-haired priest who wore a grandpa's kind face.

She began the ordeal with memorized mumblings. "Bless me, Father, for I have sinned. It has been twenty years since my last confession, and . . . and . . ."

Her mind went blank.

"Would you be more comfortable without the formalities? We could just talk. I'm Father Albert."

"I'm Elaina, and I hate the formalities. Could we sit by the *Pietà*?"

He led her to the first pew of the east transept and patted the spot beside him as she lagged behind uncomfortably. She sat on the edge of the bench, pulling her back up in an attempt to take authority over her dread.

"Something's brought you here . . ." he said encouragingly.

"Yes, and I've come a long way. I attended Saint Augustine Elementary a long time ago. A friend and I used to come here. We loved this church. She recently died." Her voice dropped, and she fought against another breakdown. "I hate confession—I mean, I used to hate it."

"I'm guessing you were one of many victims of the fear tactics and manipulation of the old church," he said. "Hard as it is to admit, there are priests and nuns who chose this vocation because the cloth guaranteed them the esteem they couldn't have gotten otherwise. Every place has its share of insecure, ego-driven power-seekers, though. Your reluctance isn't silly, but it is unnecessary, because I'm here to listen, free of judgment, if you'll allow me."

Her dark place gurgled as Father Albert took her hand and waited.

Silence simmered for all the years it had been required to hide Eric's warped deeds, for all the years it had been asked to shrink the dreadfulness of her brother's molestations so they'd fit inside a little girl's secrets. Silence demanded an explanation; it was no longer willing to accept any excuse that would make the pain more bearable and lend a sense of control. Silence was tired of waiting.

Silence had kept her seven-year-old self quiet as she hoped for an invitation to jump rope on the playground. David and Mickey must've told everyone what she'd done in the barn that summer. Good girls never played with bad ones. She'd never jump rope again.

Silence had subdued her questions as an eleven-year-old changing for gym, trying not to stare at the girl's whose chests still looked like boys. Silence forbid her to seek an answer for why her alien breasts wouldn't stop growing. Was it punishment for the silence she'd kept during the confessional interrogations, for the lies she'd invented instead, and for the things she hadn't stopped Eric from doing? Were the horrible lumps also the cause of her sinful sexual stirrings? If only she could cut them off, but, like warts, they might come back even bigger.

Silence dampened her fourteen-year-old spirit, tired of being teased, tired of pretending that the other girl's resentments had nothing to do with the attention her assets drew. Couldn't they see that the boy's overtures had nothing to do with fondness any more than her father or brothers?

By sixteen, the silent pall of worthlessness had become her truth.

Silence ached for Elaina McCroy to hug young Elaina Michael and assure her that these devastating times wouldn't last forever. One day, her failures would untangle. Keeping the uglies buried would only increase their weight and make the inevitable confrontation more excruciating.

And then the silence was no more. Every denial and deceit crash into the depravities and sexual promiscuities she'd engaged in, the hearts she'd broken and the secrets that had broken her—all of it roared out of her. Every humiliation inflicted upon her by the dregs of society and the defenders of the law spewed the silence from within her like sour bile. The night on Ron's yacht fueled the abuses at Steely's apartment and enflamed the degradation on the swap meet stage. Silence exploded, firing every detail of the cemetery rape, leaving nothing to shield the deepest horror: Eric's violations.

Her hands shook, and the walls of the church began to spin. This was the downward spiral Kurt had spoken of when coming off alcohol. She was being sucked under.

Father Albert's comforting presence disappeared as her mind's distorted shadows taunted and poked.

You're hopeless.

You've shamed me for the final time.

You're a whore who's brought disgrace to the family name.

Let's dump the bitch.

Images of Eric, Steely, Chuck, and Butch seemed so real she could smell their foul breath. Graphic scenes of the use and abuse she'd allowed with so many men threatened to plunge her psyche back into a black tunnel. Waves of sexual sewage spilled out, making it impossible to pull herself back to the reality of the present. In the rubble of this hellish place, lust licked like tongues of fire, searing *harlot* onto her heart.

She heard Father Albert's voice as if from far away. "Don't listen to the words from your past that weren't true then. Stop looking at yourself through other's eyes."

She reached through slippery memories for his hand, begging him to extract her from this godlessness. "Please, make it stop." Her hands stretched further for the old priest, who seemed as distant as heaven's gate.

"Look at yourself from truth's mirror, and truth will set you free. Say who you are, Elaina. Shout it!"

She roared. "I am the reflection of the Clover Three! I am full of Clover!"

The church, pristine and silvery-white, swam in the Spirit of the Son. Facets of possibility danced like holographs, the air charged with hope.

Baffled by this transformation, Elaina felt weightless, naked, and free from all constraints. A warmth deeper than mere temperature penetrated her skin, like lying in the sunbathed cemetery with her club. The Clover Three were so close they filled her sight, reflected in a perpetual mirror and showing breathtaking beauty through the eyes of perfection.

She could see herself as God did, sinless in complete forgiveness.

This rebirth wasn't blind to darkness, but unaffected by its presence, as if she'd jumped from the shadows of self-loathing into her original, brilliant form.

Father Albert came into focus beside her, pressing a hankie into her hand. "Faithfulness and good works can't earn God's love any more than disobedience can jeopardize it."

The door to her dark place now appeared to her an entrance of glass and mirrors reflecting a completed puzzle. She sucked in breath at the beauty of it. Hundreds of images filled every inch, framed in yellow roses—the magnum opus Imm had foretold many times. Every person and place that had shaped her life was depicted. She could see darker pieces wearing the faces of Eric and Steely, Butch and Chuck, the Tarrock police, and the crowd of bikers. For the masterpiece to be complete, they too were necessary.

Elaina offered an embarrassed smile for the sweat, tears, and mucus that had wilted Father Albert's handkerchief to a mushy mess. "Thank you for your hanky. I'll get you a new one and mail it."

"It's your grief; I would be honored to wash it for you." He took the hankie as if it were a treasure. "And now you're at a crossroads, my dear. If you continue to cling to the depravities forced upon you, fear, bitterness, and suspicion will grow back. Like mold on waste, they'll ruin your marriage, your friendships, and your ability to be a good mother, just as your struggles thus far have proven. If you choose to love, you can pray for your offenders each time you're reminded of the pain. Though your wounds will never completely heal, you can fill them with Clover. Condemnation untwisted becomes compassion. Compassion will show you the fear and darkness your offenders themselves have experienced, the reason they've continued to abuse, and you'll come to a place of sympathy. This is how the Trinity's circle of love closes the gap of sin."

He pulled her chin up, compelling her to focus on his words. "If you look, you can find at least one grain of goodness in everything. You mentioned the tragic childhood of the man who beat, drugged, and stripped you on that stage. If you can pity him, you can move mountains."

Yes, she held no malice for Steely. Even Chuck and Butch were in the realm of possible forgiveness now that the rape's horrific meaning had been extinguished. In their world, she was merely an opportunity, a lesser form of humanity for their amusement.

But her brother and especially her parents? For them, who wore *Catholic* like a badge of honor and were supposed to love her, she could find no excuse.

She shook her head. "It's my parents. Every time my mom snivels about Eric's woes, I feel betrayed. The way they overlooked his sexual infringements. I told them what he did, but to this day, my mom refuses to acknowledge it, as if I'm better off pretending too. It devalues me. The shame of it is almost worse than the years of molestations. I felt like a disappointment and disgrace to them. Eventually, it seemed everyone else saw me that way, too. That's when the secrets became lies and lying became survival."

"I understand." He squeezed her hand. "But your mother is only doing what you tried to do for decades. In refusing to face the truth, she thinks she's surviving. But she's suffering, too. She can't hide from the truth any more than you could. Secrets, lies, and denial have taken you to hell and back, yet a self-made hell isn't eternal if the Trinity remains in your heart. You can reject God, but it's impossible for him to reject you. Attempts at self-salvation merely leave us exhausted, right? Need was placed in each of us to bring us back to God."

Need?

Wonder prickled her arms as she searched his face. "You know about Need?"

"Woman, your heart reads like a book." His eyes seemed to look inside her. "Every human needs to connect with others by revealing our inner selves. This is where purpose and healing come from, deepening our understanding of who we are. Through revealing ourselves, we grow, evolve, and expand in spiritual awareness of ourselves as images of God. Then, because of how we're made, we feel compelled to make a difference with all we've learned."

There it was again: *Your heart reads like a book.* Were her Three trying to tell her something? Maybe Imm and Elaina's years of correspondence contained the story, after all.

Father Albert stood and extended his hands. "Now you're ready to celebrate Holy Eucharist in its truest meaning: thanksgiving."

25

The temperature sat just above freezing. Under the awning of the bud-swelling oak branches in Saint Augustine Cemetery, it would remain in the high thirties even though the sky was bright. How deceiving the sun made the temperature feel from the car's glassed-in perspective.

Intuition warned Elaina that she hadn't experienced her final face-off with her demons, but even in their continued scheming, they would never win in the end. This trip to the place once closest to heaven and then her worst hell would challenge her newfound strength. Here, she could measure how deeply the Son's light had penetrated her heart.

She took in the scenery while holding the memories this place summoned. They seemed both a crystal ball and a hand grenade. Images could detonate if given too much attention, but she was their master now and could dictate a short leash or their release. The Son's light made them small and submissive.

Yellow crocuses popped through the powdery snow skirting the marble pedestal that held Mary and the angels. Elaina ran her fingers aimlessly over the inscribed words on the base, thinking of Imm's words the morning after Isaac's birth. *Women are the tabernacles of human life. Man wasn't intended to touch woman's holiness except in complete reverence, and only when he is willing to lay down his life for her.*

Vince had been patient and long-suffering. Like the frozen stray mitten that lay near the tomb, she'd felt lonely and cold until Vince had slid his comfort into her emptiness like a warm hand into a stiff lump of wool.

The shadows of Chuck, Butch, Eric, and Steely stood at the edge of her mind, spineless and trembling. She watched their grotesque silhouettes dissolve to blobs, men who'd poisoned their own seeds of love for crops of self-indulgence.

She remembered Romans 8:28, when Saint Paul talked about men like them: "All things work together for the good of those who look for God's purpose." Even when the free will of one person makes a victim of another, no matter how unspeakable the deed, if God doesn't intervene, it's because goodness can be molded from it. Her job was to make beauty and purpose from the savagery those pathetic men had inflicted.

Here stood the woman they'd abused and raped in ways an animal would never have done, yet their monstrous acts had transformed her. She had become a woman who couldn't ignore suffering of any kind, even that of an insect. The threads of compassion she'd spun from their depravities continued to weave themselves into the lace of her character with generosity, empathy, and forgiveness.

In a backward way, she should thank Chuck and Butch, Eric and Steely for pushing her back to the arms of love. Their violations were feces turned to fertilizer, nourishing the seeds of magnificence asleep within her.

She was only sorry it had taken her so long to see the bigger picture. Her stubbornness and rebellion had slowed and discouraged her, while her failures had blinded her completely. But her Three's outstretched hands had pulled her up time and again, assuring her it was impossible to live in an imperfect world without messing up. Failure was a truth of real living. Adversity and painfully won wisdom had enlightened her more than any institution of higher learning.

Elaina Rose Michael McCroy was brilliant!

Feasting on the Son's warmth, she moved to the grave that dark years had carved into a throne of judgment: Edward Jonathan Michael, Born: June 1, 1915, Died: January 20, 1982

One day, you'll thank your parents even if they were wrong, because their no's and required hardships are the seeds of your character.
—Kurt Trackwald

She rested her cheek on the smooth marble, eyes pooling in gratitude for her father's love she finally recognized.

"Thank you, Dad, and rest in peace. I love you."

* * *

Crunching gravel at the apron of her driveway said welcome home. Before she was fully in the door, Max and Liam were at her side, peppering her with the questions of children who weren't used to their mommy being gone all day. Gratitude for their stay-at-home mornings prompted a silent thank you to the Three.

"I saved you a plate, love. How'd it go?" Vince came out to help her with her coat just as the telephone rang.

She slipped out from under the heavy garment, buoyant with the lightness of her new outlook. "I got it." She snatched up the receiver with a smile as he shook her coat at her in mock frustration. "This is Elaina."

"Elaina Michael McCroy?" asked a smooth, deep voice. Something in his tone brought forth the same sense of appreciation she'd found for her father's memory at the cemetery.

"Yes, may I ask who's calling?"

Time halted when he said his name. She eased herself down into the chair, wonder washing over her senses, blurring away the faces of her family as they gathered to see who was on the other end of the line.

The voice was her gift to God and God's gift to her: the gift of her firstborn.

The End

⸙ About the Author ⸙

The story in E.R. Millott's heart began to seep onto paper the Spring of 2008 after being reunited with her first born child, placed for adoption more than two decades prior. After nine years of scratching and cutting, deliberations and re-writes, ***Full of Clover*** is complete.

E.R. Millott has also spent the last twelve years as both an elementary and high school teacher of Catholic religious education and a student of basic Theology and Philosophy. Besides her annual mission trip to Tanzania, she fund-raises for a variety of mission projects in the Mbulu region of Tanzania.

For more information go to www.fullofclover.com.

Made in the USA
Lexington, KY
26 July 2018